Outcast Artist in Bretagne
WWII Heartbreak and Forbidden love

Diane Scott Lewis

Print ISBNs
Amazon Print 9780228625506
BWL Print 9780228625513
B&N Print 9780228625520
Ingram Spark 9780228625780

BWL Publishing Inc.

Books we love to write ...
Authors around the world.

http://bwlpublishing.ca

Authors Note

Many events and most people are fictional or used in a fictional manner. The special port and U-boat are entirely fictitious. Timing of events, such as the murders in Nantes, have been moved or combined for dramatic purposes.

Dedication

To Marie-Josephine and Pierre, my French friends. Marie helped me with my French. Pierre shared his experiences as a child in France during the German occupation. May he now Rest in Peace.

Table of Contents

Chapter One

Brittany, France 1941

At the sound of a boot scraping over stone, Norah peeked around the tall rock. Her pulse spiked. The Commandant stood a couple of feet away, straight as a steel beam, arrogant, gazing out over the Atlantic. His Nazi uniform was a terrible mockery to the village of Saint Guénolé.

She'd thought herself secluded here. Why had she taken the chance? She hunkered down and should slip away, since she could be apprehended for spying on the German officer. Though that's not why she was there. Loathing coated with fear rippled through her.

Almost frozen with inaction, she slid down a little more into the cove of rocks' shadows. She glanced at her drawing book. The sketch of the Atlantic Puffin, delicate in its lines traced in colored pencils. The orange legs and strong red and black beak on a body of black, pale gray, and a white underside shimmered on the page. In profile, its eye shone with life, and the puffin looked about to take flight.

A gust of wind tossed her hair into her face, a thick sweep of strawberry-blonde in the scent of brine from the sea.

Did she hear his boots scrape closer? What if he peered over the rocks? Swiping her tresses aside, she shrank deeper into a cleft and glared over the ocean, longing for her home in Yorkshire, angry and upset at being stranded. But she must pretend to be calm, in control.

The Southern Finistère coast, with its rugged, rocky outline, was a buttress against the forceful ocean waves that slapped the stone slope two yards below her toes. The dark indigo of the Bay of Biscay reflected a blue spring sky. Spray filtered through the air, a mist that refreshed her skin—except today. If she could only sneak to the north coast and be capable of swimming the channel.

Inching to the side, Norah crept, head down, out from the semi-circle of tall rocks on the opposite side from the Commandant. Thankful she wore trousers and not a skirt, plus sturdy Oxford shoes, she brushed off her backside. She hurried past the monolithic-like stones with golden lichen clinging to their bases, across an open area of grass and into the bushes then woods. Her pencils rattled in the canvas bag. Her legs grazed against the orange and yellow wildflowers.

A sentry or two always patrolled this area. She tried to remain inconspicuous, but more soldiers had arrived in the last few weeks. The Germans had started to build ports somewhere along here and a special one, heavily guarded, right below the village. She *must* be more careful.

As she pushed her way through gorse bushes and scratchy plants, sharply fragrant, she pondered the German officer's reasons for standing at the cliff, which he did often—but never so close to her cove. Was he waiting for reinforcements by sea? Or coveting England across the channel? But that view was on the northern coast of this peninsula that stuck like a fat finger out into the Atlantic.

The Nazis' bombing raids had already decimated so much in London in the Blitz. They'd also dropped bombs on York, but with minimal damage so far. Her country had been attacked by German planes from September '40 to last month—the *worst* raid ever on London. She groaned. Now June, would it start again?

Since last year, Hitler planned an invasion of England, but it had failed to land any troops.

Her stomach clenched with more anger she needed to temper. She increased her stride, sucking in the fresh air. Rustling behind her, footsteps—too close. Someone panting then a hand grabbed her shoulder.

Norah flinched and swung around. A baby-faced soldier in Nazi greenish-gray scowled at her. "What are you doing here?" he demanded in heavily accented, terrible French, two of his teeth jagged like a weasel.

She straightened, chin high, the pad pressed to her stomach. Inside, she trembled. "I live nearby. I was enjoying a walk. I draw birds." Her French was passable after the year entrenched with her cousin, and her schoolgirl lessons from a decade ago. Her arrival happened only five weeks before the Germans invaded France. A desperate year because of that and for anguished, personal reasons.

The young man pointed at her book and bag, then shouted over his shoulder in German.

Was he alerting his superior? "Please, I've done nothing wrong." She had no desire to come face to face with the Commandant. "You can search me…if you want." She cringed at that idea.

"I have no choice but to report you." The soldier shouted again. The officer's heavy footsteps thudded closer.

He burst through the bushes, tall and broad-shouldered, his expression stern. The two Germans spoke in their guttural language.

Norah wanted to collapse to the ground but refused to show intimidation. Her spine nearly crackled as she held it firm.

The Commandant confronted her, his blue eyes penetrating. "What is your purpose out here at the shore?" He had distinct cheekbones, a handsome face, his lips full; a man of about forty. An iron cross hung at his high collar. "You don't care to take instruction from we Philistines. Civilians are restricted."

"I apologize," she tried to keep the revulsion from her tone, though his near-teasing words —or perhaps a taunt—put her off-balance even more, "I was out for a walk and…I used to walk by the shore. Before—" Before you damned Germans arrived.

"What is in that book and bag? Give the pad to me, so I may inspect what you're doing." He reached out his gloved hand, his French excellent.

She hesitated, then handed the book over. "I like to sketch birds. I have a friend who is an ornithologist. We study them. Rather he studies them, I just draw."

She opened the bag at his order, and the young soldier plowed through it. "I'd appreciate it if you don't crack my pencils."

"Show me your Identification Card. What is your name, prowler of the coast?" the officer asked in his clipped, almost raspy voice. He opened and paged through her drawings. "It is only birds, nothing more?"

"I'm Norah Cooper, and yes, it's only birds." She pulled out the card residents were now required to carry.

He snatched the card and read the words, perused her picture. Then he handed it back. "Ah, I detected an English accent in your French."

His continued rough handling of the pages sent sparks along her shoulders. Would she be punished for being English, Germany's worst enemy?

She reached for her book to mask her panic, the idea she could be interrogated or shot. Her knees wobbled. "Please…may I have—"

"Your identification says you're single. Are you engaged to be married soon?" The Commandant clapped the book shut, his pointed stare on her again, though his curiosity was obvious. "Do the men in your family allow you to wonder alone?"

"I'm not about to be married." Her cheeks burned for the marriage that almost took place.

He looked her up and down, his gaze astute. "Pull out your pockets, *s'il vous plaît.*"

She did so while struggling to calm her breathing.

"Why are you in France at this particular time?" He, too, examined her bag as if he didn't trust his subordinate.

"I live here. I've lived here for years." That lie came to her easily. He might find her less suspicious if he thought her a resident and not a recent visitor.

"Is that so? I will study your drawings for hidden details. And I know where you live in the village."

Had he seen her there? She nodded, though would refuse to admit where, if she could manage it. She needed to protect her cousins. But he said he already knew where or could easily find out. Her reasoning flapped like a hummingbird.

"You can go for now. But I will keep an eye on you, as I do this entire area. Stay away from the coast. Mark my words, *Fräulein* Cooper, you must cooperate. You don't wish to come to any harm." He tugged the brim of his high-peaked hat, turned, and marched off in tall, black boots—with her drawing pad. His minion followed, shouldering his rifle.

"Wait, sir. When can I have them back?" Norah swallowed a curse, wishing she'd said nothing. They tramped into the trees.

All that work for nothing. She'd made other sketches of seabirds. She let out a long breath, eyes closed for a moment, fingers shaking. That drawing pad was expensive, with paper woven tightly like linen. She'd never find another in this ravaged country. She waited until they were out of her sight, then she slowly walked toward her cousin's cottage, measuring every step. Woozy with relief she hadn't been arrested, she still cursed inside: *bastards!*

* * *

Loeiza Menez shook her dark head in her low-beamed kitchen after Norah told her of the encounter. She'd returned, breathless and bristling.

"The Germans are watching the coast, as if it belongs to them." Loeiza hugged Norah who gleaned comfort in her embrace. "Was the Commandant threatening? You must stay cautious, *ma chérie*."

Then her cousin returned to chopping onions at her smooth wood table. A voluptuous woman with pouty lips, Loeiza's plumpness was the exact opposite of Norah's slender form.

She brushed her fingers across her abdomen. Thin, yet her still-flabby middle brought on bitter memories. A disaster she hadn't planned on, but was it for the better? "The German was a little threatening. I wish he hadn't taken my drawings. My art keeps me distracted. But yes, I could have been arrested, or worse."

"You can't send drawings to your friend, anyway. It wouldn't be allowed." Her cousin on her mother's side, Loeiza took most things stoically. A good, steady woman, of thirty-one, she was five years older than Norah. "I'm thankful you were not detained."

Four boisterous children ran into the kitchen with its huge hearth. They giggled and pushed at one another. "Do we eat now?"

"*Non*, my darlings, are your chores finished?"

The oldest boy, Jean, shrugged, his grin wide on his mother. At ten, he was gregarious but with a mischievous tinge. "Why can't we dig for clams in the mud?"

"I've told you, the guards' frown upon us near the ocean. Now take the others to the garden," their mother said gently with a sweep of her hand. "We'll plant in a day or so."

Jean ushered the littler ones, two girls and another boy, out of the room. The youngest boy, barely three, whimpered in annoyance. Norah smiled at the children's—most of them—good cheer with so much turmoil around them.

Norah went to the open lattice window that looked out on the cobbled square of the fishing village of Saint Guénolé. The warm breeze caressed her face. She'd have to sketch inland birds, in her second, inferior book, her last available. A shame, since this peninsula had unique waterfowl. Her friend would understand. She'd lost the puffin, the Purple Heron, and the Bearded Reedling in her confiscated work.

"Damn Germans, or rather *darn*." In case a child listened. "They storm in and steal everything." Norah turned and leaned against the plastered wall. She resented the humiliation of being searched while still relieved she remained free. She'd heard of others who weren't so lucky.

"Soon, we'll be eating nothing but the weeds in the field." Loeiza tossed the wild onions into a pan of sputtering lard on the stove. "Almost no butter, eggs. I was fortunate to find a chicken. But it's scrawny. Yann says meat will be even more scarce with most food given to the soldiers or sent to Germany."

"You're *poulet au cidre* is always delicious." And having a butcher for a husband didn't hurt. But stores were depleted more each month. Norah stepped to the table. "Can I help?"

"I like to cook, you know that." Loeiza waved her away. "These ingredients are difficult to come by. And we pay a such high costs, but we must make the best of what we can."

"And I'm eating your food and have overstayed my welcome." Norah propped her arms on the table. She tried to eat as little as possible, leaving most for the children.

"You have not overstayed. You didn't know the Germans would trample the French army then rush out to occupy our province. And now you're forbidden to leave." Loeiza stirred the onions, the smell pungent. Her cousin's words weren't quite so confident as before concerning Norah's residence. Or was she reading that in with her guilt.

"I'm selfish to lament my stolen drawings, with all the suffering in France." But art was her passion. "My father kept insisting I disappear into the countryside, to an aunt on a remote farm." Norah forced an ironic chuckle. Her father had also warned her not to cross the channel. The continent was being chewed apart and swallowed up by that maniac dictator, Hitler. "But I had to leave England."

"I'm happy you traveled here, even though it was risky. I haven't seen you in a few years." Loeiza's words were a balm. "No fancy breasts for this meal, we use it all." Her cousin added the pieces of chicken to the braised onions. The meat sizzled. "The scraps and bones will make a fine soup."

"And Bretons love their soups." Norah snatched a rag and wiped up the onion juice. "Father is probably still furious, but I wanted to save my old aunt from dying of apoplexy."

Loeiza laughed softly. "The older generation can be too stodgy, *oui*?"

"Aunty would have begged me to marry a man I didn't love. As did my mother." Norah fought back the gloom. She'd worked as a secretary in the walled city of York; a dull job she felt beneath her. A wild party to push back the perils of war. Dancing, laughing, then a grope with an attractive visiting supervisor that turned into more. She shivered, disgusted with herself. The wine had blurred her morals. "His offer to wed sounded more like he was being marched to the scaffold."

Her cousin smiled in sympathy, though her eyes seemed sad. "No one should marry someone they don't love. Or marry too young. Then you're stuck in matrimony… It's good we are not so strait-laced in Bretagne, *ma chérie*."

"I also wanted to check on you. I was worried with the war heating up." Norah warmed at their long friendship, though separated by the Channel. Letters *had* flown back and forth on a regular basis.

Yann, Loeiza's husband, strode in then. Medium height, thin and wiry, he pulled off his cap. His lank brown hair framed a long, bony face. He had removed his large apron, probably at his shop, but still stank of raw meat and blood.

"You are early. Our Norah had an adventure today. Don't be upset but wait till you hear." Loeiza turned the chicken in the pan.

Norah stiffened. "Yann won't need to—"

Too late, her cousin relayed the incident. Loeiza, once so sweet, appeared reluctantly obligated to inform her husband of any infractions.

Yann's mouth twisted and he turned his glare on Norah. "Are you senseless? Do you want to bring attention to us?"

"No, of course I don't. I'm sorry it happened." Norah crossed her arms and hugged her elbows. "I really am."

"We mind our own business here. We don't ask for trouble." He kissed his wife's cheek, then returned his dark eyes to her. "That Major von Gottlieb, he's a dangerous man. He might think you are drawing the coastline for the British."

"He'll find nothing in my book." Norah's voice rose in defensiveness. Of course, she did look questionable out there sketching. "I'll stay away from the ocean, I promise. It was foolish."

"You had better. We're fortunate the Germans don't house an officer here. I want it to stay that way." Yann, polite when she first arrived, definitely showed signs that she'd worn out her welcome. The ever-sparser food should be for *his* family.

Yet she suspected he was aware of any resistance against the Germans in the village. Local men sometimes gathered in the parlor, drinking fermented cider, whispering in their confusing Breton language. Though she'd learned to pick up words and phrases—the anger of the persecuted.

She left the kitchen, rubbing her knuckle along her collarbone. How could she contribute to her cousins' lives? She hated feeling useless, a burden. Or was there a way back to England? A fishing boat slipping into the night. She'd arrived with funds she thought would last her, but with the forced "stay," that money was gone. She hadn't the bribe to pay for a clandestine escape. Nor would she wish to put a willing fisherman in danger.

Shoulders slumped, Norah's throat tightened. She'd sneaked into France, a friend with a boat, who also warned her *not* to go.

Norah went to the narrow stairway that led upstairs. She tapped the banister like a drum. The Germans weren't in France in March of 1940, though England had declared war on Germany in September of '39, after Hitler invaded Poland.

The rough crossing she'd suffered that last week of March. But she'd wanted to check on her cousins, as well as hide her condition. Another stupid mistake! Her longing for home, her family, dug deep into her heart. She might be stranded in France forever.

With her original purpose shattered, and no way home, she must find a place to belong, no matter the difficulty.

Chapter Two

August tossed his hat onto the leather wingback chair of the mayor of Saint Guénolé's former office, in the village Town Hall, now appropriated as his. A musty, smoke-filled room he'd had aired out.

The desk was plain, ordinary. August had made the office neat and organized, the opposite of what existed in his mind. Two chairs faced the desk, set back slightly, for whomever he might need to speak to, or interrogate.

On top of a glass-fronted bookcase, he'd placed the photograph of Klara. A pretty enough face, with broad cheeks and a kind smile. A good woman, gone too soon—a year before he was stationed out here. He breathed over the pinch of sadness. At least his two daughters, though young, were safely married to solid German businessmen in Germany.

He was pleased they had good husbands who wouldn't suppress them. Young, unmarried girls were supposed to join the BDM. *Bund Deutscher Madel*: Band of German Maidens, where woman were taught to be wives and mothers only. A female version of the Hitler Youth.

His son, at fifteen, was in secondary school in Berlin. Klara's sister kept an eye on him.

In the bookcase he'd placed a few of his books on history, a subject he relished to learn about. Especially the historic facts of Brittany.

On a table in the corner, a jigsaw puzzle was a quarter finished. Such items gave him some pleasure, a different focus. Its irregular edges made it a challenge. Soon Renoir's *Luncheon at the Boating Party* would emerge from the pieces.

His colleagues had hinted he should recreate German paintings, but he preferred the French Impressionists.

He glanced out the window. The navy, the *Kriegsmarine*, now situated at the former French naval base in Brest, ninety-six kilometers north, were building a special port here for their new submarine. He might have to move the population farther from the shoreline. Displace these fishermen who clung to the coast. So far, they hadn't been disruptive. A simple people.

The drawing book sat on the desk's corner. There was nothing untoward among the avian pictures that he could discover. No hidden lines to show the shoreline, the shape of coves and inlets. Of course, a silly fräulein wouldn't have the skill to camouflage. The slender Englishwoman with luminescent hair seemed innocent, but she was English. You could never trust your enemy. At least, he was supposed to view her as an enemy.

He shuffled through a stack of papers, troop movements in western France, submarine and ship plans for his 'information' only.

The muscles along his shoulders tightened. Being stuck out here in the hinterland instead of Paris, or other important assignments, appeared to be an insult. Was it because he didn't toe the line, worship the *Führer* enough, as was expected? Klara's death had chipped away at his faltering zeal. Still, the perceived exile, this beautiful place, had grown on him this last year.

But he should do his duty for the army and the *Wehrmacht*. He must present himself as a loyal soldier within the limits that continued to form in his mind, until he decided on his future.

Birdsong trilled outside the window. Norah opened her eyes in the narrow bed in the tiny room, a space once occupied by a maid in previous decades. Her sleep had been restless. For an instant she recalled, from months before, when she'd awoken to kicks and movement. Thankfully, when she'd voyaged to France at four months pregnant, she hadn't shown yet. No one in Yorkshire, except her parents, should know of her disgrace.

Her cousin had found a nice couple to adopt the child. Norah swung her legs over the side of the bed, hating the memory. That morning near the end of her term she had gone into labor, the midwife summoned, but the baby was stillborn.

Norah stood, her heart in a fist. Tragic to lose something, *someone* that once thrived inside of you. The deep gash of pain hit her, and she swayed with the loss. A boy, they said. Yet she might have wondered for the rest of her life how he fared. Did her mother feel the same, as the years passed, after Norah's brother—a sibling she barely remembered—died of diphtheria at only two?

She rubbed her eyes. The crowded room contained a chest at the end of the bed, and a dresser with flaking paint. She poured water into the ewer on a tiny table and washed her face and armpits with a sliver of soap. The chilly water made her shiver. The house was primitive, with no upstairs plumbing for the three bedrooms. A full bathroom was downstairs, usually filled with a child or three.

Norah smiled at this kinder thought. She liked to take the children on walks, to teach them about wildlife, or as much as she knew; but that might be forbidden, too.

She bristled over her exile from the coast, though she could sketch something other than birds. There was a fine old church close by.

Her father had scoffed at her desire to be an artist. "Get married like your sister." Home and hearth. Norah loved her sister Agatha, but marriage had never appealed to her. She loved and respected her parents, even if they were too traditional in wanting her to be a housewife.

Dressing in olive herringbone trousers, another thing her father disliked, she pulled on a blouse with short sleeves, and cream-colored drape tie. This sailor's blouse, like all her clothing, she'd brought from England. Clothing she'd worn over and over during her extended stay.

Along with the roomier garments she borrowed from her cousin when she'd grown large with child. She fought a wince and tucked the smaller sketchbook into her bag of pencils.

The American actress Katharine Hepburn wore trousers, and Norah was thin like her. They both had defined-featured faces as well. She brushed her too fluffy hair, trying to tame it into a semblance of order as the tresses floated an inch above her shoulders. She'd never thought herself pretty, but she did have lush hair.

In the kitchen, Loeiza spooned porridge into bowls. The room was warm and hummed with the little ones' voices.

"I'm off to draw the church, to see how well I do with buildings. It's been a while." Norah greeted each of the children: Angelique, sweet and quiet, Marie-Louise, stubborn but smart, Petit Yann, spoiled. Jean, dark, flashing eyes beneath black hair, gave her a cheeky grin.

"Make certain you only draw the church." Loeiza warned. "Yann is right, we must always be careful if we are to co-exist."

"I'm well aware. My little cove of rocks is no longer safe." Norah kissed her cousin's cheek.

After a quick slice of bread and a strong cup of barley coffee, Norah left the cottage. Across the square, she passed the pretty thatched, or slate-roofed homes of stone and headed down the road. Larger buildings of stone or plaster on stone, some with chalky-blue shutters, lined the street, along with the few shops and the weathered to gray stone fish market structure. Purple irises poked up in tiny gardens.

Her plain, Panama style straw hat with a black band shaded her from the sun. Women's hats had got fancier, with bright jewel tone colors. But that would be out of place in the dreariness of occupation.

How frivolous to think of hats, she admonished herself. However, one's mind didn't always behave as it should.

A soldier marched by; his gaze raked over her, then he winked. She coiled into herself and kept walking.

Two elderly women passed her in drab gowns, black shawls draped over their shoulders, white-capped heads together as they whispered. Everyone was cautious under scrutiny.

At the Église Saint Guénolé, built in the fifteenth century, Norah admired the gothic, Breton style; the granite shone golden in the morning light. It and the village were named after a famous monk who died in the sixth century.

She sat on a ruined wall and began to outline the building with its large stained-glass windows, sinister gargoyles, and flying buttresses. She shaded with charcoal-gray around the gargoyles, under the windows, to give her drawing depth. But the cheap paper frustrated her. Plus, the drawing seemed stagnant, no ripple of feathers, twitch of a head, no life.

Norah fingered the pencil, almost chewing on it. The intense pigment of her pencils was of professional quality, a gift she'd brought from home. When she used them up, what would she draw with?

From the corner of her eye, she saw movement. A lanky man in loose trousers and shirt walked toward the village. Deniel Pichon, a carpenter, and friend of Yann's. He paused and waved to her.

She waved back and shoved her pencil into her bag.

"How are you this morning, Mademoiselle Cooper?" He ambled over, his smile easy. Under his cap, he had wavy chocolate brown hair and inquisitive hazel eyes. A dimple in one cheek gave him the look of someone of good humor. In his early thirties, he hid the limp that kept him from joining the Free French Forces in England under General de Gaulle. The majority of young men had escaped there when they heard the Germans were marching into Brittany.

"I'm attempting to draw the church, but I'm not happy with the results."

"Do you know the nave is slightly crooked in this church, due to the old priory adjoined to it?" He glanced down at her effort. "It's not bad. But I'm shocked. No more birds?"

"I'm afraid yesterday the German Major forbade me anywhere near the shore." She huffed, meeting his twinkling eyes.

"Has he? The venerable August von Gottlieb." Pichon's eyebrow arched. Hands on his hips, he gazed around. Pichon was usually the most vocal of the men who convened in Yann's parlor. "Then you'd better be prudent. We wouldn't want to upset the occupying forces." His words held a trace of sarcasm, his smile wry.

"No, we wouldn't. And I don't wish to be dragged to prison, or worse." Her arms goose-bumped. She ached to ask more; was there an ongoing Résistance group in the village? Was there hope the Germans could be chased out? But why would Yann be part of it? He'd seemed, when she first arrived, a restrained man who preferred to keep his head bent to his work.

The proud Bretons claimed to be separate from the French, a Celtic heritage. Rumor had it some even welcomed the Germans. She'd wondered if Yann straddled both positions, to keep his family safe.

"Have you ever painted, or is drawing your only interest?" Pichon asked.

"I decided not to bring my paints to France. I hadn't planned to stay long." Her stomach twisted at her reason for coming. She *must* discard the past and work on her future, to alleviate the despair that had gouged her out for too long.

"Then the invasion, I see. A shame. Our beloved village should be cleansed. *Eh bien*, I must go. I need to measure for a table. I must accumulate money." This seemingly amiable man had a fiancée, a girl in a neighboring village. They would marry soon.

"Monsieur Pichon, I once thought the entire village followed the Germans' orders. But now I wonder…"

"You are better off not to ask questions. That's my advice. *Au revoir*." His eyes flashed a warning. He tipped his cap and left her.

Norah bit back a protest. If she wanted to be of use, she intended to find out more about their group— if one existed. She'd caught words in their parlor discussions that heightened her interest. But would the men want her to be a part of any 'activities?' Was she brave enough to be an asset? Or just a desperate woman anxious to contribute but might cause further problems?

She stuffed the sketchbook into her bag, stood, and wandered over to where she could glimpse the ocean. The fishing port spread out below. Protected by two granite peninsulas, its western entrance was often plagued by rough weather. One peninsula was connected to the mainland by a sandy isthmus. Neglected fishing boats bobbed in the calmer water near the coast. A cluster of low buildings studded the shore.

The fishy scent mixed with brine swept over her. The few men left were only allowed to fish with a German escort, ten miles farther east, away from this area.

The Atlantic waves crashed the rocks as if enraged at them, the spray thrown high into the air. A few beaches broke up the harsh granite shoreline. She longed to walk along their sandy warmth. To her right, in the distance, she saw men in work clothes, carrying materials of some sort, pushing barrows, pointing down at a spot on the bank and into the ocean. Wagons were being unloaded. This work had started in March, as more sentries were posted.

If only she had binoculars. Then again, she'd be shot for certain. She blew out a breath. If she made light of her situation, she might manage to endure.

A German sentry strutted by, rifle shouldered, his head straight with purpose. His glower and rude hand gesture sent her backing away. Her curiosity could be her undoing. The confinement of being denied the shore prickled inside her.

She turned and rushed toward the village. Yann's friends whispered about what type of port the Germans planned to build in this remote place. Was that what she'd just seen? Would it be for an invasion fleet?

Germany might soon overrun her homeland with troops. Her parents' small farm, though her father worked as a solicitor, could be in the path of destruction. Their lives sacrificed for the rampaging Nazis. The thought sent a shudder through her.

What were the British army and navy planning? Prime Minister Churchill was busy trying to talk the

United States into giving Britain supplies and weapons. Help was desperately needed.

"Come sit with me," a soldier in front of the Auberge, or tavern, called, then he laughed.

Norah, eyes averted, hustled on. So much to worry about. Her Anglican family wasn't overly religious; they attended church on special occasions and holidays. However, she said a brief prayer for them and her country. Her parents were mortified by her sinful actions—and the result. Would she have the chance to make it up to them?

She forced her thoughts elsewhere. There had to be interesting birds that nested here in the spring. Her friend, James, appreciated her bird sketches, but of course, he'd prefer the unique. They'd known each other since childhood. He'd gone to Oxford, a degree in Ornithology, and was now married with two children.

A motorcycle zoomed by driven by a German officer, the fumes noxious. The invaders had taken all their vehicles, leaving the villagers to walk or ride bicycles.

She passed the large well, still used by many, near the square. A cat scurried past. Then a dog growled from somewhere.

"Fräulein Cooper." The rasp of a voice sliced into her.

Norah halted, filled with alarm. The Major walked toward her in his jodhpur-like trousers, holding her drawing pad. His medals on the dreaded uniform glistened in the sun's rays.

He held the pad out. "Your birds are attractive; you have a talent. The colors vivid." He thrust it into her hands. "Stay away from the coast, as I've cautioned, if you know what is good for you." He looked her over, his expression evaluating. "You've lived here for years, you said. I think it is much shorter than that."

Norah cringed as she hugged her pad close, thankful for its return, but aware of the danger. She must be truthful and not bring scrutiny to her cousins. Though she was weary of men ordering her about. "It's been more like one year. I came to visit family, then you and your soldiers arrived."

"So you lied to me. Don't try to be too clever." He gave her a slight smile, but menace seemed to lurk beneath it. His shadow engulfed her. "I will find out any details if needed."

"I'm fairly boring, not clever at all." Another unruly slip of the tongue she wished she could swallow back.

Now his smile looked amused. He gave a quick nod and stalked away.

Norah took a nervous breath, her hands clasped on the drawing pad. Would he uncover her disgrace? The entire village had to know, though she'd hidden inside during the final trimester. Midwives gossiped.

His threat made Norah yearn to sketch along the shore—but perhaps not birds. No, no, she *mustn't* think that way. She really shouldn't tempt fate. Her brazen nature, as her father often called it, should be used in more inventive ways.

A heavyset woman, Madame Bolloré, sweeping in front of her cottage, stared over with a frown. Norah was the outsider in the village. Now, just for speaking to the German commander, would they think her a fraternizer?

Chapter Three

"There are Golden Orioles in the poplar groves. We have choughs." **Loeiza dug her hoe into the soil behind the cottage and gouged another row.** "You could draw those."

Norah dropped the carrot seeds into the dark earth. "We have choughs in England, mostly in Cornwall. I saw a Honey Buzzard and a Serin. I don't know if I can get close again."

"I'm surprised the Major returned your pad the other day. You were fortunate." **Loeiza squeezed Norah's arm, patted it, and continued tilling the rows.** Half the garden would be carrots, half potatoes. Other vegetables were already growing in patches.

They planted late this June due to the difficultly of obtaining seeds from the *Marche Noir*, the black market. Another unfortunate expense.

"I'm surprised, too. Why not an underling? Or not at all? I wondered, for a second, if he'd changed his mind about arresting me." She stifled a shiver. People were arrested for the slightest infraction. "He said my colors were vivid, and I have a talent." A man quite full of himself, as most Germans were. She hoped they wouldn't speak again—too hazardous.

Norah debated about mentioning what she'd seen down at the port. Her cousin might already be aware. So much was left unsaid in this village. "Will you grow enough food?"

"I hope so, if the Germans don't confiscate everything." **Loeiza tugged on her straw-hat brim. She gouged the hoe in again, her strong arms brown from** the sun. The loamy scent of overturned earth was pleasing. A butterfly with blue spots fluttered through the air.

"Stop that." Marie-Louise, at five, the disciplinarian, was discouraging Petit Yann from sucking on a black-eyed Susan held with dirt-encrusted fingers. The three-year-old was adamant about putting most anything in his mouth, perhaps to fill his belly. The little boy stomped his foot.

Angelique, her dark-blonde hair waving in the breeze, pulled weeds from the garden and laid them in a neat pile. She was almost eight, inquisitive but shy. Her sweet smile charmed everyone. What future did she have now? Or any of the precious children?

Norah wondered how her cousin managed to care for them, their clothing more frayed, the food not as plentiful. Last year, Norah had been overwhelmed with the idea of bringing another mouth to… Though the baby *would* have been safe with a good family.

A rush of guilt enveloped her, after the jab of pain, that she was still here, eating their limited resources. Thoughts of how she might contribute to their coffers trickled in. What could she offer?

She glanced at Loeiza, who resembled the aunt, her mother's sister, a family Norah had visited a few times. An adventurous woman who had gone to France in 1909, five years before the Great War broke out in 1914. She'd met and married a Breton man, and stayed through that war, living in Quimper, a larger town to the east.

Now the Germans invaded for the second time. The restrictive rules forced on their country after the Kaiser's reign had caused anger and resentment—so her father and his brothers had debated. Hostility that the screaming Hitler stirred to a feverish pitch.

"Have you heard from your parents?" Norah raked the soil over the seeds, then stabbed the tines into the ground, frustrated at the chaos of their situation. She would help Angelique water when they finished sowing.

Loeiza straightened and pressed on the small of her back. Her simple, much mended, cotton dress brushed below her knees. "Not since they said they were traveling to Switzerland. The Germans curtail our mail, even the Red Cross can't send us packages. My parents begged me and my family to go…"

A plane rumbled overhead and both women stiffened and stared up, waiting, their breath held. A bomber, the allies? Should they grab the children and run for cover? Norah grasped her cousin's wrist. Loeiza reached out for her youngest; but the airplane flew north-east where the Germans had built an airfield—one of many.

When the sound of its engine faded, they glanced at each other with brittle smiles. This had happened before, but every moment brought new dangers.

Norah steadied her breathing, her mouth dry.

"I'm glad we stayed here in the village, and that you're with us, though England's countryside might be safer," Loeiza said as if little had occurred, though her face blanched pale. "I doubt Yann would leave anyway. He has relatives all over this region. He swears it's his duty to remain."

Her cousin met Yann when her family visited the Finistère coast for holidays, both in their younger teens at the time, Loeiza had told Norah when she'd attended their wedding twelve years ago. He'd appeared a much more affable man then. Norah was a mere fourteen, thrilled to visit along with her mother. Now she pondered her cousin's marriage choice. Or was Yann a different man in the privacy of their bedroom?

Jean rushed through the gate, two milk pails clanging. His cheeks flushed. "They're empty, *Maman*. The dairyman said the Germans took all the milk."

"Then we do without." Loeiza patted his dark head, her smile reassuring. "Take Little Yann inside and clean him off, please."

Jean set down the pails, grabbed his brother's hand, and tugged him into the cottage. The little boy cried out in upset as Jean soothed him with gently teasing words.

Norah raked more dirt over the seeds she'd dropped. The Germans steal milk from babies! "What do you know about Deniel Pichon? Does he have interests other than carpentry? More political?"

"You've heard them talking. You'll be fluent in Breton soon. *Mais non*, they only brag. Yann listens but discourages them." The way her cousin said it implied more. Loeiza averted her eyes and bent to her hoeing. Yann must have warned her not to talk too much.

Marie-Louise scampered by, nearly bumping into Norah. "A mole; *va-t'en*, shoo, shoo!" The little girl waved her arms and the rodent scurried from the garden.

"Why don't you settle in for good in the village?" Loeiza tipped her head, her smile encouraging. "We'll find you a nice farmer to marry."

"As if I had a choice where to live right now. Though I appreciate everything you've done. You saved me." Norah felt the stab of loss. She could never marry. Who would want her, a ruined woman? Someone who couldn't handle her basest needs in a haze of champagne. She'd attract the worst kind of husband—and she would never wish to be a farmer's wife. Or anyone's wife, now.

Perhaps her cousins wanted her to move out, and soon, despite Loeiza's previous words. Norah pushed down the anxiety that always threatened to creep up on her. Where would she go? She must never give up on the hope of returning home.

The rotund neighbor appeared at the gate between their properties. "Loeiza, did you hear?" Her double chins wagged in her round, sun-burnished face. She motioned her over. Norah followed.

"*Bonjour*. What is it, Madame Bolloré?" Her cousin smiled at this local gossip whose chickens were as numerous as her children, and just as noisy. How she kept her birds from the Germans was another mystery.

"Terrible news, that's what it is." Madame Bolloré glanced over her shoulder. Then she shuffled forward, nearly stumbling over a fuzzy yellow chick. Her faded striped gown resembled a circus tent. "The Germans arrested Pierre Kerguelen early this morning. And isn't he Yann's very dear friend? Now we'll all be under suspicion."

A chill rippled up Norah's spine. A child whined from the woman's garden, calling, "*Maman*."

Loeiza gulped a quick intake of breath.

Kerguelen was one of the men who gathered in the parlor to whisper in Breton. Norah gripped the rake handle and bit the inside of her cheek. This could mean danger for Yann and his fellows, along with the entire village. Madame Bolloré flicked a gaze to her.

* * *

The lieutenant raised his hand, the whip ready to strike the cowering Frenchman. August maneuvered down the bank of the burgeoning little port. On the large shelf of beach, he grabbed his arm. "Stop this. I've warned you not to attack the workers."

The young man flushed. "They're too slow, Herr Major."

August snatched the whip from him. "I'm reassigning you to the point. Leave at once. Beating people hardly inspires cooperation." How could he keep his men from adhering to Hitler's vicious policies?

32

The soft-faced soldier—one of many pushed too quickly through officer training—saluted, ducked his head, and marched off. August signaled to his second lieutenant, *Oberleutnant* Krause to take charge of the project. A tall, taciturn man strictly by the book, Krause stepped forward.

August rejoined Captain Schmidt, his second in command, at the top of the bank. The wind off the ocean swirled around them.

"The worker probably deserved it," Schmidt said. "Krause is a bitter man. His wife left him for an opera singer. He only regrets having no sons to join the Hitler Youth. But if we don't hurry with the port, the honor might go to Lorient."

"Our topography has the advantage." August hated to think what that advantage was bringing them. Lorient, 130 kilometers farther east, under the control of Brest, was an important base on this coast. The French general there had been persuaded into 'practical collaboration.'

August surveyed the men working below. Diligent Germans and a few forced Frenchmen—or others just seeking a paycheck. The villagers hadn't given him much trouble, until early this morning.

The construction had gone on for three months, the forms in place, concrete, and steel being positioned, along with prefabricated ceiling supports for the large bunker and pen. The naval *Kapitän zur See* would arrive soon to oversee the progress. A vice admiral had been here initially and planned to return. Arrogant men of lofty rank pushing into *his* territory.

"We should have a warship stationed here. A travesty Brittany deprived us of their fleet." Schmidt's pointed nose stabbed the sky. The previous year, after the invasion, France sent her ships to ports in Africa and England so the German couldn't use them. The *Luftwaffe* mined the waters, but their fleet escaped.

"We're supposed to be inconspicuous." August ruminated that the remaining ships were destroyed by the French and British demolition squads. Two French submarines were scuttled in front of their crew. Hitler wasn't discouraged, the war scarcely undermined. August desired an end to the insanity—lives preserved.

"We should shoot the villager in the square to show our strength, to intimidate the Breton citizens." Schmidt's thin lips under sharp cheekbones pinched. "He offers no good information."

"We'll continue to question him, to glean what is needed." August didn't care for Schmidt. He thought like a wolf and not a fox. "Then I will decide what to do with him."

"As you wish, Major. If that's what you intend." Schmidt said this with just enough sarcasm to be annoying. A man with more ambition than intelligence.

August tried to mentor his captain, teach him leadership and dignity, but the effort had been futile.

"The villager was sneaking about in the dawn, near this construction site. We will see if he's a saboteur." August put icy firmness in his words. He rubbed his tense shoulder. "Hopefully, he will give us the details of a Résistance group in the vicinity."

"I would like to assist in a harsher interrogation." Schmidt's eagerness brightened his sallow skin. Thrust into this post last year, Schmidt's father held an important position in Hitler's regime. This high-strung captain made rank through favors and not ability. Schmidt had a wife and children back in Germany, but a whore in Quimper. "I know ways of persuasion. Allow me to use my skills. I need to..." Schmidt hunched his bony shoulders.

Impress his superiors, or his father, the captain didn't complete.

"Lt. Bauer, along with a few enlisted, will *persuade* the prisoner. I'll join them soon. Information exceeds a show of brute strength." August turned his back on Schmidt and walked from the shore into the village. He wasn't a prude, but a man should be true to his wife, honor his family, and not be so anxious to commit mayhem.

It was bad enough August had to share the house he now lived in with the captain.

The sweet scent of honeysuckle reached him as he walked. Spring, the best time of the year. A pity he could hardly enjoy it. If this **Kerguelen** was part of a larger resistance, reprisals might be in order—or expected. The ugliness of occupation would rumble through the town.

His boots smacked harder along the road as he fisted the folded whip. He'd considered himself a civilized person, growing content in this village. But these people must understand who was in charge until he conceived other plans. Calculated the danger that was coming. Out of habit, he brushed his fingers over his right side, where the damage from his past happened. His frustration burned. He *would* regret any bloodshed.

Chapter Four

Yann slammed down his cup of cider. "*Merde*, if France hadn't capitulated so quickly, we wouldn't be in this situation." The others present grumbled in agreement. "But we should have stayed out of opposition to the Germans. I warned you."

"We were fooled. Don't ever believe the Boche," a husky man groused. "Germany has no intention of helping Bretagne become its own country—as we *should* be. It's their lie, a bribe."

Norah listened with held breath at the door to the tiny parlor. Her growing understanding of Breton, a dialect related to Cornish—and her several summers in Cornwall—allowed her to understand the essence of the conversation.

The Nazis had invaded Belgium, stormed through the Ardennes, then captured Paris the previous year. They eventually streamed out to the west to take the major ports of Cherbourg and Brest. The fleeing French had blown up ships, cranes, oil supplies, and other machinery so the Germans couldn't use them.

Then British soldiers evacuated in small boats out of Dunkirk after the Germans with their relentless low-flying aircraft trapped them on the beaches.

Norah had panicked, aware she'd be trapped as well, or murdered for being English. She dug her fingers into her arms to stifle her memories.

"France, so invincible, but crushed to dust by the Germans. Now the French kowtow to the invaders. But some are fighting against the traitorous

Vichy government to the south. And their German Military High Command in Paris," Pichon said, his voice pragmatic. "How will we free our partner Kerguelen? There must be a way."

"Kerguelen got caught, the worst of mistakes. They're a short-tempered family." The mayor, Monsieur Ropars, displaced by the German Commandant, threw up a hand. Norah glimpsed a portion of the chubby older man through the slightly ajar door. The door never shut properly unless jerked closed. After losing his fine home, the mayor had moved in with his brother just outside the village. He slurped his cider and poured more. "Germany made promises they'll never honor to the Breton Nationalists."

"The Boche have control of the Channel Islands to put up their Atlantic Wall, as their lunatic leader demanded," another man grumbled as he puffed on a cigarette. Smoke clung to the room as others indulged as well. "I should have escaped to the Free French. We could be massacred."

"Don't think that way. We need photographs of this port under construction, which seems more secretive than the others." Pichon spoke. "We *must* resist and protect our heritage. My father and uncles worked against the Boche in the previous war."

"It's too risky. The Germans took all the cameras," Yann groused. "And film doesn't work in the murkiness of dawn. My uncle was killed in that war."

"I doubt Kerguelen had a chance to memorize construction details or write them down. If the Germans torture him, he won't have much to give," the mayor said as he slumped deeper into his chair. "He might spout off and doom us. My wife already suspects what we do."

Yann drank his cider, swiping his sleeve across his mouth. "I won't be part of it anymore. We're only bringing danger to our families."

"My family *is* in danger. And don't call our tempers short." Erwan, Kerguelen's younger brother, struck a fist on his thigh. "We've fished these waters for years. My grandfather had the finest boat. I won't sit back and lose my livelihood. I want revenge."

The others shushed him and warned him to stay calm.

Norah lurched aside at a footstep on the flag-stoned floor. Loeiza approached with an earthenware pitcher. Her eyes wide, she indicated they step back to the stairs, several feet from the parlor door.

"What are you doing?" she whispered.

"Don't you want to know what is happening?"

"I find it easier not to know every aspect." Her cousin gave a sad smile. "Please, no more eavesdropping, *ma chérie*. We pretend ignorance."

Norah moved close to her. "But that man who was captured… Yann's friend. What will happen to him?" She pictured a firing squad and winced. Were the Résistance men wasting their time, taunting death?

"I don't know. But Yann might stop these meetings, to discourage the rest of them from risking capture and being killed. He's reluctant to be involved. Now, I must provide fresh cider." Loeiza moved past her, the pitcher raised. "You don't want to irritate some of these men here. They can be just as lethal. Haven't you come close enough to trouble?"

"Yes, you're right. I'm too impulsive. My unruly spirit, Father says. But I want to be of use. I was thinking I might offer sketches of interest, wildlife, the village, to the people of the Black Market to assist with the cost of your goods." A silly idea, Norah now admitted. "We'll discuss that later. Did Germany really offer to make Brittany independent?"

"An empty promise we realize now." Loeiza shrugged; her mouth drooped before she caught it. "But we Bretons always long for autonomy."

"Don't we all. What can I do, at this moment, to help you?" Norah shoved aside her frustration, the feel of having scant power in her own life. "No matter how small."

Loeiza hesitated, her elbow against the door, her voice low. "You could…to the left of the square, where the grass grows close to the trees, search for wild onions. Wild garlic and dandelion greens, too. Oh, and summer truffles, that's a treat. These will supplement our meals. Take Jean with you. And please don't wander deep into the woods."

Norah, with Jean, and Angelique who asked to come, carried a basket to the edge of the square where the cobbles ended. They searched the grass, around the trees, the children more proficient than she was.

The sun inched down over the ocean, the light spreading out in streaks of orange and sepia. The warm air cooled a little.

"Here, and over here." Angelique kneeled and began plucking the plants. The smell of wild garlic and onions pungent on the breeze.

"She is good at foraging." Jean laughed. "And I'm the protector of you women."

"Like a knight of old." Norah kneeled and joined in where the girl indicated. "You are stalwart and brave."

"I miss chipping mussels from the beach rocks and digging for clams." Jean shrugged. "The Germans should let us. It's food for them, too."

Norah's throat tightened for these children who had to scrounge for sustenance.

"When will the guards go away?" Angelique asked.

"I…we don't know. But don't worry. They will." Would they ever go away, or would Hitler achieve his goal of world domination as he threatened? Surely, her country across the channel could push the

Germans back, defeat them. They *must*. Whispers of deportation of foreigners to labor camps already floated through the village.

They plucked more, the green smell pleasant, the fibrous feel of the plants on her fingers reassuring for some reason. She could forget her plight for this instant. The basket filled, Norah stood and brushed off her hands. "I think we're finished. Good work."

"I wish we'd found truffles." Angelique shook out her skirt.

"Next time. We did a skilled job, *merci*." Norah patted the child's head. Then she stared off through the trees. How hard would it be to sneak down in the dark with a hooded lantern and draw the changing port? Still, it might be too soon. Wouldn't the allies need the nearly completed site to judge what it was for? She threw aside that insane idea. She'd be executed.

They walked back to the square, the shadows lengthening. Music came from the Auberge across the way, to the far right, where the German soldiers gathered to drink. The villagers' radios had been confiscated, but the Germans had use of a wireless. Usually the soldiers listened to march music, or songs about the greatness of their homeland.

The men were laughing, some drifting in and out of the bar's front door.

"Can you dance, Cousin Norah?" Jean asked. He swayed to the music.

"I can jitterbug." She sighed at her lost freedom of entertainment. The past year she'd cursed and wept for her other losses. Her homesickness and worry about her family. A draining experience. How could she work around these invaders?

"Show me the dance," Jean urged. Angelique grinned, hands pressed together.

In the shadow of the cottage, Norah hesitated. "We probably shouldn't."

"Just a few steps." He tugged on her arm. A child starved for food and fun.

Norah set down the basket, listening to the melody. It seemed forever since she'd heard lively music.

The Germans had gone back inside, their laughter grating on her. The soldiers had taken over the auberge, pushing the locals out to meet in a small café rearranged in someone's home. She rubbed her arms in anger, defiance. Could she remember how to jitterbug?

"All right, Jean. First, we'll face each other. I press you back with one hand, you step back, I go forward. Then we pull together. We rock like that, back and forth." Norah guided him, her hand on his shoulder. "Then I step and lean to the right. You step and lean to the left. We repeat as slow or fast as we want. People jitter around, putting in other moves."

They laughed as Jean missed steps. Angelique laughed, too, watching. Norah tried to stay in the shadows as the sun dipped lower. Energy surged through her, the laughter a delight. The children's happiness so uplifting. Angelique joined in, trying the steps. Norah moved faster, the boy imitating her. Yet, with a sudden tingle on her flesh, she knew someone close observed her.

* * *

August stepped from his office. The laughter carried across the square. He squinted to see in the shadows. The Englishwoman, Cooper, was dancing with two of the butcher's children. A sound that amused him for a moment. But young soldiers wandered out from the beer house, staring. Captain Schmidt was with them. Inappropriate comments from the landsers. Suggestive snickers from officers and enlisted—men too long without women.

August glared at Fräulein Cooper. She was too bold, careless. He wanted to warn her to stop such displays.

A soldier, weaving, obviously intoxicated, staggered toward the cottage. Schmidt snorted. Others encouraged the man. August stepped further from the shadows and cleared his throat. The landser turned, saw him, and stumbled back the way he'd come.

Just as August was about to call a subordinate to handle the matter, or march over himself, to reprimand *her*, Fräulein Cooper ushered the children into the cottage. The door closed, their laughter fading.

August frowned. He'd ordered his men not to take advantage of the female residents, unless the women were willing. But too many lonely soldiers were hard to contain. And such foolishness from the Englishwoman would not help.

Tomorrow, he'd admonish Schmidt to show decorum in front of the enlisted men, for what good it might do. The captain was a swine who needed reassignment.

Locking the office door, August strode down the path that wound through the trees on the left side of the Town Hall, to the mayor's former home, *Maison dans la Forêt*. The house in the forest, an obvious name.

He groaned inside at the conundrums he faced each day. He'd long thought of himself as an army officer of merit, commissioned before Hitler and the Nazi Party took hold in Germany. A position once to be proud of, but no more.

He must decide what to do with the recalcitrant, suspected-resistance Breton, who refused to name any co-conspirators. Who was he working with? He'd been seen entering the same home—the butcher's, several times—the place where Fräulein Cooper lived. The butcher must be questioned.

Despite Hitler's vile instructions, August wouldn't shoot the prisoner to keep the villagers in line. That seemed extreme for a man who hadn't killed any of his soldiers. Many German officers shot anyone for no reason—*animals*. That wasn't the way to encourage cooperation. August would make one last attempt to extract information from Herr Kerguelen. Then the fisherman could be sent away to Paris for further interrogation.

As August walked, listening to the crickets chirp in the bushes, inhaling the forest smells, he thought of the dancing woman, her sweep of light hair, her laughter. An unexpected warmth seeped through him. So far, he'd ignored his own intimate needs and stuffed them deep within. He doubted anyone could fill the hollow place inside him.

Swallowing a groan, he regretted the monster that would soon be stationed here. But wasn't that the reason he'd been assigned to this village?

Chapter Five

The thick-shouldered man slumped in the chair, though his insolent expression never changed. "I was drunk, I keep telling you." His front teeth were chipped, his lips bloody, but the Breton's story never altered. "It was dark, and I stumbled down near the port, going the wrong direction."

August stood to the side. The Town Hall's narrow back room stank of sweat and blood. "The sentry who arrested you smelled no alcohol. As *we* keep telling you. Who are your co-conspirators? The butcher?"

The prisoner shrugged and stared at the floor.

"Shall I convince him to confess, sir?" A landser raised his rifle butt.

"Don't bother." August stepped up to the man. "Herr Kerguelen, either you tell the truth and are a drunken fool, or you think that we are." The Breton was bruised, purple blotches on his face and neck, his wrist broken. Enough was enough. Torture was a method August wished to avoid. His father had been beaten badly in the last war and lost an eye. He was never the same afterwards. "I'm sending you to Paris. They will figure out whether you are lying or not. And who is helping you."

Let the higher authorities in military intelligence, the *Abwehr*, deal with him. Then the villagers will wonder what happened to Kerguelen: a man vanished. Would that force cooperation into them? The butcher, Yann Menez, might be easier to coerce.

"Major," Captain Schmidt objected. He hovered in the doorway like a vulture. "I think we can apply more *pressure* on this fisherman. Just give me a few minutes with him."

August bristled and turned to Schmidt. The captain no doubt chipped the Breton's teeth—or had one of the enlisted do it. "Don't ever question my tactics," he hissed. He ordered his men to arrange for Herr Kerguelen to be bundled off to *Oberkommando der Wehrmacht* the military high command in Paris. If they tortured him there… Some things were out of his hands, August kept reminding himself. If they extracted vital information that he couldn't, he'd tell the *Abwehr* how proficient they were—just what Hitler expected. Flagrant flattery to keep them in Paris, away from him and this village. He glared at Schmidt. "Captain Schmidt, come to my office. I have something to discuss with you."

* * *

Norah positioned Angelique and Jean on a crate in front of the church. "Sit close, good. I'm going to draw you and the church." Maybe this was what she needed to bring the picture to life. Norah sat on the ruined stone wall and pulled out her good pad and a burnt-sienna pencil.

Marie-Louise had been invited to join them, but she wasn't interested. Petit Yann was too little and squirmy to sit for her.

The children fidgeted and laughed. Norah made a quick sketch, outlining the church, the children, then filling in details to color later.

The ocean surged seven yards to their right— hopefully that distance was allowed by their captors— down a rock-strewn hill. The air tasted fresh and salty. Gulls screeched and sailed on the breeze. Surely the church wasn't off-limits as the villagers were allowed to attend mass.

Norah would pretend, for this moment, that life here was normal.

"Have you seen the *Le Château des Pleurs*?" Jean asked.

"The Weeping Castle? No, what is that?" Norah drew the waves of the girl's hair around her perfect, pretty face. She wore her best dress, in pink, which was tight around her shoulders.

"It's near here. Down that slope." He pointed. Jean was also growing out of his clothes, his shirt sleeves and trousers too short.

"Close to the water?" Norah lamented she didn't have paints. Her colored pencils didn't quite give the smoothness, the burst of color, she desired. For needed income, she might sell a few village scenes to the Germans to send back home. Or would that be considered fraternization?

"It's a ruin. What's left is half on the hill and part in the water." Jean spread his hands.

"Well, we can't go down there. Now, sit still." Norah sketched Jean's cheekbones, then his bright brown eyes. She wanted to catch the liveliness in his face.

"Romans left it," Angelique said. "Papa told me that."

"A Roman ruin?" Norah wished she could see it. Another chance to draw? "Why is it called the Weeping Castle?"

"It looks sad to be sliding down the hill." Jean made a pouty face, his thin arms drooped between his knees. Then he winked.

Angelique nodded, lips pursed. "Very sad. Only parts are left."

"It's magic, and haunted," Jean snickered. "At night it weeps for the people who once lived there."

"I don't like ghosts." Angelique hunched her shoulders. "But there are good ones."

Norah smiled and etched in more details. She'd drawn people in the past, sketches for friends, plus landscapes with farm animals. She needed to branch out again—a laugh tickled her throat—from drawing only birds.

In York, she had sold a few landscape paintings while working at the job she'd hated. Filing, typing, and fetching tea, *ad nauseam*.

Several minutes passed. The children bumped elbows, then Angelique pushed at Jean with a grin.

"Are we finished? Are you tired of sitting?" Norah drew what she could in quick strokes of sienna. "We can come again to finish."

A soldier strode by with his rifle.

"There goes another sentry." Jean frowned with ten-year-old affront. "I wish they'd go home. *Maman* isn't happy. Neither is Papa."

"We all wish they'd leave. But we must put up with the Germans for a while." *Or forever*, Norah didn't want to say. What kind of world would they be forced to live in if no one stopped the Boche? She sketched in more of the church with nervous fingers, trying to capture the majesty of the stained-glass windows. "We remain polite and stay far away from them."

"Why are they here?" Angelique twisted a strand of her hair. "They don't like us, Papa says. They should be nice. *Eh bien*, a few are."

Norah stopped and straightened. "Some think they have to be the leader of everyone. And put rules in place to keep people under their thumb. But these soldiers—"

"They want to own us and our land." Jean stood, summing that up. "I wish I could go to war."

"No, you don't, Jean. But we must be brave and try to ignore them when we can." Norah drew the grimace on a gargoyle directly to the left, high on the church's façade.

Jean stretched tall. "I'm very fast. I think I could sneak down and go inside *Le Château des Pleurs.*"

"But you won't do that. You'll be smart and stay with me. We're done for the day." Norah slipped her pad and pencil into her bag. "Let's return home. I can help your mother prepare lunch."

Angelique stood and fluffed out her skirt. "We have to behave around soldiers, *Maman* warned."

Jean rocked back and forth on his feet, a glint in his eyes. "I'm quick enough to run down and back before anyone catches me."

"No, don't you dare. We're returning to the cottage." Norah rose and shouldered her bag. "You don't want to upset the Germans."

Jean laughed and took off at a run to the top of the slope and down the hill.

"Jean! Come back here!" Norah started, astounded. She grabbed the little girl's hand and hurried to the crest. "Come back, right now!"

Angelique gasped. "*Non,* Jean!"

The sentry shouted, gripping his rifle. He skidded down the slope, dislodging dirt and pebbles, yelling in German.

"Please, don't hurt him. He's just a child." Norah watched the boy reach a ruin of columns and an arch partly visible on a curve of rock, water slapping around it. Terror clutched at her heart. "I beg you!"

The sentry reached Jean and snatched his arm. Jean cried out, more in surprise than fear. The sentry glared up at her.

"Help him. *Please* help him." Angelique pressed a hand to her mouth, her eyes huge.

"Bring him to me," Norah pleaded. "He made a mistake, *s'il vous plaît.* Be kind to a child."

The sentry shook his head as if he didn't understand French or refused her request. He dragged Jean along the shore, toward another man who had stalked over. An officer.

"What'll we do?" Angelique burst into tears, her body shaking.

"I'll take you home and—go to the Major. He's the one in charge." Norah had no choice; she squeezed the little girl's hand, grabbed her art items, and rushed her into the village. "Don't worry." Her own fear threatened to stagger her steps. "They can't hold your brother."

She had no idea what the Germans could do. Her breath heaving, Norah stopped at the cottage. She caressed under the child's damp chin. "Go inside and calmly tell your mother what happened." She had little confidence, only determination. "Take my art bag. And assure her I'll get Jean released."

Angelique nodded and wiped her tears. With a last look over her shoulder, the seven-year-old entered the cottage.

Norah faced the Town Hall, or *La Mairie*, the mayor's former office. Her body trembling, she walked toward it, dread and prayers competing inside her. She had no wish to face the Major but *must* rescue Jean.

* * *

August put his fists on the desk. "Never question me before the soldiers. And the night with the radio blasting from the bar? Do not act that way, taunting toward a woman, laughing with the enlisted men. You are an officer and a leader. You show by example how to behave."

Captain Schmidt stood on the opposite side of the desk, his posture more insulted than intimidated. "We were having a little fun, sir. These villagers shouldn't be the ones enjoying themselves. That girl was dancing, parading herself, when she shouldn't have been. She doesn't even wear skirts like a decent woman would."

"Never mind that. You are under my orders and will do as I say. You should have called the man who attempted to get close back." August should send a note to the butcher's house, warning them about overt displays. "Now go and do your duty. Check the sentries, the on-going construction, and the immediate area for any forbidden activity. I am done with you."

Schmidt clicked his heels together with a slight bow. "*Ja*, Commandant. My father too enjoys a constant correction of me. I'm used to conflict." He thrust out a raised his arm. "Heil Hitler."

"Be your own man." August raised his hand in a quick imitation, one he regretted each time. "Heil Hitler."

After the captain left, August sat, refusing to take the bait of Schmidt's obvious antagonism. He drummed his fingers on his desk. He'd write a letter to his superiors, asking for Captain Schmidt to be reassigned. His snarling objections and sloppy behavior were not to be tolerated.

Jerking open a drawer, August pulled out a sheet of paper. His secretary would type it up in proper format.

The Breton had given them nothing, but his visits to the butcher's home would be the next investigation. Yann Menez must be questioned as soon as possible.

Chapter Six

At the Town Hall, a guard stepped before her, eyes flinty, his rifle tight against his chest. "What is your business here?"

Norah tensed, her arms rigid at her sides. The ugly swastika flag flapped above her, adding to her distress. "I need to speak to Major von Gottlieb."

"For what purpose?" The young man's chin lifted higher, his French adequate.

"It's urgent." She swallowed hard. Each moment counted for her to rescue Jean. "Tell him it is Miss Cooper, the woman who draws birds. He knows who I am. I must speak to him, *please*."

The guard hesitated. She took a step closer, breath heaving. He finally turned, stepped into the alcove, knocked, and entered the office.

He returned after a minute and motioned with a slice of his hand for her to follow.

Norah walked stiffly in, her courage waning, but her resolve anchored. She'd never been in this office before. And now with the Germans in charge, changing everything—and a child's fate in her hands.

Major von Gottlieb stood behind his desk, tall and imposing, his expression curious. "What can I do for you, Fräulein Cooper?"

"My young cousin did something foolish, but he's only a child." She rubbed her knuckle along her collarbone and explained what happened in barely controlled words. "Please, don't let anyone hurt him. He's ten years old, and impulsive." Tears dampened her eyes, despite her effort to appear tenacious. "Release him to his mother. It's all a mistake."

She saw the Major's gaze change from surprised to concerned.

"Extraordinary. I will investigate at once. Wait here, Fräulein." The Major thrust on his hat and indicated the chair in front of the desk. He marched from the room and shut the door. She heard strong words exchanged in German, the shuffle of feet.

Norah sank into the leather seat, unsure what to do. Her heart beat so fast, her chest ached. She glanced about the office. A picture of Hitler on the wall made her cringe. On a glass-fronted bookcase full of books was a smaller picture of a woman. Broad-faced but attractive. The Major's wife?

Mahogany furniture filled the cramped room. The desk was neat, with a tan leather inlay. The room smelled pleasant, of lemon oil. She tried to balance herself as her mind spun.

A small table held a partially finished jigsaw puzzle. She stood to see what it was, to distract her upset.

The door opened behind her. She nearly jumped.

The Major strode in, his gaze fixed on her. He removed his hat. "Fräulein, it's been taken care of. The child is being escorted to his mother as we speak."

She pressed her hand to her breast, almost swaying. "Thank you. I'm so relieved."

"Warn him he should not be so impulsive. It's dangerous." Without his hat, she saw the Commandant's hair was sandy-colored, almost golden, a wave over his high forehead. He had a strong cleft chin.

"I will, I promise." Her words came out too breathy. She still believed it unfair the villagers hadn't access to their own coast, but she couldn't allow her resentment to show.

"It seems a problem in your family, this impulsiveness. You should not have been dancing before the cottage the other night either." He raised an eyebrow, but the glint in his eyes was somehow a challenge. "The soldiers notice these things."

Her cheeks burned. Had *he* watched her dance? "You're right. It won't happen again. I'll restrict my dances to the rear garden."

"Good. See that you do. I'm only trying to keep you out of mischief, if that is possible." His tone wasn't harsh, his glance almost teasing.

"I must go and see how my cousins are." Norah inched toward the door. She should have asked about Mr. **Kerguelen**, what happened to him? But wouldn't push her luck. "Thank you, again. I'll try not to be such a problem."

"You're welcome. Be warned to follow the rules no matter how you might object. *Guten tag*, Fräulein." He bowed his head for an instant, like an aristocrat in a play. He smiled wryly. "Yet I imagine this won't be our last meeting."

Norah blinked then left the office and hurried across the square.

Was Jean home already? Surely the Major hadn't lied to her. He seemed a gentleman. She gasped and clapped a hand over **her mouth. What a bizarre thing to think about a Nazi commandant. What sort of man would follow the dictates of a tyrant like Hitler?**

* * *

After calculating the budget and finances for the Southern Finistère occupation, August read the latest messages from Marshal Philippe Pétain—a WWI hero and collaborator with the Axis powers— head of the Régime de Vichy. Updates from the Military Administration, the *Militärverwaltung in*

Frankreich, in Paris. The reports contained standard information for all German commanders. But his thoughts kept slipping back to Fräulein Cooper. A spirited woman who could cause problems.

Why was she here? He'd heard different stories. She had to have arrived in a clandestine manner if she'd crossed the Channel last year. Then she'd supposedly hidden inside the butcher's house for months. If she were a spy, sheltering inside would make little sense. There were rumors of more unseemly motives of a personal nature. He must confront her again and ask sharper questions.

He sorted through more papers. The fräulein sketched seabirds, according to his sources, and what he'd seen in her drawing pad. And now the children at the church. An artist with talent. He should have someone keep an eye on her. But that idea displeased him. A soldier might not act respectfully.

He sat and stared at the paper he'd began to write, requesting a transfer for Captain Schmidt. But another notion struck him that had nothing to do with the snide captain.

First, he had business to attend to. "Fritz!"

His secretary rushed in and stood at attention. A slender private with thick spectacles and unruly blond hair, Fritz usually looked fairly-well turned out. And he was efficient.

"Send one of the landsers to the butcher shop." August struck his pen tip on the desk. "I wish to talk to the butcher, Herr Menez. Bring him to me, now."

When Fritz left, August went to his puzzle and moved pieces around, the people on the boat, the man in a sleeveless shirt. The colors delighted the eye. Hitler intended to rearrange the map of Europe, all under Nazi rule. Wouldn't it have been better to concentrate on Germany alone, make her a sustainable country after the devastation of the first war? And why this extreme hate of the Jews? Many were being shipped off to labor camps.

Twenty minutes elapsed. He grew impatient.

Finally, a landser brought in the butcher: a sullen-faced man with stringy hair and a thin body. His eyes looked defiant, no fear in them. He wore a blue shirt and corduroy pants, a common garment out here, and stank of raw meat.

"Herr Menez. I have a few questions for you. Sit." August pointed to the chair. He should have had Fritz swap it out for the hard, wooden chair that kept people uncomfortable.

Menez slowly sat, his expression changing to leery.

August remained standing. "First of all, you live in a decent-sized house, here on the square. Surely a butcher in a tiny village can't make that much money."

"My grandmother's second husband did well in shipping. He leased the house to me once he moved to Brest." Menez slouched in the chair. "Now, with the German occupation, the bombings, he may not be doing so fine. I don't know."

"I see. You must give me his name. I also noticed you have guests now and then, which included the man we just arrested. Herr Kerguelen." August chilled his voice for emphasis. "What do you meet about?"

"We are old friends." The butcher flipped up his hands, as if trying to appear casual. "We talk of fishing, the price of bread, the scarcity of certain foods, common topics."

"You don't discuss resisting the German occupation?" August allowed a German accent into his usually impeccable French.

The butcher forced a laugh. "That would be absurd. There are so many of you, and too few of us. A bizarre idea."

"A perilous idea." August stared off as if in contemplation. Then he glared at the butcher. The man didn't appear very shrewd, or it could be a facade. "We're keeping an eye on you and your friends, so be aware. I won't tolerate any such resistant activity or sabotage."

"I'm just a butcher who wishes to run my business, and support my family," Menez shrugged, "even in difficult times."

"Because we Germans are here?" August raised his eyebrow again and gave the butcher a frosty glower. The games they all must devise to keep order.

"Soldiers take the cows and goats, leaving little for the villagers. Some people are eating horse meat." Menez didn't sound indignant, only relaying facts as he saw them. "My family's been here for generations as butchers and farmers. My wife, she deserves more, but never complains."

"You are fortunate to have a good woman." August pictured Klara; that twinge of pain at her suffering the final year as the cancer progressed. She was also a dutiful wife.

"I am blessed. What's happened to Kerguelen?" Menez asked, almost like an afterthought.

"He's being taken care of." August made it sound ominous, which it could be, in Paris. But what other choice did he have? "Your son was recently caught running down to the shore, despite the restrictions."

Menez straightened, his gaze sharper. "My oldest, Jean? Are you certain?"

August paced the length of his desk. "Your houseguest, Fräulein Cooper, came to me to rectify the situation."

The butcher trailed a hand through his hair, oily and drooping. "She did? Is my son safe?"

"You will find he is. As his father, you must advise him better." August stilled, thumbs in his uniform pockets. "Now, about Fräulein Cooper. She arrived in France last year, is that true? In the midst of her country being at war with Germany. Why did she take that chance?"

Eyes hooded, Menez glanced away. "She was worried about my wife; they are close, first cousins. Norah is a careless woman."

The butcher's lack of empathy for Fräulein Cooper sent a flash of annoyance through August. He had a sudden feeling of protection for her, which unsettled him. Yet he wanted further information. "She crossed the Channel, in the middle of war, just to check on your wife? Then hid herself away? I think there is more to it." He leaned over his desk. "You would do well to tell me everything."

Menez stared up, expression calculating. His lips twisted into a semblance of a smile. "I could be persuaded. Do you have a cigarette?"

Chapter Seven

Norah, basket on her arm, reached the stand at the edge of the square, past the auberge, where the old women sold fish. She rose early to make certain she could purchase her share. "Are the sardines fresh?"

"*Bien entendu*. They are the freshest." The elderly woman, her face leathery from the sun, turned up her nose. The tiny fish, one eye staring, lay in rows, their scent not yet pungent. "Do you have your ration book?"

People milled about at different booths, but mostly grumbled at the slim offerings. The venders shrugged in apology. Some women sold linens and lace, items famous in Brittany, along with the local pottery. But the villagers wanted food, which the invading army bought up quickly.

Several German soldiers were already at the booths, jostling for space to inspect the wares.

Norah pulled her book out and the coins she had. She clinked them down.

"I can't take those; you know the rules." The woman glared at the livres as if they were vermin.

"I'm afraid I ran out of the other money." They were all forced to use German money since the occupation. Even many of the towns had been given German names, the streets changed as well. All clocks were switched to German time. The Jerries wanted domination.

Someone moved beside her. The woman shrank back, eyes lowered. She plucked at her white cap. Norah turned, then started. The Commandant stood next to her.

"Is there a problem?" he asked, his tone inquisitive and not confrontational.

His nearness unnerved her. Norah found her voice. "No, I just don't have any more of the Reichsmarks."

He pulled coins from his pocket and laid them on the booth's wooden counter.

Norah held out her French coins. He acted as if he wouldn't take them, but he must. She set them down and nudged the livres further in front of him. She couldn't be seen given favors.

The woman quickly wrapped up the fish and handed them to her, eyes darting between them. She snatched up the Reichsmarks.

"The offerings here seem sparse," the Major said after a glance around.

Norah stuck the package in her basket, wanting to move away. "It's because you…the Germans buy up most of the food before we have a chance." She sighed inside. There was her wayward tongue again.

"Ah, I see." He scanned the scattering of booths again. Then smiled at her. "Hungry soldiers are a problem. I wonder what can be done."

The Major's half-smile sent a flutter through her belly—so wrong! What was the matter with her? She stepped to the side. *Would* he do something about the food?

"How is your young cousin after his unfortunate experience yesterday?" He walked beside her, and she forced herself not to be rude. Tall for a woman, Norah's five-foot seven-inch height barely cleared his shoulder.

Several women stared and whispered.

"Jean is fine, thank you again." She was careful not to gush. She didn't dare take the children back to the church. Her cousin had been distraught over what happened with Jean.

The Commandant bowed his head. "It was only fair, Fräulein Cooper. I'm a reasonable man."

His caring about fairness surprised her.

"If you'll excuse me, I need to take this fish to my cousin." She moved in that direction.

"I can see you're anxious not to be seen with the enemy." The Major put his hands behind his back, his smile wry. "Since you're English, are you registered as an enemy alien?"

Her stomach plunged. "I suppose I should, but we're so far removed." She'd tried to blend in with her French cousins and hated to call attention to herself. Would he demand that she comply?

"I'm sure there are many who haven't." His tone seemed to excuse her actions, but she remained wary.

"As pleasant as this conversation is, I really must return home." She hesitated when she felt a strange pull toward him, a spark that was totally improper. Her body stiffened.

"People are watching? I am rather obvious." The Major raised an eyebrow, his blue eyes intent under his high-capped hat. He took a step back. "Don't forget your Reichsmarks again, young lady." He said the last just loud enough for people to hear. Then he walked away, his boots clicking across the cobbles.

She left the open market, heart in her throat. How could she feel that strange attraction to the Commandant, a Nazi? She was only overwrought, caught up in the sudden, unasked for, meeting.

Loud laughter caught her attention. A soldier, pale as a fish's underbelly, stood over a buxom woman, who crouched in the street. Her torn package of sardines littered the ground.

"Why did you do that, monsieur?" the woman groused, eyes down, her scarfed head drooping. "Swipe aside my food."

"Because we're in charge here, and you are clumsy." The soldier snickered. "You will address me as Corporal Flach. Never forget I'm your superior. Watch where you step next time." He swaggered off. Norah, in the heat of anger, hurried to help. The Commandant was nowhere to be seen.

* * *

August hefted a stone in place in the wall behind the house in the forest. With a wriggle, he fitted it in just right. A storm last winter had sent a tree crashing into the wall, knocking a few stones loose. He'd meant to repair the wall for months. The sun warmed his bare arms, as he'd pushed up his shirt past his elbows.

"You should hire someone to do that, sir." Lt. Bauer approached, carrying a cup. Lean and muscled, he was third in command, a man August could usually count on. "Your cook was kind enough to pour me some coffee."

August wiped his hands on a cloth. "I enjoy the work and being outside. I used to help my father repair walls on my grandparent's estate in Germany. My brother and I." He checked the symmetry of the wall, nice and even now. He inhaled the earthy smells around him.

He'd ridden horses on their estate as well, and thought about purchasing a horse here, to ride in the hills. He smiled at thoughts of his *Oma*. She had been a wise woman who warned Hitler's greedy policies would ruin Germany.

"Where is your brother? Is he in the military?" After permission, Bauer sat on an iron chair on the stone terrace. His chiseled face wasn't easy to smile.

With his dark brown hair, he was hardly the Aryan perfection Hitler preferred.

August stepped closer. Terracotta pots full of red geraniums lined the terrace, giving it a bright appearance.

"He's a businessman in Vienna." August's brother, Walter, had followed the Nazi ideology, and they didn't speak as often as they used to; letters had dwindled. Sadness over their estrangement briefly darkened his mood. "Do you have anything to report?"

"Only that two privates were arrested late last night. Drunk, and with some unsavory women they'd brought to the village. Venereal disease is rampant among soldiers, unfortunately." Bauer grimaced. He was a man who wrote his wife in Germany frequently, appearing a loyal husband with values.

"It's difficult for so many men without women, so far from home. However, I want no prostitutes brought here." August rolled down his sleeves. How long had it been for him? Since Klara. The image of Fräulein Cooper slid into his mind.

Why did she intrigue him? Why did he wish to talk to her again?

"I will make certain no more girls of that ilk arrive." Bauer sipped his coffee. "How I wish this war would end and I could return home."

"Very good, on both counts." August turned from his lieutenant and stared off through the pine trees. "Does your family support the war?"

"Only on the surface. My wife objects but feels helpless." Bauer's gaze saddened. "My children might forget me."

"As it continues, we all have less control." August pondered what could be done to slow the barrage. His life needed a change of course. "What do you think about the vessel which will soon arrive at the port?"

Bauer groaned. "It won't be good for any of us who still have a conscience."

"I agree. Much needs to be done." August clenched his hands together. What about the effect on the village? For now, could he make food more available to the inhabitants as he'd mentioned to Fräulein Cooper?

He'd been impressed by her courage in approaching him about her young cousin. And her dancing, if he was honest with himself. Her green eyes were bright and intelligent; her blonde hair with that hint of red, lustrous. He mentally shook himself and must *stop* thinking that way. She was someone he should leave alone.

Chapter Eight

Norah cocked her head to get a better view of the Eurasian Hoopoe nesting in a hole in the chestnut tree. The bird was fairly common, but she couldn't resist the bright orange feathers, the black striped wings, and the unique black and orange striped crown feathers that sprung from its head. The French called it *huppée.* Its long, thin, tapering bill for foraging, and butterfly-like flight also made the bird stand out.

Morning light filtered through the branches at an angle. The air grew warmer as the green forest smells enveloped her. She was only about eight feet from the square, sitting on a rock.

Here, in the quiet of the woods, with no view of the coast, Norah contemplated she was wasting her artistic efforts. Yet drawing calmed her, usually; but it hadn't kept her out of trouble.

The Commandant's face wormed into her mind. His voice, with its raspy edge, his elegant manners. His smile and probing blue eyes. She quivered with that spark of attraction—tainted with repulsion for what he stood for. *Damn.* He was a dangerous man she should stay far away from. But his kindness at the market two days ago confused her.

She worked on the bird's eye, adding white to the dark, to make it shine.

Yann had been questioned after Jean's escapade, while she and Loeiza had scrubbed the house with vinegar and water to keep busy once Marie-Louise rushed in. The five-year-old had seen her father enter the Town Hall with a soldier while she swept the front step.

Was the interrogation about Norah or Jean? Norah feared she would be thrown out now for causing strife, bringing the Commandant's attention on them, *again*.

Yann had shrugged it off, though he'd gestured toward her, warning, "*You* must behave yourself." Treated like a child, she'd sucked in her pride. Jean acted like his run-in with the sentry was a great adventure, yet he promised never to do it again.

Madame Bolloré had accosted her on the way out of her front door two hours earlier. "You should have known better than to take the children so close to the coast. You cannot be trusted." She clacked back to her cottage in her wooden sabots. A bitter woman since her oldest son had been transported away by the Germans to work in one of their factories. The fate of too many.

Norah had bitten her tongue to keep from retorting. She sympathized with the woman's situation.

In sweeping strokes, she added more orange to the bird's feathers. The family had acted quiet the next day after the incident, not saying much to her. Yann gave her a gruff look before he left for his shop. A definite chill in the air. Perhaps she should look for other relatives to stay with elsewhere, if there were any. Or find a way to sneak back across the Channel. She pressed harder with her pencil, almost breaking the tip.

Footsteps, slow and deliberate, came from her left. The hairs on her nape prickled. She turned.

"Good morning, Fräulein Cooper. You've a fine day for drawing." The Commandant walked toward her.

Her stomach flopped and bumped against that strange flutter she wished she didn't feel. Was the Major following her?

"Good morning. I'm back to drawing birds. Nowhere near the coast, as you can see." Her words clipped out. Irritation wrestled with apprehension, and a twinge of excitement underneath—a bewildering mixture.

He came closer and loomed over her. "I can see that. And you've caught the colors beautifully."

She fisted the pencil, unable to concentrate. "It's a beautiful bird."

"Beauty is ephemeral. What was the name of that dance you were teaching the children that night?" His cologne smelled pleasant, bergamot with a more peppery scent.

"The jitterbug, a tamer version. I'm sure it's disapproved of in your country." She chewed the inside of her cheek. What could he want?

"There is so much that has changed. I grew up in the village of Jüterbog, near Berlin. A similar word. We have a thousand years of history there."

He sounded proud. She almost said, *Hitler wants to destroy other countries' history.* She dared to glance over. The major's shoulder-boards were white, braided around a silver disk. His greenish-gray tunic had the iron cross on his high collar and medals of various sizes. How many men had he killed?

"Is there anything you wish to discuss? Have I broken another restriction?" She tried to keep her tone even, to show she wasn't intimidated—though she was.

The Commandant straightened, hands behind his back. "I'm wondering how you traveled here to France in the midst of war."

A slight wince. "I had a friend, or rather friend of a friend, who brought me over on his boat. Before the invasion." The truth about this was best. But what had Yann told him?

"Why make such a perilous voyage in the first place?" He sounded almost thoughtful. Or he was a fine actor.

She shifted on the rock with a pierce of the pain she wished to forget. How much did she dare admit? Did he already know? "I needed to see my cousin on an important private matter. Things were calmer, here in Brittany, then."

And she hated to face her immediate family with the growing evidence of her disgrace. She closed her drawing pad, about to rise and excuse herself. But a stubborn part of her didn't want to be chased away. Her muscles felt twisted.

"I'm making you uncomfortable?" Was he taunting her again? "I wish to offer you a business proposition, Fräulein. All very proper. Would you be open to drawing me?"

She stared up in surprise. This might be a challenge. Her breath stilled.

* * *

August watched the astonishment in her eyes. She looked about to take flight, like the birds, but then a contemplative expression crossed her face. The color that rose in her cheeks made her even prettier. Was he stepping where he shouldn't, his decision to leave her alone banished?

"I'd like a portrait to send to my son. I can offer you a good fee." He said this quickly.

She settled back on the rock, glancing away. "What about…your wife? One for her? I saw the photograph in your office."

He slowly inhaled over that sadness. "Klara died two years ago."

She stared up at him again. "I'm sorry."

August hadn't meant for the conversation to turn in this direction. He wanted to ask about what the butcher told him, but now it stuck in his throat. Distressing personal subjects that were really none of his business. But did she know of any secretive discussions at the Menez home?

"Again, I can pay you well for a portrait." He named a price. His urge to bring her closer, know her better, was still unformed, wavering. Wasn't it simply nice to talk to someone he didn't command in the military? Or did he just seek information?

Her fingers tightened around the pad. "I would do much better if I had watercolors, though they'd be impossible to get. But I don't know if I should. Don't I cause enough problems?"

"Because the villagers will think you are fraternizing? Many already collaborate." He scrutinized her; she *was* interested.

"I'm better with birds. I might make you look like a hawk." She pursed her lips.

She stalled, he knew. He smiled. "I have no hawkish beak."

She studied him again, head tilted. "True, you have a fairly straight nose."

"We can do the drawing discreetly." The heat of pleasure threaded through him at her tease. "At the summerhouse in the woods. On the mayor's former property."

Her eyes widened before she seemed to tamp down the response. "Alone, in the summerhouse? That would be inappropriate."

"Bring one of the children with you. Except not the one who ran to the ruins. Is there one who can keep a secret?" He leaned closer and winked.

"I couldn't bring a child. My cousins would object. I'd be tossed out on my head." She slowly stood, her face flushed, her amused smile brief. "But, still, I don't know—"

Gunfire echoed through the trees. Birds squawked and flapped from the branches. Squirrels chippered and scattered up tree trunks.

"*Was ist das?*" August's chest clenched. "I must see what that is. Wait here, or return to the village, Fräulein." He ran through the trees, past gorse bushes, across a field, toward the shore. What the hell was going on?

An artilleryman was shooting one of the machine guns they'd recently mounted on the rocks. Out in the ocean a fishing boat bobbed. The stink of gunpowder and fire swarmed the air. An incident in August's past threatened to overwhelm him, a horrible murder. His too often nightmares. The sound of the gun banged through his head. He thrust the memory aside as best he could.

Captain Schmidt stood to one side, arms akimbo.

"What has happened?" August demanded. The sea breeze swept over him.

"That fisherman is sneaking off to England, taking young men with him. Men we can use for labor." Schmidt pointed with his nose and finger. He resembled a woodpecker.

"Are you certain? What blatant disregard." August snatched the binoculars his captain held. Anger seared along his neck. His superiors would investigate incidents like this.

More gunfire, the *rat-a-tat-tat*. The boat had taken down its sail and motored beyond the reach of the bullets.

August stared through the lenses. It looked like one man was down, perhaps bleeding. Others hunched in the cabin as the boat grew smaller on the shifting blue sea. *"Das Arschloch!"*

He lowered the binoculars. Schmidt stared at him as if shocked by his foul language.

"Halt shooting, sergeant. You are wasting ammunition now." August thrust the binoculars at Schmidt. The artilleryman stopped firing. August relished the relief of silence. He also preferred capture to killing. "You must keep a closer watch on these local people, Captain. In broad daylight they sail away?"

Schmidt stiffened in affront. "I was elsewhere, but… I don't know how they slipped off. I try my best. I should be appreciated. Your lieutenant might be to blame, sir."

"And you oversee him when on duty. No excuses." August had been ignoring *his* duties, dallying with the Englishwoman. "We must add more sentries, but men are limited. You're supervising the bunkers and blockhouses being built along this coastline. Soon, this will be an official forbidden Zone for civilians, the village included." He turned, swearing to himself. He wasn't enthusiastic to order the villagers inland.

Fräulein Cooper, ever recalcitrant, stood at the edge of the woods, observing him, before she backed away and disappeared into the trees.

Chapter Nine

Norah pulled Loeiza into a kitchen corner. In surprise, her cousin dragged the old sheet she'd held with her, as if reluctant to let go. A few squares she'd cut on the table slid to the floor.

"I couldn't see what happened from where I was in the woods," Norah said with as much calm as she could muster. "And I didn't dare go any farther. The Germans fired on an escaping boat, but I think the villagers slipped away."

"The sound of gunfire ricocheted everywhere; it was so frightening. We haven't heard this much since…last year." Loeiza scrunched the sheet to her chest. "But why choose this late in the morning to flee? Who would be so idiotic?"

A pot of soup simmered over the hearth fire. The smell of cooking vegetables and greens gave the room a welcoming atmosphere that Norah wanted to cling to after the incident.

"And there's more." She patted her chest and tried to steady her breathing, nerves pinging along her shoulders. "Major von Gottlieb approached me as I drew a bird. He asked me to sketch a portrait of him, for his son."

"Oh, no. *Mon Dieu*." Her cousin snatched up the cloth squares and returned them to the table. "More unwanted attention. Was he aggressive, demanding?"

"No, he was very polite, almost teasing." Norah rubbed her arms. *He was too nice.* "He offered me a lot of money. Money you could use to buy food."

"You won't do it, will you?" Loeiza sloppily arranged the sheet on the wood surface and cut a few more squares, her mouth bunched. "You can't."

"I know I shouldn't." Norah's mind swirled with confusion. She pressed on her temples and watched the scissors slice through the material. Her cousin was part of a group of women who sewed, and they sold their items on the black market. "Are you making more napkins?"

What was so vital about napkins? When she'd asked, Loeiza always acted vague. She had also turned down Norah's offer to help.

"We sew napkins, head caps, among other things. My friends like to embroider little designs on them." Loeiza kept snipping. "Norah, it could cause difficulties if you're seen with the Commandant."

"I realize that. We'd be discreet, he said. The Major would sit for me in the mayor's old summerhouse." A ramshackle building surrounded by overgrown weeds. Norah knew it was a bad idea, so why did she dither? "Think of the money."

Loeiza stopped and stared at her. "What if he wants more than a drawing?"

Norah felt a rush of warmth at her own totally improper reaction to the Commandant. "No, I'm sure he has no interest like that in me." But if the Major knew of her actions in England, her shame, he might consider her an easy mark.

"But Germans, especially soldiers, are known to rape women," her cousin whispered. "He seems too focused on you."

Petit Yann ran into the kitchen with Marie-Louise chasing him. The three-year-old shouted *boom, boom*, as if imitating the gunfire that must have unnerved the entire village. Marie-Louise told him to be quiet. The children rushed out again.

Norah leaned against the high table. "He's too cultured to force himself..." But did she really *know* this? She winced. "Who would be attracted to me, anyway?" Although, she'd pondered the same in the woods. Why did his interest entice her? She certainly didn't need the complication. "It's the fraternization I worry about. The taint on you."

"Then don't, *ma chérie*. Please." Loeiza folded up the material she'd cut. "You must stay far away from the Commandant." Her cousin gripped Norah's wrist. "Avoid him."

The front door slammed. Yann stomped into the kitchen, swearing in Breton, a scowl on his face. He threw up his arms. "I can't believe this has happened."

Norah almost insisted she was nowhere near the machine gun. He couldn't blame that on her.

"Stupid men. They hid too long in a cove, then tried to escape anyway. Who knows if they made it to England. The Germans patrol the waters. Their planes scout the skies." Yann shook his head. "Pichon arranged for the escape. Now he regrets the attempt."

"Was this part of a plan you knew about?" Loeiza asked in a soft voice.

"*Mais non*. He was warned not to attempt anything so soon after Kerguelen's arrest." Yann placed his hand on his wife's shoulder, his eyes with a flash of worry. "I want no part of this. The Major already watches our family too closely." His gaze shifted to Norah.

"It's not my fault. I've been careful." Norah groaned inside after that evasion. She hoped Loeiza wouldn't tell Yann about the Commandant's portrait request. But the tension on her cousin's face conveyed the worsening atmosphere in the house.

"Erwan was involved with this escape, too." Yann trailed fingers through his lank hair as he spoke to his wife. "He's an angry young hothead."

Erwan, Kerguelen's brother. What *had* happened to Pierre Kerguelen? He appeared to have vanished after his arrest by the Germans.

"If we continue to infuriate the Boche, we'll be sent away from our village." Yann scratched under his arm. "There are already whispers we might be. Our home is here."

"Others have been moved from the coastal areas," Loeiza said sadly.

Norah felt caught in a maelstrom. She needed to be circumspect and forego the tempting allure of money and avoid Major von Gottlieb. She stuffed deeper her disturbing response to him. Maybe men of power intrigued her, that was all.

* * *

August scanned the letter Fritz had typed up concerning the special request from Paris. Could such an item be located? "This looks fine. Make certain it is carried with the courier this afternoon."

"*Jawohl*, Major." Fritz took the paper and left the office, his blond cowlick bouncing free from its pomade. A good young man, his secretary kept his opinions to himself. He came from a decent family, his father a respected winemaker.

August had also sent a letter requesting Schmidt's reassignment days before. Word had probably reached Paris about the escaping boat. A reprimand for Schmidt, or for August as well?

He rubbed the back of his neck. So much to mull over but appear serene and in charge while performing his duties. He'd sent in his own report on the incident, just not what he himself was doing at the time it happened.

Opening his desk drawer, he slipped in the letter he'd just read from his oldest daughter, Gerta. At twenty-one, she was with child. Soon he'd be a grandpapa. He smiled at that notion. Would the war be over by then?

Hitler once expected England to sign a peace treaty, but that would never happen. The British had proven themselves stalwart in this fight against German expansion. August had to admire that.

He put his mind back on his family. His younger daughter, Erika, nearly nineteen, had married right before he left for France. Her mother would not have approved due to her young age. However, their husbands should keep them safe from this chaos. August and Klara had married young, an agreement between their families more than a passion. They'd been good friends and helpmeets. He missed his children. Too bad his fifteen-year-old son didn't write often. But Christoph was busy with his studies. He'd make a fine engineer.

A short, heavyset man waddled through the office door, without knocking, wearing the midnight blue, double-breasted uniform of the **Kriegsmarine**.

"Good morning, Major. I slept well last night. The house is in a lovely grove. Much quieter than Brest." A chubby officer whose uniform belt strained to hold in his belly, Port Captain Ziegler had thick, prematurely white hair. He couldn't have been much older than forty, August's own age.

"*Hafenkapitäne* Ziegler, I'm glad you approve." August wished he didn't have to share the house in the forest with this man who'd arrived yesterday. It was bad enough Captain Schmidt was billeted there. Now he'd have two captains to deal with in close quarters. "Would you care for coffee?"

"Do you have actual coffee? That would be welcome." Ziegler plopped into the chair without asking permission. A man with bad manners. "Is there a good pastry shop in the village?"

"There is, though flour isn't easy to come by. And many here roast barley to make coffee." Not the best flavor. One of his landsers had obtained coffee on the Black Market. August should shut down that enterprise. But if he and his men could profit as well as far as sustenance, he'd let it continue. "Fritz, two coffees, please."

"I can't wait to see the progress at the harbor." Port Captain Ziegler would be stationed here to oversee the completion of the submarine port. He grinned; his round face had a reddish tinge, as if his skin never tanned. "I expect good results."

"You'll find we are on schedule, the workers diligent." August strained to sound proud, though this U-boat was a hazardous prospect. He'd experienced these worrisome thoughts as the savagery of this war repelled him. Where was the honor in attacking non-aggressive countries?

"Do you use French laborers?" Ziegler asked. "Are they good at taking orders?"

"We've had no issue with them." Scooping up paperclips, August tossed them in his middle drawer. He must hide his negativity about this offensive. When he'd entered the army at twenty, after the Great War, he thought he'd be protecting and perfecting *his* country.

Ziegler said, "The main office for warship construction, the *Hauptamt Kriegsschiffbau*, has inspected and approved the location for this port. The *Führer* is pleased."

"I was present during that inspection. I am aware of the approval." August refrained from replying about Hitler's pleasure.

"Naval Command believes Brest may not be the suitable base they'd sought, with only one serviceable dry dock," Ziegler went on. "They might build up St-Nazaire to become the premier base."

"Brest is also close to England and suffers attacks from the RAF." August arranged his pens neatly in the brass penholder. St-Nazaire was further southeast, along this coast, over two hundred kilometers away.

"Brest took heavy RAF bombing in April, a battleship damaged," Zeigler spouted.

"I remember. Several cadets were killed." Terrible loss of life—a sad state. August pictured his son, vulnerable in Germany.

"Then the British navy sank the *Bismarck*. A tragedy." Zeigler snorted in affront.

"Indeed, for the sailors." August wished it would slow the tide of the war. Though he had been aware they were coming, the chubby naval officer and his sailors were an intrusion on his growing appreciation of Bretagne.

Fritz rushed in with two earthenware cups steaming with coffee. The aroma, a panacea to the nose. He nudged his thick spectacles into place with his arm. "I'm sorry, sirs, but we are currently out of cream and sugar."

"This is good enough, thank you. You've done well." August took his cup and tasted the delicious, dark brew.

Ziegler sipped from his cup, rubbed his belly, and smiled like a satisfied cat. "Ummm, quite good. The tiniest things mean so much now." He looked around the room. "You have a nice setup here, very cozy."

The port captain sounded covetous.

August's gut tightened. Certainly, he wasn't about to be stationed elsewhere once this fat man settled in? August would fight, or maneuver around any attempt in that direction. He must protect his place in Saint Guénolé, and his own interests. He admitted his wishes had changed—or only sharpened—since he'd first arrived in Southern Finistère.

Chapter Ten

Norah walked through the swathes of pink campion and rosebay willowherb, absorbing the piquant scent of nature. Angelique and Marie-Louise followed along. Angelique marveled at the wildflowers; Marie-Louise held fast to the serious set of her face. They had to convince her to join them.

They strolled through the woods on the opposite side of the village, far from the coast. A farm sat in the distance, the house spread out in ancient granite stone. A *pigeonairre*, like the turret of a castle, stood on one edge of a meadow where cows grazed. The Germans usually commandeered the eggs and beef.

"We can't go too far," Marie-Louise warned. Her baggy blue dress, a hand-me-down from her sister, drooped around her sturdy legs. She had the full face of her mother, under similar black hair.

"Only to the hill up ahead." Norah glanced around, wary of being noticed, or stopped and a guard demanding where she was going.

She widened her pace, slow and even, feeling her muscles extend. "We are stretching our legs, keeping strong." She filled her lungs with fresh air; surely a walk with the children would not look suspicious, but the forbidden drove her forward.

"I like it out here," Angelique said, her own yellow gown tight across her shoulders, and short to her knees. "If there are no sentries."

They climbed the small hill. Below sat the mayor's summerhouse, though it was a former cider house with an apple press inside. Low slung, crumbling stone in places, the little building was half obscured by weeds and grass. Loeiza said the mayor's wife, Madame Ropars, once used it to pot her flowers.

"There's a stream on the other side," Angelique said. "It's very pretty. A nice place to sit."

"That's too far." Marie-Louise frowned at her sister, her dark brows knitted.

"We won't go there today." Norah chafed at the restrictions. Over a week had passed since she'd spoken to the Commandant in the woods nearer the coast. She'd stayed close to the cottage and the rear garden to avoid him. Why did she long to hear his voice, or catch a glimpse of him? Foolish woman!

Angelique plucked a handful of herbs and held them up. "Verbena, it's good for fevers."

"Need egg whites," Marie-Louise said, ever practical. "We have none."

"Be sweeter, Marie. You need fun." Angelique ran the herbs over her sister's dark head. Marie-Louise swatted them away.

"Bring the plants home, anyway. We'll find a use." Norah gazed around. She could draw the summerhouse. The aspect was beautiful, the forsaken building swallowed by nature. But her drawings were piling up in her tiny bedroom, with no purpose.

And the Commandant wanted her to draw *him* in this structure. Norah shivered with her conflicted feelings. But the money could buy food, and material to make the children clothes.

"Did they kill anyone on that boat?" Angelique whispered. "Papa won't say."

"We shouldn't ask," Marie-Louise warned. She kicked a pebble.

A red squirrel, flicking its bushy tail, rustled in the pine branches above them.

"The men must have sailed safely across to England." Norah let the lie slip out. She had no idea what had happened to them. A terrible worry for a seven-year-old child and her younger sister.

Yann continued to grumble at the stupidity, and no one came anymore to meet in his parlor.

Something, or someone, moved through the grass. A young German soldier, walking in another direction. He gave them a menacing glance. A girl met him beside a tree. They argued, arm gestures flung about. She slapped him and ran off. The soldier stalked after her, his fist on his rifle stock.

Norah cringed, though acted unperturbed in front of the children. She hoped the girl stayed safe. How could *she* ever trust the enemy?

"We should go home now," Angelique said, eyes huge. "The soldier might grab us like they did Jean."

"Told you." Marie-Louise crossed her arms. She rolled her eyes like no one ever listened to her five years of wisdom.

"I'll protect you if you stay beside me. But we've had our exercise. Let's go." Norah herded the little girls back down the path.

In the village, the Market was set up. Booths of what food and goods were still available to sell. Scents of fresh fish and pastries. White-capped women with baskets moved among the offerings. Some of the older women wore the pointy, black headdress called the *jibilinnen*, showing they were widows of sailors lost at sea.

German soldiers also scouted the items for sale. The women scuttled away from them if they hovered too close. Norah didn't see the Commandant, half relieved, half disappointed.

One soldier set down his payment and picked up a parcel of seabass wrapped in paper.

"That's a fraction of what it's worth" the proprietor, an elderly woman, complained.

"It's good enough, *Frau*," he insisted and stalked off.

Norah wondered what would be left for the villagers. Frustration that she had no income twitched, like the squirrel's tail, inside her. Should there be a quick drawing of a dangerous man? A payment in secret.

At the cottage, she glanced across the cobbles at the Town Hall. No activity over there.

"Look, Mademoiselle Norah." Angelique bent and pulled out a box that was half hidden in the buddleia bush near the front step.

Marie-Louise opened the front door, as if anxious to be away from them, and stepped in.

Norah took the wide, flat box. The words '*pour toi,* N.C.' were scribbled on top. *For you*? She glanced around again, mouth dry. "Who could have…? Let's go inside."

In the parlor, she tore open the box. Angelique sat beside her on the sofa.

Norah slid out a leather case. She unbuckled and opened it. Her pulse jumped. A beautiful set of watercolors with brushes nestled inside. Underneath that, a pad of watercolor paper. Angelique cooed in excitement. Norah swallowed an exclamation of dismay.

* * *

August stood with Zeigler atop the slope leading down to the sea. The wind swirled around him, the sun obscured by a few clouds. "The construction is on schedule, as I informed you." He forced pride into his voice, for the diligence not the outcome.

"It appears so, *sehr gut*. We must build our military power. A shame the French destroyed their ships or fled with many. We've had to commandeer trawlers in Lorient for minesweeping." Ziegler patted his fat belly. "At least in Brest, there was still equipment to be had. Including depth charges of various sizes."

"Our good fortune." August nodded, though he knew most of this. The idea of men blowing each other up, or assassinating those in power, or in the way, was too personal. These memories haunted him, disrupting his sleep. His chest tightened. He was no longer the commander above it all, but once again he'd be knee-deep in the destruction.

A gull cawed as the blue-gray waves smacked the rocks with watery fists. A wild, yet bucolic scene that pulled him from the past.

"Now with the 'armistice' the French supply us with what ships they have left, guns, and so forth." Ziegler sniffed loudly. "But the British still mine our ports."

"The British will protect their interests since we're at war." August tried to sound pragmatic. The previous year, a British submarine sunk a German catapult ship, the *Ostmark* southwest of St-Nazaire. Losing that ship had been a huge blow for Germany.

Hitler was a fool to think a powerful nation like Great Britain would roll over. And what about the United States? They'd make a formidable enemy if their President Roosevelt decided to enter the war. They'd signed the Lend-Lease policy in March, giving ships and weapons to England. A policy that infuriated the Nazi High Command.

Ziegler leaned forward. "Things are going well, I commend you. A quiet place for the most important U-boat. An extra deep harbor. The RAF won't suspect something here."

A towering crane had moved materials in place for the *Dom* bunker to protect the submarine, the noise of the motor loud, sometimes screeching. The stink of fuel poisoned the air. Previous equipment had smoothed out a bunkered lock. An ugly, low, concrete building with a rounded top was three-quarters formed, a pen underneath for the larger U-boat. A submarine, while slower, that could carry far more torpedoes, further devastation.

"A storage area for additional torpedoes and fuel is nearly finished. The bunker will have an area inside for minor repairs." August gritted his teeth and kept his words officious. "Camouflage netting has been ordered to hide the dome from air reconnaissance."

"*Gut.* And you have experienced shipyard workers from Lorient, as was requested. How do you keep the regular people away from this construction?" Zeigler asked.

Below, workers smoothed out a concrete path leading from the torpedo storage. Stairs had been cut into the slope.

"They are restricted from the coast." August glanced far to the right where soldiers were rolling out barbed wire along the sand. A shame to scar the beauty of the coastline. "We've had a few incidents, but they were handled. My *Oberleutnant* Krause oversees this port."

Ziegler nodded. "We will work with him. I checked and the steel carrier frames, the *Melan-Träger*, will strengthen the bunker from bombs. The *Fangrost* reinforced concrete beams are huge."

"High Command made certain we'd have quality equipment." Could August wish the RAF would attack this bunker? Sadly, lives would be put in danger.

"As for incidents, your Captain Schmidt said a child broke through the sentries." Ziegler snickered.

August bristled with ire. Schmidt should keep his mouth shut. August thought of Fräulein Cooper, begging for the release of her cousin. Her tearful green eyes. "A miscalculation; a willful but innocent child. And it wasn't near this port."

"What about Schmidt?" The port captain nudged him with an elbow. "He likes to brag, that one. I hear he has a mistress and a wife. Though many men do."

Ziegler was too friendly and careless in his ways. He should never 'nudge' a superior officer. August moved a step aside. "Excuse yourself. Captain. Schmidt is a man who acts as a prig when it comes to the army, but not in his personal affairs."

August was disgusted that the transfer for Schmidt was turned down. Officers were being sent to the Eastern Front, and there weren't enough men to go around. Reports had it that Hitler intended to invade Russia at any moment. Madness!

"My wife and I have an understanding while I'm away. Are there any women of, let's say, easy reputation in the village?" Ziegler laughed, almost a bark. "I don't mind a little fun."

"I forbid my men from taking advantage of the village women," August snapped. "You might have to travel to Quimper for such entertainment."

He reined in his irritation—the dreadful aspect of the U-boat—and placed his mind to more pleasant thoughts. And his were mostly innocent, he told himself. Would Fräulein Cooper accept his offer to draw his portrait? If she liked the watercolors he sent, she could paint him. He relaxed his rigid muscles. One couldn't dwell on war constantly.

Yet he might coax intelligence out of her useful to his importance to remain here. Snippets of information to keep his superiors satisfied. If he enjoyed her company as well, more's the better.

The Military Commander in Paris, Otto von Stülpnagel, would find Major August von Gottlieb invaluable in this village. He squared his shoulders.

It was best to keep your enemies close, and Fräulein Cooper *was* English.

Chapter Eleven

In the rear yard, Norah turned the handle of the mangle, squeezing the rinse water out of one of Yann's shirts. Her arm muscles were sore as she and Loeiza had already done the children's clothing. Their garments hung on the line, in the sun and slight breeze, like different shaped flags. "I know I got the best of the barter. A sketch for the watercolor kit."

Norah hated to lie to her cousin again, but how else to explain her 'gift' without upsetting her. She wished she could confide her conundrum to Loeiza.

"I never realized you knew Madame Ropars. She was a snooty woman before her husband became mayor. A Parisienne who prefers those of noble breeding." Loeiza's tone skeptical, she used her paddle to slosh around her husband's trousers in the big wooden tub of rinse water. The soapy water with the scrubbing board sat cooling in another tub.

"She liked my flattering depiction of her in pencil. I promised to paint her, and her silly dog, next." Norah would have to catch the mayor's wife out walking her white curly-haired dog, no bigger than a cat, and offer this service.

"Where would Madame have acquired such a fancy item in these difficult times?" Loeiza's gaze remained pointed. She handed Norah the dripping trousers. The scent of rosemary in the rinse water, which combated the harsh soap they had to use, perfumed the air. "That set looks expensive."

Norah laid the corduroy on the bottom roller, pushing the waist between the rollers. Then she turned the handle. "The Black Market, I suppose."

She buried her turmoil that the Commandant had no doubt procured the paints for her. At first, she'd resolved not to use the kit. But her enthusiasm grew at the beauty of the watercolor cakes. How could she not utilize them?

Now the Major would expect her to do his portrait. Those opposed emotions, fear and attraction, filtered back. How would she refuse him? Yet she must. She pulled hard on the handle and pain shot to her shoulders.

Norah massaged her shoulder and neck muscles. Her mother had an electric machine that did this work.

Angelique and Marie-Louise carried watering pots, sprinkling the garden where the carrots grew. Petit Yann crouched, building a fort out of pebbles.

Jean rushed through the back gate. "Did you hear the news? Germany has invaded Russia." The boy huffed his breath. "Men in the square are talking about it. Millions of soldiers sent to attack!"

Norah paused her cranking to listen.

"Hush, don't frighten the little ones," his mother scolded. "Did you get what I asked for?"

"*Oui, Maman.* My friend's mother had two extra skeins." He handed her the dog hair yarn. One in yellow, the other in green. "The dye isn't perfect, she said."

"It looks lovely. We'll knit sweaters for the children." Loeiza addressed Norah, making no comment on Russia. "Perhaps skirts for the girls, if we can trade for more."

Norah flexed her aching fingers. "You should make blouses out of those old sheets and other scraps of material people bring you."

Loeiza glared, then softened her look. She smiled, though it seemed phony. "We'll see."

What was her cousin doing with the napkins and caps on the Black Market? What was being embroidered on them? Messages? A tingle passed through Norah. Whatever Loeiza was involved in, she intended to keep it a secret.

Norah cranked one more time then pulled the trousers out from the rollers. She draped them over the line. "I'm surprised people comb and card dog hair to make yarn."

"Long-haired dogs work well. When you're desperate, you do what you can. I'll fashion a pretty scarf with embroidered roses in return for this yarn." Loeiza with Jean picked up the rinse tub and dribbled water over the rows of plants.

Millions of soldiers sent into Russia, could that be true? Norah rubbed her cheeks. Now the insane Hitler fought on two fronts. England was under constant threat of invasion, since Churchill had first refused a peace treaty, and now refused to surrender. The RAF had bombed German cities for months.

"We'll be caught in the middle, massacred in our homes!" Madame Bolloré hung over the side gate, double chins wagging. The gate creaked as her chickens squawked. Her herd of children argued in the background. "Angry Russians will overrun us."

"Enough, *please*. That won't happen, Madame." With a scowl at her neighbor, Loeiza hurried her progeny into the cottage. Jean hesitated, eyes sparkling, ready for action.

"Go inside, Jean." Norah stuffed down her turmoil and pressed on the boy's back until he complied. She turned to the large woman. "Your harsh words were unnecessary in front of the young ones."

"Wait until the Boche and Ruskies savage all of us. And don't talk to me about young ones. At least mine are legitimate." Madame Bolloré scanned her up and down.

Norah resisted shrinking back and throwing a wet shirt into the woman's face. "That is extremely unkind."

"I'm barely surviving and have children to feed." She lifted her chins, her flowered gown snug over her ponderous breasts. Her husband had vanished when the Germans invaded France. Gossip was he'd run off with a woman half his age. "I have responsibilities you can't imagine." Madame Bolloré snorted in affront and left the gate.

Norah suspected the woman sold her chickens and eggs to the Germans and used arrogance to mask her guilt. "Shall I paint your portrait for a chicken or two?" she called out.

Arms gripped around her, Norah held herself still, and closed her eyes, her thoughts skimming over the stab of pain over the lost baby, then back on the possible invasion of England—or would fighting in Russia take up Germany's resources?

Hopefully, her parents and sister, with her children, had relocated away from the coast. Norah whispered a prayer for her family. How she wished she could find out their situation as she figured out ways to improve her own.

The monetary solution niggled at the corners of her mind, even knowing the peril.

* * *

A private served brandy in *Maison dans la Forêt's* parlor, to August and Captains Schmidt and Zeigler. They'd shared a meal of stringy beef and potatoes.

A few lamps on small tables illuminated the plaster-walled room. A maroon carpet covered a portion of the slate floor. Dark-wood bookcases lined one wall. August could live here happily, though he'd change the almost feminine décor, if he could rid himself of these two.

He wished to secure his place in Bretagne, something permanent, and benevolent—no longer a conqueror. But if the army assigned him elsewhere, he'd have to find a practical reason not to go.

He missed his homeland, in simpler times. The quaint town he grew up in. **Saint Guénolé** brought back his youth, despite the occupation. Germany was being ravaged, her cities bombed to rubble—as the Luftwaffe had decimated towns in England, especially London. He sought a serenity he wouldn't dare admit.

August settled into the wingback chair near the hearth, though it was too warm to start a fire. He sipped the brandy, a rich fire in its own right. It burned down his throat and heated his stomach. "Time to relax, gentlemen. And be grateful for a decent meal."

Here, they spoke in German, the two captains' French not as fluent as his. August prided himself on learning French from his uncle's wife, a kind woman from Lyon. Their bilingual son, a close cousin, reinforced his skill.

"To the *Führer*, and our success in Russia." Zeigler lifted his glass as he took up half of an old Victorian sofa upholstered in pale rose.

"Heil Hitler." Schmidt raised his glass from his chair, arm straight. "And England will be next if they continue to refuse our terms."

August raised his glass a few inches. "We'll be stretched thin on two fronts. Hitler ignores the pact he made with the Russians."

"The *Führer* believed Stalin was dealing with England behind his back." Schmidt lit a cigarette. The pungent smell of smoke filled the room.

Zeigler snorted. "The Luftwaffe has destroyed over a thousand Soviet aircraft. Stalin is in shock, the wireless said."

Now Stalin would gather forces and attack the Germans, August didn't point out. Russia was a vast country with many men to engage in battle. Germany *had* promised France they'd protect them from Communism.

"I'd hoped to be promoted. And involved in the fighting." Schmidt puffed on his cigarette. His gaze slid to August. Did he know of the unsuccessful request for reassignment? "I want to prove myself to the *Wehrmacht*. My talents should be rewarded. And my wife and children could use an increase in pay."

Along with his whore, August refrained from saying. Schmidt struck him as someone who would recoil and burrow beneath a rock if under fire. "Have you put in a request for a more front-line position?"

"I have contacts in Berlin. Though my skills aren't often appreciated." Schmidt crossed his skinny legs, a smirk on the face of his egg-shaped head with thinning brown hair. "When will this damned port be finished?"

"Very soon, I should think." Zeigler took a gulp of brandy, then coughed, his ruddy, round cheeks darker. "Over the radio that coward General de Gaulle, who hides in England, calls for the people in France to join the French Free Forces there."

"De Gaulle has announced such before. That's why we must keep the Bretons from escaping." August tapped his glass. And prevent undue shooting of civilians.

Schmidt's face reddened. "We need to empty this village. Move people away, inland."

"We await further orders." August's hand tightened around the crystal. Surely Schmidt would not go above his head. He intended to protect the people here, leave the village intact. "And *you* take orders from me. Keep the coast guarded, that is your job."

"My men are here now, the coast will be secure," Zeigler said with a satisfied grin. "Especially the port. I wait in earnest for the U-boat to arrive. She'll be a marvel."

August suppressed his consternation. And he had the added policing of the sailors and soldiers who now intermixed. Several fights had broken out in the tavern.

"I heard another rumor." Schmidt sipped more brandy. "That supplies meant for Germany from this region will be short-changed."

"What exactly does that mean?" August leaned forward in his chair.

"Food, held back, and kept locally. That's the new…instruction." Schmidt glanced away, swinging one booted foot.

Zeigler stood, his cheeks flushed. He'd consumed three beers with dinner. "If you will excuse me, friends, I think I'll retire for the night." The chubby man made a quick bow and left the parlor. His footsteps thudded up the stairs.

"Do you expect the villagers to starve?" August finished his brandy and stood. "Even an occupying army should attempt good relations."

"We are here to subjugate these people, that should be all, sir." Schmidt stubbed out his cigarette and slowly rose to his feet. "Hitler wouldn't care what happens to them."

August fumed inside. Hitler had no soul, it was obvious. August could never be like that. The reality of this grated deeper each day. "Well, you *will* care, under my command."

"Germany should have the supplies, sir." Schmidt's 'sir' held no respect.

"We also have sailors to feed now that Captain Zeigler is here." August stepped up, close to his subordinate, half a head shorter than he. His hand gripped Schmidt's collar. "I'm tired of your attitude. If you don't follow my orders, you will be put on report. Do you understand?"

Fear sharpened Schmidt's eyes, though resentment shone through. "I don't… I'm only thinking of our soldiers. I understand, sir."

"Good, make sure that you do." August bunched the man's collar and gave a slight jerk. This idiot did have friends in high places because of family connections, but how far would he go? His father seemed to have little respect for Schmidt.

A weariness at the position August was in, hating Hitler's policies, threatened to drain him. "Don't force me to carry out my warning, Captain."

Chapter Twelve

Norah and Loeiza set out the dishes for dinner on the two small tables pushed together in the kitchen. Norah tried to dismiss the flinty way Yann watched her, as he obviously wished her elsewhere.

"Seaweed cakes, again, *Maman*?" Marie-Louise poked one with her fork as if it might crawl away and leave her alone. The cakes were made by squeezing the moisture out of long strands of seaweed, called *goemon*, then rolled into a cake-shape and dried in the sun. The Germans allowed a group of older village women to collect seaweed a half mile from the port. "It's a bad taste."

"You will eat what is served, *ma fille*." Loeiza smiled at her stubborn child.

"Don't be rude to your mother." Yann sat at the head of the table with a groan. "Business isn't thriving; there's less meat to butcher," he muttered to Loeiza.

"These cakes are full of good health and will make you grow tall and strong." Norah placed cups of watered-down cider before each child. "Your mama soaked them in juice for flavor." The cakes were still a chewy, slightly fishy meal.

"A German soldier brought whelks and sea-snails to the market. He didn't charge too much, to my surprise." Loeiza set out the dish of simmered *bulots* and *bigorneaux*. "I had enough lard to cook them." A fishy aroma mixed with the fatty scent of lard.

"If they let us pick our own on the beach, we'd find more." Jean winked and scooped the seafood onto his plate.

"You will not go near the coast again, young man." Yann jabbed his fork in Jean's direction. "But how much longer can we exist like this?" Yann slipped a cake onto his plate, along with the fish and a salad of greens sprinkled with vinegar. "A Corporal Flach threatened me today that the Germans will push us from—"

"Not now, Yann, please." Loeiza pressed his shoulder, her eyes beseeching.

"These look delicious." Angelique speared a sea-snail and ate it. She sliced into a cake. "Yum. I'll be taller than all of you."

"*Non, Maman.*" Petit Yann stuck out his tongue when his mother cut up a seaweed cake for him. She stroked his golden locks.

"Food will become scarcer because of German greed, that's all I know. And now their sailors are here." Yann shoveled a cake into his mouth and chewed. "Shipping of supplies is interrupted everywhere because of German patrols."

"We are managing, *mon cheri*," Loeiza said with a comforting smile—though it wavered— obviously to calm the children.

"Are we? I wonder." Yann's glare shifted from his wife to their unwanted house guest. "We should find you a husband. I know a few intrigued men in the village."

"I'm not interested but thank you." Norah scraped over the least amount of the meal she could cope with to keep her stomach from growling. If she continued to eat their ever-sparser food, she must bring in money. She groaned inside, her hand trembling as she ate the pungent greens. Could she do the forbidden, risk being caught, and suffer condemnation?

The next morning, she packed her drawing pad, pencils, and the leather case with the watercolors. She strolled close to the Town Hall, the office windows winking in the sun. She even hummed a tune. The guard stared at her.

She shoved aside her reservations, the voice in her head that warned her to turn back.

Walking around the back of the building, she followed the path that led to the right, away from the Commandant's house nestled in a beech grove. She steadied herself with the woodsy, fresh scent of morning air as the path twisted through the trees. A chirp of birds and the rustle of squirrels accompanied her. A rabbit startled and hopped away.

A particular bird call brought thoughts of drawing coastal birds in Yorkshire near Whitby, for her ornithologist friend. Even in summer, the weather there could be cold and foggy. A pang for home briefly filled her. But lamenting the past did no good. Here, the bright sun lit a flame inside her. And she must forge on.

She reached the summerhouse, sat on a hillock, and pulled out her pad. She made a rudimentary sketch of the low, granite building with its slate roof. Paint could be applied later.

Impatient, nervous, she opened the leather case. She admired the watercolor set again: Italian pigment cakes in twenty-four colors. Two round tip brushes and one flat tip. A palette for mixing paint. Would he come? Would the guard report on her movement?

She outlined the crumbling stones, the high grass and weeds. The broom shrub with yellow flowers, and clumps of goldenrod. Bees buzzed about the blooms.

With quick strokes, she delineated the slate tiles on the roof. Maybe the Commandant wouldn't come. She should forget this crazy idea. More minutes passed.

Slow bootsteps along the path. She held her breath. A glance to her left confirmed his approach. Her body quivered.

"Am I to understand that you've changed your mind about the portrait?" The Major's shadow draped over her.

"Perhaps." Norah didn't look up at him. She was doing this for her cousins. "I'd like…more money than you offered."

"That could be arranged." He crouched beside her. The peppery aroma of his cologne drifted over her. "Shall we go inside and see what condition the summerhouse is in?"

She took a long, slow breath. Was this an innocent invitation? Do *not* show fear. "Yes, we should." Norah packed up the case and pencils, stuffing her pad in her bag. Her feet pulled in, she began to rise.

The Major clasped her elbow and stood, assisting her up. Her pulse tripped. Then he released her.

They walked to the weathered door. The Major turned the latch and pushed on it. The ancient wood creaked. He put his shoulder to it, and the door gave way with a shudder.

Inside, it smelled of mold, rotten apples, and dirt. The one room was full of creeping shadows. Small windows on the opposite side were dingy and gave little light.

"This is not an ideal place to draw someone." She took one step in. His close presence unnerved her. She was beginning to regret her decision. Could she trust this man, alone?

"I agree. It is dark and needs a thorough cleaning." The Major stepped farther in. He swiped cobwebs from the old cider press. Cast-iron gears and handles were attached to two wooden baskets on a wood stand.

Splintered, warped barrels sat near the press. A high, narrow table stood to one side. Various plant pots lined the wall, some cracked. Cobwebs clung to a low, raftered ceiling.

"Even clean, there won't be enough light. This is a gloomy place to call a summerhouse." Norah walked to one of two windows. Outside was the stream Angelique had mentioned. Several flat rocks poked up from the grass on the near side. "We could do the portrait out there."

The Major stepped beside her, his upper arm almost touching her shoulder. Her stomach flipped. She cursed herself and must learn to curb her unruly emotions.

She needed to keep to her purpose, not only on earning money, but to learn about what the Germans were planning with this secret port—if feasible. Her cousin could embroider *that* information on her napkins. A good reason to spend time with the Commandant.

* * *

Standing this close, August felt an unsettling heat in places he'd forgotten he had. Fräulein Cooper smelled clean, like soap. Should he move away from her? This was not what he'd planned. "Out there you risk being seen with me, your most devious enemy."

"In here it's too shadowed." She sounded stiff, almost remorseful. "And there are enemies everywhere."

"Why have you changed your mind?" Her hair looked soft, and he wondered what it would feel like to touch. Such thoughts!

"It's a business proposition, isn't it?" She shifted the leather case in front of her. "I'd like to purchase better food for my cousins."

"Ah, of course. Understandable." He glanced down at the case, where her fingers gripped the handle. "Are the watercolors suitable?"

"They are quite suitable. Can we open this rear door?" She moved toward it.

She must know he'd purchased the kit for her, but obviously didn't intend to say so. A spirited, and perhaps complex woman, as he first surmised.

After three wrenches, August dragged the door open, fingers clenched on the metal handle. A few splinters flew as it squeaked.

"I've made plans to bring additional food supplies to the village. Allow more fishing boats out to catch fresh fish for the inhabitants. Let that be our secret." He brushed his hands together. He'd test her; would she keep silent on that accord? If she didn't, no harm—despite Schmidt's vindictiveness—but then he'd know her level of loose lips.

She stared at him. He'd surprised her. "We'd all appreciate more available food." She stepped outside to the edge of the stream. The water burbled past, in and out of shadows from the trees. A bird chirped. She pointed to a large, flat stone, mostly in sunlight. "You could sit there. But take off your coat and hat."

"Right to business. Very good, Fräulein." He smiled at her gumption. Removing his hat, he unbuckled his belt and undid his tunic. He laid these items carefully on one of two weather-beaten wooden chairs up against the building's wall. The air felt good through his dark green shirt, yet a vulnerability he hadn't expected seeped in.

August watched the stream, with steaks of foam, bubble over the rocks beneath its surface. A reminiscence of fishing as a boy with his father and brother, Walter, in a stream outside the ancient wall of Jüterbog entered his mind. Sweeter days, though the rise of aggression that accumulated in the Great War under the Kaiser already rumbled around them. Peace was such a fragile thing.

He turned to observe Fräulein Cooper. A slender, graceful form. Would she pass on any intelligence, by mistake, from the village? Then again, he'd only use the information to keep the village safe from his superiors. To retain good order, keep the villagers in line, and quash any forms of resistance.

She placed the kit and her canvas bag on the other chair. "I'll draw you on the watercolor pad, which might take a couple of days, and then start to paint at another time."

August sat on the stone, warm beneath him, hands on his knees. This felt peaceful. Words gentle, he said, "Take as long as you require, Fräulein."

Chapter Thirteen

As night closed in, August sat on the mayor's former bed and rubbed his freshly scrubbed face and damp hair. He wouldn't have displaced the mayor and his wife for the finest house in the village if they hadn't had a place to go. A brother, with a farm outside of town. It was a civil as could be possibly managed transition.

For once, part of August's day had been pleasant. A breeze, a stream, and an attractive young woman he probably liked too much. But perhaps tonight, he'd sleep with happier thoughts. And avoid the nightmares.

Of course, he couldn't escape the ongoing war. Fritz had given him a dispatch which said German soldiers and the Waffen-SS murdered Jews in Lithuania and the Ukraine. Hitler blamed all his and Germany's problems on the Jews. A vicious retaliation. Hitler called them ideologically guilty.

When August first arrived in **Saint Guénolé**, he was informed all the Jews had fled. And he'd never ordered his men to make certain.

A slight reprimand came from Military High Command in Paris for the fugitive fishing boat, but praise for the port progress. August dug his palms into the mattress. As Commandant, he took the brunt for any mistakes.

He worried about the dangerous U-boat near completion at St-Nazaire, though Lorient was the main base for repairing U-boats. Would she be too unwieldly to operate and have to be scrapped? If not, soon the beast would be docked here, awaiting orders. He lamented the reality of such a damaging vessel.

And if he was ordered to move the villagers farther inland, it would ruin their lives. Their simpler existence, something he longed for, and he wanted to preserve it.

He stretched out on the bed in his cotton pajamas, hand behind his head on the pillow. When he closed his eyes and drifted into half-sleep, instead of the sweet smile of a blonde girl who drew birds, Operation Hummingbird, *Unternehmen Kolibri*, intruded, *again*, on his thoughts. He tightened his fingers on the sheet he'd jerked up to cover himself.

Seven years before, in 1934, a purge with mass assassinations had taken place. Hitler ordered the murder of top officials, allegedly to prevent a coup—but he wanted complete power. Göring and Himmler had urged him on, aided by the SS and Gestapo.

August pressed on the knot in his stomach that usually formed when he had these ugly memories. He was a captain then.

Kurt von Schleicher, the former chancellor of Germany, had been a friend of his father's. Schleicher had dared to criticize Hitler's government, allegedly working behind the scenes against him. August, alerted by his father, had rushed over dressed as a civilian to Schleicher's home near Potsdam to warn him, to take him and his wife to safety. Almost immediately after August had arrived men in trench coats drove up, knocked, and opened fire.

August grimaced and closed his eyes tighter. Gunfire, the stink of gunpowder, Schleicher and his wife both murdered. Their bodies sprawled in pools of crimson in the hallway. The men had fired at him, hitting him in the side. He felt the sharp spike of pain, the sticky blood on his hands. He'd fallen to the floor and pretended to be dead. A coward! He should have shot one of them. But he had been outnumbered.

He felt the rumpled scar along his right side. He'd nearly died, but had dragged himself to a physician, a friend of his family.

So many were murdered in those three days, about this same time of year, leaving Hitler with no competition. The madman demanded the military rearm and prepare for war.

A shudder passed through him. August, unreported or unrecognized as being present in the whirl of slaughter, should have left the army then. But Klara was already ill and needed expensive, specialized care.

He blew out a shaky breath. Each day he had waited for his own arrest and execution, but it never came.

* * *

After she positioned the Major once again on the flat rock behind the summerhouse, Norah laid out her pad and pencils.

At their first sitting, she'd sketched the details of his face, his high forehead, full, well-formed lips; a classic face with vivid blue eyes, so they hadn't talked much. A woman's laughter in the distance two hours later had broken up the session and they parted.

Today, as June slid into July, the heat rose faster, the air not as refreshing. Birds squawked at their intrusion. The stream rumbled over the rocks. Bursts of yellow marigolds lined the edge of the water.

She sat on a tree stump, leery of the rickety, warped chairs, and put more details into his shirt and trousers.

"Where are you from in England?" he asked, after several minutes of quiet where he seemed distracted.

"North Yorkshire. I grew up in a village not far from the city of York. Amotherby." Her village had a railway that carried supplies, but she wouldn't tell him that. "There's an old church there with interesting effigies. Our most famous resident was Sir John de Bardesden, fourteenth century; he was ex-communicated by the Pope for disputing rights of pasturing."

He smiled. "You have family still there?"

"My parents. My sister is married and moved ten miles away." Sadness at missing them, plus her nieces and nephews, slowed her hand. A bee buzzed around a clump of lavender, the scent soothing away her upset.

"But you never married?" Was he implying something? Did Yann tell him of her humiliation? She fought a cringe.

"No, I intended to be an artist, but my father wouldn't pay for art tutors. He called it a waste of time for a woman. I worked as a secretary to earn enough to pay for lessons." Every clumsy boy she'd went out with never interested her for long. And her night of alcoholic-infused lust had derailed her artistic plans.

She concentrated on his hands, elegant in his lap. What could she find out about him to assist her country? Other than money, that *had* to be why she did this. "Did you marry young?"

"Yes, very young." He stared off as if recalling the loss of his wife. "We have, or rather had, two daughters and a son."

The Major seemed so human, especially without his tunic and hat. He no longer scared her. This close, she was curious about him. He still put her on edge, but in a different way—a layer she should never explore.

"And you joined the army young?" she asked.

"I was twenty. I graduated early from the *Kriegsakademie*. Before Hitler took over our country." Worry etched in lines at the corners of his eyes.

She stopped her drawing as irritation flared. "Why didn't you leave the army once Hitler's plans were apparent? Or do you endorse his policies?"

She stiffened. Would she anger him?

He gripped his hands together. "You are blunt. My original reasons were to please my father. Then I had a family to support."

"That's important, but you could have found another line of work. Away from the army." Now she wanted to provoke him.

The Major shifted on the rock, his gaze sharp. "I kept telling myself I was better than the others. With me in an important position, I prevented an evil adherent from committing atrocities." Hands untwisted, he settled his chin firmly on his right palm, mouth tight. "I see now it might be a fool's errand." He shook his head. "I should not have admitted that."

Was he telling her the truth? He sounded sincere, even frustrated. Caught up in over his head like she was? She sketched more of the stream, the shadows, and trees. How could she believe him? "But you joined the Nazi Party?"

"Can I trust you, Fräulein? I tell no one this, but I'm not a Nazi." His eyes gleamed with affront, which switched to challenge. "Will you report that to your comrades?"

Her heart thumped. "No, that's personal. I wouldn't tell anyone." He seemed to have put his career, perhaps his life, into her hands. A heavy burden—as if he *did* trust her. Or was it a ruse?

"Until recently, the branches of the *Wehrmacht* were not permitted to hold membership in political parties." His words came out grim. "Even if permitted, I would never align myself with a group bent on nothing but power and annihilation."

"Then you don't support Hitler in any way?" She resisted feeling sympathetic.

"I'm a German soldier. I'm loyal to my country, but I see the honor of Germany has eroded." He shook his head again, then chuckled in irony. "You are too easy to talk to. I mustn't reveal my weaknesses."

She laughed, then caught herself and quickly continued to sketch the finer points of his boots, the rock he sat on. The laugh *only* came from nerves.

"How are you related to the butcher, Yann Menez?" The Major's question sounded casual yet put her on alert.

"His wife is my first cousin. Our mothers are sisters." Norah smiled at the idea, relieved she could. Two very different women, one adventurous, one who preferred to stay in her village. "My aunt traveled to France, met her husband, and made her home in a larger city in Brittany. My cousin met Yann on holiday, in this village, and they eventually married."

They spoke more of their families as she worked. His French fluent, hers catching on words occasionally. A normal conversation, as if between friends—or two people finding their way to become friends. An odd feeling for her, to know better this man she once hated in theory—an enemy to her country. She shivered.

Should she push the growing easiness aside and ask him about the port being built, and nearly finished the rumors said? It might be a home for an intended ship or submarine with weapons against England. Though she doubted he'd tell her.

Norah once considered sneaking down and drawing the port. Should she still attempt it? Or was it only a death-wish of a scheme?

"I've brought more food to the village as I promised, and I intend to protect the people here," he said after a moment.

Now she heard truth, or only wanted to. Was this why she was drawn to him, she'd sensed the decency underneath? Doubts filled her head. Attraction and friendship were two different things, both dangerous in this situation. She swallowed a sigh.

"I would appreciate that, as would my family." She nibbled the end of her pencil, then stopped as noises, someone walking quickly, came from the woods to her left.

"Major von Gottlieb, sir!" A man's voice sounded from the path that led into the village. "You're needed at the office. Something has happened."

The Major stood. A chill rippled through Norah.

"It's my secretary, Private Fritz. He's discreet. I had to let him know where I'd be." His expression stern, von Gottlieb walked to the chair and donned his tunic and high-capped hat. The imperious Commandant once more. "Until next time, Fräulein. Take care."

The Major left her. She stayed sitting and listened to the stream burble, the birds calling out. Her body and brain buzzed with confusion, but she must keep up her guard.

She slowly packed away her pencils and reordered her ideas about him—good or bad. She churned in the turmoil of actually *liking* him.

Chapter Fourteen

August moved to the edge of the ravine, up a slope from an inlet of water—a bite into the land from the Atlantic. The surf sucked at the rocks below. Loose dirt sprinkled into the ditch at his footsteps. A landser sprawled below in the soil and grass, a blotch of blood, spreading like a starfish, on his stomach, blank eyes staring at the sky. The copper scent of blood mixed with the loamy earth.

Gott verdammt, August cursed, his neck muscles bunched. "Did you hear the gunfire?"

"Nothing, sir." Lieutenant Bauer stood stiff as a rod. "I was going off duty, and a sentry ran to inform me."

Schmidt hovered close, yet barely glanced at the boy. "As I was informed as well."

"No one saw anything?" August turned from the slain soldier who was too young to die. The landser's cap was half off under his straw-colored hair, his face drained and pasty like wax. His Gewehr-41 rifle missing.

A lamentable fact, in war, they all took their chances. The ramifications weighed like a stone on August's chest.

"It must have happened during the night patrol. When they came up a man short, they searched." Bauer shook his head. "The unfortunate sentry. Hours passed before he was found."

"Were you aware of the search, Lieutenant?" Schmidt demanded, head thrust forward, his woodpecker nose striking the air.

"Of course. I sent word to both you and the Major as soon as I was notified." Bauer remained at attention. "A regrettable loss."

"It's Sunday, my day off." Schmidt shrugged, though the gleam in his eye made August suspected he'd been in Quimper with his mistress—a woman of the worst reputation.

And August had again been dallying with the Englishwoman; but he didn't care. He savored his time with her. "I want a thorough investigation. Schmidt, you are in charge. Bauer, get me that boy's name and other information for my report. And I must write to his family. Cover him up!"

"Won't our superiors in Paris demand retribution?" Schmidt appeared to gloat over this, and care little for the human life lost. "A villager for one of our landsers? Or we could shoot two."

"Let's make certain we find the correct individual." August fought down his anger. His second in command made these snide remarks to exasperate and poke at him. "I'd rather *not* kill innocent people."

August would detest such an act. It was something he'd never done, though pressure from the *Wehrmacht* always crowded around him.

He stomped off, back toward his office. The poor young man. A mother and father would weep over their beloved son. Had one of the villagers killed him? That seemed likely. The group that once met at the butcher's would be August's first contact.

At his desk, he pulled out paper and scribbled notes.

This development might upend everything. Now a local was armed with one of their rifles. Should he extract information from Fräulein Cooper since she could name these people? He needed suspects, folks to interview.

August gripped the desk edge. He could never intimidate Fräulein Cooper, or demand information. He looked forward to their interludes. Stiff in the chair, he couldn't deny he was very attracted to her, the first woman since Klara's death. Or was he just lonely?

He'd slipped and admitted too much to her today. He might have put his head in a noose, though somehow he believed she would keep his secrets.

He tossed down his pen. Nothing could come of their relationship, and he must never let his resolve waver.

"Fritz, send a landser to the butcher shop," he called through his open door. "I want to speak to Herr Menez, right now."

* * *

Norah walked home the long way, around the other side of the village, close to the turret that housed the pigeons. She heard them cooing and rustling inside. Gray heads poked out from the window slits and the birds gabbled at her passing.

What had happened to pull the Major away? Was anyone in danger? She liked his company, his attention, far too much.

And his confessions! Was he trying to link the two of them together, engage her empathy? Or did he seek intelligence about the resisters? Her pulse skittered. A terrible conundrum she must steel herself against.

She swung the case, tapping the side of her leg. He'd given her half the money she asked for already. And the last Market had been stocked with more food, just like he promised. She'd purchased fish, vegetables, and fruit for her cousins. Material to sew the children new clothes.

Loeiza had given her a suspicious look. "Where did you get the money?" she asked.

"I sold a few paintings," Norah had replied, and left it at that.

Her cousin watched her with circumspection for a while afterwards.

Norah entered the village through an alley near the tavern. A group of men were playing the game of *petanque*, where they tossed a metal ball at little wooden spheres called *cochonnet,* or piglets.

Two teams stood in a circle etched in the dirt. It was similar to the English game of bowls. The balls clicked as the men laughed.

A young German soldier stood to one side, watching them, as if he longed to be included, or listened to their conversation for radical information.

"Mademoiselle Cooper." Pichon, Yann's lanky friend, left the game and approached. "How are you today?"

"I'm fine, *merci.* When do you marry your fiancée?" She continued to walk, and he fell in step beside her, grimacing as he disguised his limp.

"Quite soon. We plan for the end of July." He chuckled. "My friends think I should marry a girl from this village, as though you can switch what's in your heart at will."

Her heart squeezed with the growth of illicit feelings. "That's very true."

They reached the stone well in the square near Yann's cottage and stopped.

"The people in Bretagne are very particular about outsiders," he shrugged in his loose blue shirt, "even if just from a different village."

"I know. They'll never accept me." Norah shrugged, too. She had planned to go home as soon as she could save the money for a clandestine sail across the Channel. But now, she wasn't sure she could, or even wanted to leave. *Mon Dieu*, as her cousin would say. Had she lost her senses? She bit on her lip.

"I must warn you, Mademoiselle, the village is whispering about your drawing sessions." Pichon kept his voice low. "Some have seen you at the stream with the Commandant."

Her cheeks burned, but she wasn't surprised; they were out in the open. The villagers had long given her cagey looks since she was English, but she'd tried to ignore them.

"I'm gathering important data and being paid to create a portrait. My cousins need food."

"Fraternization isn't unknown around here. Some Bretons prefer the Germans to the French." He pinned her with his hazel eyes. "Have you discovered anything? Perhaps you discussed the port?"

As she'd been informed, and Pichon just verified, many villagers collaborated with the Germans. Though it didn't make her situation less troubling.

She glanced at a passing cat to formulate her evasion. How could she find out any details without being obvious? Nevertheless, she *wouldn't* repeat their private, personal conversation, unless the Major's actions harmed her family. He appeared to have placed confidence in her, and she staggered under the burden.

"I was about to ask for port information, but the Major was called away."

"If Gottlieb is smart, and cunning, which he seems to be, he'll say nothing about it. Still, women have their wiles. But be very careful. Don't go too far." Pichon sounded concerned. "Unless…"

"I'm doing nothing improper; tell your friends that." Her words clipped out, defensive. This accusation didn't surprise her either. And she wasn't as insulted as she should be, which disturbed her. She teetered on a narrow ledge and must step carefully. It also surprised her Yann had yet to confront and scold her.

Norah moved away from Pichon toward the cottage. She could *never* allow it to go too far. She only wanted a man who cared about her, loved her, and would encourage her art; no indiscriminate affairs to regret in the cold light of day.

Obviously, a German officer was out of the question. Even, despite her efforts, her affection grew. And, she suspected, so did his. How could she manipulate such a powerful man?

"*Un moment.*" Pichon followed in one long stride with his good leg. "Did you know one of the German sentries was killed during the night?"

She flinched and faced him again, hands tight on the case handle. "*No.* Oh, dear. Do they have the person who did it?"

Pichon gave a shrewd smile. "Not yet, or perhaps never. You, my friend, be aware of this Boche commander with far more experience—and murders to his credit—no doubt. Don't be tricked. We want freedom from the occupiers but protect your cousins and yourself. *Bonjour.*" He turned and loped awkwardly off, back to his game.

"I won't be tricked." Norah shook, and the case rattled. A dead sentry? That's why the Major was called to his office. What would this mean for the villagers? The Germans were known for retribution. Yet now she couldn't picture the Commandant allowing such a reprisal. He said he intended to protect the people. Or was she fooling herself?

A soldier left the Town Hall, rushing across the cobbled square and down the street. Norah hurried inside the cottage as her stomach lurched. Had matters already spun out of control?

Chapter Fifteen

August grimaced at the butcher's back as the man ambled out to the square from their discussion in the Town Hall. Menez acted blasé, though appeared to hide something wily inside. He claimed to know nothing about the murdered landser, but August suspected otherwise. He warned him he was not fooled. But he held back a too harsh interrogation because of Fräulein Cooper. The butcher provided a home for her.

"I'd be happy if our guest had *stayed* across the channel," Menez had grumbled. "We don't need the English here. But she showed up without notice. And my wife, she is too kind."

August stuffed down his loathing. He felt the need to protect the young woman, and was quite aware of being too close, too soft when it came to her. Their banter gave him the happiness his life lacked, though he must watch what he revealed from now on.

If this damned war would end, Hitler defeated, could matters be different between them?

With a groan, August entered his office and turned to his jigsaw puzzle to quiet his mind. The bottom edge proved difficult with the white tablecloth. But he'd completed the striped canopy at the top and the straw hat of the man in the sleeveless shirt on the far left. Now he worked on that man's reddish-brown hair, face, and beard. A character enjoying life at the boating party. To have such indulgence! August's movements jerky, he nearly knocked a piece off the table.

Fritz rapped on the office door. "Excuse me, Major. An urgent message." His secretary handed him a telegram.

August read it, dated July 1st. "The Royal Air Force bombed the harbor in Brest. Our cruiser, *Prinz Eugen,* is severely damaged."

Zeigler would have a fit. Brest was once again the premier naval base. August didn't care as much about the cruiser—unless men were injured—as he did about keeping the bombing from Saint Guénolé.

"Bring me Herr Ropars. We'll see what the mayor knows about my dead landser. I'm certain he's part of the group who met at the butcher's." He slammed the telegram down on his desk. These people would hardly give up their own, but August needed results.

"Right away, sir," Fritz said, his whip-thin body at attention, his cowlick bouncing despite the glisten of pomade.

"Give this telegram to Post Captain Zeigler." August snatched up the telegram and flapped it. "Send orders to all lookouts. Be on immediate alert for enemy planes."

"Of course, sir." Fritz turned. "You have…just the visitor you seek." He indicated the lumpy form of the former mayor who the guard had brought up behind him.

"Herr Ropars, come sit. What may I do for you?" August forced a smile.

"If you'll excuse me, my wife would like a few items we left at the manor." The man wobbled in, his wide nose full of burst blood vessels. Clothes stained and rumpled, he didn't look well. "She misses our home. As do I. I have no duties left."

"Are you comfortable? Take better care of yourself. Leave me the list, and I'll see what I can do." August took the paper Ropars held out.

"You know how women are, always demanding. Never happy." Ropars swayed as if he'd been drinking. He stank of cider. "Now that you have a 'friend'. You can appreciate—"

"I don't know what you refer to. Do not make assumptions. Sit down, I want to talk to you about other matters." August's words were angrier than he intended.

* * *

Under the call of a Red-backed Shrike, Norah rounded the summerhouse at the appointed day and time. Yann and others had been questioned about the sentry's death four days before. Yann said little in front of Norah about his interrogation. The atmosphere in the village was tense, with lots of whispering, conjecture, and cautions.

Norah had wondered if she should continue with the portrait, then decided not to be intimidated. None of the villagers had spit on her. Perhaps the increased food at the Market was more important, and they might think her perceived actions precipitated this.

She needed the rest of the payment—and truthfully to her wayward self, to see him.

The Major stood there at the stream, his back to her, his tunic and hat already removed and placed on the rickety chair.

"I thought you'd be too busy, but I came just in case." She took a slow breath, sat on the tree stump, opened the valise and arranged the paint items. "Today I'll start the actual painting."

He turned, his smile fleeting, but it looked genuine. "It's good to see you. I needed this 'sitting', to clear my head."

Norah resisted her own smile. Her pulse did the dance that unbalanced her. She pulled a tin cup

115

from her canvas bag. "Would you mind dipping this into the stream?"

"I don't mind at all, Fräulein." He took the cup, crouched, and caught it half full of water. After handing the cup to her, he sat on the rock.

"I realized instead of drawing just you, I've included the trees and stream. Is that acceptable?" She pulled the pad of paper onto her lap.

"You are a woman who appreciates nature. It's quite acceptable." His flattery also sounded genuine. A tingle she regretted passed through her.

She dampened the smaller brush, mixed yellow and a smidgen of brown onto the pallet. Studying his hair, a golden, sandy color, she dabbed on the hue she created to her sketch.

"I also appreciate nature, I've found, since coming to Bretagne." The Major darted his gaze around the landscape.

She finished his hair, pleased with the outcome, but she hesitated on painting his face. She wanted him to talk, as if her strokes would prevent him. Instead, she mixed hues of brown and painted the tree trunks. She set aside the small brush and used the larger, pushing it flat at intervals to invoke bark. The silence seemed to thicken between them. The burble of the stream the only sound.

"The villagers talk about us meeting here." She added lighter streaks of beige to the bark.

His gaze met hers. He frowned. "Is it uncomfortable for you?"

"I'm all right." She enjoyed their sessions, more than she should. He had a profound effect on her, despite her misgivings. Again, she wondered if men of power simply attracted her. "I can take care of myself."

He looked away. "I thought it might happen, but I don't wish to put you in difficulty." Was he having the same battle with forbidden attraction? He might be lying or testing her.

Still, she wanted to believe him. "I use the excuse that I'm spying on you." She said it off-handedly, then lamented her honesty.

His blue eyes flashed. Then he smiled. "As do I, Fräulein. We are both on assignment, it seems."

Norah smiled this time; two spies, real or deceptive. "You questioned my cousin's husband, Yann." She kept pushing. Everyone warned her the Major was dangerous. Was she struggling to see it while checking their boundaries? "But those men no longer meet at his house."

"So he has said. He isn't an affable person, rather sly. Do you know any of those men?" He asked this as if reluctant.

"Not really." Her nape prickled. She rinsed the brush, mixed blues, back to the smaller brush, and painted the current in the stream. "They conversed in Breton, a language I don't understand." That was a lie; she understood enough of it.

"Breton," the Major said thoughtfully. "A Celtic language like Cornish, brought over by Britons in the early Middle Ages."

"You know your history." More long strokes for the water, she made darker and lighter shades, then white streaks to show movement. Should she stop this inquiry? Her efforts grew clumsy.

"I'm not a Neanderthal. I once thought I'd teach history. There were scattered tribes on this peninsula that the Romans supplanted. Then the Bretons took over as the Roman empire crumbled." The Major resettled himself on the stone.

"Now the German empire is taking over the Bretons, and elsewhere," Norah said, keeping her tone matter-of-fact, hiding her aversion. "The circle of war."

"England captured Brittany for a time." Hands stiff on his thighs, the Major pinned her with his gaze. "I hate to ask, but must perform my spy duty. Have you heard rumors about who might have killed my landser?"

The sky clouded up, blocking the sun.

"No. But I couldn't tell you if I had." She mixed shades of green and stroked over the leaves, her lip caught between her teeth. Her stomach knotted, but she plunged on, challenged. "Can you tell me about the port being built? Why is it so important?"

"You'll understand if that is information I cannot speak about." His words sounded disgruntled, but not towards her. He raised an eyebrow at her audacity.

Thunder rumbled. The air grew cooler, with a slight wind.

"Do you intend to move the villagers away from the coast?" Many worried about this.

"Not if I can help it. But people must cooperate." His voice remained even.

"Well, thank goodness we've got our interrogation out of the way." She made light of it, though discomfort trickled through her. Was he here only to extract information? That should *not* disappoint her. "Then we'll discuss other things. The more you question Yann, the more …unpleasant it is for me."

He nodded slowly. "I understand. I will try not to put you in any disadvantage with the butcher."

Perhaps she did have some influence with him. She mixed and dabbed more paint; the dark green of his shirt, his broad shoulders, muscled arms. "You could retire from the army soon, couldn't you?"

"I have plans. Do you intend to return to England, or make a place for yourself here in France?" He acted like she could easily cross the channel, though she heard real curiosity in his question.

"I have wanted to return home…we'll see." She declined to bring up the war, the fact all their lives could be destroyed by the whims of a maniac.

"What I admitted to you last time, you must keep to yourself." He said it gently, no threats in his tone.

"Yes, I will. I said I would." Again, that weight on her shoulders; but she needed this man on her side. She tried to squelch the depth of that need.

The Major's gaze softened, and she had to look away. She rinsed her brush, squeezing out the water, tapping the rim of the cup.

A raindrop fell onto her pad. "Oh dear. We must move inside, or the painting will be ruined." She stood and headed for the summerhouse. More drops fell on her head.

He rose, packed up her paints, grabbed his tunic and hat, and joined her at the rear door. He pushed it open.

Inside the dim building, she placed the painting on the high table. "How odd. This table has been cleaned." She glanced around. The room had lost its musty smell. "The entire place looks tidy."

The Major draped his tunic over the cider press basket, his hat on top. "I confess. One night, I so tired of my house mates, I came over and scrubbed."

"Did you?" She laughed, trying to picture that. The tension between them seemed to evaporate. She watched him in the shadowed room; an interesting man, and at this moment, not a dreaded officer of the Third Reich.

"I should bring over chairs and lamps." His smile was teasing. "And books to read in peace."

Norah almost asked if she could join him. What a loaded thought. "You'll have your sanctuary."

Rain battered the roof and the windows.

"Indeed. I will. People need sanctuary." He stepped close to her. They stared at one another. He touched her cheek, his fingers gentle. She shivered and drew in her breath.

* * *

August stepped back. "Forgive me, I shouldn't have done that." He'd promised himself not to compromise her, no matter his feelings. The village gossip no doubt already condemned them. She'd become important to him, someone he cared about.

"It's all right." Eyes bright, she moved away and about the room. Trailing fingers over the cider press, she said, "You did a fine job of cleaning."

Rain pattered steadily on the roof. A flash of lightning, then more thunder boomed.

August put his hands behind his back. "One of my many skills."

She wandered the room and back toward him, but stopped. She cocked her head. "So, in all truth, that's what we're doing, spying on one another. Have we been successful?"

He rocked on his feet. A quiver started in his chest. Should he be honest with her? "I must admit, it was an excuse on my part. I suppose I've enjoyed your company."

She brushed a hand through her hair, the lush blondeness. He wanted his fingers to be where hers were. "At first I thought… I did need the money. But now, I've enjoyed your company, too. In this limited capacity." Her voice came out breathy.

"Only in this limited capacity?" He put it frankly, baiting her, or longing for a deeper confession.

"What else could there be, given our circumstances?" She stepped toward the table, her manner almost jittery. "I knew the denunciation would begin, the hazards."

August should throw his tunic over his head and leave for the Town Hall, out of this room, away from her. An impossible situation for them both. Yet he stayed rooted to the spot. "What does one do, in such a hazardous predicament?" He ached to know her exact feelings.

"I wish I had a good answer to that." She stared up at the rafters for a minute. "We should part as friends and say *adieu*."

"Is that what you want?" A sadness crept over him. "Of course, it is the wisest choice."

"Anything else would be foolish." She touched the watercolor pad, the painting of him, eyes downcast.

"I realize that." But he still yearned to know; it had been so long since someone cared—*if* she cared. "Tell me what is in your heart."

She turned and met his gaze. "I'm not one to mince words. I'm rather blunt, as you've pointed out."

"Then let's be honest, please." His throat felt raw. He should let it go, allow her to dismiss him.

She sighed and blinked quickly. "I have feelings I shouldn't have."

"*Ja*. As do I." Two lonely people, or something more? Silence followed, punctuated by rain and the whistle of wind around the building. Her eyes looked huge, and startled, even in the shadows. A woodland creature; but was he a savior or a predator?

Finally, he said, desperate to say something, "May I see what you've done so far on the portrait?"

She smiled, looking relieved by the change in subject. "No, not yet. I want it to be completed first."

He moved toward her, playfully. "Just a peek won't hurt."

She spread her arms as if protecting her masterpiece. "*Mais non*. I'll tell you when."

August took a long step toward her. Fräulein Cooper came forward at the same time. They bumped into one another, her breasts right below his chest. He clasped her upper arms. She stared up at him, lips parted, inviting, yet wary. Past helping himself, he lowered his head and brushed his lips against hers. A tightening started low in his body.

She quivered beneath his hands, but didn't move away, her breath warm on him.

Thunder boomed and rattled the windows. The rain pounded like drumbeats on the roof. The gunshot sounds from his nightmares faded.

"This is wrong, especially for you," he whispered into her mouth.

"I know. Terribly improper. We shouldn't." She remained in place, her form delicate under his fingers, and kissed him back with a tiny moan.

"Norah." Her name felt right, sounded poetic. He pulled her snug into his arms, their kiss deepening. She tasted sweet and *verboten* at the same time. The heat of desire radiated through him.

Chapter Sixteen

Norah concentrated on knitting the stitches her grandmother taught her, maneuvering the long needles in her cousin's parlor, a small room with shabby furniture. Her mind kept slipping back to the Major's kiss three days before, the passion that had vibrated through her. Caution wrestled with this memory. She should have objected, though she'd decided to be truthful in her desires—unsuitable desires! She shouldn't allow it to happen again.

"You're very quiet." Loeiza's knitting needles clicked away, the yellow sweater forming an attractive rib stitch. "Is everything all right?"

"I haven't knitted for a while." Norah performed the basic garter stitch for the jumper panels in green. The Major, or should she think of him as August, said he'd bring chairs and lanterns to the summerhouse. A bottle of cognac? A friendly talk only?

"You seem troubled." Loeiza sounded distracted herself.

"I have a lot on my mind." Would the Major try to seduce her? The idea excited her, but also threw up her guard. Norah must keep him at bay. Until...until she could figure out where their irrational relationship might go. She flushed like a fever ignited inside her.

Petit Yann hissed. He sat on the floor making snakes out of the snippets of yarn, his honey-blond head bent in concentration. The other children were in the garden.

"As do we all…have a lot on our minds." Loeiza continued to knit, but her movements slowed. "You might wonder why I married Yann."

"Oh? No, I wouldn't pry like that." Norah hid her surprise. This subject jolted her from her thoughts. She *had* wondered now that she knew Yann better, but the topic seemed to crop up out of nowhere. "I remember he seemed a nice man at your wedding."

But he wasn't a jolly fellow; a man strict in his narrow beliefs. The Major called him sly. And she'd seen little affection between Loeiza and Yann since moving in.

"He has changed, become less patient. Or in my youth I hadn't noticed. We women seldom have the chance to know someone well before we marry them. The invasion has altered us all." Her cousin tugged more yellow yarn from the ball she'd made from the looser skeins. "But a good wife is supposed to make her husband her priority and preserve his peace of mind. I loved him, or *try* to love him."

"You are a loyal wife, that's obvious." Norah lowered her needles. A good Catholic like Loeiza would never divorce. "Is everything all right between you?"

"I protect my children. And I shouldn't have said anything. He's caught between his Résistance friends and his own wish to not be involved." Loeiza shrugged quickly and resumed her knitting.

"Is he angry about his questioning over the dead sentry?" Norah jerked a length of yarn from her ball.

"He says he handled the matter. He knew nothing." Loeiza completed another row in stiff precision. "The murdered sentry has us all nervous."

Norah didn't want to know who killed the German. She refused to be a snitch and put someone's life in peril.

"Am I causing the problems?" Her regrets over that rushed to the surface. "Should I find another place to live?" Where could she go? Camp out in the summerhouse?

"*Mais non.* I know it's difficult right now. We're all under pressure." Her cousin smiled, though it never reached her eyes. "Strange, there is more food available in the Market than before. But I'm thankful."

"We should all be grateful." Norah's words tripped out. Loeiza appeared to be digging for information. But the Major had fulfilled that promise. *Let that be our secret*, he'd said.

"More food is…welcome, as long as..." Her cousin flicked her a glance, then back on her work. "I hope to have these finished by autumn." She held up the needles, dangling the sweater panel with her elegant stitches.

"I'm happy to help." Norah paused and took a sip of coffee, half real coffee, half roasted and ground barley. They were stretching the precious resource now available. The straight barley brew did not taste like coffee but had a tolerant roasted flavor. Her hand trembled. "Whatever you need."

"You continue to have enough money to purchase food for us." Loeiza now sounded suspicious, wary. "Your painting is going well?"

Norah felt her face heat. "The mayor's wife, Madame Ropars, introduces me to paint pictures of her friends and their pets." The lies piled up around her. Still, she was protecting her cousin by keeping her actions to herself.

"I trust you're not doing anything you shouldn't be." Loeiza sipped her coffee, but watched her, as if expecting a confession. Like Pichon, her cousin had probably heard the rumors.

"I try my best not to." Norah bit the inside of her cheek. Was it collaboration to paint the Commandant's portrait? To kiss him? To care about him? Those last parts, *definitely*.

As August had said, many in the village did business with the Germans. The Bretons assumed themselves separate from France, an independent people. And her time with the Major might make him even more amiable toward the locals, especially her family. But now he'd kissed her, and she had enjoyed it. Her feelings for him increased. She skidded to a ledge, one of her feet dangling in the air. "What do you embroider on those napkins and caps you sell?"

"Snake!" Petit Yann giggled, tossing the yarn fragments into the air.

Loeiza blinked and stopped her knitting, her plump lips pursed. "We embroider pretty designs, nothing more." Her cousin leaned close. "Norah, be *very* careful about what you do. I ran into Madame Ropars at the market yesterday. I praised the watercolor kit she gave you. The woman had no idea what I was talking about. She's never met you, she said. The gossip in the village hints at your actions. Can it be true?"

Norah nearly dropped a stitch, her fingers tangled in yarn. "I'm sorry I didn't tell you. I…really regret the lies. I'm painting the Major's portrait. I'd hoped to keep you out of it. He pays me well. We need the money."

She hid the painting under her bed and cleaned her room herself. Had her cousin peeked?

Loeiza groaned and rolled her eyes. "I worry so much about you. Women who fraternize can be roughly treated, heads shaved, paraded in shame through the streets." Her needles resumed clacking along. "Not that we're so judgmental in Bretagne. Still, he could demand more."

"He's kinder than you might think. Please trust me." Norah relished her time with the Major and looked forward to seeing him as she strained to separate the man she conversed with from the Commandant. "I'm gathering information, too. That's why I do it."

Loeiza huffed but didn't look at her. "*Ma chérie*, you are… Don't make our occupier suspicious in

126

asking too many questions. Remember, Yann wants to ignore the Résistance. Finish the painting and be done with it."

"I'm keeping you and the children safe." What would Norah do when the painting was finished? She felt a jab of disappointment. Her attraction to the Major was intense; to her shame, she craved more kisses. But where would it lead? How well *did* she know him? If she unearthed any sinister details of his past in the army, would that turn her away from him?

And Yann could insist that she leave his house.

Norah clenched the smooth needles. She and Loeiza were both lying, or hedging about their activities. With more secrets between them, they seemed at an impasse. Everyone did what they must to survive. Their knitting clicked on, both trying not to look at one another.

* * *

August stacked the papers on his desk. Germany had taken Minsk and began the battle of Smolensk, an important communication center. The Gateway to Moscow, supposedly. Latvia was occupied and the army advanced into Ukraine. Yugoslavia, a country formed after the Great War, was dissolved. Greece and the Balkans attacked the previous month. Hitler gobbled up the world, now dealing with the Japanese to start trouble in the East, ostensibly to distract the United States.

August crumpled one of the papers. Wasn't there anyone at Hitler's side who could put a bullet where it belonged?

Would the United States step into the war, join Great Britain and stop the madman? There were rumblings about it. How would it effect *his* position if France was attacked? He still needed to discover who killed his landser. A particular local man was suspect. Schmidt had him in once for questioning.

A swift knock, and Port Captain Zeigler waddled in. "Good morning, Major." He puffed out his chest like a rooster, which strained the buttons of his dark blue tunic over his plump belly. "I was wondering, now that I'm here, if I should, eventually, have total control of the port and village." He grinned wryly. "My admiral has asked about my situation."

August stretched tall behind his desk, but he was ready for this, given the man's swagger. "This area is under my purview. I'm still the superior officer. My men are also coordinating in building an airfield at Audierne, on the tip of this peninsula."

With the airfield, the Luftwaffe would have more places to land, in case further bombing of England was ordered. Which, for Norah's sake, and the world's, he hoped would not happen. He was weary of bloodshed.

August shoved papers in his drawer. "You keep watch on your submarine port and the behavior of your seamen."

Zeigler's mouth twisted. "The army is often the start of these fights in the tavern. But I apologize, I may have overstepped in my suggestion."

"When will this U-boat be finished?" August wished for delays, foul-ups, anything to keep it from arriving.

Zeigler shrugged; his saccharine smile returned. "That's still weeks away. Now, let's have more of your excellent coffee and have a friendly discussion." He winked. "I hear you have a girl—"

"As pleasant as that sounds, I cannot share coffee. Fritz will prepare you a cup. I have an appointment. Good afternoon." August thrust on his hat and left the office. Zeigler was about to mention Norah. His shoulders prickled. Whispers from his officers had already started.

And if Zeigler wrote to Paris about taking over Saint Guénolé... The port captain could make things difficult, especially after the U-boat arrived. What could be done about that bloated killing machine?

August must prove *he* should remain in charge here. How to keep control and not be brutal in his administration? He increased his stride, relieved to be out in the air and smell the piney woods, hear the rush of the stream; but mostly to see her, setting up behind the summerhouse. His heart swelled.

She smiled shyly when she looked up. "*Bonjour*. You are punctual."

"To a fault. Good afternoon, Fräulein." He removed his tunic and hat, sat on the rock and wanted to say more, but was unsure what. "May I call you Norah, when we're alone?"

"I suppose that would be fine." She mixed her paints, now not meeting his gaze.

Did she regret their kiss? Disappointment dampened his previous elation at seeing her. "You can call me August. When we're here, the two of us, of course. To protect you."

"Thank you. We do need to be…circumspect." She caught her lip between her teeth, studied him, and began to paint.

"Norah is Irish, isn't it?" The Luftwaffe had bombed Ireland the previous month, in Belfast. Bad news everywhere. He gripped his thighs and shook off the concern so he might savor this time with her.

"Irish ancestors, on my father's side," she replied. "Father's grandmother was named Norah."

August sat very still. He was too fond of her, too attached. How did one sort lust from—more lasting emotions? He said he wouldn't compromise her, yet he had. Without thinking, he massaged his temple. Then dropped his hand to his lap, the 'subject' once more.

A squirrel skittered up a tree, and a bird tweeted before flying off.

"You're certain you won't allow me to see the portrait?" he asked after several minutes.

"I want it to be perfect." She rinsed her brush, mixed more colors, then dabbed at the paper.

"Nothing is perfect, no matter what we might wish." He let the silence fall over them again as he pondered the difficulties, the ramifications for her, if he pursued this growing infatuation.

"True. But as perfect as I can make it." She studied him again and worked on. "I'm not exactly Mary Cassatt."

That pleased him; she liked the Impressionists, too. "What will we do when you're finished?" he asked gently.

She stopped and straightened. Disturbance clouded her eyes. "I don't know. My cousin, Loeiza, wants me to finish for good."

"Your cousin knows?" He nodded and frowned. "I understand her concern. When you're done today, let's go inside the summerhouse, and we'll converse."

Her cheeks blushed pink, though a smile tugged at her lips. She worked for another half hour, then rinsed and dried her brushes. "We do have much to talk about."

"You promised to share a cognac with me." He stood, his smile hesitant. "Come in and see what I arranged."

Inside the building, she glanced around.

"You see the ugly chairs I brought over." He indicated the Louis XV style Bergere chairs he and Fritz carried from the mayor's house. Wood framed with gaudy floral upholstery, they looked out of place. A small table sat between.

She smiled in amusement. "They are quite fancy. But a nice effort."

"Come, please sit." He pulled the stopper from the decanter he brought earlier and poured two glasses. "Let us talk about our conundrum. I have yet to bring a lantern. But there's plenty of light, still."

She slowly sat and accepted the crystal glass. "This is nice." She tasted the brandy; her eyes darted to his. "First, I don't know what Yann told you about me, if anything. The reason I came to France to begin with."

"The butcher wasn't subtle." August sat in the other chair. He sipped the fiery cognac, spicy on his tongue, hesitant to discuss what must be painful for her. "I wouldn't think badly of you. Not that I'm in the position to judge. I'm sorry it happened to you."

Norah met his gaze head on with a flicker of sorrow. "Thank you. But despite what Yann might have said, and what it appears to be, and the fact I'm sitting alone with you in this secluded structure, I'm not a woman of easy virtue."

"*Ach nein*, no, I never thought that." August reached over and touched her hand, caressing her soft skin. "Don't think I'm trying to take unfair liberties with you."

"I'm making certain." She sipped her drink. "I know our situation is filled with hazards."

"Especially for you, yes." He sat back, the glass between his hands. Sadness settled over him. "Are you sorry we kissed? It meant a lot to me." Should he admit how much?

She fidgeted in the chair. "To me as well." Her words almost a whisper, the light slanting in the window brought out the reddish tint in her blonde hair. "I realize you have your duties, but as far as I know, Yann, nor any of my cousins are part of the Résistance."

"And I promised you I would leave them out of anything." August whispered *if I can* in his mind. He wanted to believe her, though that subject surprised him at this moment. He was certain the butcher knew the suspect they'd questioned. A defiant young fisherman with ties to a previous arrest.

"Also." She caught his eye again. "To me you act kindly and are a gentleman. But as an officer in the German army, have you... This is so hard to ask, but I need to know. Have you caused the death of anyone?"

August raised his eyebrows. "You are straightforward, as always." He sipped more cognac as his career stumbled through his mind. "Do you mean have I ever commanded or committed any executions? No, honestly, I have not." He was proud of this, too—but how much longer would he have that choice?

"That's important to hear." She looked relieved, her shoulders relaxed. "As long as you're truthful."

"I have been. Do you wish to be finished once the painting is completed?" He must measure her feelings for him.

"I don't wish to be done, no." She smiled, her voice tender.

"We mean much to one another, don't we?" he asked. She might walk away, reject him, though she seemed too sincere and brave for that. Or so he hoped.

"We do, it seems. But what else can I paint?" She tilted her head as if waiting to see if he had the solution. Her mouth firmed with intensity. "What excuse will I have?"

Reaching over, he clasped her hand and squeezed it, his thumb rubbing along her fingers. He shouldn't offer to do this, to put them both on open display. "There is a fine palace about sixty kilometers from here. The *Château de Keriolet*, in Concarneau. A magnificent place. I'd like a painting of that. We could go for a day."

Her eyes lit up, then darkened. "It sounds wonderful, but won't we both be under scrutiny?"

"We will be taking that chance. It's up to you." He continued to caress her hand. How could he shield her completely? "I'll dress as a civilian, of course. We'll be as subtle as possible."

This woman, an *English*woman, could weaken him, if he gave in to what he felt. His supervisors would be suspicious. But he needed her.

She sipped more cognac and squeezed his hand. "I'm hesitant… I would like to see more than this village—and spend the day." She paused, as if mulling it over, then her smile reappeared. "I'll be daring. When shall we go?"

August raised her hand and kissed it. A warmth flowed through him. He yearned to be with her, away from here. He leaned closer and kissed her lips. Their kissing lasted, her mouth so sweet, though he had to pull away before he went too far, too quickly. He steadied his breath and touched her cheek. "As soon as I can clear my paperwork and arrange to borrow a vehicle."

Chapter Seventeen

In the early morning hours, past the church in the thicker woods of a feeder path, Norah settled into the sidecar. She tightened the scarf around her head in the still cool air. The Major kick-started the motorcycle, which roared and juddered the sidecar. She peeked at him, her mouth dry. In his leather jacket and cap, he cut a dashing figure.

The sun was barely rising with feeble rays of ginger and rose. She glanced around to see if anyone was watching.

The bike rumbled to the main road, then off they sped, away from the village. She'd told Loeiza she'd be gone all day, drawing various structures on a farm. She met the Major—no, he'd asked her to call him August—beyond the village outskirts, hoping no one would notice them leaving together.

The sidecar vibrated, along with her nerves. Her cousins would be angry if they found out. Why had she agreed? The thrill, the influence over her occupier. Her deepening attachment, though she couldn't let August think her too willing. Her daring and desire for him might be her undoing.

Hair blowing out behind her, she watched the countryside fly by. Trees, flowers, farms. A man leading an ox. Quick glimpses of the ocean, sand dunes, and bright azure bays. Little villages of low stone houses and quaint churches.

The stink of petrol was whipped away by the wind, replaced by the smell of nutty fields and briny ocean. The sweeter scent of wildflowers.

A German truck with soldiers halted them at one point, but August flashed his identification. The sentry stared at her then waved them on.

Norah glanced away and tugged at her scarf. She felt exposed but also privileged, then guilt seeped in at that last reaction. She swiped a few insects from her face and wished she had goggles, a disguise of sorts.

The road twisted along the coast, where high cliffs jutted up on one side. A stone weathered to an arch stood on one flat, sandy beach with surprisingly calm waves. *Menhirs,* the vertical Neolithic rocks like craggy fingers, studded other points along the road.

Sheep or cows grazed in fields divided by thick escallonia hedgerows with clusters of red flowers.

German sentries in front of barbed wire marred the landscape in places. They were stopped two more times, with the same result.

After about an hour and a half, they passed a huge bay with a long island in the harbor. Norah craned her neck at the walled town that occupied it.

August veered inland, off the main street, to a smaller road. Past hills and clumps of trees, around a curve, up to a long sweep of a drive. He slowed and Norah gasped.

A sprawling gothic, golden-stone structure spread out before them, imposing and huge.

August shut off the engine. Norah stretched her jostled neck and back.

He strode around and helped her from the sidecar. "A rough ride. Can you still hear?"

She laughed. "A little. The ride was exciting. And this castle *is* magnificent." She rubbed her spine, anticipation rife. She couldn't believe she was here, with him.

He removed his goggles. "The *Château de Keriolet.* The original mansion was thirteenth century. A Russian princess had it renovated in the nineteenth century to Neo-gothic."

"Who owns it now?" She hoped the Germans hadn't seized it, though couldn't tell him that. Were they even allowed to be on the property? She saw no guards.

"It's passed through many hands." August picked up her canvas bag and the watercolor pad. He offered his other arm to her. "I should have found goggles for you, I apologize."

"I'm fine, just a few insects." She ran her fingers through the knots in her hair, then took his arm, absorbing the warmth of leather. An abrupt tingle rippled inside her at his closeness, their arms entwined. She realized she'd never been *this* engrossed in a man before. A German officer she should never encourage, but the heart wanted what it wanted.

They strolled across a stretch of grass. "Part of it resembles a church." Norah scanned the elaborate structure, the one huge façade with high, arched windows, and the front entrance, which wasn't as grand as she expected. "Beautiful. Who needs this much room?"

"No one. A waste of extravagance, but it is a feast for the eyes." He glanced at her.

She kept walking, absorbing the flutter in her belly. His blown, light hair gave him a rakish look, a man of strength as well as vulnerability.

About thirty feet from the castle, they stopped. "This should be a good place to draw." She sat cross-legged on the grass, pad in her lap. He sat beside her.

She sketched the roofline, the pinnacles and chimney pots, acutely aware of his nearness, like the heat from a stove. Minutes passed in silence.

"The Princess Zénaïde, related to Tsar Nicholas II, fell in love with Charles Chauveau. It was during the time of Napoleon III. She bought a count's title for him." August spoke in a soft voice. "Am I distracting you?"

"No, I want to hear the history. I can draw and listen," she said, though his voice with the raspy edge that poured over her was very distracting.

"It was built in this style about 1863. Inside, it's supposed to be sumptuous." He studied her, she could *feel* his regard, which further unnerved her. "But the count didn't live very long to enjoy it."

"An unhappy history." *A tragic love story,* she bit back with a swallow. "I'll only do a small section, or I'd never have enough time, unless I came back again and again." Trying to concentrate, she sketched in finials, gargoyles, the long, lancet windows, and fairytale towers, all on a grand scale.

He plucked and fingered a blade of grass. "We could return if you like. It's a nice break from duties. Your drawing is excellent already."

Norah wanted to return, with him, though said nothing. She filled in the shadows and light, the way the sun caressed the stone, with a sepia pencil. "How many women have you shown this castle to?" she asked in a tease.

He chuckled. "You are the very first." He paused with a sigh. "I've had no women in my life since my wife died."

Norah tapped the pencil against her cheek. Everything was changing and she wasn't certain how to navigate. For this one day she'd pretend they were two ordinary paramours, getting better acquainted. "Were you passionately in love with your wife?"

He plucked more grass, twisting it through his fingers. "Klara and I were great friends who worked well together. And we had our three beautiful children."

She pondered that answer; no mention of 'love.' "You must miss her."

"I do. She was a calming force in my life. A good wife and mother." He stared up as a large buzzard soared overhead, then vanished in the trees. "What about you, anyone special?"

"No. Just that one stupid…" She found herself telling him about the party, too much champagne, the supervisor, her resulting pregnancy. The loss of the baby. The pain roiled inside her. She kept drawing, though in slower strokes.

Yann obviously told him much of this, but she put in the anguished details, as she fought off the sadness. She needed the truth out in the open. "So, you see, I'm a ruined woman."

"Are you trying to scare me off? Don't disparage yourself, please." August clasped her free hand, warm and comforting in his. "I'm so sorry about the child, everything that happened. I realize our relationship is not ideal. But I care sincerely for you."

She turned her head to face him. His gaze on her was penetrating, with a yearning wrapped around it. Was she trying to deter him? "We are star-crossed, as you said, yet I care deeply for you, too."

He leaned close and kissed her, his mouth gentle. She kissed him back, her pulse in a frenzy, body aching. Her resolve to keep him at bay had shattered.

* * *

August reveled in the soft warmth of her lips. He found he more than *cared*, but neither seemed ready to bare their hearts. He could only hope she felt the same, despite the complications. Her story of the dead baby, her sorrow, drew him closer to her. He reached to embrace her. Snug in his arms, he caressed his fingertips down her back.

Norah pressed her face onto his shoulder, then pulled away after a moment, cheeks flushed. "We're being bold, aren't we? Though I enjoy our time."

"I'm delighted to be with you. I can't resist." He straightened, calmed his breathing, then brushed his hand through her hair, silky on his fingers. He had so much more to say. Instead, he stared at the chateau—built for love. His lips burned with the taste of her. "Please, draw some more and I'll sit here quietly."

He heard noises, a rustle of feet in the grass. Norah stilled. August sat straighter. A woman appeared, struggling to contain a large dog on a lead. She glanced at them and kept walking.

Norah blew out a breath and sketched on, but he noticed she flicked glances at him. The sun moved high in the sky, then passed its zenith. He'd removed his jacket already, the heat relentless.

"We should find a café, and have a meal, before we return to the village. If you're finished." He touched her hand. "We could come back another day. You'll need to paint it."

"I'd like to." She smiled and slipped her pencils into her bag. "I do need to paint. After all, it's a commission for you."

Twenty minutes later, seated at an outdoor café overlooking the Bay of Concarneau, August ordered food and wine. No one else was at the outside tables.

"Are we, or rather me, allowed to sit here?" she asked, scanning the area.

"You're with me, don't worry. On that island out there is the Ville Close, the walled medieval town, once a center for shipbuilding." He pointed to the island nestled in the azure bay that flowed into the Atlantic. A golden-stoned city with ramparts occupied the curved atoll. The fishing village on the mainland was built in tiers. Fishing boats bobbed in the harbor. A sea breeze refreshed.

"You know so much history. You're trying to impress me." She sipped the Muscadet, glistening clear in her glass. "I like it, very light and crisp."

"With hints of lemon and tart apples. The French know how to produce the best wines." He clicked his glass with hers. He reveled in seeing her smile, relaxed. "Have I impressed you? *Bon appétit.*"

The waiter served steaming bowls of *Cotriade*, the local fish stew, made with bass, eel, mackerel, other fish, potatoes and onions. A rich smell with a hint of fishiness.

Norah dipped in her spoon and tasted. "Delicious. So much bounty. And the perfect spices."

They each spoke of their childhoods and later years, trying to find common ground. He left out the growing chaos in Germany, the march toward totalitarian authority that corroded his youth. He almost told her of the day he was shot and nearly died, but didn't want to ruin the pleasurable interlude.

"I'm surprised the Germans haven't taken over this city with the expansive harbor." She glanced down across the coastline. There were a few sentries.

"I couldn't say if we have." Many bunkers were being built here. He poured them another glass of wine. The wine relaxed him, and he wished they didn't have to leave. He had the urge to trace his finger along her collarbone and lower.

She looked at him with a wry smile. "We each have secrets, though you know most of mine now."

"That might be so. I still need to find out who murdered my landser." August said it casually, certain she wouldn't admit if she knew. He finished his stew. "I'm sorry, the commandant returns in me."

"Are you trying to scare *me* off?" She ate more stew, her tongue licking juice from her lips, eyes sparkling. "I haven't heard anything; that's the truth."

He laid his hand over hers. "I believe you. And again, forgive me for asking." He curled his fingers around hers. "This is a perfect day with an exceptional woman."

Norah drank her wine. "Please continue. I'm listening in earnest to your flagrant flattery."

He laughed. "I'm telling the truth, my dear." He was a fool to think this relationship wouldn't disgrace her. She'd be shunned by her family. Yet he was selfish in this instance and wanted her. She'd opened up his heart like no one else. His body throbbed with urges, and he raised her hand and kissed it. "I want to do more of this. Or you should run away from me now."

"I should dash off." She shrugged, her gaze flashing with amusement. "But how would I get home? It's a terribly long walk."

"And I wouldn't let you attempt it. Not in those shoes." He kissed her fingers again.

They both laughed. He held her hand to his chest as he stared into her green eyes. He could get lost there, a tempting thought.

"I won't run away," she whispered, their lips close.

Three German officers ambled by them, speaking in rapid German. August and Norah pulled apart. The trio sat at a table not far off. August heard them talk of the scenery, the day, recent conquests of whores. Then one looked over at them and muttered to his companions.

The young officer rose and approached. He stank of smoke and alcohol. "Are you French? You should not be here at the harbor." The stupid man had asked in German.

Norah hunched her shoulders, staring away from the officer.

August tossed money on the table and stood. "I can go where I wish, lieutenant." He flashed his identification.

The man backed off a few steps. "Of course, Major von Gottlieb. But to bring your woman here is not wise."

August bristled at the way he'd said 'woman.' "Don't question my judgement or make assumptions. She is a lady." He turned to Norah and switched from German back to French. "Let's go, *ma chérie*. We still have a long ride."

When they reached the motorcycle, he helped her into the sidecar. "Pay no mind to those smug officers. We must enter the village before dark, or risk being arrested," he teased with a wink. "The dreaded curfew."

She tied her scarf about her head and gave him a quick smile. "I'm glad I don't understand German. I trust in your abilities."

Cap pulled low, goggles on, August kicked the bike into a rumble. He'd savored the day, yet his emotions were on the verge of reckless.

He roared down the road in a waft of petrol, the bike vibrating his body. As commander, he must be careful to handle business and pleasure, to figure out something for the two of them together. His dreams of her disturbed his sleep—as the nightmares had—and misted his thoughts in the waking hours.

Chapter Eighteen

Norah rushed past the auberge, her arms full of packages. The wormy-white corporal who hung out in front, leered, and stepped in front of her. Her skin prickled.

"What's your hurry, *Fräulein?*" He winked and made ugly smooching noises. "I'm lonely, *ja*. Share your charms."

"Pardon me." Norah darted around him. She'd seen him do this to other women. He snatched out a hand, but she dodged him. Quickly entering the cottage, she elbowed the door shut, and set her purchases from the open market on the high table near the sooty hearth. She groaned in relief.

"I see you've earned more." Yann leaned in the kitchen doorway, suddenly there as if waiting for her. The stink of bloody meat drifted from his clothing. "I've left you alone, but I know about you and the Major. We all do. I like the money you bring, and it's your reputation. But does he ask about me?"

Norah braced herself for this expected barrage. "I assured him you are not a member of any resistance." No surprise that Yann wouldn't mind the money. She turned from him, heart clenched. She'd fallen hard for a German officer, and danger lurked everywhere. "The Major will be kinder to this village, since I'm friends with him."

"Friends? That's what you call it?" Yann snorted and, she saw from the corner of her eye, realigned his long body against the jamb. "Do you please him?"

"Stop such talk. It's disgusting." She flushed but pushed down her upset. "Believe what you wish." Of course, with her past, he would think the worst of her. And what were her intentions, plans, with August if—*when*—their relationship evolved? She tore open the larger package she'd bought, trying not to rip the paper to shreds.

"Does he ply you with questions about the villagers? Who might have murdered the sentry?" Yann's mocking tone grated on her nerves.

"I don't know anything, so I have nothing to tell. Not that I would, anyway." She might end up caught in a corner, but she wasn't a rat. "At least now, with the Major's help, you have meat to butcher."

Loeiza slipped past him into the kitchen, Petit Yann in her arms. "What are we discussing?"

"My luck in purchasing flour that's not made from turnips or potatoes." Norah pulled down an earthenware jug and filled it with the fluffy flour, her fingers soon coated in white. "Now you can prepare your delicious crepes, the gavottes, though I know you prefer buckwheat."

"Ummm." Petit Yann clapped and grinned at his mother. "I like gavottes."

Loeiza rocked her youngest, her dark eyes sad. "Norah, I appreciate the food that's available, but I think you should stop whatever future commissions you might have."

"I'm also fostering good relations between us and our invaders." She replaced the lid on the jar, careful not to reveal her growing love. Was that it, *love*? August had asked her about 'more.' She saw in his eyes he felt the same. His kisses reverberated in her mind. Her throat constricted. She was a branded woman, a fraternizer. "I'm keeping us safe."

Yann pushed himself from the door frame. He leaned over and ruffled his son's hair. "As long as you protect *this* family with your, uh, actions, Norah.

That's what I expect. Remember whose house this is." He shambled down the hall.

"Where did you go yesterday?" Loeiza asked in a whisper. "I think you went somewhere with the Major."

"I'm hungry." Petit Yann whined. His mother rocked him again, her mouth in a thin line.

"I went to draw a castle, that's all. For pay." Norah placed the flour jar back in the cupboard, her motions slow. She opened the package of cloves and cinnamon sticks, the aroma piquant. She was almost done with the portrait. And finding out the details of the secret port still hovered at the edge of her mind—should she forget them?

She felt as if she tumbled down a hill, with little to grasp onto, but the slide was exhilarating. It had to be more than lust she felt.

"You're too close to him, admit it. Perhaps intimate? I'm constantly worried." Loeiza's voice softened. *After what happened in England,* hung unspoken in the air.

Norah turned and clasped her cousin's shoulders, the little boy squeezed between them. Her pulse rippled. Was she always to be denied happiness? "You're right, we are closer; but it's my life, let me manage what I do. The Major is a good man, that's all I can say. And your husband just admitted he doesn't mind."

"Kindness can be a trick," Loeiza said quietly. Did she speak for herself, her marriage? "And Yann has anger you don't see."

Norah moved away and plopped the spices into a smaller jar. She voiced another worry for her cousin. "Is Yann being hostile to you because of me? Are the villagers?"

"*Mais non*, there are only whispers, questions if it's true. Yann's family has lived here for ages." Loeiza pressed her cheek to her son's. How much did the three-year-old comprehend? "He's proud of his roots."

Yann had sisters who married and lived in nearby villages, brothers on farms or worked as butchers, and innumerable cousins spread about Finistère . His parents died of the measles five years ago, a disease they caught from a younger brother, who also died.

Loeiza added, "the village treats me well, but I tell them nothing about you."

"And nothing has happened between us." Not yet. Was Norah shameless for enjoying her day with August, for wanting him? She was entranced with the *man*, not the Commandant.

"Be careful, *ma chérie*. I have your best interests in my heart." Loeiza turned away, her son cuddled close. "It cannot end well."

"I love you for being so concerned, but…" Norah could echo the sentiment that it wouldn't end well. Filled with remorse, she also faced the very real fear that she'd have to move. But again, to where? She could hardly crowd into the *Maison dans la Forêt* with August and his officers.

In the hallway she bumped into Jean and his two sisters. The ten-year-old stared up at her. "Papa ordered us to go inside. I wasn't finished with picking tomatoes." He held up a basket half full of bright red tomatoes, his mouth in a smirk.

Angelique cast Norah an anxious look, her smile tremulous. "Papa has company, but he's not happy."

"I want to be done with our work." Marie-Louse glared at them all, obviously resenting any interruption.

"You will finish later. You'd better do as your papa says." Norah smiled, confused. She patted their heads.

The boy and girls hurried past her.

Norah went to the rear door and peeked out the window. Yann stood at the far corner of the garden, in the shadow of a beech tree. A stockier man was with him. By their actions, they looked angry.

She eased the door open to listen.

"I don't want to. It's my prize," an irritated but sullen voice said.

Norah recognized Erwan, the younger brother of Pierre Kerguelen, the man arrested for trespassing at the port. Supposedly, Pierre had been sent off to Paris, to God knows what fate.

"I'm warning you, throw the damn weapon into the sea," Yann groused. "Don't be any more stupid."

"The bastards deserve to die." Erwan gripped a rifle to his chest. "I might take out another."

"Don't do it, and *don't* come around here again. I want no part of your actions." Yann shook a fist in the young man's face. "I have to safeguard my family. My interests."

"Then I need money so I can flee to England," Erwan hissed. "And join the Free French."

Norah softly shut the door, her stomach in knots. She hadn't heard every word, but it sounded like Erwan had killed the sentry. She wished she hadn't overheard. Why was he even here when able-bodied men his age had been mobilized into the French army at Germany's advance? French soldiers were killed or captured, but some escaped and snuck home. Was Erwan one of those?

She pressed on her forehead. Now she had information that would fester inside her—but she must keep it secret.

* * *

Inside the summerhouse, after they left the stream, her paints packed away, August smiled when Norah held up the finished portrait. They'd kept the rear door open to let in more light. His image looked serene in soft watercolor, amid the beautiful background of nature. A man not trapped in the ugliness of war.

"Excellent. I should pay you twice as much." He kissed her forehead. "Your talent amazes me."

"Thank you. I worked hard, but you're not an easy subject." Norah's smile and gaze seemed preoccupied when he'd hoped for an easy warmth between them.

He shut the door, leaving them in shadow. "Are you all right? You act a little nervous."

"There's a lot of pressure on me from my cousin to stop seeing you." She laid the pad on the high table and faced him. "Though her husband welcomes the money."

August put his hands on her shoulders, feeling her tension, his fingers massaging. A lump formed in his throat. "What about you? What do you want?"

She stared up at him, her gaze intent. "I know it's wrong for us, but I want to," she huffed out a breath, "to keep seeing you. But we must be discreet. And I need to know that it's more than a man needing a woman—"

"Norah. I want *you*. It is more, believe me." He really meant it, his heart blooming in his chest. He pulled her to him and kissed her. A passion he'd never experienced, even with his wife, unsettled him. Yet he desired more, along with the comradery they shared. He hugged his arms tightly around her. Then he broke away with a groan. "But are your feelings genuine for me?"

"I've been confused, but yes, they are. Despite the obstacles." Her mouth trembled. "I've never felt like this. It's heady, and…"

August kissed her again, inhaling her scent. He ached for her body to be against his. "And beautiful." He ran his thumbs slowly down her cheeks. "I love you, Norah. I'll protect you." If he could, if the war didn't intrude.

"Don't forget to protect my cousin's family." Her eyes glistened and she caressed the back of his neck. "This is happening fast… But I love you. Like I've never loved any man."

August kissed her forehead, then the tip of her nose. "I know we're in for a difficult time, but we'll figure it out, nourish our happiness." He kissed her lips, again, their mouths hungry. His breathing rapid, he traced his fingers along her back, caressing her hips, as they pressed together. His body reacted, with a heaviness and desires he wanted to give in to.

* * *

When she entered the village through the alley by the auberge, Norah's nerve-ends tingled at her embrace and caresses with August. The heat that threatened to consume them. But they'd slid apart to steady themselves before their passion overwhelmed. Their declaration of love still stunned her, and it opened a whole new set of intimate pitfalls and possibilities.

Love, so wonderful, even in precarious times, even in her bewilderment over how to cope with the stress of her choices. She must cherish the glow.

A rat scurried by her, and she sidestepped it with a start.

Norah shifted the case. August had taken the painting to find a frame for it. He'd package it up to send to his son at his school in Germany.

Out of the alley, she passed Germans who sat in front of the tavern in a haze of smoke, laughing. They stared at her. Now the idea of Erwan darkened her mind. A secret she must bury deep.

A thin, uniformed man rose and followed her. She cringed and must remember not to take this shortcut again. She hurried toward the square. The click of boots, then a hand grabbed her and pulled her into the doorway of a shop. She gasped, winced then glared into the face of Captain Schmidt, August's second in command.

"Let me go at once! You have no right." She kept confidence in her voice and jerked her arm, but he held tight, his fingers bruising.

"How are your assignations with Major von Gottlieb? Are you taking care of all his needs?" The captain gave a lurid wink. "You're deterring him from his duties. He's been too soft on this village." Schmidt poked his nose near hers, his breath foul. "Our High Command won't like the privileges he allows here."

Norah fought a shiver. She mustn't anger this brute. He had a harsh reputation. She replied as calmly as she could manage, "You're mistaken. I paint pictures, portraits, that's all."

Schmidt snickered. His gaze traveled slowly along her body as if undressing her. "I'd like you to paint mine. Then perhaps you can show me how you perform *other* tasks in the summerhouse with the Major."

"I'm not taking commissions at the moment. And again, you are mistaken about whatever you're insinuating." She pulled free this time, certain her face had seared red. "Excuse me." She stepped away from him.

"I have important friends in Paris. I might write to them about what is happening here. The food that is available to all instead of being sent to Germany." His voice chilled. "Major von Gottlieb could be transferred."

Norah scrunched her muscles to hold in her alarm. "You wish to cause problems. A good officer shouldn't do that. Where is your dignity? *Adieu.*"

She walked across the cobbled square, her heart racing.

"I'll be around when you come to your senses and change your mind, Fräulein," he called after her with a laugh.

She kept her pace even, head high, the paint case bumping her leg. The captain could cause so many problems, but surely he hadn't the power to have August transferred. Her warning August about Schmidt might cause unneeded friction, further complications. She tripped on an uneven stone in anger as she neared her cousin's front door.

A siren shrieked. The sound of heavy aircraft reached her ears. She rushed between the cottages. In broad daylight, bombers were flying low along the coast.

"They're RAF." Pichon limped up beside her. "They bombed a German battleship, *Scharnhorst*; they're following up the coast to sink it. The Germans tried to hide the vessel." The carpenter obviously had a forbidden wireless.

Shouts came from the soldiers. The anti-aircraft guns the Germans had mounted were turned toward the planes. Would the British see the secret port? Norah's anxiety high, she readied for bombs to drop, guns to shoot. More people gathered, their voices sharp. Mothers hurried their children to shelter. Norah's calves bunched, she turned to run. One of the guns fired, shattering the air, shaking the ground. But the planes zoomed away, farther to the north.

Chapter Nineteen

"I was fortunate Madame Bolloré offered me a chicken in exchange for my knitting mittens and scarves for her children." Loeiza set the platter on the table; breaded chicken with garlic butter, surrounded by turnips, wild onions, and dandelion greens. She smiled at their guests.

"We still don't know how that scold holds on to all those birds." Yann chuckled. "Other than she sells eggs to the Germans."

"We Bretons do what we must, in many ways. The food smells delicious. You are very kind to share your meal, *mon ami*." Pichon grinned, his dimple flashing. His bride to be, Gwénola, shyly dipped her head.

Norah looked briefly at Pichon. How much did he suspect about her? "We are happy to finally meet you," she said to the pale, dark-haired woman. Norah helped her cousin dish out the meal, the pungent scent of onions with the mouth-watering poultry and garlic. They were fortunate for the bounty.

"*Merci*." Gwénola lowered her large brown eyes. "You are very generous."

Pichon seemed too lively a man for such a shy bride, but perhaps new people intimidated her.

"Deniel will finally tie the knot." Yann raised his glass of cider, in rare good humor this evening. "May he prosper and enjoy his life as I have."

Loeiza went to check on the children. Already fed, Jean and Angelique were bathing the younger two in the large, rusted bath. Then they would take a turn in the slowly cooling water. She returned and sat down. "No one has drowned yet."

"I've been helping Gwénola's parents with their farm. Agriculture suffers from worker shortages." Pichon sliced a turnip. "People still send packages with whatever food they can find to our soldiers in labor camps."

"We used to grow peas and green beans for the canning industry, but so many young men are gone." Gwénola shook her head and took a bite of chicken. "In my village, we stand in long lines for food. And it's sparse. But the Germans eat well."

"Ask our Norah here for advice. She has influence with the Commandant." Yann winked, his gaze probing.

"You overestimate me." Norah gave him a brittle smirk, then attended to her meal. What would Yann say if he knew she'd fallen in love with August, and she was poring over ways to keep their relationship viable? She stirred her food. "I paint, that's all."

"Please, Yann. You shouldn't tease." Loeiza said it softly, the dutiful wife resigned to her situation. "We are all united here."

"I wish the Germans would allow our *Tro Breizh*. But travel to other villages is restricted." Gwénola smiled sadly. "I miss our customs."

Loeiza had told Norah the Tour of Brittany was a Catholic pilgrimage that linked the towns of the seven founding saints of Brittany. These Celtic monks from Britain had brought Christianity to Bretagne in the fifth and sixth century. Norah could never talk August into permitting that.

Conversation ebbed and flowed as the food disappeared. Loeiza and Norah cleared the table then made certain the children had their night clothes on and said their prayers. Petit Yann slept in a cot in his parents' bedroom, the other three on a larger bed in the middle room.

Norah inhaled their sweet, clean smell. Then she felt a twinge of guilt that because of her the children were crowded together. Though because she took up space, no German officer was billeted in the house. How much longer would *she* belong here—or had she ever?

Downstairs, Loeiza took Gwénola out to the garden as the sun was yet to set. Yann was in the storeroom behind the kitchen, fetching more cider from a barrel.

Pichon caught Norah in the hall, a determined look on his face. "One week to wed, the end of July. At least the war is concentrated in Russia for now. The Red Army attacked the *Wehrmacht* in Leningrad."

Norah nodded, unsure what to say. Would Pichon deride her for her rumored closeness to the Commandant? It was no one's business but hers. "I wish you a long, happy marriage."

Pichon grinned, though his gaze was sharp. "I'd like to ask you something." He lowered his voice. "With your artistic skills, would you be able to forge identity papers and passes?"

Norah held her breath. How could she? Betray the man she loved but help the people she *should* be helping by such an activity? "That may be beyond my skills."

"My fiancée has brothers who need to leave France and travel south to the unoccupied Zone. But they require new identities." Pichon leaned close, his words a whisper. "They have Jewish friends they'll be taking with them. Those people must have different names. They have children."

Norah closed her eyes. She could use the excuse that Yann would be angry, since he wanted nothing to do with such intrigues. But children? She'd heard the rumors of Jews being hauled off like cattle to work camps.

She looked at Pichon once more and felt like a coward, when she was already in peril, loving the enemy. "Perhaps I shouldn't get involved."

"We all need to be involved. Don't forget the children, their lives are at stake," Pichon whispered.

Her neck prickled like a spider crawled along it. *Mon Dieu*. If I could do this, where would I get the correct type of paper?"

"I'd provide it, plus the ink." He glanced around as if to make certain they were alone. "You would fill in the names and forge the official signature."

"What about the proper stamps?" She gripped her elbows, still unsure.

"We're working on that." Pichon waved away her concern.

"The poor children. I might try...you cannot tell Yann." Her fingers already trembled at the idea. What if she failed and was caught? Could August protect her? He might be furious if he found out. Their tender attachment ruined. "You know how my cousin feels."

"I won't tell Yann." Pichon patted her shoulder. "You can do this. I have confidence. I'll show you my papers so you can see the official signature. I've had to travel to other regions of Brittany for my carpentry work."

Yann entered the hall with earthenware cups brimming with cider. Pichon stepped to the hall's other side. Loeiza and Gwénola came through the rear door.

"Your garden is lovely, and with vegetables to feed your family," Gwénola said. "We have trouble getting seeds."

"I will give you some seeds and vegetables to take home," Loeiza replied.

"Let's drink to celebrate friendship and marriage." Pichon took a cup and raised it, his smile wide, voice joyous.

Yann followed suit, his angular face in a grin. "May you have many healthy children."

"Excuse me, I forgot something upstairs." Norah hurried up the narrow staircase while the others drifted into the parlor, voices bright. In her tiny room, she sat on the bed, feeling queasy, her head pounding. She *should* do this, she had to help—but feared adding more complications, risking her life perhaps. She'd be balancing precariously on both sides, in danger of slipping off each.

* * *

August rushed through the woods, his boots tramping along the dirt path leading west from the village. He swiped low-hanging branches out of his way, the pine smell sharp.

"The fisherman seems not right in his mind." Bauer kept pace beside him. "I warned the sentry not to shoot him. You'll want to question him again and find the truth."

In screeches, birds flapped away. A deer darted through the brush.

"We must make certain he is the one." August kept moving. Sweat dampened his collar. A clearing opened before them. "He has our dead landser's rifle, you said?"

"*Ja*, the Gewehr-41." Bauer slowed, breath puffing, and they both walked toward the three men arguing. "He was found deep in the woods and tried to run, but we stopped him."

Schmidt stood, arms akimbo, chin tipped high. "You lied to us about your bloodthirsty deed. You incompetent *dummkopf*."

"I killed the bastard and I'll shoot more." The stocky young man waved the rifle about, his grin sloppy.

A sentry raised his weapon.

"Hold your fire." August stepped up to them. "Herr Kerguelen, give me that rifle."

"Why haven't you disarmed him?" Bauer asked the sentry.

"We were about to," Schmidt cut in. "I had everything under control."

August held out his hand. The Breton stared at the weapon, then finally passed it over.

The stock and barrel gripped in his hands, August demanded, "Did you kill my landser? I asked you before, and you denied it."

Kerguelen laughed, his broad cheeks scarlet and damp with perspiration. His clothes wrinkled and dirty, he stank like a man who'd hidden out in the wild and drank too much alcohol. "I snuck up on him and shot him in the chest when he turned. It was so easy."

"Why do you admit it now? Were you protecting someone?" August wondered who else might be in a local network of Résistance.

"We must execute him," Schmidt snarled. He sounded far too rapacious. "As soon as possible. To show these people we are in charge."

"Do you swear you are the culprit, Herr Kerguelen?" August's throat tightened. He hated to admit that Schmidt was correct. He'd avoided any executions up until now. But Military High Command would expect this retribution for a murdered landser. "And you did this alone?"

This man had also been seen with the butcher. Did Norah know anything about him? Of course, they kept secrets from one another, but she needed to be careful. Schmidt was anxious to cause trouble.

"I did it alone." Kerguelen spluttered. "All you Boche should be killed for fouling up our country. And for my brother being sent away. Is he dead?"

"Now your mother will lose two sons. I have been a patient man. You are a fool." August turned to Schmidt. "Arrest him. I want to question him further at the Town Hall." Precise information needed to be extracted before the execution. "Then we will arrange the ultimate punishment."

"We should shoot other fishermen to make our point," Schmidt said airily.

"Only the guilty will suffer." August thrust the rifle at his second in command. He knew other German commanders ordered such retaliation, but he would not. "I want this kept quiet for now."

He turned away to hide his scowl. His nerves scraped through his body; but he must order death if the man was to blame. An eye for an eye, he had no choice.

August stormed down the path, his gut in a twist. He'd hoped to keep his reputation decent and shield the ones he cared about. Norah might despise him for this deed. The weight clamped down on his shoulders.

Chapter Twenty

Through the trees, Norah watched the sun dip close to the Atlantic. Sepia and auburn rays sprayed around the dimming ball of yellow that touched the silver sea. She leaned into August's warmth, the firmness of his chest behind her as they sat on a blanket, leaning against a smooth stone that formed a backrest about forty feet from shore.

"This view, over in those groups of stones, is where I used to sketch the seabirds. Then your sentry caught me and called for you." She lightly laughed. "You intimidated me."

"Oh? I remember. The English girl and her pad of paper with pretty birds." He spoke softly, his arms around her, just under her breasts. "Who later boldly told me she wasn't clever."

"You recall that, too?" She wondered at his distracted manner, a quietness when they'd first arranged their 'sunset viewing.' A mood she longed to penetrate. "You used to stand out there, staring across the ocean."

"Trying to clear my mind." He kissed the top of her head. "This position is much nicer, with the two of us." He handed her the flask and hugged her against his chest.

She drank the smooth yet potent brandy, which burned in her stomach. The heat of his body against her back sizzled through her as well. An owl hooted in lament from high in a tree. The muskiness of him enveloped her as the air cooled, and the scent of sea brine carried on the wind.

"Thank you for bringing me here to watch the sunset." She sighed. "If only life were so simple, the sea breeze could whisk away our not so perfect situation."

"It never is simple. So much is beyond our control." August wrapped the blanket edges over her shoulders, then pressed his face into her hair. "We must grasp any moment we can."

Norah quivered with the feel of his breath, but her unease at his words increased. She hated to ruin the moment but wanted to know August's thoughts. "How do you suppose the war will end?"

"Hmm? My theory, if the Americans join forces with England, and combine their ships and planes, Hitler might be defeated." He spoke so softly, she barely heard his reply.

"And you'll be happy about that, won't you?" she asked as crickets chirped in the nearby gorse bushes.

He nipped her ear. "I will. I don't agree with Hitler's policies. He's gotten more erratic and malevolent."

She wanted to ask what would happen to *them*, but no one could predict their fate. Her stomach dipped. "What do you plan to do after you retire?"

August was silent for a moment. "I once thought to make a place here, in this remote village. But now I fear the battles to win will cause further destruction in France and Germany, other countries as well." He trailed one hand across her stomach. "I might move to Switzerland and live with an artist, a woman who painted my portrait."

He included *her*. Could that be possible? The idea sent a rush of pleasure through her. Did they have a future, or were they only dreaming? She caressed his arm. The difficulties must be forgotten this evening.

The silhouette of a sentry shouldering his rifle passed on the crest of the shore. The outside world intruded. Obviously, the soldier knew they were there.

She wanted to ask about August's children. When did he plan to see them again? Would she ever see her own family? She swallowed. "Is there a way I could send a telegram to my family in England? To tell them I'm all right? They could send one back, to let me know how they are."

"That could be arranged. Only twenty-five words are allowed. And no coded messages." He nuzzled above her ear.

Elation filled her that she might open communication back home, discover if her family was well. Though again, his tone seemed on edge.

"I'm no spy, and thank you." However, she might soon be a forger. She nestled further into his warmth. But now the purpose of that clandestine activity niggled at her. "In the town you grew up in, Jüterbog, did any Jews live there?"

"Your mind travels in mysterious circles. You're no spy? I hope you tell me the truth." He shifted behind her. "My mother had a Jewish friend. A nice lady. The ones who lived in my village were upstanding people."

Norah thought again of what Pichon proposed. "Why does Hitler hate the Jews so much?" She handed him back the flask, her muscles relaxed though the subject was disturbing. "What is being done with them?"

"*Mein Schatz*… must we?" August sighed. "He blames them for controlling the finances, Germany's terrible depression, worshipping a different religion, whatever he can think of." He kissed her left ear. "He orders them into ghettos. To work camps. Many are fleeing to other countries. I hope they make it."

His lips on her ear sent a tingle low inside her. What would happen if he found out about the passes she'd decided she must create? But he seemed to agree they needed to escape. She wanted to trust in his humanity. Was she being naïve? "I hope they make it, too."

The sun sank halfway below the horizon. Its last rays formed a shiny path that rippled along the sea toward shore, like a rope to keep it from slipping further. Soon they'd have to return to their homes.

She clasped his hands and held his fingers to her body, snug to her ribs. Several minutes passed with just the crash of waves against the rocks. "I wish we could stay like this forever."

"As do I." His heartbeat increased, a vibration on her shoulder blades. "Norah, no matter what happens, you will always love me?" he whispered.

She heard the doubt in his voice, the worry. Was something big about to happen? Her pulse throbbed. There were rumblings in the village about an arrest.

"Yes, of course." Though how could she make such a promise, ignorant of the future? The man she wanted to embrace to her soul was the one she should be wary of. "Why do you ask? Is everything all right?"

"We'll talk of it later." His hand brushed beneath her breast, thumb rubbing.

Sparks ignited inside her, a sinuous flow through her chest. She bit back a moan, then caught his hand. "*Mon cheri*. It's getting late."

"You're right, and we are very exposed here." Now his words were brisk, though regretful. "Time for us to go."

They rose and he folded the blanket, then kissed her on the lips. She sank against him, tasting the brandy, the passion they shared. "Don't forget, I love you, too," August said softly. He caressed her cheek. "More than I've ever loved."

"I would never forget that." She kissed him back, wishing to wrap her arms around him, and hold him against her, preserve their devotion somehow.

Norah feared something bad was about to drag them apart.

August walked her to the edge of the square, keeping to the safety of the shadows, and squeezed her hand. His gaze looked troubled. Norah wanted to ask why, but he stepped away from her. She hustled across the cobbles and entered the cottage. She heard the children upstairs, Loeiza's cajoling voice.

A loud knocking on the front door made Norah jump.

She opened it. Madame Bolloré loomed there with another woman. They pushed inside in a clatter of sabots.

"You are the commandant's woman. Beg him not to shoot Erwan Kerguelen." Madame stuck her florid face into Norah's, her double chins tight in anger.

The other woman, head wrapped in a gray scarf, her cheeks wide in a square, plain face, held up gripped hands. She blinked back tears. "Please don't let him kill my son, mademoiselle. He's the only boy I have left."

Norah sucked in her shock, head reeling. "Have they arrested him?" She feared the truth; and recalled Erwan, careless with the German's rifle in Yann's garden. Would there be an execution? What could she do?

"He's confessed, my poor son," the woman wailed.

Norah choked back her misery. So this is what bothered August this evening. She *must* talk to him first thing in the morning.

* * *

August trudged behind the Town Hall, the sun barely risen. Nerves taut, he observed the young man tied to a tree, hands behind his back. Three landsers stood at the ready, rifles at their sides.

Kerguelen had insisted he alone shot the sentry. He would give no other information. There was no way out for the Breton.

Zeigler stepped beside August and adjusted his belt around his plump belly. "You will have your pound of flesh today."

"I have no choice." August gritted his teeth to keep from scolding the man for his cavalier tone. He'd been deluded to think with his rank that he would never be in such an appalling situation. "I know what my responsibilities are."

"Shall I do the honors?" Schmidt joined them, legs spread, puffing on a cigarette. "These worthless—"

"There is no honor in killing. And you will not." August resisted an angrier retort. He motioned Lt. Bauer over. "You will give the signal, Bauer."

"Of course, sir." The lieutenant's chiseled face remained stoic as a rock.

Muttering and groans came from behind. August turned to see Norah with two village women. Herr Ropars, the mayor, was also there. Norah's eyes were huge, pleading, cutting deep inside August. The woman in the scarf was weeping. The heavier woman hugged her, a sneer on her lips.

Kerguelen glanced at the women, then hung his head.

August turned away, hating that Norah was here, regretting this, but the sentry's life must be avenged. If he'd only been wounded, other arrangements might have been made.

He almost ordered a landser to chase the spectators off. His body felt like a fist.

"Bauer, take your position." August clenched his hands in his gloves.

"I'd have done better." Schmidt tossed down his cigarette and smashed it beneath his boot. Zeigler rubbed his wide nose.

Bauer walked to the far side of the three soldiers and stood stiff. August took a deep breath, then nodded.

"Ready!" Bauer ordered. The rifles were snatched up. "Aim!" The men pointed their weapons at the prisoner.

August cringed inside. The scarved woman cried, "Noooo! God help us! *Mon fils.*"

"Fire!" Bauer chopped down his arm.

The rifles barked. Bullets struck the prisoner. His body jerked, legs flailing. Then he sagged, kept standing by the ropes around his middle. Blood spurted from his torso in red blobs, his shirt soon soaked.

August closed his eyes and swore under his breath. The stink of gunpowder billowed over him.

The scarved woman screamed and collapsed. Norah and the heavy female, both crying as well, dragged her up and away, down the path. The mayor drooped his shoulders and followed. August feared Norah might reject him after this.

"Well, that's finished." Zeigler blinked rapidly. "Efficient, in its way. I suppose the—"

"Quiet, port captain. Show some respect." August stuffed down his anger and shouted to Bauer. "Cut him loose."

Schmidt said something, but August thrust a finger in his captain's face. "Silence. It is done. Two young men are dead." Then he strode to the rear of the Town Hall and entered.

Fritz met him, eyes wide, cowlick bouncing. "Do you want coffee, Major?"

"No, nothing, thank you." August entered his office and closed the door.

He dropped into the chair at his desk and stared at the door. The execution played out in his head. He had no choice, *Gott verdammt!* Why were ordinary men caught up in this brutality? War had turned them into wild animals. Brought out the beasts to devour the weaker.

Removing his gloves, he slammed his fist down on the desktop. Pencils rattled. A pen rolled off and clacked on the floor. Pain shot up his arm and struck like needles behind his eyes.

Chapter Twenty-one

"I had no time to speak to the Major." Norah pressed her hand to her mouth, afraid she'd be sick in the parlor. Tears blurred her eyes. The image of Erwan jerking with the shots, the gruesome blood splatter, churned in her brain.

The sunset and brandy together with August were only last evening, followed by a dawn execution. She'd no notion of Erwan's fate. What could she do now? How would she react to August after what happened? "Poor Madame Kerguelen. And Madame Bolloré almost ripped off my head."

Loeiza wrapped an arm around her. "I'm sorry you witnessed it. I pity Erwan's mother, the poor woman lost both her sons; even if they were careless. The village will be in an uproar."

"Erwan ran the risk. We warned him. He asked me for money to leave Brittany, but I had none." Yann shrugged, though his gaze looked troubled, then he leered at Norah. "Your charms wouldn't have been enough to save him."

"Erwan had the rifle, and he acted alone? Isn't that true?" Norah shook with anger and despair; she searched for justifications, something to cling to.

"It doesn't matter. Now you see what kind of man the Major is. More will probably be shot." Loeiza spoke firmly, yet her eyes glistened with tears. "Let it be done. He isn't worth your affection."

"You don't understand. There's…" Norah started to protest over something much deeper than affection, but her excuses would fall on closed off ears. Was she too embarrassed to profess her love for a man who ordered a firing squad? How well did she really know him? Her mind in a spin, she was falling off the cliff this time.

The parlor door swung open, and Jean poked in his head, frowning. "Did the Boche really kill Monsieur Kerguelen behind the Town Hall?"

Loeiza hurried to her son. "That's enough, dear. Don't say another word." She embraced her boy and left the parlor with him.

"The village *will* be in an uproar." Yann pushed back his hair. "It's best we stay quiet for a while. The food may be taken from us again. More retaliation."

Norah, consumed by confusion, with so many crashing emotions, staggered toward the door. The man she loved and thought decent… August had acted in retribution; but if Erwan had murdered the sentry—it *was* war. His own mother said he confessed. Still, if the Germans hadn't invaded in the first place. She scrubbed at her face, swiping aside tears.

"You're certain you knew nothing about this?" Yann asked as he followed her.

"*Mais non.* Nothing." She paused in the doorway. Why hadn't August told her last night? Of course, he wouldn't want to ruin their evening. Or discuss an execution that couldn't be halted.

She left the parlor, wishing to hide, to kick something, perhaps scream; but should she speak to him, to uncover further consequences?

This was why he'd asked if she would always love him. Could she? And what would she say to him now? She trembled with dread for the future.

"You must convince your *friend* to take it easy on us, no retaliation, and no cutting off of the food supply." Yann hovered over her. "Because where else would you live, if you can't assist us?"

"I appreciate your hospitality," she spat. *As grudging as it's always been.* "But it's wise to keep your friends from killing sentries." Norah trotted up the stairs, hand gripped on the banister. She fought the urge to kick Yann, but called back to him, "August, the Major, has been good to this village, don't forget."

Now she defended a Nazi, though he'd promised he wasn't one. Brain on fire, she fought the bile in her throat and felt crammed in a corner, unsure of which direction to run.

* * *

August crumpled the proclamation dated July 31, 1941. Hitler called for the extermination of Jews. August had told Norah they were being sent to work camps. Now he feared what that implied. Under Hitler's orders, through Nazi official Hermann Göring, SS General Reinhard Heydrich was forming a plan for a Final Solution. An action horrendous to contemplate. August would never allow that to happen here. The atrocities of war pressed too close. No, the viciousness had arrived with the execution, turning him into someone he detested.

After a quick knock, Schmidt stepped into the office. "Did you read the Führer's announcement, sir? Working the Jews to death is too slow. This will be much more effective."

"Why do you approve of such definitive acts?" August almost said 'ghastly'. He tightened his hands on the desk edge, probing what made this man who he was.

"My father was cheated by a Jewish banker, nearly bankrupted." Schmidt shrugged his narrow shoulders. "He had little money to provide for the wedding my youngest sister deserved."

August kept his voice level. "Unfortunate, but is that a reason to condemn an entire race of people?"

Schmidt's eyes narrowed. "Don't you want *our* race purified? My family had spent so much to send

169

me to the finest schools, to get my commission into the *Heer*. Of course, as the only son, it was expected I join the army." He rubbed a finger over one of the medals on his tunic, his gaze sly. "They couldn't afford to lose money. I have five sisters. All obedient wives to their husbands. Don't you have daughters?"

"They are both newly married. Simple ceremonies that my parents, and my wife and I, approved of." August didn't care to discuss his loved ones with Schmidt, and Klara hadn't been alive for his youngest girl's wedding.

He thought of his mother, tall, blonde, devoted to her family and her roses. His father retired and slowing down. Head stuck in his books on the Great War. How had *this* war affected them? Letters were slow, he should send a telegram.

Schmidt stared down his pointed nose at the jigsaw puzzle on its little table. "My father was very strict, especially with me. He's now a colonel in the SS. We are an honored family."

Schutzstaffel, the SS, a notorious organization. Anti-Semites, the elite of the Nazi party, and very lethal.

"Have you inspected the bunkers along the coast, and coordinated with Port captain Ziegler and Krause over port security?" August shifted in his chair, muscles constricted. He couldn't tell this braggart that his attitude outraged him. He had the sneaking feeling that Schmidt leaked information to High Command about matters out here. The fact August wasn't as steel-fisted and cruel as other commandants. He must keep an even sharper eye on Schmidt.

"If I must, I will join the port captain now." Schmidt clicked his heels and left.

August stood abruptly, squeaking back his chair. Today he must check the progress on the airfield in Audierne at the tip of this peninsula. He needed fresh air to blow the concerns and cobwebs

from his mind. He'd kept a low profile after the
execution two days ago.

Sadness crept over him. He must think of a
way to bring Norah close again, to explain the
situation. He missed her and yearned for her sweet
presence. A love that stirred him so profoundly. A
warmth he craved. But he must be careful not to
behave too weak when it came to her.

Fritz stepped to his open door. "Pardon, Major,
but Herr **Kerguelen's** father is here. He wishes to
speak to you."

August tensed, hesitated a moment, then
nodded. "Show him in."

A round-shouldered fisherman, face weathered
by the sun, twisted a hat in his blunt hands. He
smelled salty, like the sea. "Major Gottlieb, my wife
pleads for the body of our son, to give him a proper
burial. I beg for this consideration."

The boy had been cleaned up and put in a pine
box. The intention was to bury him in an unmarked
grave.

August took a slow breath, staring at this man's
misery. There was little reason not to grant his wish.
"You may have his body; but the funeral must be
quiet, no talk of martyrdom, your immediate family
only. Make certain of that."

* * *

Rushing from the miller's with the buckwheat
flour Loeiza preferred, Norah was relieved the man
had any left to sell. The food supply remained in good
order for the village.

The local women stepped to the other side of
the street as Norah passed, their noses in the air.
Three widows in the pointy *jibilinnen* headdresses and
flowing *robe noirs* turned their backs on her.

Norah cringed, though shouldn't have been surprised. Had they all assumed she had the power to rescue Erwan? Frustration and regret flooded through her.

Passing an alley, a hand reached out and snatched Norah by the hair. Wincing in pain, she grabbed a thick wrist.

"You should be shaved and shamed for the whore you are." A young woman snarled into her face. Her head wrapped in a scarf, her squarish face was pinched in fury.

"Let me go." Norah struggled to untangle the woman's fingers. "Who are you?"

"I'm Erwan's sister. My mother is devastated. And so am I." She jerked harder on Norah's hair, dragging her down the alley. "And where is my other brother, Pierre? He just vanished. We should strip you and parade you through the street like a dog."

"Stop this; there was *nothing* I could do." Fear coated with anger rose up and Norah dug in her heels. She scraped fingernails into the woman's wrist as her scalp burned. She drew blood.

The stocky woman grimaced and released her. She rubbed her wrist, then slapped Norah across the face. "You will regret your whorish actions, bedded by the Nazis."

Norah recoiled and shoved her hand away. "I didn't deserve that. You don't know…"

"We should fight. I want no husband, no babies, just revenge." The woman whirled and strutted down the alley.

Norah touched her stinging cheek. She wrestled with more retorts, but instead she hurried on. This is what her life had come to.

Madame Bolloré plucked dead leaves from her geranium plants as Norah neared her cousin's cottage. She straightened. "You visited with Kerguelen's sister. Was it pleasant?"

Norah clutched the package of flour, bristling, her words choking out. "Erwan committed—he knew the risk he took. I'm sorry that it happened." She steadied herself. "But you Bretons first welcomed the Germans, hoping they'd allow Brittany to become its own country."

"And protect us from Russia. Those ideas proved false. And now you warm the enemy's bed, instead of helping us." The woman waved a chubby arm. "You're English, you should know better."

Norah struggled to keep her exasperation stuffed deep. "I'm doing no such thing in anyone's bed. Don't forget the extra food we receive thanks to the Major. And that France capitulated to Germany; they signed an armistice."

Her biggest worry was that more men would be shot in retaliation, but she couldn't imagine August behaving that way. A week had passed since the execution; it seemed they avoided one another. Perhaps he was protecting her. Unhappiness dragged her down.

Madame Bolloré stepped closer, her large bosom bumping Norah. She smelled like stewed chicken and onions. "No more of our men better die, remember that," she said as if reading Norah's thoughts. "Your being a *collaboration horizontale* must count for something."

Norah massaged her scalp and swallowed an outraged response; hair came loose in her hand. She walked around Madame and entered the cottage. She was condemned as a whore, though she could hardly blame them. Was she even safe walking these streets anymore?

The flour put away in the kitchen, she headed upstairs. In her room, cheek still stinging, she locked her door and slipped the official documents Pichon brought her from under her bed. He said he obtained the blank forms on the black market. She didn't ask for details.

Setting the ewer aside, she used the little table as a desk. She must work to divert her troubled mind. Breath blown out, she studied the official signature she'd practiced for days, the loops just right. The block letters and dates where needed. Her right hand ached with the effort, her fingernails stained with ink she had to scrub off with harsh lye soap.

Utilizing a mapping pen with a fine metal nib, and appropriate ink, she filled out the paperwork for passes, birth certificates, and naturalization papers. Jewish names were changed to more French or Breton names.

She was proud that her endeavors might save lives, yet her body sagged with exhaustion from sleep-deprivation.

Each night when she tried to sleep the hole in her heart opened deeper. In her half sleep, she felt August's kisses on her neck, her lips, his soft words of love, his humor and smile. She awoke aching for him. How could she approach him and feel he was that man again, and not the one who ordered the execution?

The pen etched on as she strained to steady her hand. The faked signature was of a German official in Nantes, on the eastern border of Brittany, someone she hoped to never meet. Her forgery was perfect.

A quiet funeral service was held for Erwan at the church that past Sunday. The villagers grumbled and whispered. Furtive in their movements down lanes. A village holding its breath.

Tomorrow, after this brief delay, Pichon would marry his fiancée at the church. Norah said she couldn't attend, she was ill. She didn't wish to spoil their special day by being the one stared at.

A warming August breeze drifted through the open window. A motorcycle zoomed along the road. Her nerves twitched.

Sighing, she continued to fill out the forms. She prayed Yann would never find the forged passes. If caught, the Germans might execute her. Deep down, she dithered over whether August would safeguard her; and would she ever trust him again? Or he her, if he ever found out. A heaviness settled behind her eyes. How to rectify this situation, to bridge the emptiness, her need for him?

She laid down the pen and wiped her hands on a rag. She should finish the jumper she was knitting for Marie-Louise. Not that the little girl would ever thank her, but she'd need the warmth when winter came.

Reaching for the yarn, Madame Bolloré's and the sister's cruel words came back to her. Norah shivered with the apprehension she'd made a huge mistake by encouraging a relationship with a German officer. How could she love the enemy of her country? Yet his declaration of love had sounded so genuine.

A light tap on her door. Norah stared at the drying documents, then went to it and inched the thick wood open. Jean stood on the landing. He smiled, then handed her a slip of paper.

"Don't tell my parents. The soldier gave me a coin." He winked, a child conspirator.

Norah's pulse jumped. "Which soldier?"

"The young one who works for the Commandant." Jean rocked on his feet, his manner casual. He'd grow up fast in this environment.

She bent down and whispered. "Where were you?"

"I got more dog yarn for *Maman*." He shrugged. "I was walking home."

Norah pressed his shoulder, hard. "Thank you for bringing me this. But, please, stay away from any German soldiers if you can."

She closed the door and unfolded the note. Her thumb and forefinger pressed hard on the paper.

I need to see you. Meet me this evening, 7 pm, at the summerhouse. A.

Chapter Twenty-two

While he waited in the summerhouse, August checked his watch. Ten after seven. Would she come? What if she didn't? He massaged the knot in his stomach, the scar that rippled his skin on his side. He'd find some way to bring her back. Dreams of their tenderness eased his lonely nights. But the nightmares from seven years ago had started again. The blood sticky on his hands. He tightened his fist. Young **Kerguelen**, tied to a tree, gunfire; this too crashed in his brain.

Another scheme punctured his nights; something extremely dangerous. He must speak to Bauer.

August stepped outside near the stream and rubbed the nape of his neck. The water flowed in rivulets around the rocks, finding the easiest way to move forward. His path was not so flexible. His thoughts pulled him in so many directions, the depth of his responsibilities. Was he foolish to allow a woman to have this much sway over him, even one he loved?

He once thought his love was a desperate lust, but now he knew for certain that Norah was a part of him. More nestled in his soul than placid, dear Klara had been. His failing over not loving her enough was something he'd long dealt with.

Soft footsteps. He turned. His heart lifted to see her rounding the summerhouse. But her expression was cautious, at the same time, analyzing.

"Norah. I'm glad you came." He almost said 'relieved.' He smiled and nodded, hoping she wouldn't sense his nervousness.

"It's important we talk." She didn't smile and stopped near the rear wall. "I have the words for my telegram to my family. Will you still send it?"

"As quickly as possible." He approached her, yearning to hold her against him. But he slowed two feet before her, feeling her anxiety. "You must understand with Kerguelen, I had no choice."

She frowned, eyes moist. "There should always be a choice."

"Kerguelen admitted he killed my landser. It was murder." His hands held out, palms up, he ached to touch her. August refrained from telling her that he'd have faced possible punishment at a military tribunal if he hadn't acted.

"Couldn't he have been sent elsewhere?" Her voice broke; she turned her head, and her blonde hair brushed the shoulders of her rose-colored blouse.

"No matter what I wished, an example had to be made to prevent further resistance. Military High Command would've demanded it." He moved closer, into the scent of her.

"It was so brutal." She backed to the wall, flat against it. "I thought you were different."

"Even the English would shoot someone who killed one of their men." He reached out and touched her arm. "I regret that his mother was there. If I could have spared her the sight, I would have. And you shouldn't have been there either."

She balled her hands, tears welling in her eyes. "I see the reasoning, the rules of war. But I have all this anger and sorrow I don't know what to do with."

He clasped her upper arms as if to keep her from running off. "I understand your misery. However, it was my responsibility."

"Why did it have to happen?" She pressed a fist against his chest. "I know, that's rhetorical. But I'm—"

"I wish it hadn't. I really do, though the outcome was inevitable given the sentry's death. And if Kerguelen hadn't bragged about the shooting." August kissed her forehead. "*Ma cherie*, please understand."

"I can't forgive what this war has done to us all." She pushed at him with the heel of her hand, but not overly hard.

"This war has torn apart the world. We are in a storm, trying to be normal." He traced a finger under her chin. "I missed you."

"I…missed you." She thumped her knuckles on his collarbone. "Dammit. My instincts are a mess. And I'm caught between two worlds."

"You're in an untenable position. Don't let this tragedy change what we have." He rubbed his thumb over her cheek and opened the summerhouse's back door. "Let's go inside."

"Everyone… The villagers, my cousins. I'm condemned, marked as your woman."

Despair pricked at him; because of his position he couldn't be a proper choice for her. "I realize that. And I'm sorry, if only—"

"I may not even be safe, there's so much anger." She swiped at her tears.

"I'd never want you to feel unsafe." They entered the shadowed building. He squeezed her shoulder. "Do you wish us to stop seeing one another?" Could he deny his feelings? Give her up? His chest tightened, crushed by stones.

"I'm confused by what I should do." Her gaze met his. "But you'll still be good to us?"

"Is that why you're here, for me to be good to the villagers?" His voice rose in sadness, a heaviness gouging inside him. He did not want this sort of relationship. Was she using him? He couldn't think that of her.

"*Mais non*, I didn't mean it that way. I swear. But the people need to think I have some influence, so they don't denounce me." She groaned and shook her head. "They thought I could save Kerguelen."

August shut the door, encasing them in dimness. "You couldn't have saved him. That was my decision." The commandant reared up, then he groaned. "We all face that, the opinions of others. You mean so much to me." He caressed both her cheeks, the damp softness. "I love you. I need you. But if it's impossible for you..."

"It is, but... No matter how difficult, and I've thought about it over and over, I love and need you, too." More tears dripped from her eyes.

August kissed them away, salty and sweet. She smelled like lavender. His lips covered hers. His body heated just being next to her. "And I thought to leave you alone, but couldn't, if your love is sincere."

Her arms tightened around his neck, her breasts pressed against him. "Very sincere. What do we do?"

"How do I make you safe?" he murmured between kisses.

"I wish I knew." Her lips searched his. She pulled back. "Can you do something special? Let my cousin have more cows to butcher for the village? Then maybe he'd stop resenting me."

"I could do that. Your cousin should not resent you." August kissed her again. She was influencing him; his boundaries were crumbling. But he wanted her secure. "And more supplies for the inhabitants."

"That would help." She gasped for breath. "And ask your men to pay twice the money for the eggs they purchase from my neighbor, Madame Bolloré."

"Yes. It will be taken care of." Arms wrapped around her, he kissed her for a long moment. "Just remember, there's only so much I can do."

"We all have our limits and expectations." She trailed her fingers through his hair when he kissed her throat. The sweet taste of her skin.

The heat of urgent desire rose. He yearned to make her his. "Norah, I want you, in every way. Selfish ways. But if this is not the right time or place."

"Will any time be perfect, I don't know." She kissed him, slowly. Then her green eyes met his, shimmering in the shadows. "I want you to respect me."

"I do, you're a portion of my heart; but if you have doubts." He pulled back, breath heaving. "You need time to think about it."

"I thought about it. Just kiss me." She caressed his face. "We both love one another."

"We do. Most assuredly." August wanted to devour her, but still be tender. He intended for their time to be memorable and obliterate her past experience. Their kissing intensified, every nerve in his body thrumming. He untied the bow of her blouse.

She unbuttoned his shirt, breath rasping. "Here? But where?"

He snatched the cushions off the two chairs and dropped them on the floor. "There? If that isn't too awkward." Had he lost his mind, here in this inappropriate place?

She laughed nervously. "Yes, there."

He kneeled on one cushion and pulled her down, hands framing her face. That lively, lovely face. "Are you certain? I don't want to take advantage of you."

"I am certain." She kissed him, her lips lingering. "As long as you stay true."

"You're my great love." He was admitting to everything, laying himself bare, but it didn't matter at this instant. He tugged her blouse from her shoulders and kissed the bare skin. His brain fogged with desire.

"Make me forget all that's happened." She murmured, then moaned, her fingers pressing on his back. "Cherish me."

"Oh, I cherish you." August fumbled with their clothes, soon touching the silkiness of her thighs. He unhooked her bra, revealing her breasts. Then he kissed her nipples, the soft buds, and she groaned and arched her back. His urges grew, and he knew he couldn't stop. He wanted to bring them both pleasure.

*　*　*

Snuggled to August's chest on the hard cushion once they'd spent their ardor, Norah inhaled his peppery cologne and musky skin. Her breath calmed, heartbeat slowing. Her body tingled with pleasure, a soreness lower inside. Their legs draped half on the other cushion, and half on the dirt floor of the summerhouse.

"That was wonderful, my sweet Norah." August kissed the top of her head, his raspy-edged voice tender. "Though not the most comfortable place to share our first time. How do you feel?"

"Happy. It was magical." Far better than her first encounter of drunken lust. She felt the passion he had for her in his caresses and kisses. His whispers of love. She pressed her face to his throat, still hot and moist from the exertion. "But you're right. My hips could use a softer landing."

"My knees took a beating, too." He chuckled and held her snug against him. "Not that I minded too much."

She fingered the buttons on his open shirt and mulled over her next statement. "I know I shouldn't ask yet, but given my past, what if I become pregnant?" The despair from her lost baby often cut deep and her breath hitched.

He rose on one elbow and cupped her face, his expression earnest. "Then we will have a child, don't worry. We'll be together, somehow, in this morass of war." He kissed the tip of her nose, then slowly lingered on her lips. "I want to marry you, Norah; but I realize you would face even more condemnation. We'll have to wait for now, to see how this war progresses."

His offer of marriage sent a tremor through her. Could that ever be possible? Did they have a future? Or would the war destroy them?

So many problems to consider. She traced a finger over the slight cleft in his chin and his lower lip. The lips that had given her so much delight. The gaze she once thought arrogant now adored her, assuring her as best he could.

She smiled at his confidence. The memory of their union sent warmth throughout her body. She brimmed with love, though the danger lurked beneath the surface.

He sat up and smoothed down his hair. "Let's dress and get off this floor."

Sitting, she pulled her clothes on. August finished dressing, stood, and offered his hand. Once on her feet, she picked up a cushion and so did he. They fitted them back in the chairs.

She ran her fingers through her hair, then retied the bow on her blouse. Another concern surged up. "When can you contemplate retirement from the army?"

"The earliest would be next year. I want my son graduated from school, then sent off to college." He brushed off his trousers. His gaze met hers. "A college in Switzerland being preferable."

"You want him safe." Had August been making plans all along to keep his son out of Hitler's claws? Norah wanted August out of the madman's clutches, too.

"Yes, safe. But I have important business to take care of here before any thoughts of retirement." He tucked in his shirt. "Something I've recently realized needs to be done."

"What is it?" She rubbed low on her back.

"I'll tell you when the reason for it is closer." He tugged on his tunic, fastening his high collar where the Iron Cross hung.

She glanced away from the reminder of what he represented. "You can't tell me anything? I want you to confide in me."

He pulled her close and kissed her, thoroughly. "I'll confide when I can. Don't worry, you will approve."

"Is it dangerous for you?" She gasped after the kiss and now grew apprehensive about this new information. The idea of the guarded port stuck in her mind for some reason.

He opened the door and peered out. "I'll give you the details later, I promise."

"Not too much later, please." She cocked her head and clasped his arm. "I hope it's something to slow this war. We must all make that effort."

He pressed on her fingers, his smile sweet, then gestured for her to exit. "Goodbye for now, *meine liebe.* We'll meet again as soon as it can be arranged. I'll discreetly leave notes for you in the terracotta pot of geraniums in front of your cottage."

"Yes, very soon. But that reminds me." She pulled a paper from her pocket and handed it to him. "The words for my telegram."

"I will take care of this tomorrow morning." August slipped the paper into his tunic pocket. His smile now looked sad. "Don't forget, I have limited power out here. There are constraints."

"I understand. I'll check the pot daily. Be careful in whatever you plan." Stepping out into the warm air, her mind swirled with fear for him, herself, and the need for more of what they'd just shared.

"I love you," they both whispered, gazes intense.

Norah's step quickened away from the summerhouse. She'd turned into the worst of wanton women, a fraternizer. The English called it a Jerry-bag. But her love for him gripped her, staggering her as she hurried around bushes and under trees. The green scents washed away the sweat of lovemaking.

She chewed the inside of her cheek. How much time would they have if Hitler clamped down harder here, in Brittany—and across the channel? She could lose August, lose her country.

Her heart twisted as if squeezed through a mangle. Norah knew she'd have to be stronger than she had ever been before.

Chapter Twenty-three

The long, sleek Mercedes limousine rumbled to a stop in front of the Town Hall. The two pennants with swastikas on the hood now drooped.

August snapped shut the office curtain. The colonel from Paris was here. A telegram arrived yesterday, warning of this visit. An inspection from *Oberkommando der Wehrmacht,* Military High Command. An unwelcome intrusion into August's personal situation in Brittany. Why this sudden visit?

"Fritz, have the coffee ready!"

The sentry stationed outside shouted, "Heil Hitler."

August straightened his tunic, chin high, as he stood stiffly behind his desk.

A large square of a man strode in, hat tucked under his arm. "Major von Gottlieb. Heil Hitler." The colonel thrust his other arm into the air. He looked in his fifties with sparse, light brown hair.

"Oberst Albrecht von Burmester, you honor us with your visit. Heil Hitler." August raised his arm. He could have bitten off his tongue at that greeting. He gestured to the chair.

"Indeed, you should be honored. I rarely like to leave the comforts of Paris." Burmester sat, his back straight as a rod, a once handsome face a little jowly. He smiled, though it didn't reach his stern eyes.

Fritz came in with the coffee tray. He set it on the desk. A plate of butter cookies, the Breton *Sablés,* was included. Dismissed by August, the young man bowed to the colonel, adjusted his spectacles, and left.

"How do you like your coffee? Black?" August poured the dark liquid into a white porcelain cup. "To what do I owe this long, tedious effort on your part? We are doing well here. The port is almost finished. The airfield on the tip of the peninsula is close to half done."

Burmester took the cup, dwarfed in his large hands. "I'll get straight to the point. I've had word that things are, to put it bluntly, too lenient out here."

August's neck muscles crimped. He knew this was probably the reason the colonel came. "Ah, and what has made you think so?" He poured his own cup, added a dash of precious sugar. He put two cookies on a smaller plate and handed them to Burmester.

"We had an anonymous letter." Burmester sipped his coffee. Then he bit into a cookie and nodded in approval. "Food meant for Germany is being distributed among the local population."

August sat. An anonymous letter? Was it Schmidt? He tightened his fingers on the cup. "I decided, to keep opposition to a minimum, to not starve the villagers." He took a tiny sip, not enjoying the rich flavor. He had no appetite for a cookie. "However—"

"However, you had a sentry killed, is that not so?" The colonel leaned forward, the medals on his broad chest glinting. He'd seen many campaigns.

"It is true. The culprit was quickly caught and executed. He was an unstable young fisherman." August kept his face impassive. If it was Schmidt, he'd like to strangle him. "With the building of the special port, we need cooperation from French workers with experience or strong backs. I want no sabotage. A full belly encourages this."

"Why were no civilians shot, along with the fisherman?" Burmester leaned back again, the chair creaking, his smile slick. He finished his coffee. "That is the proscribed method."

"Once more, that would foster sabotage among the villagers." August fingered his cup, jaw so rigid it ached. He tamped down the worry he could be stationed elsewhere, or worse. "We have a delicate situation with the port. Many are collaborating with us in Brittany. We need that. I can arrange a tour for you with Port captain Ziegler."

Burmester arched an eyebrow. He held up his cup. August came around the desk with the coffee pot and refilled it. He'd briefly act the obedient underling—to rid himself of this intruder.

"How is your father?" Burmester nibbled on the second cookie. "Wasn't he close friends with Kurt von Schleicher, Germany's former chancellor?"

"They were acquainted." August touched his side where the bullet had ripped his flesh. He took a slow breath. "My father is well, enjoying his retirement."

"Schleicher was an enemy of our *Führer*. He disapproved of the Third Reich." Burmester brushed crumbs from his chest, gaze flinty. "A man dangerous to associate with."

"Schleicher is dead now and no threat to anyone." August's pulse thumped, but he met the colonel's gray eyes. The bloodied bodies of the chancellor and his wife sprawled on the floor stabbed into his memory. "My father tends his garden, studies German history, and bothers no one."

"I see. Well on another matter, I hear you have an English mistress. A young one." Burmester flashed a suggestive grin.

August picked up a pencil, pressing his thumb hard into the wood. "My private life should be of no interest."

The colonel coughed into his large hand. "The English are enemies of Germany. Have you forgotten?"

"She is only half English," August lied. He'd protect Norah at any cost. With their recent intimacy, his love for her had intensified. "A little Prussian is also in her ancestry." He stood and called for Fritz. "Find Port captain Ziegler and have him come here at once. There's an important guest I'd like him to meet."

Forty minutes later, August stood on the hill that sloped down to the port, the wind off the Atlantic ruffling the sedge at his feet. Seagulls cawed and swooped in a pale blue sky.

"Our special port will be finished in a day or two, Colonel Burmester." Ziegler preened in his rooster way, rubbing his belly. "And the U-boat should be ready to sail soon from **St-Nazaire**."

"*Sehr gut*. This should be a priority. The *Führer* anxiously awaits news of this operation." Burmester scanned the bunkered concrete lock with its rounded *dom*—the house for the bulky submarine. The camouflage nets were in place, brown and green colors that blended into the landscape.

"We are very proud of our progress," August said. He ran his mind over ways to disable the huge U-boat when it arrived; machinations that disturbed his sleep. He'd realized these past weeks that the deadly object could never be allowed to sail from here loaded with extra torpedoes. His own act of sabotage was the only recourse.

"What do you think of the management in **Saint Guénolé**, Port captain Ziegler?" Burmester lit a cigarette and blew smoke into the air.

August stiffened his posture. The ocean below swirled and crashed against the rocks and the invasive bunker.

Ziegler drummed his fingertips on his belt. His ruddy face reddened deeper. "Well, I… I find it, comfortable, and well-run. With only the one incident, the sadness of losing our sentry. But we had a proper execution."

'Our' sentry. August didn't care for the possessive tone, but Ziegler had responded decently enough. August stilled his breath and glared down again at the bunker. Two or three explosives strategically placed, with the help of Bauer, the officer he trusted—another man sick of this needless war. He could never allow the U-boat to destroy Norah's homeland. "I've written to the young man's parents in Germany to express my condolences."

Ziegler faced the colonel, his smile tentative. "Will you honor us by joining us for dinner, Herr Colonel? I have instructed our cook how to prepare Braten, the pork roast and sauerkraut."

"I wish I had time. I'm headed to Brest to check the port there." Burmester nodded his large head and puffed the cigarette, the smoke snatched away by the salty breeze. "But also to a farm near that city. They breed racing horses. I have interests in strong horse flesh."

"I've thought myself of purchasing a horse. May you find a good one." August mused on his previous wish, to ride like he did as a child on his grandparents' farm.

"Then come with me, Herr Major. We can discuss many subjects of importance." Burmester's tone wasn't friendly, and his offer was more of a demand than an invitation. "Such as the errors of leniency in command, family relations, and inappropriate women."

"I'd be happy to, sir. An inspection of Brest and horses, perfect. Let me pack a few items and tell my second-in-command." August clamped his hands behind his back. He wasn't the least happy, but he might soften the colonel toward him, so August didn't end up at the Front, or in prison. He could *never* allow this pompous superior to ruin his presence in Southern Finistère. Not before his plans came to fruition. And he and Norah could find a solution to their predicament.

Verdammter Schmidt—if he was the anonymous letter writer. Now August had to put the cretin in charge. And spend too many days with the powerful colonel, a man who could crush his future—if he didn't destroy it himself. Shards of dread sliced through him.

* * *

Jean pushed through the broom shrubs, the golden rod withering in the heat, as Norah and Angelique followed him over a hill, a quarter mile behind the big house.

A once pretty little cottage sat tucked among overgrown hedges and clumps of purple iris.

"That's the gardener's cottage," Jean said. "He worked for the mayor but left when the Germans invaded. No one has lived there since."

The three of them approached the stone building with chalky-blue shutters and a slate roof. Pots with dead plants lined the walls. Norah tried the doorknob, but it was locked.

Jean crouched, pulled out two nails and jiggled the lock. It clicked and he pushed the door open. The old wood creaked, almost a squeal.

"I hope you don't make a habit of breaking into houses," Norah said lightly, though she did wonder.

The boy, who just turned eleven, gave her a smirk. "I'm very talented."

Angelique rolled her eyes and laughed. "It's not a talent to boast about."

Norah peered in. The place smelled dank and musty inside. A small flagstone foyer separated a bedroom and parlor.

"Did the gardener have no family?" she asked.

"*Maman* says no family. He joined the French army we think." Jean cocked his head. "But he's probably in a prisoner of war camp now."

"The poor man," Angelique said as they entered the cottage.

Norah stepped into the parlor and the children followed. Dust covered the few pieces of furniture, a table and two chairs, and a worn sofa. The bedroom had an iron bedstead. Cobwebs covered the dark-beamed ceilings in both rooms.

"I suppose no one has ransacked the place out of fear of the nearby German officers. Do you think I could set up to paint here?" Norah walked to the windows where, if scrubbed, would let in a good light.

The gardener's cottage was part of the estate of *Maison dans la Forêt*, where the Nazis now lived. Would the other men object to her presence, no matter the decent distance? She needed to ask August.

"It should be all right." Jean shrugged, then grinned. "You could meet with friends, too."

Norah darted her gaze to Jean. Did he mean the Major? How much did the boy know or understand?

"Jean." Angelique elbowed her brother. She swept her wavy, long blonde hair behind her shoulder. "I'll help you clean in here."

"Thank you, *ma chérie*." Norah smiled. "Some vinegar and water, a good sweep, and pounding the dust from the sofa." She walked to the sooty parlor fireplace, which would need a thorough scrub. A tiny kitchen was to her left. A stove, an ice box and a rack for dishes above a sink. The place had no electricity, with no switches on the walls. An oil lamp sat on the fireplace mantel.

Could she imagine the little place as hers? But would she be safe here, alone, when she painted, surrounded by the occupation army? She was surprised no Germans were housed here.

"I'll clear out the grounds," Jean said. "There should be rakes and shears in the shed."

"I need to ask your mother's permission, first." Norah couldn't involve the children if Loeiza objected. They hadn't spoken much in these last few days. As if Norah's sin showed on her face.

Had August provided more meat for Yann, and higher egg payments for Madame Bolloré? He'd assured her that he sent her telegram to England.

Norah glanced at the bedstead again. It needed a mattress. Her insides tingled. Was she setting up a love nest? Or had she made a huge mistake with her morals again?

Four days past, she'd traveled once more with August to *Château de Keriolet.* A lovely day, with her quickly painting the chateau, more Impressionist than realistic. Then luncheon at the same café as before. If they could only have more outings like that.

August had praised and paid her for her depiction; this time she'd earned her pay with honest work. Though at times she almost felt 'bought', after what she asked him to provide for the village. She'd shook off her doubts after more kisses and sweet promises, neither was certain they could deliver. He still wouldn't expand on the plans he promised she'd approve of.

They hadn't made love since the awkward pairing on the summerhouse floor six days ago. She dreamt of his intimate caresses, the simmering low in her body, the need to hold him close.

A heavy crunch sounded outside. Was someone there? Norah's arms goose bumped. Jean and Angelique's eyes widened. Norah went to the ajar door. She heard footsteps moving away, through the brush. Someone had been spying on them.

Chapter Twenty-four

The French trotter, a breed originally bred in Normandy, galloped across the paddock. A horse bred for racing, but August would ride him for pleasure. His house in the forest had a small stable behind it. A few soldiers had mucked out the structure and cleared the dead brush from the paddock.

A stallion, it had a chestnut coat and three white socks. He'd named it Maler, 'painter' in German. A homage to Norah. A young landser, a former farmer, would break the horse. August briefly thought of doing it himself, but at age forty-one the chance of a broken bone would bungle his plans—his very precarious plans. Chest tight, he concentrated on the stallion.

Large for the breed, at over 170 centimeters, Maler was muscular in his chest and shoulders, with a straight back. His withers rippled as he ran, his face noble. A chocolate-colored mane and tail flowed in the air as he loped. Horses, a memory of freer times as a boy.

August leaned on the fence. The animal was the only highlight from his journey to Brest. Burmester had drilled him over his kindness to the villagers, and his liaison with an Englishwoman; a woman he could keep as a mistress, but nothing more, the colonel warned.

August had stuck to his reasons. The colonel, in a veiled threat, said he'd keep an eye on matters. They'd parted on wary terms.

Maler galloped by, snorting, tossing his head. The tangy smell of horse.

Hands gripped to the fence rail, August almost told Burmester he wanted to marry Norah, the one person who made him happy. However, that would have been a mistake. And August hadn't admitted to her that all officers of the *Wehrmacht* must ask Hitler's permission to marry a non-German woman. *Ridiculous!* He must wait until Hitler had no control over his actions.

Fritz walked up beside him, shuffling a few papers. His hat held down his cowlick.

"How are your parents, Fritz?" August asked, anxious to delay anything official. "Does your father still produce the finest *Liebfraumilch* in Rheinhessen?"

"They are well, and he does. I'll ask him to send you a bottle, Herr Major." Fritz smiled briefly, then his gaze followed the horse's progress. "He's a handsome beast. Here are the latest reports, sir. We've taken Smolensk. And cut the Soviet forces in two in Estonia." He didn't sound enthusiastic. August had the notion that this young man also cared little for the war, but they'd never dared discuss it.

"Hitler is stretching his resources too thin in Russia. Fighting on two fronts is a risk. I heard Roosevelt and Churchill are having another meeting." August watched the stallion lope around the other side of the paddock.

"Colonel Burmester asked me many questions." Fritz again watched the horse. "I told him you are the best of commanders."

"I appreciate that, *danke*." August smiled at his secretary. Then his shoulders bunched with the duty before him. "Tell Captain Schmidt I want to speak with him in my office, now."

* * *

Norah found Loeiza in the parlor, hemming a skirt for Marie-Louise. Another hand-me-down from Angelique. At her mother's request, the little girl turned to the right as she eyed Norah with suspicion, as if she knew all her carnal pleasures.

Loeiza knotted then broke off her thread. "There, all finished, my dear. Go and see if your sister needs help with Petit Yann." She kissed her daughter's cheek.

"*Merci, Maman.*" Her words even, Marie-Louise flapped the skirt and strutted out of the room.

"She's so serious, I often worry about her," Loeiza said as she packed up her sewing basket. She swiped emery paper over her needles to keep off rust from the sea air.

Norah sat on the sofa beside her. "She is very serious for one so young, not quite six. Maybe we could set up games to play more often. Are you sure you don't mind Jean and Angelique helping me clean the gardener's cottage?"

Loeiza met her gaze, her full mouth firm. "Yann doesn't mind, and Jean begged me. I have several misgivings. Will you be all right out there when you're alone?" Her cousin rearranged her sewing basket, then stared at her again. "My absolute rule is, the Major can't be there when my children are."

"No, of course not." Norah shifted on the couch cushion. She'd yet to ask permission from August to commandeer the cottage. He'd been gone for three days, *on a port visit*, his note said. This worried her, but she heard he had returned. She clasped her hands on her knees. "Would it be better if I moved out, so I'm not bringing shame to your family?" Could she move into the cottage, with August? The villagers would definitely denounce her.

Loeiza sighed. "I'd rather have you in this house, where you're safe. And I know you've done favors for the people here. Yann has received more animals to butcher. Madame Bolloré says the

Germans are paying more for her eggs, over twice as much as before."

Norah relaxed. August had kept his promises. "That's good to know."

"It's…dangerous for you, this 'friendship'. And I hope you aren't selling yourself because you have no choice." Loeiza pressed her hand, her words sad.

"Our love is real, I swear. Inconvenient, ill-advised, hazardous, yes. My heart went where it shouldn't, but I can't imagine loving anyone else. He feels the same." Norah's throat constricted as she squeezed her cousin's wrist. "Just tell me if I need to leave when the time comes. I'll understand."

"We all make compromises. And love…it changes." Loeiza stood, fingers gripped on the basket. "But again, be extremely careful. I'll prepare a Queen Anne's Lace tincture for you, to prevent—"

"*Merci*. I will drink it." Norah stood, flushing hot inside. "I appreciate your attention to, uh, that issue." Another baby was *not* what she needed. She pushed past that anguished event from last year.

Loeiza nodded quickly and left the parlor.

Norah blew out her breath. She moved to the foyer, opened the front door, and inhaled the warm air with the sweet hint of honeysuckle. She rubbed her cheeks—so many worries. Had she given up her body too easily?

She glanced around and no one was about. Rustling among the geraniums in the pot, she saw a note. She plucked the tiny paper from the soil and unfolded it.

There is a good reply- A. The telegram, word from her family? Could she be so fortunate? Relief filtered through her.

She sat on the edge of the well, smiling, her thoughts slipping to their lovemaking. Warmth stroked through her at the idea of his touch, his lips on hers, and eyes filled with passion. Their flesh pressed together.

The click of shoes over cobbles. Norah turned. Madame Ropars, the mayor's wife, stood there, her narrow face haughty. "I've been wanting to speak to you, Mademoiselle Cooper." She puffed on a Gauloise cigarette, the tobacco smell harsh, her red lips in a twist.

"I apologize for telling false stories about sketching you and your friends," Norah said quickly, stuffing the note in her trouser pocket. "It was—"

"Your lies to your cousin about drawing me, *oui*. A miscalculation." She waved her cigarette around. A thin, beautiful woman in her forties, she wore a wide-shouldered suit jacket with a pleated skirt, both a faded purple, her brassy blonde hair caught up in a snood. "Do you know my sister was chased from Paris by the Nazis in the mass evacuation? Starving and sleeping in the hedgerows."

"How awful. I heard the horrible stories about that exodus last year. I hope she's all right." Norah tried her best to sound kind but wondered what the woman wanted. A niggle inside made her suspect the worst.

"She'll never be the same. We lost our home to these damn oppressors." Madame Ropars strutted closer in scuffed high-heels, her seamed stockings riddled with snags. A strong floral perfume drifted off her. "And now you're sleeping with the commandant. Isn't that so?"

"My personal business is just that, personal." Norah stood, holding tight to her indignance, when she had no right to be indignant. "And don't say any action of mine affects the village in a negative way. It's the opposite."

Madame Ropars looked her up and down, her eyes assessing. "Tell your lover, I wouldn't mind two pairs of new stockings. I should make some use of you." She puffed her cigarette again, her pale eyes sharp. "I'll ask my friends to look the other way when you're cavorting with the enemy. We would all appreciate stockings, cigarettes, and perhaps, some chocolate. But be discreet."

"I'll try my best, but these items might be unavailable. Furthermore, you need a lesson in politeness, Madame, if you wish me to be useful." Norah bit on her lip and waved the smoke away, back in the woman's face. She sauntered into the cottage, knuckles white in her fists. The glint in Madame Ropar's eyes spoke of more than she admitted. And now Norah was expected to be her private Black Market.

They all sought to better themselves, to take advantage—to survive. When most of what Norah desired from August was his love. She squeezed her eyes shut for a moment against the turmoil.

Loeiza folded her napkins and caps into a basket in the kitchen. She cast a furtive eye at Norah. What was she doing with these embroidered items? Her cousin had to be involved in something mysterious—perhaps dangerous.

Norah hurried up the stairs to forge more passes, with a new list from Pichon. Locking the door, her fingers fumbled when she checked the ink reservoir in the fountain pen. They clung to too many secrets for survival.

Chapter Twenty-five

A blast shook the manor house. August, jerked from sleep, jumped from bed, threw on his robe and rushed down the stairs. Ziegler and Schmidt joined him in similar attire. Plaster from the ceiling sprinkled on August's head as he reached the front door. He swiped the debris away.

Outside, in the murky dawn light was the stench of gunpowder and a waft of smoke. Chips and larger pieces of stone littered the ground. Gunshots sounded from the forest.

Landsers stood at the corner of the house where a hole had been blown into the heavy granite, partially revealing the inside of a storeroom. A thickset woman stood a few yards off. A sentry pointed a rifle at her.

"What goes on here?" August demanded over his drumming pulse.

"An attempt on your life. We've sent men to search the area, sir," a landser said. "We found her here."

"I tried to stop them." The disheveled woman held a bleeding arm against her black cotton dress frayed at the sleeves. "*Mon Dieu*."

"Who are you, Frau Kerguelen?" August approached, his stomach like a fist. "Who did this? You know them?"

"They're from the Maquis, avenging my son's death." Her eyes were full of angry tears, her expression mutinous. Stone dust dirtied her arms, chest, and face. "But I warned them to do no more."

August reined in his own anger and sent a man inside for a towel. He wrapped it around her scraped arm. "You must seek out a doctor. Were these men local people?"

"We should start to shoot the villagers in reprisal." Schmidt thrust his hands on his slim hips encased in an ebony robe. The captain had been unavailable the day before to speak to. He stomped over. "Who were they, Frau Kerguelen?"

She lowered her scarf-covered head. "I don't know them personally. No villagers."

"We will send a special detail into the woods to flush out the Maquis," August declared. The Maquis were guerilla fighters who'd escaped into the forests to avoid conscription into the *Service du Travail Obligatoire*—the forced labor in Germany. Now they performed acts of sabotage.

Ziegler puffed out his broad chest in a mauve satin robe, his thick white hair a mess. "*Ja*, we have important…" He glanced at the woman and stopped. He waddled back into the manor. "I require my coffee!"

Lt. Bauer loped into the group in full uniform. "I heard the explosion. Is everyone all right?"

"We're fine." August massaged his scalp, thinking of what might have happened. How could he keep order in the village? "Everyone, back to your positions. Frau Kerguelen, seek out the doctor. Return home after, then stay there until we have more questions."

"We are decent Bretons, our roots deep. Hard workers. You Germans invaded, forcing my sons to protect our homeland. *Our land!* You murdered a hero." The woman, head down, scurried along the path toward the village.

"We should arrest her," Schmidt protested as he swept into the house like a bat.

August understood her anger. Chest heavy, he was caught in an untenable position. "We have essential business to take care of when the U-boat arrives," he whispered to Bauer. A scheme they'd discussed on and off in secret. "Are you still onboard with the plan?"

Bauer nodded, his mouth in a grim line. "I will be ready, Herr Major. This war has done nothing but destroy our country, too."

* * *

August fitted the jigsaw pieces depicting wine glasses, bottles of wine, and the woman with the straw hat sporting an orange flower into place. The luncheon at the boating party was taking shape. He turned to Captain Schmidt whom he'd kept waiting. "I had a visit from High Command's Colonel von Burmester. Do you know him?"

Schmidt sniffed through his pointed nose, his gaze roaming the room. "I have heard of him."

"Did you write him a letter, complaining about my actions out here in Saint Guénolé? And don't lie to me." August crossed his arms, the resentment a hot coal burning inside him.

Schmidt briefly met his eyes. "*Oberkommando der Wehrmacht* might notice the leniency that is happening. Look at the explosion this morning. That woman should be interrogated."

"I questioned her before you arrived. She claims she's told us all she knows." August didn't believe her, but she'd suffered enough. "Our men are searching for the Maquis."

"Rougher methods against her might be required." Schmidt stood taller.

"Herr Captain, if you aren't satisfied under my command, you could ask for a posting elsewhere." August cocked his head, straining to sound calm. "I'm sure the delights of Paris would be more to your liking."

Schmidt's sallow skin turned pink on his sharp cheeks. "I'd hoped to be part of something historic out here, the largest U-boat in Hitler's arsenal." He walked to the opposite wall where the painting of *Château de Keriolet* hung. "Did your… Fräulein Cooper paint this?"

"That is not the topic we are discussing." August refrained from jerking the man away from the precious painting. Did his love for an Englishwoman spur on his rash decision to destroy the U-boat, not yet in port?

"I prefer realistic paintings, rather than these impressionistic efforts." Schmidt waved a flippant hand. "This looks careless."

"In Paris, they might require your art critic skills." August strode close to Schmidt, anger searing along his nape. "Again, if you don't like being under my command, request a transfer." August fumed over his previous failed request to have Schmidt reassigned. "You say you have important friends in Paris; contact them for another position."

Schmidt slid away, skinny body drooped for a moment. "I might do that, Herr Major. But my father hates people who shirk their duty."

"Well, keep *my* private business to yourself, if you think you know something." August kept the menace in his tone from exploding, though it crept out. He moved close again, very close, and clamped a hand on Schmidt's shoulder, fingers digging into his bony flesh. "I hope you understand?"

"*Jawohl.* I understand. I only did what I thought right. Is that all, sir?" A bead of sweat formed on his subordinate's sloped forehead, his gaze evasive.

"Opinions aren't always facts." August released him, moved away, and stuck in the last pin, to keep his captain off-balance. "Remember, *you* were in charge of security. The sentry died under your watch. The manor's sabotage as well."

Schmidt's entire face blotched, his eyes like slits. He went to the door, clicked his heels, and thrust out his arm. "Heil Hitler."

August swept up his arm, teeth clenched. "You're dismissed. Heil Hitler."

After the captain left, the door shut again, August leaned hard on his desk. Schmidt's father was in the SS. He could make life dangerous, or deadly. August swallowed slowly. He had a fine line to tread.

He felt the paper in his pocket, grabbed his hat, left the office, and slipped out the rear door of the Town Hall.

Chapter Twenty-six

As soon as the summerhouse door shut, Norah and August embraced. She pressed against his warmth, savoring the clean, Alpine smell of him. "I missed you. That bombing at the manor terrified me. I wanted to see you sooner." She quivered with the fright, and had almost run to the manor to find him.

"And I missed you, *liebchen*. We are still investigating, but a sentry watches the house closely. A lax young man from that incident has been reassigned." He kissed her until they both gasped for air. Then he pulled the telegram from his pocket. "Here it is. I'm sure you're anxious to read this."

Norah smiled, unfolded it, and read the static words. "My father says they're fine. No damage to property or family. They're relieved to hear I am well." She pressed the paper to her chest. If they knew what she was really involved in would her parents ever speak to her again? "Thank you for sending mine."

"I'm glad your family is well." He hugged her again, his mouth in her hair. "I want you to be happy more than anything."

"But I fear for them. Are there any plans to attack England? Can you tell me?" She'd avoided questions like this—their time together a haven from the war—but they constantly burrowed inside her.

"As far as I know there are no immediate plans, but there are forces on the Channel Islands. And I'm not on Hitler's high staff." He sounded sincere. "But I must explain to you why my sudden excursion." He told her about Burmester.

"Oh no. A colonel to beware of. Are you certain it was Captain Schmidt? Can you dismiss him?" She recalled the one time Schmidt had accosted her near the tavern; her worry for August skittered inside. Strange to worry about a German commandant—but the man mattered, more than she ever thought possible.

"He has been a thorn since assigned to me. I tried to get him transferred but was denied. No puffed-up colonel will ruin what we have." August stepped back, his hands cupping her cheeks. "Let's talk of more pleasant subjects. I have another surprise. Do you like horses?"

"What?" She looked into his mischievous gaze. "You weren't inspecting the Brest harbor. You got me a pony." She laughed.

He kissed her forehead. "You make me happy with your laugh. I purchased a stallion. Indulgent, yes. I used to ride as a boy. Happier times, until right now. We can sneak away and ride him together, deep into the hills."

"I'll enjoy that. We can take a picnic lunch. Tell me about this horse." She clasped his hands as he described the stallion, his eyes bright.

"As soon as he is comfortable with a saddle, we'll plan our outing." He pulled her close again and kissed her. Her body grew heavy with desire. And to think, she'd almost lost him.

"*Maler*, the 'painter'; he sounds magnificent. And I'm honored you thought of me." She almost giggled, behaving like a love-sick schoolgirl. "I also have a thorn. I was approached by Madame Ropars, the mayor's wife. She says she and her friends will look the other way about us if I provide them with stockings, cigarettes, and chocolate. I've asked enough of you and resent her request."

"What a shrew. I'm sorry you must cope with these judgments." August squeezed her fingers and held them to his chest. "I'll do what I can, but silk stockings are difficult to procure. Let's hope she doesn't become too avaricious."

"Please don't go to any trouble for her." She watched him as the shadows of the summerhouse played off his handsome face and vivid eyes. In here, they could pretend their relationship was carefree, but the truth was darker. She blinked it away. "I have another request, a personal one."

"You want me to wave a royal scepter and make the war disappear?" He smiled sadly and cocked his head.

"I wish you could. Do you know of the gardener's cottage on the estate? I'd like to fix it up and use it for painting and storing items." She touched the collar of his green shirt. "If that's all right."

"I have seen that cottage on my walks. It's a forlorn place tangled in weeds. Do you need my excellent cleaning skills?"

"I want to surprise you. I'll prepare it with the help of my young cousins, Jean and Angelique. We've already been inside." Embarrassment flickered through her. "Jean picked the lock. I don't know where the key is."

"You broke in? Shame on you." His admonishment was a tease. "I wish you'd waited. If a sentry had caught you…" He put his hands on his hips. "There's a set of keys in the main house. Perhaps one will fit."

"Also, the bed needs a mattress." Her words faltered.

"Do you plan to stay the night? I wouldn't advise that."

"Not without certain company." She trailed her finger down his chest. Was she being too bold, too wanton? She had lost her bearings when it came to him.

"Ah, and I insist on *being* your company." August sat in one of the chairs and pulled her down to sit on his lap.

"I'd have no other." Norah nestled against him, their combined warmth comforting. "I mean that, no matter our obstacles." If she was being naïve, let it be so for now, these fleeting moments of joy as storm clouds gathered.

"*Meine liebe*. I want no other. I'm sorry you must suffer being my woman." August tipped up her face and kissed her passionately, his lips so hot and soft, their tongues exploring.

She moaned and squirmed on his lap. Then felt his desire beneath her.

August broke the kiss, his breath rapid. His eyes were tender with longing. "To continue like this, there may be consequences."

She smiled, her chest heaving. Her mind clouded with need, the heaviness of desire. "You must show me a new way of…accomplishing that."

"It will be my pleasure. Both of us, *ma cherie*." He seared her with another kiss, his hand caressing up her thigh.

* * *

In her tiny bedroom, Norah folded the forms and stuffed them down the front of her trousers. The bulkiness was too obvious. She slipped on an old cardigan of Loeiza's.

Yann was asleep, his snores rumbling from his bedroom. Loeiza was outside with the children, playing a game in the rear yard.

Norah told Pichon she'd come to the rectory behind the church where he worked on a cabinet for the priest.

She left the cottage, holding the cardigan close. The sun was setting, but the air remained warm. The slight rustling as she walked kept her on edge. Now she thought twice about being so daring.

German soldiers watched her from the tables in front of the tavern. Music, a marching song, sounded from inside. Comments circled among the men. Her neck prickled as she evened her pace. To distract her mind, she thought of the awkward pairing with August yesterday. Messy, fumbling sex, in a chair. A desperate passion? She smiled to herself.

Past the gray stone market building, then the majestic Église Saint Guénolé, she approached the granite rectory, a foursquare building, dour in the fading sunlight. A noise made her jump. A cat ran out from behind a bush.

At her knock, a woman in cap and apron opened the door.

"Is Monsieur Pichon here? I need to talk to him."

The round-faced woman flicked a disapproving glare over her—the commandant's woman, or worse—turned and strode down the short hall. Norah followed. The housekeeper opened a door and pointed.

Norah entered a dining room furnished with plain but heavy, elegant pieces. The room smelled of linseed oil.

Pichon crouched by a small cabinet; he was in the process of fitting in a drawer. He stood and smiled his easy smile. "Mademoiselle Cooper, you didn't need to come here. I've already told you that."

She moved closer. The housekeeper had shut the door. "I know. But you said you needed these…items right away. And I needed a walk."

He wiped his hands on a cloth, his hazel eyes serious. "I hate to ask, but now that you and the commandant are, if the rumors are true, involved, can I trust you?"

She'd expected this; the entire village whispered. "You can trust me. I know these passes are important. The major and I, we don't share our secrets." A slight shame crept up, but she banished it;

she *had* to. And it had become so much easier. She pulled out the forms and wouldn't try to convince Pichon that August was a good man. "It's complicated."

"Is it for your own gain?" He said it gently, without accusation.

"No, it's two people who love one another, as simple as that." She knew nothing was simple, not even the basic truth.

"All right, but don't deliver like this again. It's too dangerous." He looked the papers over. "Perfect as usual. I will use them later this evening."

She glanced at a large cross with Jesus, a crucifix, on the wall over a sideboard. *Oh, dear.* "I'll fill out whatever you require, any time. I want to help."

He tugged at the drawer to make certain it slid. "Soon we'll need papers for downed airmen who must escape over the mountains. I'm trusting you when I say this."

She'd heard of British men parachuting out of bullet-ridden planes and spies guiding them over the Pyrenees to safety. She'd rejoice in helping her countrymen; it might diminish her torn loyalties. Would the war soon turn in England's favor? But what would that mean for August, arrest, a firing squad?

She nodded over her jab of fear. "Don't give me any unnecessary details."

"My wife and I are repairing a larger cottage to live in. The roof needs re-slating. Married life is good. But you, now you must be careful. It's twice as dangerous if you're discovered. You will anger the Major." He smiled, though he looked disappointed by her situation. "You'd better get back home before it's dark."

She appreciated that Pichon didn't chide her for her relationship with August. "I would only anger those who have power over him. Good evening."

Norah left the rectory. More shadows draped the landscape, the sun disappearing behind the trees.

She wrapped the cardigan around her and walked past the looming Gothic church, now a stark menace in the gloaming. Insects hummed in the bushes.

She passed the tavern. The soldiers had gone inside and pulled the blackout blinds. The music was not quite so loud.

Further into the village, she saw a woman with a large basket duck into an alley. It looked like Loeiza. Norah shook her head. She reached the alley and even in the shadows, the woman's walk matched her cousin's. Norah stepped into the narrow lane. The footsteps sounded ahead, around a corner. She crept after her, pulse thumping, and peered around the corner at the side street. The ocean rushed beyond the road, from down the slope.

Loeiza stood in darker shadows, talking low with a tall man in a long coat and fedora. Her cousin handed him the cloth items in her basket.

Norah gripped the stone at the wall's edge. Loeiza must be working for the Resistance.

At the stomp of boots from the alley entrance, Norah turned. A sentry? Was it close to curfew? Fear coursed through her. She ducked into a deep doorway, flattening herself against weathered wood.

A soldier trudged by, a rifle slung over his shoulder. Norah held her breath. Her stomach sank into a pit. The soldier passed her. Would he catch Loeiza? She wanted to shout out a warning but froze. She'd be shot if she called attention to herself.

She heard more bootsteps echo where the soldier went, but no raising of alarm.

Shaking with apprehension, she edged from the alley to the area where her cousin had been; no one was there now.

Keeping to the shadows of the back street, the village shrouded behind blackout curtains, she hurried on. Norah had taken a huge risk to be out this late. If she counted on August's protection, this put him under suspicion.

Her breath rasped in her lungs. A dog growled, and she cringed. Chickens rustled in their coop when she passed **Madame Bolloré's**.

Norah stared about and saw no one. She slipped through the back gate into her cousin's garden. She crouched near the wall, heart pinched. How could she face Loeiza, after what she observed?

Chapter Twenty-seven

August slid the key into the lock. After trying four others, this one fit; the lock clicked and he opened the cottage door. He twisted the key off the ring and handed it to Norah. "*Voila.*"

He kept his voice ebullient while glancing over his shoulder. Would the Maquis try to kill him again, or this woman he loved? He let out a slow breath.

Norah stepped inside. "We've finished most of the cleaning. My cousin gave me a tablecloth to spread on the table. Jean will help me carry over my paintings."

"This is not a bad little place." August crouched and inspected the flue of the fireplace. He almost felt they were viewing their own new home. A contentment filled him for a moment. "A good cleaning up there is needed." He stood and faced her. "Just never come here alone after dark."

"I won't. I know better." She walked to the kitchen. "I need dishes; Loeiza doesn't have any to spare."

"I can bring you some from the manor house." He scanned the room. The faded green sofa, small table with two chairs, and he noted the lack of electricity. Primitive but tidy; he approved. "You'll need oil or kerosine for the lamps. I could provide a small rug."

"I'd like that, and I want to keep it simple." She pointed to a glass jar on the mantel where purple flowers stood in water. "My little cousin, Angelique, picked lavender to perfume the cottage."

"The smell is wonderful." He gazed around again. "There is a phonograph with records the mayor left behind. I'll bring it here."

She laughed. "I'll teach you the jitterbug."

"I'd prefer we dance slowly." He winked then entered the bedroom. "*Ja*, a mattress is required, and bedclothes. I'll haul one over from the manor." He smiled when she came to stand beside him. More sensual thoughts seeped into his mind. Time for them together, in a decent setting, worthy of her.

"We'll finally have a proper place to…enjoy…" Her cheeks flushed pink.

He slipped his arm around her, eager to hold her close. "You won't miss the summerhouse floor?"

She laughed and leaned into him. "It was memorable."

"It was. Special, as our first time." He kissed her cheek, savoring the sweet taste of her. "Will you regret our being this obvious, here together? Everyone will know."

"I won't lie; there'll be objections, and anger, but we must put up with it." She gazed up at him with a light of love deep in her eyes he'd never experienced. "Everyone already knows."

He heard no sadness in her tone. He swiped aside any fears for her fragile predicament. He must believe he could keep her safe. "Yes, of course. It won't be easy, as we are aware."

She had proved she really loved him despite his official capacity and his country's war against hers. He felt it in her kisses, her caresses. The way she looked at him as her paramour and not her oppressor. The precariousness of their difference in position, heritage, even age, would always be obstacles to overcome. He detected no betrayal in her love, though there were layers inside her she held onto. Could he count on her being stalwart? He liked to think so.

He felt like a schoolboy, discovering his first love. He'd respected Klara, her gentle presence, but there had been no passion in their practically arranged marriage.

August kissed Norah on the lips, his hands on her soft body, the flare of her hip. If he could only linger here now and forget his odious duties. "Fetch your paintings with the boy. I must return to my office." He wouldn't tell her that Ziegler had requested to house some of his sailors in this cottage. August had said impossible, it's a ruin. He hadn't wanted them on the estate property. The seamen were housed in tents scattered on the outskirts of town.

At his desk twenty minutes later, he stood and read the latest bulletin. Roosevelt and Churchill had offered assistance to Russia to thwart Germany's advances there. Hitler was outraged. But on August 16th, yesterday, Hitler's forces occupied the vital Soviet naval base at Mykolaiv, and they captured warships, ammunition and repair facilities.

Yet the previous week the Soviets had attacked Berlin. And the RAF carried out daylight bombings in Germany, when most of the Luftwaffe was on the Eastern Front. The paper rattled in his hands. Were his children and parents safe? This hung over him constantly. He must send them additional telegrams.

Back to business. The Luftwaffe was also anxious for the airfield at Audierne to be completed. August hadn't rushed the workers out there and hoped any stalling would remain unnoticed.

The war swung back and forth. August grimaced. He must speak to Herr Zeigler about the progress of the submarine. Would it arrive before winter? Could August accumulate the explosives needed? Was he mad to pursue this? Perhaps the unwieldly vessel would implode or sink under its own weight. But that would mean the death of German sailors. He detested this war as it was not for

Germany's honor, but to destroy everyone who wouldn't submit to Hitler.

Schmidt knocked on the doorjamb. "Herr Major. We have a problem." He strutted in. "My informants tell me there is a forger in the village. This person is falsifying documents to help Jews and other undesirables escape."

August stacked papers into a neat pile and slowly pondered this possibility. Rumors had trickled in concerning such activity throughout France. "Do you have any additional information on this?"

"It might be a local carpenter, or one of the people who used to meet at the butcher's house. Or the butcher himself." Schmidt gave his sly, irritating smirk. "We should raid that house."

August clenched his hand on the back of his chair, his glare on Schmidt. Did the man taunt him? Was it a lie? August had promised Norah not to interrogate the butcher, the cousin who provided her a home. Yet he must act as the commandant. Was someone in that house a forger? It *could* be the carpenter or anyone else in the village.

Schmidt said in an oily tone, "Herr Major, an artist would make a fine forger."

"No raids. Find out more information, quietly. Do not approach anyone in the **Menez** residence. Bring Menez and the carpenter in for questioning. I will make my own inquiries. We proceed slowly." Certainly not *her*—though an artist would be suspect. The apprehension unsettled him. He must question her, gently, if she would even tell him if she knew about such activity.

August wrestled down a shout in his next command, "Do nothing without my permission."

* * *

Norah watched Loeiza fix the pedal on Jean's beat-up bicycle in front of her cottage on the square. The hot summer sun beat down on them, hardly a breeze stirring. The Nazi flag over the Town Hall drooped, hiding the ugly symbol.

Loeiza gripped the handlebars. "Here, *mon fils*, it should be tight now."

Jean chuckled as he swung his leg over the seat. "This is a bumpy ride without inner tubes." He started off down the street, his wheels making a strange, grinding sound. Inner tubes were impossible to find, so people filled hosepipes with sand, and tucked them under the tires.

Norah turned to her cousin. She'd stewed on this for hours; should she cause more animosity? "You often ask me if I'm making a mistake in my relationship. I wonder if you might be…involved in something clandestine."

"What do you mean?" Loeiza's dark eyes flashed, her mouth pursed.

Norah stared at her scuffed oxfords for a minute. "Can we be honest? I was coming back from the rectory two evenings ago and I saw you—"

Loeiza sucked in her breath. "What were you doing at the rectory in the evening?"

Norah inspected the scrapes on her hands from pressing against the door. "I'm only concerned that you're safe."

"As I am for you." Her cousin's words clipped out, but she looked away. "You say you know what you're doing with the commandant. Don't doubt anyone else, as you wish not to be doubted."

Norah stifled a groan at Loeiza's incisive comment, but she still worried.

Petit Yann hovered at the terra cotta pot where August had his messages hidden. The child dug his fingers into the dirt, rustling the geraniums.

Norah hurried over and scooped up the boy. She brushed off his hands. "No dirt, sweetie. Don't hurt the flowers." She glanced down at the disturbed dirt to make certain no note was there.

Loeiza took her boy and kissed his plump cheek. "You behave, my naughty one."

"I'm hungry, *Maman*." He patted her ample chest.

"You're too old for that. We'll eat soon." Loeiza set him down, her laugh forced. The boy saw the yellow tabby cat that seemed to own the square and chased after it, giggling.

"Are your embroidered items messages helping the Résistance?" Norah whispered.

"I cannot tell you. You have the ear, and more, of the Major. Please don't put me in a more difficult position." Loeiza stared at her, eyes moist. "We must keep our secrets."

"You're right, I'm sorry. Your husband would be angry, too." Norah had her answer. Despite Yann's claim to stay out of the Résistance, his wife was of a different mind. Concern for her cousin piled in atop her own hurdles. "As you warn me, be careful, please."

Loeiza clasped her shoulder, her gaze pleading. "Don't follow me, ever. Never tell anyone about this; especially…you know who I mean."

"I would never do that. I wouldn't put you in harm's way."

Her cousin's eye softened. "And you should not be out in the evenings either."

"I agree, it was foolish." Norah recalled the sentry marching by. A shiver crept up her spine.

Jean rode back, the wheels of his bike wobbling as he bumped along. The sifting noise of sand shifted inside the hoses. "I couldn't ride very far like this. But it might make my legs stronger."

Norah wondered if August could find inner tubes for the bike; but she'd asked too much of him already. She never wanted him to think she was using him, though it worked to her advantage if the villagers believed it. They would 'look the other way', as Madame Ropers said, if they thought Norah's fraternization benefited them.

They would never understand the depth of her love for a man who happened to be a German officer. She was still amazed herself.

Norah felt the cottage key in her trouser pocket. August had a duplicate made for him. She and Jean would carry over her paintings in another hour to set up her studio, with Loeiza's permission.

A skinny male, arms swinging, stomped toward them from the village's far end. He came into distinct view and scowled at Norah. Yann!

Chapter Twenty-eight

Yann waved Norah inside the house, his long face glum—as it usually was—and now creased with anger. "I must speak to you in the parlor."

Norah bit back an exasperated 'what is it now', and rearranged her face into impassive. This couldn't be good. "What would this discussion be about?"

"What is wrong?" Loeiza asked. She entered the foyer with Petit Yann by the hand, and Jean behind her.

Yann opened the parlor door, eyes narrowed. "I'm having a private word."

"I'll be all right." Norah wouldn't come between a husband and wife, no matter the state of their marriage.

"Yann, please be kind, whatever it is." Loeiza briefly met Norah's gaze, then called into the parlor. "Angelique, bring your embroidery items. We'll try to interest your sister in sewing. She's weeding. Let's go to the garden, children."

Angelique, who'd been sitting in the parlor diligently working on her embroidery, eyed her father, nodded to Norah, then quickly left with colorful threads, material, and a small basket.

Loeiza forced an exuberant air. "Jean, gather your cousin's paintings for her studio at the cottage."

"No, please, I'll collect the paintings. Some are still damp." Norah leaned out from the parlor, afraid Jean might find her forged, hidden documents. The boy looked at her with one eyebrow raised. He seemed to know something.

Yann shut the parlor door. "Mayor Ropars told me there are whispers about a forger in our village." The coppery stink of animal blood rolled off his clothes and from under his red-stained fingernails. "What do *you* know about it?"

"I've heard no such whispers." She tried to sound indignant but dreaded she might be caught out. Her stomach roiled. "Why do you ask me?"

"The Major might have said something to you about any suspicions." Yann lowered his dark brows.

"He wouldn't tell me such things." Norah turned from his glower. Did the Germans know? "Where did Monsieur Ropars hear these whispers?"

"The group who once met here puts me under suspicion." Of course, Yann would think of himself first.

"But again, why ask me? I know nothing." She crossed her arms and gripped her elbows, mind racing. She couldn't quit and jeopardize the escape of Jews with their children. The rumors of what went on at the labor camps and other places grew increasingly horrendous.

"You draw; forgers need to have that talent. You're English, and your name might have been mentioned, among others." Yann's growl crawled up her back. "Ropars didn't say where he heard it."

Her name was mentioned! She bit on her lip, struggling to hold herself together. She resisted staring up at the ceiling, beneath her room, where the documents and permits that would condemn her were hidden. Was August aware of the accusation? And if he found out about her forging, how would he react? Her life would be worth little unless he shielded her. Then that put him in danger. What if he decided she wasn't worth shielding?

She tightened her fingers on her elbows until it hurt. "I draw pictures not words."

"You know I want no part of the resistance activities." Yann's voice rose in anger. "I should never have allowed them to meet here. At first, I thought I'd help, but realized it's too risky. Look what happened to the **Kerguelen** brothers." He seemed to talk to himself now, lamenting his status. "I'm a simple man who desires a simple life with my family. My parents raised me that way. The invasion was bad enough."

Norah turned to face him again, making her expression sympathetic. She had to placate. "I understand you want no part of—"

"I could demand you leave, no matter what my wife wishes." He swaggered close to her, his limp brown hair flopping about his ears. "She wanted to help you, but you've been nothing but trouble. You don't even wear dresses like a proper woman."

"I'll find another place to live if that's what you decide." She'd feared this so many times. But she *was* the intruder here. Where would she go? The gardener's cottage? She sank deeper into the mire of her choices. Forging right under August's and Yann's nose.

Yann thrust a greasy finger in her face. "You'd better not be lying to me about knowing nothing. Who would trust you? You're screwing our enemy."

Norah winced and swallowed down any retort or plea. She was in the worst possible conundrum. A pariah for love. Her own family would disown her and be shamed. And now, perhaps her cousin would agree that she leave—no matter Loeiza's own actions. "I fell in love. I'm not a mercenary."

"Your friendliness in his bed brought food to our village, but if true, *this* is too far." He stomped over the well-worn rug. "I need to speak to others, especially Pichon."

Yann would get nothing from Pichon, she was certain.

Yann had condemned her without evidence, though her guilt kept her silent on that complaint. She had overstayed her welcome. Mouth dry, she said, "I'll abide by your decision."

"You have no choice. I want my wife devoted to *my* wishes." He didn't sound confident on this last part. Yann slammed through the parlor door and out the front entrance. The house rattled.

Muscles rigid, Norah stood stiff, like a megalith upright in a windstorm. Shoulders pushed back, she left the parlor and dragged her feet up the stairs. Her hand trembled on the banister. She must find a better place to stash the documents, travel permits, and identity cards. In her suitcase, under her knickers and brassieres for now. But where could she stash herself?

* * *

August kissed Norah's naked shoulder, her skin warm and moist after their lovemaking. Her lithe body felt natural against his in their mutual musky scent. Crickets chirped through the open window where a slight breeze filtered around blackout curtains, into the dark room of the gardener's cottage. The moonlight outlined them both. "I love you, *mon amour.*"

"I love you…so much. And this is nicer on a mattress," she murmured, her back to him as they snuggled under the sheets on the iron bed.

"You seemed a little agitated earlier; is something wrong?"

She turned and touched his face. "I'm fine now. Can I ask where you got that huge scar on your right side?"

"I was shot seven years ago, trying to warn friends." He really didn't want to go into the details, the pain, at this moment. But he was naked, like she was, to be explored in all his flaws. He shoved away those ugly memories, brushed his lips over hers, then traced his fingers down her silky, soft back. "I'll tell you more later. In the morning, we'll plan our picnic, and you can meet my stallion, Maler. He might like his picture drawn, then painted.”

“Another handsome portrait. I’d be happy to.” She reached up and ruffled his hair. “Even in the shadows, I like your hair mussed up.”

He smiled. “No military strictness?” Wouldn’t it be ‘freeing’ to not have to wear that uniform each day, which wrapped him in the menace of the *Wehrmacht*?

She nestled her head on his chest. “My cousin’s husband might ask me to leave their home.”

“Why? What has happened?” His mind immediately went to the rumor of a forger, an inquiry he’d yet to begin.

“He thinks…I’ve been there too long already.” She sounded evasive. Or he read too much into it.

“Is it as straightforward as that?” Here was the source of her anxiety. A shame to have to discuss these things after they’d shared such sweet passion tonight. He did need to find out what she knew. “Is it because you are with me?”

She sighed and ran her fingers down his abdomen. “That’s part of it. I was wondering, though you might object, if I could move in here.”

August closed his eyes, enjoying her touch, but now these other problems pushed in. “You’d be alone, though I could come most nights; unless I leave for inspections. Let me think about it.” He could throttle the damn butcher. He wanted to recapture that languid, satisfied feeling he’d just had. However, her fingers were raising another potent condition.

“You could provide me with a pistol, for protection,” she whispered.

He grasped her wandering hand. “That is dangerous, too.” Non-Germans weren’t allowed weapons, for obvious reasons. “I would worry about you out here.” But where else could she go? Anywhere close by, without her family, she’d be open to worse scrutiny and hazard.

She kissed his chest, her mouth warm on his skin. "I know how to fire a gun."

"I'm not surprised." He pulled her against him and kissed her firmly on the lips. "We should sleep, then talk about this soon. I'll think of a solution." Another, more personal question niggled at him. He hated to continue to dishonor her when he felt this intensely about her. He let the question slip out. "Norah, would you marry me?" *Though as a German officer I might be a threat to you and your people for a short time more.*

She breathed in slowly. A few minutes of quiet. "As difficult…yes, I would. We'll go to Switzerland, you said. You can retire next year?"

"That is my intention." As soon as he could take his son with them—after graduation—away from the Nazis, and count on his daughters being protected by their husbands.

He kissed the top of her head as he hugged her, holding on to his dream, making it real. He needed her love, though other troubles such as the direction of the war, and the business with the U-boat, kept him from any true peace. But negotiating life was always a challenge. She couldn't be involved in the clandestine activities in the village—he must believe that. Yet Schmidt was certain to cause problems.

August closed his eyes, trying to drag himself into oblivion. He knew his family wouldn't be thrilled when he married an Englishwoman. One thirteen years younger, and his mistress. But his love blurred all these battles.

He rested his cheek on her lush, fragrant hair as she snuggled against him. Her name was whispered in the allegations. The picnic—he swallowed a groan; he must question her then.

Chapter Twenty-nine

The jeep sped along the narrow path through the woods. August clung one hand to its side in the dark. Schmidt was in Quimper with his mistress, Bauer searching for petrol farther north. But information had arrived about a Maquis group hiding in an abandoned farmhouse, east of **Saint Guénolé**. The jeep bumped over potholes, as it swerved around trees. The headlights were fitted with metal covers, with a slit to allow a little light out.

The zealous Corporal Flach drove. The son of a soldier who'd served the Kaiser, Flach had failed officer training—and made up for it with aggressiveness. Unmarried, he bragged about surviving a rough upbringing with an alcoholic mother. A man who clawed and devoured to outrun his past.

August gripped the door's top, cold on his fingers. He must be seen as an officer in command, willing to attack, to keep his position until he could retire next autumn.

A shadowed building slid into view. The corporal stopped the jeep in a crunch of tires. Landsers scrambled from the vehicle and spread out. Four soldiers crept toward the house. August touched the pistol at his side.

"We're certain they're holed up in there, sir," Corporal Flach hissed. A pale young man with pale blond hair, he practically glowed in the dark.

"Good work, Flach." August left the jeep. Flach always gave him a feeling of distaste. "These could be the guerilla fighters who tried to blow up the manor house."

A window flew open in the farmhouse, a rifle slid out, shots fired. The landsers fired back, the noise cracking through the woods.

August and Flach advanced, ducking down under fire behind a derelict wagon.

A man staggered from the house, shooting a long rifle. Chunks of wood burst off the wagon. Animals thrashed away through the bushes.

"Charge the building!" August raised his pistol and fired back, along with the soldiers. The man jerked and fell.

More gunfire filled the air, smoke, the stench of gunpowder. The landsers rushed into the house. Further shots. A bullet flew by August's cheek. He touched it, no blood. His pulse sputtered.

Then silence. August and Flach entered the farmhouse. The dingy place stank of unwashed bodies. They stepped over a dead figure in the hallway. Two men lay dead near the flicker of a lone candle on a table. Two guns and a scattering of ammunition were also there. The rear door was open. Three mothers or more had lost their sons tonight, others had escaped.

Flach shoved at one body as he searched the ammunition, but August grabbed him. "No need for that, Corporal. Respect the dead."

"I'll never respect these French maggots, sir," Flach grumbled. "We Germans must keep the upper hand, no matter who we crush."

"There are more subtle procedures. I don't recognize any of these people. They are outsiders, and not from the village." August strapped his pistol back at his side. Sweat formed on his collar. Regret dampened his spirit. Perhaps this would frighten the Maquis away from this region. He hated to kill, but Paris' Military Administration, the *Militärverwaltung in Frankreich*, would receive an excellent report.

Norah held tight to August's waist, her hips moving with the undulating pace of the horse. The warmth of man and horse seeped through her. The scent of trees, grass, and August's cologne made her smile. She felt safe and ready to laugh pressed against him. They galloped over a field, then trotted through the woods, to the north of the village, past hedgerows blooming with pale yellow primroses.

In a small clearing, he reined in Maler. Rocks poked up through the earth with tufts of grass and the wild purple lobelia.

They dismounted, and she rubbed her lower spine. "It's been a while since I rode. I enjoyed it."

"My muscles have had to remember what it's like as well." He tied the horse to a spindly tree and patted the animal's haunch.

She stroked the stallion's velvety nose, then ran her hand down his neck. "You're a fine horse, aren't you? With those three white socks." She used to ride in her early teens with her sister. A sudden sadness that she might never see Agatha and her sister's children, as well as her parents, weighed heavy on her heart. But she'd made her choice, no matter where it might lead.

"I'm sure he agrees he's a fine one." August smiled, spread out a blanket, then set the basket he'd tied to the saddle on it. "Maler is still a little skittish, but is settling down."

She sat, opened the basket, and laid out *Andouille de Guémené* sausage, Saint-Paulin cheese, and plump peaches. Also, a fragrant baguette. Loeiza had helped her pack it, saying she was sorry about Yann's anger. Norah would not ask her to intercede. He had a perfect right to demand Norah leave. This morning he'd given her until the end of the week. Glancing at August, she must get permission for the cottage.

She sliced the sausage, her fingers soon greasy. Her hair fell in her face, and she swept it back with her wrist. "I need a haircut."

"No, I like it long." August sat close to her and twirled a strand around his fingers.

Her neck tingled and she laughed. "We'll see."

They settled in with earthenware plates. A shrike flapped overhead. A rusty-colored squirrel skittered up a tree. Maler snorted. The sky shone bright azure, the air warm, soon to be hot.

Dressed in his civilian clothes, a light blue shirt over broad shoulders and gray trousers, shoes not boots, August again became that man separate from his disturbing duty as a German officer. His dark golden hair ruffled in the breeze, this lover who kissed her hungrily in their nights.

He bit into a sausage slice. "Pork? With good spices. Delicious."

"My cousin's husband provided it."

He arched an eyebrow. "You do not like this man, I can tell."

She nibbled on the soft cheese, which tasted buttery and nutty. "He doesn't bother to be likeable. But he is a good provider for his family." Her voice even, she opened the flask of cider and sipped the potent apple drink.

"And has he asked you to move out?" August cut the bread into manageable pieces.

"At the end of the week." She forced a smile over the sinking feeling she'd fought all day. She resented being so vulnerable. "I plan to camp out at the summerhouse, like a gypsy."

He pressed a piece of bread into her hand, his gaze concerned. "You will have to move into the gardener's cottage. It's the only solution, I'm afraid. I want you secure." He cocked his head. "I received cigarettes and even a pair of silk stockings for the mayor's wife. This is all I could get."

"It's enough, thank you. I'll ask for no more." Norah felt easier with a home to go to, her body relaxing, though she'd been fairly certain he wouldn't disappoint her. She ate the fresh bread with its crispy crust. "Madame Ropars better keep her word about insisting people don't harass me." Especially after Norah took up residence on the manor property. She handed him the flask.

They ate for a few minutes in silence. Maler swished his tail. A fly buzzed. It was nice, like two regular people on an outing—no troubles, no war.

She bit into a peach, and juice dribbled on her chin. He tugged out his handkerchief and dabbed at it as they both laughed. Then he patted the tip of her nose with the cloth. She clasped his hand, pressing his knuckle into her cheek. "We need more moments like this."

He smiled, his gaze warm. "I hope we'll have many."

She wiped her hands from the juicy fruit on a napkin and pulled out her sketchbook and pencils. "Now to sketch this handsome creature." She raised her knees, steadied her pad, and outlined the horse. "Oh, and you promised to tell me about your scar."

"I'd rather watch you sketch." He took a long pull from the flask. "Very well, but it is a hideous story." He began to tell her the details of a horrific day of murder and blood, assassins sent by Hitler, and the couple August tried to save. The bullet meant to kill him.

Norah stopped her drawing, her throat clogged. "How awful. You could have died." She reached over and squeezed his hand. "I can't imagine."

He grimaced. "I've had too many nightmares about it." He touched her face, along her jawline. "But with you, they've faded."

"I'm happy about that." She kissed his finger, holding his hand to her shoulder, her sympathy bursting. They gazed at one another for a long moment. "And no one suspected you as an officer were there?"

"I wouldn't have been promoted. I'd have been shot, again. This time they'd have made certain. Hitler forgives nothing." He gave a rueful smile, but it was full of pain. "I should have left the army, left Germany, but my wife was already ill, embroiled with doctors and tests."

"I'm sorry. I'll be selfish and say I'm fortunate you're here, despite the circumstances." She ached to hold him but redirected her upset and started to sketch again, the long lines of the horse's legs, fetlocks, and hooves.

Gunfire sounded not that far away. Norah stopped and stared at him. "What is—?"

August palmed the small of her back. "It's my soldiers, holding drills."

Maler snorted, glancing in that direction, ears twitching.

Were the Germans planning an attack? She didn't dare ask. Of course, war was always around them. She awkwardly sketched two more lines. "I was thinking, I'll need to get my birth certificate for us to marry."

Would it really happen, or did they play a game of a conventional future?

"That might prove difficult." August fell silent, staring off. Birds chirped. "We may have to get one falsified to expedite matters. My own as well, perhaps."

She concentrated on the horse's head, his eyes and nose, her hand tight on the pencil. *Falsified?*

"Norah, have you heard about a forger in the village?" He asked it softly.

Her shoulders hunched as her hand stilled. Here it was. She inhaled over the jump of her pulse. "Is there one?"

"Your cousin Yann was mentioned."

"No, not him." Surprise prickled her scalp. How could he be a suspect? She must sound calm. "He wouldn't have the intelligence."

"If there is such activity that you know of, to be safe, you must distance yourself from it." August's words were solemn with a brisk edge. "It would be very dangerous."

She turned and saw his blue eyes flicker and sharpen, his mouth firm.

A defensive stubbornness flared up like a flame inside her. "Do you know what happens in those work camps where the Germans send Jews and the crippled people?"

He raised his eyebrows, eyes wide. "I have heard appalling talk, reports. Why do you bring—"

"People are being shot, children, too." Tears sprang to her eyes. "They need to escape."

"That's why I want out of this army," he said. "These acts are reprehensible. But I want to protect you. If you're involved, and I hope you're not, you must stop."

"Didn't you once say you were going to do something I'd approve of?" She squirmed on the blanket, changing the subject, her thoughts in a tumble.

"I have plans, yes. I now realize I'd put you in more danger if I told you." He grasped her arm. "This forger is being investigated by Captain Schmidt. Your cousin may be questioned."

"He's innocent, I swear." She might not like Yann but wouldn't condemn him with a lie. It was her fault. "That's part of his anger toward me, not that—"

"Norah." Sorrow filled August's eyes. He shook his head. "Please, I beg you to stop if you are doing anything. Or stay away from who is. I'm extremely serious."

She couldn't, wouldn't stop, but needed to ease his mind. "There's nothing to be anxious about. It's fine." She leaned over and kissed him, the sweet peach taste on his lips. "Please don't worry."

Her emotions warred inside her. She was putting them both at risk. But they kept many secrets from each other. It was the nature of their situation. Still, the guilt she felt for deceiving him surged through her; guilt for doing the right thing! If only she could confide in him.

"I do worry. You must listen to my warning." His voice grew sterner.

"I'm listening, always." Norah stifled a quiver and bent to her drawing again, to look away from the disapproval and unhappiness on his face. He wanted to scold her more, it was obvious. She delineated the muscles in the horse's body, the sweep of mane and tail—and hated their discord. She felt squeezed in a vise, barely able to breathe.

Then, suddenly, she had the sense they were being watched. Further iciness crept along her shoulders.

* * *

Yann Menez slumped in the chair in the Town Hall's back room. He flipped up a hand. "You think these hard-worn fingers could forge anything?"

Schmidt leaned over him, his sharp nose jabbing. "But you know who it is, don't you? Is it someone in your house?"

August stood against the wall, watching. How far would he allow Schmidt to go against this man he resented for his treatment of Norah? Suspicion wouldn't leave him alone that *she* could be the forger. She was too jumpy and evasive at the picnic. Or was it his own leeriness after the Maquis raid? A raid he'd never tell Norah about.

Still, he must make certain she stopped any forging if it was true.

Menez shrugged. The man stank of sweat and blood. "I don't know anything. I've heard the same talk as you."

"Liar!" Schmidt raised his fist. "You will regret not cooperating. We've been generous to you villagers so far. Too generous."

Menez didn't even flinch. In fact, he looked scornful.

Two young landsers hovered close, ready to assist.

"What about the carpenter, Pichon? Isn't he a friend of yours?" Schmidt growled. "Is he the one we're looking for?"

"You should ask him. I'm just a poor working man trying to get by." Menez picked at his fingernails.

No defense of his friend, typical. August shifted in his boots.

"I'll have him dragged in here, but you'd do well to tell me what you know." Schmidt paced away, then back, both hands clenched. "Before I use measures to force you. *We* are in charge here!"

August was surprised he wouldn't mind if Schmidt struck the butcher. Was he becoming too vindictive? He didn't like that side of himself. Chest stiff, he'd allowed Schmidt to interrogate Menez because he didn't trust himself to contain his ire.

Now that the man refused to provide a home for Norah, August didn't need to be soft with him.

August stepped out of the room for a breath of air. He'd warned Schmidt he had already questioned Norah yesterday, no matter her avoidance. Schmidt must stay away from her. August rubbed his face.

Bringing up the plight of the Jews raised his suspicions about her activities. He hadn't told her the worst when she asked if he knew what was happening. The Nazis used sealed vans to round up the Jews, then filled them with gas, or other poisons, to exterminate them en masse. Entire camps for such murder were being discussed.

He cringed. What the hell had his country come to? *Gott verdammt.* He loathed this sickening conduct. And Norah might be helping Jews escape? If not for his position, he'd encourage her. But he couldn't risk being reassigned if Colonel Burmester got word he wasn't performing his duties. Still, he'd never allow her to be caught and punished.

A chair crashed in the other room. A groan. August opened the door. Menez sat on the floor, wiping blood from his mouth. Schmidt rubbed his knuckles, his smile wry.

"That's enough. Beating people to tell us what we *want* to hear is not the solution. Release him," August ordered. "Bring in this carpenter, Pichon. Find out what he knows. In a civilized manner."

He had to commend the butcher for not implicating Norah as far as he could tell. The man might have a shred of integrity. Or was she innocent and only knew the true perpetrator? Did she have any connection to the carpenter?

She might be implicated out of fear, jealousy, from whomever started the rumors; or over her relationship with him. He must consider all of that.

Back out in the hallway, August put on his hat. He'd walk to the port and talk to Port captain Ziegler. He'd almost forgotten he hinted at an intention to Norah, but never revealed the destruction of the submarine. He shouldn't have even broached the subject.

He stepped out the front door and stalked down the street. Where was that damn U-boat? Had it proven too out of proportion and was being scrapped? A too fat, whale of a vessel? He could only wish for that resolution.

The U-boat destroyed, his son graduating next year, August retiring. If he could only speed matters along. Eventually, he'd need a forger to draw up papers for an entrance for both him and Norah into Switzerland.

The hot sun beat down on his shoulders. Women with baskets or small children scattered out of his way as he marched along.

Chapter Thirty

Norah, her few finer clothes draped over her arm, stepped through the brush toward the gardener's cottage. She decided to leave earlier than requested, to save Loeiza any animosity from Yann. Her cousin was sad she had to go. Angelique had tears in her eyes. Marie-Louise gave her the 'you got what you deserved' look. The little minx.

Jean hauled her battered suitcase behind her. "You won't be afraid out here alone?"

In a way, she liked the idea of her own place. The nights, she hoped to be snug in August's arms. "I'll make sure to lock the doors."

"I know the Major will come to visit you." He spoke matter-of-factly.

She slowed, denial on her tongue; but everyone knew. De Gaulle might soon broadcast it over the radio from London to the Free French. "You shouldn't repeat such things."

Jean hopped over a small gully. Yellow butterflies soared from a pink hydrangea bush as he brushed by, releasing a sweet aroma. "Is he nice to you?"

She walked through the low, rusty gate and blew out her breath. "Of course. We wouldn't be friends if he wasn't truly nice."

"*Très bon*." Jean trudged through the garden he'd weeded and cut back himself. He set the suitcase down in front of the door. "Be careful. This place crawls with soldiers."

They both stared up as a sentry trekked by on top of the hillock that separated this cottage from the manor house.

Jean grinned, obviously used to having his every move watched. "The Major will protect you because he wants you for his sweetheart."

If only life were that simple. She fumbled for the key in her pocket and fought her own smile. "You know too much, young man."

"I listen, and see things." He shrugged, his brown eyes bright.

She clicked the key in the lock and opened the door. They entered. An excitement that the cottage was hers, but *would* she stay safe, passed through her.

Jean placed her case in the bedroom. Norah laid the extra clothes on the bed. She glanced around. Her paintings and paint kit they'd brought over the day before were stacked against one wall. She scanned the room again. Where could she hide her forging materials where August would never find them?

"Is there an attic?" Jean asked.

Norah started; was the boy reading her mind? "I don't know. Why would you ask?"

"Attics have interesting stuff in them…sometimes." He wandered through the parlor, staring up at the ceiling. "There. See the trapdoor?"

Norah looked up. There was a rectangular shape cut into the ceiling.

Jean dragged over a chair. "Let's see if we can open it."

"*Mais non*. It's probably filthy up there." She gripped the chair back. "Another time."

"I know you have things you need to store." Hands on his hips, he scrutinized her.

"How…how would you? You're mistaken." She pulled the chair back over to the table. "I don't know what you mean."

"I want to help. Monsieur Pichon can't come here."

Her body sagged, and she leaned on the chair. Was she that obvious? But he was right, Pichon could never come out here. "Jean, you must stay out of this. You're too young. And your father would be furious."

"I'd make the perfect courier. My father won't know."

She turned and forced a smile over her tripping pulse. "You will not put yourself in any danger. I forbid it. Now, thank you for your help, but run along home."

"I already stopped him. Papa searched your room days before your fight."

"What?" She nearly sank to the floor, fear in her throat. She knew Yann was being questioned by the Germans. If August found out, would he ever forgive her? "Why would he do that?"

"It's all right." Jean stood tall and winked. "I offered to look under the bed and in your dresser. I said I found nothing."

"What did he hope to find?" *Before* the rumors. She bristled at her lack of privacy. Again, she was too vulnerable.

"He wondered what you did in there, besides painting."

"Jean, I…" Was she putting too many people in danger? Her noble actions wavered. "*Merci.*"

"See, I'm useful." He went to the door, his gangly limbs and taller frame swaggering. "Ask the Major to bring his horse over so I can ride it."

She joined him and touched a dark curl on his head. "You're very brave. But your mother wants you nowhere near the Major. Please, don't speak of any—"

"I would never tell. I'm not stupid." He opened the door and stepped out with a wave. "Let me know if you need me. *A bientot.*"

Norah closed and locked it. She pressed her forehead to the wood. "Bloody hell."

Did the child know as much as he hinted at? He'd saved her from Yann's further wrath? At eleven, he grew up too fast. She could never involve him. But how to get the finished documents to Pichon? He usually came to Yann's cottage, on the pretense of visiting him, but to really collect the paperwork.

If she visited Pichon's shop too often, whispers would be frantic. August upset and suspicious. His disturbance at the picnic had rattled her composure. She must be discreet with the forging.

She hurried to the bedroom and opened her suitcase. She'd forge until it got too risky, the heat impossible for both her and August. If Schmidt, or anyone, approached and threatened her, she'd quit.

She pulled undergarments from the case, leaving the papers, ink, and pens inside. She'd had to utilize different colors of ink, and different textures of paper to make the documents look genuine. The attic might prove useful for these supplies. However, her need to help people—children—escape couldn't put her life and her lover's in ultimate peril.

She dragged the chair back under the rectangle, climbed up, and pushed on the trapdoor.

* * *

August joined Ziegler on the crest of the hill overlooking the port. The cranes had gone, the concrete dome awaiting its lodger. The netting sagged over the bunker. The ocean slapped the rocky shore, but there was little breeze. The sky looked bleached of most of its blue. "When will this magnificent U-boat arrive at our port?"

Ziegler preened, a grin on his ruddy face. "It will amaze you, I promise. A grand *Unterseeboot*. A coastal attack boat, a Type XXIV, the only one of its class. They expect it will sail from St-Nazaire in early

240

October. An impressive repair yard is setting up in that port, but it's getting too crowded. A few days after that, the U-boat should arrive."

Six weeks, August calculated. Tension rippled through him. Would Bauer be prepared, as he'd pledged? The lieutenant had demolition experience. The sentries must be distracted, everyone safe from the destruction. "Will it sail toward England shortly thereafter?"

"*Nein*, final staffing, specialists brought down from Brest, testing, all that must take place." Ziegler tapped his belly under his dark blue tunic that hugged him like a sausage skin. "I hear you have a mistress now, when you seemed averse to taking advantage of the village women."

August bristled, but on this he could be truthful. "I'm not taking advantage of her. I intend for her to be my wife."

"Ah, you are a man of honor. How virtuous." Ziegler said this as if it were a slight insult, though his tone remained amused.

"I try to be." An uphill battle in this war. How did so many ignore what was happening: fear, indifference, anger at Germany's suppression after WWI? Or the raw need for power? He felt the heavy weight of it every day he put on his tunic.

Two sentries passed, going in opposite directions, rifles balanced on their shoulders.

Another disturbance flashed into August's mind. Men would still be aboard the U-boat, even in the middle of the night. How could they be evacuated, and the vessel still disabled? He wanted no casualties. No matter what, August must be above suspicion to retain his position until his son graduated next year.

The year before, at the age of fourteen, Christoph had to join the Hitler Youth; it was compulsory. A step to being a true German, according to Hitler. *A heartless step to infamy!* He worried for his boy's peace of mind.

August stiffened his arms at his sides and nearly kicked a pebble down the slope.

"Why wouldn't they have tested it at St-Nazaire? Not that I'm familiar with U-boat particulars." August turned to the port captain with a faked smile. He should have done this earlier but must admit his time with Norah had distracted him. "Ziegler, *mein Freund*, we must share a drink, and with your vast knowledge and experience, you can enlighten me on submarines."

After Ziegler spoke to one of his officers, and the diligent Krause, the two of them walked into the village.

When they entered the tavern, the few German soldiers and sailors in there stood, chairs scraping the wood floor.

August waved them down. Zeigler nodded. August had only been in here once since he'd arrived in Brittany the previous year. Loud, drunken men had no appeal for him.

The auberge had low-beamed ceilings, a bar to the right, and a scattering of small tables and chairs. Shelves above the bar held various sizes and colors of bottles. A few photographs on the plain plaster walls showed a woman in a Breton costume, and men hauling in fish from small boats. The scents of beer, smoke, and other alcohol leached into the room.

The owner came from a door to the left. A short, chubby man in a long apron, his head bald, he smiled, though it didn't twinkle in his eyes. His eyebrow twitch showed his surprise at seeing the two top enemy officers. "*Bienvenue*, gentlemen. Please have a seat. What may we serve you?"

"Do you have Deutsches Reichsbräu?" Ziegler asked as he settled in a chair at a table near the back wall. A window looked out past stone buildings into the woods.

"I'm afraid we don't," the owner replied, a flicker of distaste in his eyes over the German beer most associated with Nazis.

"Order something French. *Bière de Garde,* a strong, pale ale. We'll have two." August sat across from Ziegler. The man dipped his head and left. "You know many small breweries were put out of business because their equipment was turned into ammunition?"

"We should bring German brewers to France. German beer is far superior." Ziegler leaned forward, as much as his bulk allowed. "I have found a willing young woman in the next village. And, as I've said, my wife doesn't mind."

"She's an understanding woman, your wife." August had never cheated on Klara, though he had offers. He had respected her too much.

"My wife is the daughter of an admiral; a good marriage for me. She prefers me in France, while she entertains her friends in Germany." Zeigler chuckled. "She gave me fine sons."

They fell silent as the owner placed two glass mugs filled with amber-colored ale on their table.

"Anything else, officers? Monsieur Commandant?" The man's pretense of fawning rang false. He resented their existence.

"No, nothing, thank you." August sipped the ale with its toasted malt flavor.

The soldiers and sailors at the other tables hunched close to one another, their conversations low as if they didn't wish their commanders to hear their remarks and complaints.

"I once thought I'd take over here, but you seem well established." Ziegler grunted. "We must build barracks for my sailors at the port."

"And an air raid shelter to protect the people," August put in. RAF raids were increasing.

"Now, for the more personal, how will you marry the Englishwoman? You need the Führer's permission. He likes good German brides, making Aryan babies for the Fatherland." Ziegler sipped his drink. "Umm, not as good as German beer, but not too bad."

"I will find a way to marry. We all must make adjustments." August ignored Ziegler's remark on 'taking over', since his own plans had changed. It wouldn't have been his decision anyway, but someone higher up the chain of command. And August wouldn't discuss Norah with him.

"Your second lieutenant, Krause, he's an odd one. A man of few words. You wonder what he hides." Zeigler grinned. "Not like me."

"As long as he performs his duties." August didn't add Krause seemed a humorless man with little imagination, while Zeigler was too outspoken. He'd use it to his advantage. "So, tell me more about this grand U-boat. Are there more engines to account for the extra weight of crew and weapons?" Extra engines would also increase the load.

"*Ja*, we use 9000 PS for the diesels, and 1000 PS for electric, with battery backup. The sub will carry two extra." Ziegler nodded with pride. "It will have a special class number, U-2000."

"That is impressive." August drank more ale, slowly savoring it for a moment. "Won't this make it awkward, the extra weight?"

"This is an experiment in many ways." Ziegler shrugged his plump shoulders. "Your coastal attack boats are usually smaller, to slide into shallow waters, so this one has limits."

"And additional crew, of course." August's concern grew for the young men trapped in a metal cylinder. They might hate this war as much as he did.

"Up to fifty-five men, and twenty-six torpedoes with two 105-millimeter deck guns." Ziegler gulped his drink, then covered his mouth as he burped. "The forward torpedo room will contain six torpedo tubes. The aft, the usual two."

"It will move slower in the water with such mass." August rubbed his thumbs on the glass mug. He pictured the U-boat, pieces of metal flying, fire, and smoke choking the air.

"Unfortunately, that is true." Ziegler sniffled loudly, though their voices remained barely above a whisper. He gave a self-satisfied smirk. "Only up to sixteen knots. Submerged up to five knots. But such a magnificent blast it will make into any major port, or fleet."

Two soldiers snarled words at the sailors who snarled back from the next table. The animosity grew thick between them. Chairs shifted. One soldier stood, face flushed. Another hopped up, fists raised. A chair fell over with a clatter.

"Calm down, men," August warned, rising to his feet. "Or you will spend time digging latrines."

"*Jawohl*, sir!" They quickly bowed their heads, cheeks red, as if surprised he was still there.

August sat and asked Ziegler the vital question, the one he'd brought him here to ask. "How long do you think before it is ready to approach England's coast?"

"If all goes well, by mid-November." Ziegler held up his mug for a refill when the owner scurried through.

"Excellent. I can't wait to see this prime vessel." August swallowed a curse. His blood boiled. He had hoped they'd wait until spring. Perhaps a little sabotage here and there would delay the U-boat, closer to when he could solidify his plans to retire. Enough sabotage to disable the vessel permanently was even better, and safer than an outright explosion. It might also preserve the lives of the crew members. "I've enjoyed our conversation. Now I must return to the Town Hall. Duty calls."

August tossed coins on the table, his smile fixed. He rose and left the auberge. He must seek out Lt. Bauer right away. Would he have any small explosives ready in eight to ten weeks? Before the U-boat had a chance to slither like a fat serpent toward England.

Chapter Thirty-one

Lt. Bauer lived in a cottage one street over from the main street, now called *Hauptstraße,* with an older couple. German officers were forced on the populace for billets, but August knew his lieutenant got on well with these people and helped them around their home.

"You're a good man to look out for them," August said when they entered the side gate. He placed a basket of fresh eggs on the rear porch.

"I even scrape salt from their windows after the Atlantic storms." Bauer led him across the patch of lawn in the shadows. "They're like having grandparents close."

"We're both too good." August was certain *his* non-kowtowing to the Nazis had prevented his promotion to *oberst*, or colonel. "I still miss my *oma*."

At a gardening shed in the back corner, Bauer pulled out a key. High hedges hid them from the other cottages adjacent to the rear garden. "I should have ingredients to make small explosives. The old folk never look in here anymore."

August stilled his hand. He made a quick scan of the area. An apple tree stood in one corner, throwing shade over a neatly weeded vegetable patch. The earthy scents surrounded them in the fading light.

"Can we start with something simple, a subtle damage to the engines, the fuel lines? I don't want the crew harmed if it can be avoided." August shook off the stress that coursed through his veins since his conversation with Ziegler. So little time!

Bauer thought for a minute, his chiseled profile an outline in the increasing dark. "The simplest way would be to put sugar in the fuel, and metal shavings in the oil. That should ruin the engines, foul up their mechanisms."

"*Sehr gut.* It will be a beginning. We can't act too quickly after the U-boat arrives; perhaps two weeks later. We need to distract the guards I'm certain Ziegler will station around it. And our watchdog Krause. I'll take care of that." August massaged the taut muscles in his jaw. "An official visit for a tour for both of us to understand the U-boat's layout would not be too much to ask. Ziegler will be anxious to show it off."

"I'll be ready. This thing should never be allowed to sail." Bauer pocketed the key. "But there's still danger in simple sabotage."

They fell silent at a rustle in the hedge. August touched the pistol at his side, his breath sharp in his throat. A badger scurried out and along the garden perimeter.

He exhaled and whispered, "We'll come up with a plan for such close work. I don't want your life put at risk." August pressed a hand on his subordinate's shoulder. "You need to get safely back to your family when this abominable war ends." He wanted to believe they all had a future.

"It will never end if decent men don't act." Bauer walked toward the porch. "No matter what my father wants from me as a loyal German son."

"As well I know." Loyal to a madman. August rubbed the back of his neck; so much to consider— months earlier than he'd planned—and any error would cost them their lives. The happiness he counted on. But he could never leave here without destroying such a monster.

* * *

Carrying her canvas sack, Norah walked under the trees and past the church away from the village. A woman rode by on a bicycle and shouted, "*Putain!*"

Norah winced, though this wasn't the first time she'd been called a whore. Once, a rock had sailed past her head. The price of her love. She stifled a curse and kept her head high. A quarter mile later, she strode up the path to the farmhouse, a low rambling stone building. The mayor and his wife had moved in here with the mayor's brother after the Germans invaded. The occupiers 'requisitioned' the manor house where August now lived.

He'd said nothing these last nights of his interrogation with Yann. Had Yann kept his suspicions to himself?

Chickens clucked from a pen near an outbuilding as she approached. A goat bleated from another enclosure. Should she even be here? Yet how else to deliver these ill-gotten items?

Norah knocked on the weathered front door. A fragrant wisteria vine tangled through the stones to her right.

Inside, a dog yipped. A young woman opened the door. The brother's daughter, a plain girl of about nineteen with a round freckled face.

She raised her snub nose as if Norah smelled bad. "What do you want?"

"I need to speak to Madame Ropars, please." Norah smiled, ignoring the obvious insult.

"Who is it?" Madame appeared behind the girl. The little white dog, a ball of fluff, bounced and yipped near the woman's feet. "Oh, Mademoiselle Cooper. Please come in." She nudged the girl aside. "I'll take care of this, *ma nièce.*"

The younger woman bustled off, nose still in the air.

249

Madame Ropars gestured for Norah to enter and follow her into a bright parlor. She wore a crisp white blouse and a gray pencil skirt on her slender form. "It isn't as nice as *Maison dans la Forêt*, but we make do. Please sit." Her tone conveyed she resented 'making do.'

"I brought you those items you requested." Norah indicated her sack and sat on a worn sofa with a colorful scarf draped over the back. The room was plainly furnished, but with touches of a woman who liked elegance. A doily, under two silver candlesticks, graced the sideboard. A vase of red and pink geraniums sat on a table under the window. Stylish paintings, in the surrealist trend, hung on the walls.

The woman sat beside her. The little dog sniffed at Norah's feet. She bent to pat its furry head.

"Go lie down, Blanche." At her mistress's order, the dog romped over to a folded blanket and sat, but watched them with lively black eyes.

Norah pulled out the stockings and seven packs of Gauloises cigarettes. "I couldn't get chocolate. Silk is also nearly impossible to obtain. It's being used to make parachutes for the soldiers."

"I'm aware of that." Madame Ropars took the stockings, a wide smile on her angular face, her red lipstick intact. "Very fine. Not that I have anywhere to wear them these days."

These days had changed them all. "You said your friends would…look the other way if I brought you such items. Though there's no stockings for them, I hope that still stands."

"Straight to the point. I like that." Madame Ropars tapped her fingers with chipped red polish on the cigarette packs. "And you're from England, related to the local butcher and his wife?"

"My mother and Mrs. Menez' mother are sisters." Norah wondered if the subject of her 'reason' for coming to France would arise. A hollow feeling opened inside her and she mentally locked it down.

"I see no resemblance, but that often happens in families." Madame's red lips pursed. "I'm not from here either. I spent most of my life in Paris, back when it was the center of fun and fashion." Norah sensed a loneliness in the woman.

"I haven't yet had the pleasure of visiting Paris." Norah doubted she ever would, not that she really cared. Switzerland with August was her goal.

"You wouldn't like Paris now, from what I've heard. A drab city under occupation." She opened a pack and pulled out a cigarette. "Are you required to register as an enemy alien, since Germany is at war with England?"

"I've been…ignored so far. All the way out here." Norah speculated on how long that might last. With the war heating up, anything could happen.

"And now you have the best of protection." Madame Ropars tilted her head. "So, what is it about Major von Gottlieb that attracts you? I'll admit, he is a handsome man."

Norah stiffened, hands on her thighs. "I'd rather not talk about him, but my feelings are completely sincere."

"I see. You're in love with him." She didn't sound surprised, only curious.

"Yes, I am, very much." Norah's throat tightened. She stared straight into the woman's pale blue eyes. "We try not to take advantage of one another, Madame."

"Call me Giselle." Her expression softened in sympathy. She lit the cigarette. "I think you really are in love. I trust he loves you, too? I'll insist that everyone leaves you alone, as much as they'll listen. I'll pass them cigarettes. It's difficult to love someone who isn't approved of, isn't it?"

Nora reined in her churning emotions and kept herself from being too open. You never knew whom you could trust. She kneaded her sack and nodded.

"Is he good in bed?" Giselle grinned; the lines around her eyes crinkled.

Norah felt caught off guard, again. "The very best, of course." She grinned back, playing along—though she fidgeted and now wanted to leave.

"He looks like he would be. You're fortunate. *Excusez moi,* I should have my niece bring us coffee." Giselle started to rise.

"Don't bother, I can't stay." Norah slid to the cushion edge.

"A shame." Giselle puffed on the cigarette; smoke curled around her. "I've heard other things, such as, you might know a forger in the village. My husband said as much."

Norah's stomach plummeted—the culmination of this entire conversation. She raised her chin. "I don't know anything. Who else was mentioned?"

"Anyone could be under suspicion. Forgers are needed. My sister said the latest news from Paris is the Germans are rounding up thousands of Jews to be sent to internment camps." Giselle watched her closely.

"That's horrible." Norah prayed that many escaped, and her efforts helped.

"It certainly is. If you need help, let me know." Giselle waved the cigarette, the smoke harsh and stinging Norah's eyes. "I could be of use."

Norah slowly stood. Was this a trick? "I wouldn't mind the war ending, and peace resolved. That's what I need. I wish you well, but I must be on my way now." Everyone seemed to suspect her. August's disturbance at the picnic had bothered her, though she'd pretended otherwise. How much longer could she continue?

"Why don't you come by and sketch me with my dog, as you once told your cousin you already did?" Giselle walked her to the door, her tone almost teasing.

"I would be happy to. My fees are reasonable." Norah opened the door. "How about tomorrow at two o'clock? *Au revoir.*"

Norah hurried back down the path, the sweet smell of wisteria washing away the burnt-rubber stink of smoke. She had an art assignment, but would the woman ply her with more questions? She should have turned her down. Speaking to Pichon must be next on her agenda.

A greenish-gray uniform flashed to her right. A skinny man, ducking into the tall bushes. The chickens squawked. The goat hopped. Norah nearly stumbled but rushed on. Was someone following her, a soldier? The icy feeling she had at the picnic, and previously at the cottage, chilled through her.

Surely August wouldn't have her watched. Nausea rose in her throat. She increased her pace along the road.

After a quick glance around, as she'd done the entire way, when she reached the village Norah stopped to admire the wares of a woman selling flowers. Then, after this stalling tactic, and no soldiers in sight, she meandered to the wide-open doors of the carpentry shop. She entered, intent on requesting an item for her cottage—an excuse for being here.

Later, she must speak to August about her fears, and trust he wasn't behind it. He couldn't be! But who else would want her followed?

The smell of new wood assailed her, and she tried to even her breathing. Tools hung from hooks on the walls, wood shavings littered the floor. Deniel Pichon stood at a high, narrow table, scraping a plane over a hunk of wood. Tables and chairs, freshly sanded, lined the perimeter, along with wooden toys.

"*Bonjour*, Mademoiselle Cooper. What brings you here?" He gave his easy smile, the dimple flashing in his cheek.

"I'd like you to make me an end table, nothing fancy." She walked close, checking every corner. "Are we alone?"

"*Oui*, my assistant is making a delivery. Is something the matter?" He wiped his forehead with his arm. Wood dust clung to his wavy, dark brown hair. "I've been on my wife's farm the last few days, helping her parents."

"I just left the farm where the Ropars live," she whispered. "Monsieur Ropars apparently started the rumor of a forger, according to Yann. Can they be trusted?"

"That was a blunder. The mayor was drunk and spouting off." Pichon shook his head. "He can be a fool sometimes. He's angry at losing his position. He's from an old Breton family and thinks he's the black sheep."

"So he puts his own village in danger?"

"He was drinking with Yann, and considers him a friend." Pichon scraped the plane again, wood curling from the device's sharp plate. "I don't know how the Germans found out."

"Neither do I. August and I don't share our clandestine activities. It works better that way." However, she hated deceiving her lover. A slippery conundrum. "Ropars' wife asked me about it, and I denied everything."

"She's a clever woman, a Parisian. Too cultured for our community. I heard she was 'talked' into that marriage when a teen." Pichon rolled his shoulders. "Her sister returned to Paris, and I believe she's helped to aid the Jews there. I'd still be discreet."

"She wants me to draw her tomorrow. I'll find out more about her intentions." Norah leaned against the table to balance the burden of her concerns. "August has asked about the forging, too. He's warned me to distance myself. I'm torn in two, it seems."

"And now you're practically living together. It won't be easy." Pichon half-smiled, the slightest of scolds in his tone. "I have another list of names for you." He reached into his pocket. He seemed to assume it was a foregone conclusion that she'd continue.

A boy barged into the shop, his eyes wide. "Monsieur Pichon, two German soldiers are coming. I think they want to speak to you."

Norah flinched, the bag clutched to her chest. "They *can't* find me here."

Pichon frowned, then opened a door on the rear wall. He handed her the paper. "Hide in the storeroom."

Norah rushed inside and shut the door. She stuffed the list into her brassiere with quivering fingers. Heart hammering, she gulped in her breath and pressed her ear to the crack.

A minute later she heard a march of boots. "Herr Pichon, the commandant wishes to speak to you." A youthful voice rang out. "Come with us."

She stiffened with dread. Had they been discovered? What would they do to Pichon? August would be livid, and so much more, if she was mentioned. But that 'list of names' that crackled in her brassiere, how could she ignore it?

Chapter Thirty-two

August stared down at the carpenter in the Town Hall's back room. Herr Pichon sat straight in the chair, his expression relaxed and confident. His blue chambray shirt and corduroy trousers were dusted in sawdust. He'd remained calm during this last twenty minutes. But was he overly calm, a mask?

"You deny everything else, but are you a member of the Maquis?" August doubted it yet had to ask. Perhaps he knew who was involved in the manor explosion.

"The Maquis? I'd never endanger my family like that. Those men are volatile." Pichon squared his shoulders, his gaze steady. "I keep to my carpentry, a little farming. I recently married and hope to start a family."

"And you were eliminated from any hard labor because of a limp, is that so?" August had seen him around the village with his uneven gait.

"It is. I injured my leg as a child." Pichon rubbed his right thigh as if reliving the pain. "But I do the best I can to design furniture and other wood items."

"You travel about the region frequently. For carpentry work, you stated. You must have all the correct travel permits?" August's nerves on edge, he hoped this man had nothing to do with any illicit activities, the village accusations false—no one guilty or under suspicion.

Pichon nodded. "I'm much in demand. Do you need any carpentry work, Major? I'm quite skilled. My family is long renown for our furniture building."

The door opened and Schmidt strode in. He looked sweaty, like he'd rushed to get here. A leaf clung to his trouser leg. Where had he been skulking?

"As I said earlier, your name was mentioned as a person possibly involved in forging documents not authorized or issued by the German authorities. Tell me the truth." August put more accusation in his tone, though he hardly cared if this man helped innocent people escape. He just had to give the illusion that he did. But would he find out something he regretted, as in who was assisting?

"Do you work with artists in this forbidden venture? Someone in this region?" Schmidt pulled out a handkerchief and wiped his damp cheeks.

August glared at his captain. Schmidt had jumped right into the subject August feared but cared about most. Schmidt strived to implicate Norah. August's fingers itched to jerk him outside.

"There is no forbidden venture. I woodwork and help my wife's family with their farm." Pichon slid his gaze from August to Schmidt as if sizing them up, though his expression remained congenial. "Young men are in short supply since the war."

"The soldiers are searching your home and shop as we speak. Will they find anything illegal?" August gritted his teeth and hoped they wouldn't.

"*Mais non*. There's nothing to find." Pichon gave a slight, one-shouldered shrug.

"If we discover you're lying, there are methods to get the whole truth from you." Schmidt, always ready to threaten physical violence, the last bastion of the weak-minded, sneered.

"Where is your proof other than rumors?" Pichon asked in a cajoling voice. He was too calm, too cavalier. He definitely hid something.

"We will be watching you, and anyone associated with you." August injected more threat into his words, and dearly hoped it wasn't Norah. "You are warned. You must stop any illegal activity."

Schmidt spread his legs in an arrogant stance. "We've seen certain people at your shop. I—"

"We're finished here." August had a terrible feeling his subordinate was up to more mischief. He scrambled to regain control. "You may go, Herr Pichon. I'll bring you back if we do find proof. You want to start a family, protect them by staying away from trouble."

Pichon put on his hat and left, out the rear door.

Schmidt sidled up to August in the hallway as he headed back to his office. "I saw her, your girlfriend. She entered the carpentry shop about thirty minutes ago."

A blast of heat flooded August, staggering him. Would the soldiers find her? He'd never had her cottage searched, not even the attic. Perhaps he should have now that she'd moved in. "You'd better not be lying to me."

"I swear it. I know you don't like me, but this is the truth." Schmidt's smirk was too self-satisfied. How did his wife and mistress stand his oily personality?

"Why are you watching Norah? It could be innocent." August's gut in tangles, he restrained himself from committing his own physical violence. A smash of Schmidt's pointed nose. "I am the one who will speak to her."

"But I'm in charge of security. You said so yourself, sir." Schmidt's effort to sound offended came out petulant. "I saw the soldiers march in and apprehend the carpenter, but I didn't have time to tell them to search for her. I'm only performing my duty."

August loomed over him, doubts and recriminations sparking through his mind. He had to safeguard Norah above all else, preserve their love, until he could leave the chains of this blasted army behind. "You seem too anxious on this point. I've warned you before. Stay *away* from her. That is an order."

* * *

Norah placed the record on the portable Decca phonograph August had brought to her cottage the week before. The black-out blinds drawn, the candles on the kitchen table provided a mellow light.

He moved up behind her, his hands on her shoulders. She inhaled his bergamot cologne and tried to relax. Would he mention his interrogation of Pichon from earlier in the day? She'd left the shop out the back door shortly after the soldiers escorted him away.

"Are you ready to dance?" The glasses of wine they'd drank partially calmed her, but she felt a tension in the air between them. She cranked the handle to start the player. Then placed the needle on the record. A crackling sound emitted as the record turned.

"I'm ready to hold you in my heart." August turned her to face him, sliding his arms around her, his gaze penetrating.

The French singer and actress, Fréhel, began to sing in her rich voice, "La Java Bleue" from 1939. A lively, waltz-like song.

"She's of Breton origin." Norah smiled, unsure how to read the intensity on his face. "She uses the seductive but controversial java dance. Like the waltz, but the partners dance extremely close."

"In a way it's like a slow polka with that beat. Except, I like that we dance this close." August pulled her against him as they moved to the music in a leisurely manner. The heat of his body sent quivers through hers.

"It is decadent. But perfect for us." She swayed her hips to match him as the singer's voice urged them on.

"If only the rest of the world would vanish," he murmured.

She heard an underlying tone that instantly put her on alert. "Is anything wrong?"

"*Meine liebe*, I hate to ask." His warm lips touched her cheek. "Were you at the carpentry shop this afternoon?"

She felt the tautness of his muscles as hers went rigid. *Was* she being tracked? "Yes, briefly. I took Madame Ropars the stockings and cigarettes. She inquired about you. I wondered if I could trust her. Monsieur Pichon is friends with her husband, the mayor. So I asked him what kind of person she was."

August's hand traced from her shoulder down her back, pressing her even tighter. "What did she want to know about me?"

"If we loved each other. I said, of course we do. She promised to keep people from harassing me, if she could." Norah smiled again and hoped it didn't waver. "At her request, I said I'd draw her tomorrow."

"Can you trust her? Will she want to know more about us?" He moved her in a circle, much slower than the beat of the song.

"I don't know yet. I'll be circumspect." She tried to take comfort from his embrace, and wished to lock out everything else, but another issue niggled at her. "Do you have someone watching me?"

"Why do you ask?" He pulled back slightly, his steps hesitant, gaze sharp.

"I saw someone in uniform near the farm. He was trying to hide." She stared into his eyes, his full of concern. "And how else would you know I went into the carpentry shop?"

"You saw a soldier hiding?" He frowned but didn't look that surprised. "Norah, I have no one following you. But people see and report things. My captain is overzealous." His expression changed to sad, dismayed. "You should be careful where you go."

"I want Monsieur Pichon to make me an end table, to put next to the sofa. But I *also* asked him about Madame Ropars. He's a friend of Yann's and just married a nice girl from the next village." She took a slow breath, trying not to sound defensive. She squeezed against him again and laid her head on his shoulder, absorbing his musky scent. Perhaps this list she had would be her last endeavor.

"As long as that's all you did, we should have nothing to worry about." His voice was low and raspy, though full of doubts. He caressed his hand up her back and along her nape. She shivered.

The music stopped. So did they. She looked up into his face and prayed he wouldn't press her about the forging. She only wanted to see love in his expression.

"Could you bring your horse over here for my young cousin to ride?" She had to jump to another subject. "You mustn't be here, though, when Jean comes."

"Evil villain that I am." His humor was forced, his hands on her upper arms firm. "I could do that for your impetuous cousin."

"You are far from a villain; and thank you." She pulled his head down and met his lips, their kiss hot and hungry. "I love you so much."

"And I love you." He brushed his fingertips over her breasts. "But you are certain everything is—"

"Let's talk another time and enjoy ourselves now." Her body throbbed at his touch; she needed him. When he dropped his mantle of a German officer, he filled the longings inside her no one else could. A coil of warmth deep into her soul. She trailed her hand lower, past his abdomen, feeling his desire.

"I'm not fooled. You are manipulating me, in more ways than one." He groaned, his gaze clouding. He slipped his hand under her blouse, his fingers hot on her flesh. "Not that I mind at the moment."

"We deserve our happiness and passion." She clasped his arm and tugged him toward the bedroom where they could forget their problems with forging suspects, his power of authority over the village, for tonight.

Chapter Thirty-three

In the old farmhouse's pretty, cobbled garden with pink and white hydrangea bushes, and beech trees for shade, Norah sketched Giselle who held her squirming dog. They both sat on hard cast-iron chairs painted white and adorned with Victorian-style swirls. The scent of plants lingered strong, as no breeze stirred the air.

"I brought these chairs from our former home. But my husband made me leave too much behind. The gardens are bigger at *Maison dans la Forêt*." Giselle slowly patted her dog's head. "I once thought to cultivate roses with that much space. Have you seen the gardens there?"

"No, I've never been to the manor." With her pencil, Norah delineated Giselle's sharp cheekbones and full mouth, her short sweep of blonde hair. An attractive woman eroded by life.

After her sensual night with August, Norah had spent the morning falsifying for the list of names, Christianizing Jewish names, filling in identity cards and travel permits, signing the official signature she'd perfected. She must decide whether to stop this dangerous endeavor. She *should* stop.

"My husband's brother was married, but his wife left on the pretext of helping her mother in Toulon. And never returned." Giselle gave a dry laugh. "That's why his daughter is unfriendly."

"Or just unhappy." Norah drew the woman's discerning eyes, but not the beginnings of crow's feet. She sketched her purple, empire-bust, short-sleeved blouse. "Was this around the time of the German invasion?"

"Years before the invasion. Since we Catholics don't divorce, I suppose that was her solution." Giselle stared toward the farmhouse as if she contemplated something similar.

Were there no loving marriages in **Saint Guénolé**? Loeiza seemed trapped in her marriage as well. Norah was satisfied to be Anglican, where divorce was possible, though frowned upon. But for Catholics, it was a sin.

"I suppose we must be thankful for any crumbs. We've been lucky out here; the Major is a fair man." Giselle adjusted the dog on her lap. "What are your plans with the dashing August?"

"Eventually, to marry." Norah drew the woman's slender arms as they encircled Blanche. Then she worked on the dog's fluffy exterior. She'd said too much.

"That's bold. While he's still in Hitler's army?" Giselle straightened. Blanche struggled to get off her lap.

"We'll work something out." But would they? Was it all a fantasy? So much could go wrong. A slice of apprehension cut through her. "Hold Blanche's head still and I'll draw her pert little face."

Giselle slipped her hand under the dog's chin. "I toyed with drawing as a girl. I was adequate. What skills are needed to falsify documents?"

The hairs on the back of Norah's neck prickled. This is what she'd expected. She quickly drew the dog's black eyes and nose in its nest of fur. "Good copying skills, I guess."

"I only ask because my sister is trying to assist Jews into the unoccupied Zone, but they need papers." Giselle's voice fell to a whisper.

"You shouldn't tell me these things when you know my situation." Norah rubbed her temple with the back of her hand, her mouth dry. She laid the drawing pad in her lap.

The dog yipped, and Giselle set her free to sniff about the garden.

"Monsieur Pichon made the mistake of telling my husband about the growing actions of resistance. And Ropars can't handle his cider or ale—and he's become so much worse." Giselle's eyes filled with sadness. "I'm tired of being useless. I want to help my sister. Refugees need documents before they reach the demarcation line into the Free Zone."

Norah fought the urge to rise and leave the garden. Her loyalties split and twisted. She flipped the page of her pad. "Copying, tracing, and block letters are probably used." Could she pass the mantle to this woman? Or was Giselle trying to trap her? Norah's fingers tightened around the pencil as she drew the letters. "That would be the skill required, I'd guess, from what I've seen on my own identity documents."

Giselle dragged over her chair. "What about the official signature? Was that easy to recreate?"

"I wouldn't know for certain, but are you adept at tracing?" Norah fisted the pencil, her knuckles white. "Lots of practice, to get it just right, I imagine."

A squirrel chucked from the beech tree. The dog barked at it, her little rear end and stubby tail wiggling in excitement.

"I know you don't trust me, but who would I turn you in to?" Giselle gave her a sad smile. "I want what's best for my country. And I'm not..."

"Sleeping with the enemy?" Norah regretted the defensiveness of her reply. Giselle could turn her into any German official in the larger cities. But would she?

"I realize you love the Major, and I won't judge you." Giselle touched Norah's knee. "And he doesn't suspect?"

"Everyone suspects everyone these days." Norah stared at her, then glanced around. August hinted at his suspicions. She scrutinized the woman's pleading eyes and had to take this chance. Or was she desperate and risking everything? "If you're sincere, come by the cottage tomorrow, after lunch. I might have…things to show you. But don't put our lives in danger."

* * *

August looked up from his paperwork as Fritz stood before his desk, smoothing down his cowlick. "I'm sorry, Major. Sugar has become a rare commodity. But I'll check my contacts who may know people who deal in the…excuse me, black market."

"Thank you for trying. I'll think of other supply avenues." August handed his secretary a paper he'd scribbled on about the continuing investigations into the local Résistance. Was his report too vague? "Type this up to send to Paris."

"*Jawohl*, sir." Fritz clicked his heels, re-adjusted his spectacles, and left the office.

August leaned back in his chair. If not sugar, then what? He thought of the carpenter covered in sawdust. Would sawdust foul up a U-boat engine? Or sand, direct from the beach? The trick was to slip it into the lines undetected. He must ask Bauer.

His mind drifted back to last night. Norah was keeping something from him; she was too anxious to quiet his questions, luring him to bed. Her erotic actions had fogged his brain. He didn't need to wonder where she'd learned any of it because he had taught her. Actions he never asked of prim Klara, but had read about in books as a teen. Books that were banned now. He'd reverted to a randy young man with Norah.

His lovely Englishwoman, soon to be wife, if all went well. Their love entwined together. In

266

Switzerland, if they could escape, he a mere civilian, she could paint, and he might teach or research history. Study totalitarian regimes and why they rise. The brutal conceit of men.

He sat up straight and must prepare for his inspection of the airfield at Audierne tomorrow. Plus, more bunkers were being built along the Finistère coast. Military High Command demanded the airfield be completed next month. No more slowing down the progress, or he might become too obvious.

Unfortunately, he had to contend with Schmidt. The swine! If his captain's father was in the SS as he bragged, why hadn't he transferred his dear son elsewhere, to a higher position? Or was the captain here to spy on him?

Tapping his desktop, August came to another dreaded conclusion. Next time, while Norah was out sketching, he'd search the cottage to ease his own mind. And make certain she was out of harm's way.

* * *

Norah stood tiptoe on a chair and pulled the documents from the attic, the narrow place she'd dusted the best she could. Giselle was coming over for coffee, and to look at what she had. The mayor's wife had friends who could distribute paperwork and collect information. She had to trust her. Norah felt a burden lifting from her shoulders at no more sneaking around, no more deception.

Last night, as August slept beside her, she decided this was the best option.

She balanced and went to step down from the chair. A paper floated to the floor. The door unlocked and opened. She sucked in her breath.

August stood in the doorway. "What are you doing up there?" He was supposed to be gone, inspecting the airfield.

The chair seemed to shake with her jolt of emotions. She stepped off, the documents smashed to her chest. Her pulse pounded in her ears. "I'm cleaning up some old paperwork. I thought you'd be at Audierne."

"The inspection was delayed." He walked forward and picked up the paper from the floor. It was a sketch of her recreation of the Reichsadler, the Nazi eagle over a swastika, required on travel permits. He held it up. "What is this? Norah, *mein Gott*. You are forging, aren't you?"

Her breath came in rasps. "Please. Think of the Jewish children."

"You lied to me. I thought I could trust you." The hurt in his face jabbed at her, nearly spinning her to the floor.

"August, I…" She had no viable excuse. "I didn't exactly lie. I never admitted the truth."

He took the documents from her shivering hands. "Do you know what would happen if Captain Schmidt discovered this? From *you*, my fiancée. You would face arrest, even torture. Colonel Burmester would be contacted to implicate me. I could be sent from here to Russia, or elsewhere. How would I find you or protect you? I thought you understood."

"I'm sorry. I thought only of the children, not what could happen to you." It made such sense when he spoke it. Her head swirled, knees weak.

He slapped the papers on the table, eyes wide and sharp. "What else have you been doing behind my back?"

"Nothing, I swear." She leaned on the chair for support; icy fear shot through her veins. "I'll be careful from now on."

"You must stop at once." His glare sliced through her, but pain shadowed it. "Do you hear me?"

She knew she was defeated, and she had planned to give up her work. She couldn't put him in jeopardy. Her body sagged. She struggled to breathe. "I won't do it anymore. I was quitting anyway."

He raked a hand through his dark-gold hair, eyes flashing. "How can I believe you? Who else is involved?"

"I can't reveal that." *Please don't insist on it!*

"If you're found out, there's no telling what will happen." He gripped her shoulders, his fingers on her flesh painful. "Again, how can I trust you? I want so much to. I thought we had something special."

"We do. I'm so sorry. I wasn't doing this when we first grew close." Her eyes dampened with tears. "That sounds worse, but I was convinced my actions would help people."

"You deceived me." He cupped her face, his thumbs caressing her cheekbones, his expression miserable. Then he stepped away, shaking his head. "After I warned you, you continued." He swept his hand toward the table, forehead creased. "Burn those documents and whatever else is up in the attic. Our lives are at stake."

She nodded, straining to balance herself. "I will. I swear I won't do it anymore. I want you safe from retribution. I was reckless."

He stood tall, the commandant once more, as he reached for the doorknob. His flushed cheeks betrayed his upset. "Norah, I understand why you did it. But you should have told me before this. I cautioned you." The disappointment on his face was obvious, the hurt in his eyes condemning her.

"I'll destroy them, I promise." She hated to do it, yet yearned to embrace him, to hold him close. Her pride, her confusion, kept her from begging that he stay. She must not collapse into a grasping female. "Forgive me."

"I must return to my office. I've much to think about. The risks you took. You were dishonest, so heedless." Words stern over an anxious voice, August was out the door, shutting it after him. A swift, stormy wind had blown over her, scattering her life like dried leaves.

"I didn't lie. I just didn't admit to the truth." Heart like a rock weighing down her chest, she bent to the hearth, blinking back tears. A sob erupted. She must bring him back to her, make him understand. They still loved one another, didn't they? But to destroy all her hard work. She felt frozen in place, her world crumbling. *It's not fair! I was doing the right thing.* She reached into a basket for the kindling August had split for her, as her soul felt cleaved in two.

Chapter Thirty-four

A light knock on the kitchen door startled Norah from her lackluster search for matches. The papers remained on the table, important, yet their existence mocked her. How could she burn them? And now someone was here. Should she jump up and hide them? Her body felt bolted to the floor.

The door squeaked open. "It's me, Giselle." A woman's soft voice.

Norah then remembered Madame Ropars and their visit. She swiped the tears from her cheeks but remained in front of the hearth, fingers clenched. A sliver of relief. "Come in."

"I heard everything." Giselle hurried to the table and stacked papers, identity cards, and the rest into a tidy pile. "You're very talented. Is there any more in the attic?"

Norah, as if in slow motion, rose, mounted the chair, and pulled additional items from the tiny attic. Pens, blank forms, ink.

"Do you have a sack I can carry these in?" Giselle sounded calm, efficient. "I'll take care of it, don't worry."

"Take it to Monsieur Pichon. Tell him I can no longer do this. I've been caught. He needs to beware. Especially of Captain Schmidt." Norah spoke in a monotone, August's words spiking in her ears. She'd betrayed him, or so he felt from his perspective. She went to the bedroom and brought out a canvas sack.

"I loved an inappropriate man many years ago. My parents didn't approve." Giselle stuffed the items in the sack. "I was very young. They forced my engagement to Ropars. They thought he had a fine future. Except, he never aspired to being more than the mayor of this village. In my sadness, I allowed it. And now the Germans are in charge, instead of being brave, he drinks himself into a stupor every night. Ropars also resents we never had children."

Norah rubbed her temple, her mind still fuzzy. "What happened to the man you loved?"

"He left France in the '20s. I don't know what happened to him. I once heard he'd gone to America. It seems he wasn't as invested in me as I thought." She eyed Norah with a mixture of firmness and sympathy. "Too many regrets. You are in a very precarious position, my dear. But then, you know that. We can't help who we love."

"No, we can't." Nora's stomach churned with turmoil, as if mangled in barbed wire. Had she lost August's love? She couldn't believe that about him—or she'd fall into deeper despair.

"I'll tell Pichon to stay away from you," Giselle said when they stood at the kitchen door. "You're no longer involved."

"Thank you." Norah felt a like failure, on all sides, but the feeling would improve with effort—it *had* to. "I appreciate you carrying these away. And hope you make good use of everything. The work is important. I'm counting on you."

Giselle's bright red lips smiled. "I'm very aware of the importance. I'll practice the signature and meet with Monsieur Pichon for additional names. Then contact my sister to help her with evacuating Jews. Don't worry. If the Major loves you, he'll get over his anger." She slipped outside with a small wave.

Could August discard her, his career taking precedence? Her doubts pulled and poked at her. He said he detested this war. Norah choked down the bile in her throat. The cottage felt chilly, empty, but she had to collect her strength. She *would* bring him back. They had plans for their future.

And with Giselle taking her place, she felt she'd achieved something for the refugees.

Norah filled a large pot with water from the garden pump and plunked it on the stovetop. She shoved wood pieces into the stove and fumbled to light it. A hot bath might soothe her anguish. August had given her a bar of jasmine-scented soap. She'd accomplished so much at, perhaps, a heart-wrenching price. She had taken too many risks. Managing an even breath, she'd scrub determination for love, marriage, her art, a new life, back into her body.

* * *

In his office, August tossed back a few drinks of Calvados, the apple brandy popular here. The beverage was too saccharine, but a gift from an admiral in Brest. Perhaps the tart sweetness, the burn through his body, would numb his mind. Was Norah using him?

He moved the puzzle pieces around on the small stand, completing the table, glasses, and bottles of wine, then on to the woman on the right in blue and the man leaning over her. So much white, the men's shirts, the tablecloth, but hardly his thoughts. His fingers faltered; a piece dropped to the floor. He had the urge to dump the entire "Luncheon at the Boating Party" to join it. He flexed his fingers.

He'd tried to bury his reproaches and apprehension in reading *Die Geschichte von Bretagne,* a history of Brittany, but nothing would settle in his mind.

Norah deceived him, putting their very lives in peril. He knew she was in an indefensible position, but they needed trust. His heart ached; he yearned for peace, with *her*. Her sweet smile, comforting warmth, and infectious laugh, her teasing. She made him feel desired, cared about, like no one else ever had. Klara had been dutiful but seemed more a sister than a wife.

He might have been impulsive to ask Norah to marry him the first time, but time proved his wish was solid, his love pure…until now. He smacked his fist against his thigh. *No*, he still loved her. But was hers honest for him? He wanted to spend his life with her. It was fear of what could happen if she were caught that drove his anger. His ego was also bruised. She *couldn't* be using him—he must hold fast to that.

He snatched up the latest report from his desk and re-read it. Trouble was brewing in Paris. Rumors of a more lethal resistance to the occupying army. All German Forces were on alert.

Fritz tapped on the doorframe. "Can I get anything for you, sir?" The private eyed him warily.

"Nothing, no. You may leave for the day, *danke*. I think I'll take a long ride on Maler." August had to do something with his restless anxiety.

He headed for the stables. Should he have stayed at the cottage to make certain she burned the documents? His upset had forced him out the door before he said anything else he'd regret. How could he protect her if Schmidt found out the truth? Additional news from Paris said they were putting enemy aliens in internment camps. British citizens. Another obstacle to overcome. His head thumped with pain as he tried to come up with solutions and control his misery.

The scent of hay and horse distracted him a little. Maler shifted in his stall. August removed his tunic and hat. Putting on the horse's bridle, he tossed on the blanket, settled the saddle, cinched it, and stroked the horse's soft nose. "Are you prepared to take a fast ride?"

Maler snorted and eyed him warily. August's sorrow must be etched on his face.

He mounted, hugging his calves to the warm body, and rode out of the stables. Once away from the paddock, he nudged his horse to a gallop. He leaned into the movement, trees flying by, as Maler's hooves ate up the ground beneath them.

After dark, August would walk around the cottage to make certain Norah was safe. He'd rather go inside, cuddle her body to him, but his pride wouldn't allow it; not yet. Her deception cut deep. Though how could he blame her for wanting to save innocent children?

* * *

After a lonely, sleepless night, Norah knelt in the back garden and dug a hand-rake into the earth, determined to plant vegetables. Her solitary time in bed, the recriminations, kept her in a haze. Every time she felt the gaping hole inside her widen, she swore to herself: *He must forgive me; he said he understood my motives.*

She'd often wondered, after her disastrous night of lust in England and the stillborn baby—her heart still pinched over that—if anyone would ever love her. Then she'd found love in an impossible situation. Now she might have ruined it, but for a selfless reason.

Tears threatened. But a slight irritation as well. He'd left her alone last night as if she hadn't mattered. She scraped and clawed the rake through the hard ground, the scent of weeds, pungent plants and dirt, filling her nose. Would Giselle be able to falsify documents without her help? She must *not* be involved anymore. But how could she aid her adopted country?

The back gate creaked open on rusted hinges. Norah caught her breath. Angelique peeked around. "I knocked at the front door, but you didn't answer."

"Oh, *Cherie*, what is it?" Norah sat back on her heels, hiding her flash of disappointment it wasn't August. "Join me in my attempt at tilling the soil."

The child knelt beside her. "The mayor's wife visited *Maman* this morning and asked if I could keep you company."

Giselle knew she'd be in a devastated state. Norah sighed. "How kind of her. I'm glad you did."

"Radishes, turnips, and beets are good to plant in midsummer." Angelique dug her fingers deep into the dirt and pulled out a weed.

"I'll need seeds. Any vegetables will be welcome." Norah heard the cities were suffering food shortages, but here in the country where they could grow their own it wasn't as bad. She chopped at the earth again as if she could tame it, spin it backwards to alter time.

"I'll get seeds. Go slower." Angelique touched her hand, then studied her face. "You've been crying."

"I'm just tired. I had a bad night." Norah squeezed the little girl close, her cheek in her soft hair. She smelled like soap.

"I try to stay happy, too; but it's hard. I do it to please *Maman*." Angelique spoke in a quiet voice. "Marie-Louise is grumpy enough."

Norah smiled despite herself. "It's a turbulent world. We'll be all right, you and I. We have to be."

"Work hard and keep our heads down, Papa says. Or pretend." The girl, at age eight, was full of wisdom.

More gate creaks, and Loeiza stepped through into the garden, Petit Yann in her arms. "I came to see your new home." Her big brown eyes were full of sympathy.

Norah stared in surprise. She'd wondered if her cousin disowned her after she moved in here.

"I want down." Petit Yann squirmed and Loeiza set him on his feet.

"I'll loosen the dirt." Angelique took the hand-rake. "You visit with *Maman*. Yann, come pull weeds with me."

Norah stood and brushed off her hands as the little boy knelt beside his sister, their two blond heads close. She embraced Loeiza, her plump body a comfort. "It's good to see you."

They entered the cool dimness of the cottage.

"I've wanted to visit and see how you are." Loeiza gazed around. "This is very nice."

"It's a simple place; I like it. I'd visit you, but Yann would probably object." Norah went to the kitchen and brought out a jug of cider. She poured the beverage into two glasses.

"I'm really sorry about what happened with Yann." Loeiza laid the canvas bag Giselle had used to carry off the documents on the table. The one August inspected when filled with Norah's pencils, the first time they'd confronted one another near the coast.

She swallowed past the lump in her throat. "It's your husband's house. I don't blame him. He's protecting his interests."

"Madame Ropars said you quarreled with the Major, but not the reason why." Her cousin briefly met her eyes, then took the glass and sipped.

Norah ran her knuckle over her collarbone and bit her lip to redirect the stab of potential loss. "She's right. He…thought I was doing something illegal. He was worried for both of us."

"Were you doing anything illegal? As Yann accused as well?" Loeiza's voice exuded concern.

"Not anymore." Norah gulped the potent liquid, and thought of her cousin's embroidered cloths, the handoff to a mysterious man in the dark. "I've sworn to be above suspicion."

"As long as you're all right." Loeiza strolled the small parlor, sipping the cider. "I didn't know you were actually friends with the mayor's wife."

"We're not exactly friends, but I am drawing her and her dog, as I once lied to you about." Norah's shoulders drooped; she felt swamped in a web of lies. "I'm sorry about that."

"I only want you happy." Loeiza glanced out the front window. "Are you safe here? Are you and the Major still…"

"We'll be fine." Norah refused to sink into the mire. August needed time to cool off, she kept telling herself. "Romantic relationships are always difficult."

"And happiness is never guaranteed. Not that I'd encourage yours, with him." Loeiza turned and met her gaze. "He is good to you, isn't he?"

"Yes, very good, I promise." And he *would* be, again. She'd make certain. "We love each other."

"It may not end well, wartime affairs. I can't help cautioning you." Loeiza walked close and clasped her shoulder, her plump mouth in a moue. "I'll bring over more Queen Anne's Lace tincture. The priest would be scandalized."

Norah smiled. "Thank you." She wouldn't mention that her period was a week late, but that could happen with high emotions. Too *early* to add that worry. "I'm so glad you're here."

They hugged again, then sat and talked for another half hour, until Petit Yann ran in and whined, his hands filthy. "No more weeds!"

"I should go." Loeiza grabbed a rag from the kitchen. In the rear garden, she pumped water and cleaned his fingers. "It's primitive here."

Angelique glanced up and waved her mother off. She'd tilled a good portion of the beds at the rear hedge, and now started on the right side.

"I'm a true pioneer." Norah forced a laugh. "I'll bring Angelique home in an hour or so. I know she wants to prepare my garden for me."

"My perfect daughter. I often worry about her." Loeiza scooped up her son, then stroked her daughter's head. She joined Norah at the gate. "Take good care of yourself, no matter what."

"No one is perfect; that's what we must accept." Norah opened the gate. Her spirit sagged, then tightened like a knot. "I'll walk with you to the road."

They strolled through the gorse bushes and sprouts of wildflowers, yellows, pinks, and orange, the slight fragrance baking in the August sun, back toward the village. Norah's exhaustion impeded her steps, but she pushed on.

As they neared the main road, several motorcycles zoomed by and German soldiers rushed past on foot, brandishing their rifles.

Norah lurched backwards, grasping Loeiza's arm. Petit Yann clapped his hands as if they were watching a parade. A jeep roared by, leaving the stench of petrol.

Captain Schmidt stormed past them. He gave Norah a quick glower. "Search every house for weapons, soldiers! Or we'll be under assault. These people must be punished."

Soldiers knocked on doors, and entered homes, all down the street. Whimpers and objections sounded from open windows. Boots thudded everywhere.

"What is happening?" Norah whispered to her cousin, heart hammering.

Loeiza squeezed her child close. "I don't know."

Petit Yann stuck his fingers in his mouth, now sensing danger. "*Maman*?"

An older man was dragged from his home by a soldier and marched toward the Town Hall. "I forgot I had that pistol," he insisted.

Norah hurried with her cousin over the cobbles to stand in front of Loeiza's house. She quaked with fear at this uproar and prayed Giselle had hidden the forging materials.

Madame Bolloré lumbered over, her chubby cheeks blotched. "Damn Boche. A communist killed a German officer in Paris. The first deadly attack in the capital on our occupiers."

"*Mon Dieu.*" Norah and Loeiza hissed at the same time.

"Now Germans are shooting hostages in the occupied zone. We're all under suspicion." The hefty woman scowled at Norah.

August stood in front of the Town Hall, under the Swastika flag, towering in uniform, glaring down the road. Norah shuddered with confusion and apprehension. Had everything been ripped apart at the seams?

Soldiers pushed past them to pound on Loeiza's door.

Her cousin gasped. "I must go inside. Jean is there with Marie-Louise."

"Do you want me to come with you?" Norah asked, tearing her attention from August, whose gaze swept over her. Full of concern or skepticism?

"No, return to your cottage, and see to my daughter, *s'il vous plaît*. We have no guns, I'm certain." Loeiza pressed her shoulder.

Jean opened the door. The soldiers barged in. "Do you have any weapons here? Search everywhere, men."

Loeiza hustled inside with Petit Yann, who burst into tears. The door slammed shut.

"Did you know this was going to happen?" Madame Bolloré accused. "Now that you live with the Commandant and share your secrets, and your body."

"Are you jealous? Do you hate the Germans paying twice the worth for your eggs?" Norah swung around, away from the woman, regretting her taunt. "I'm as shocked as you are by these actions."

A young officer rushed up to them, rifle raised. "Get off the street, back to your homes, before you're arrested, *schnell*!"

Madame Bolloré huffed and rammed herself into her cottage, where several of her children had been peering out the door. Norah rushed down the path around the now empty front of the Town Hall, back into the woods, her head reeling. She must get back to Angelique.

Would the soldiers search her cottage? August couldn't allow shootings here, not of the innocent—Norah had to have faith in him. She used every ounce of strength to hold herself together while she stifled a howl.

Chapter Thirty-five

August unlocked the cottage door. The area was quiet, with only crickets chirping in the darkness. He stepped into the dim foyer. His anger and the sense of betrayal, mixed with injured pride, had started to dissipate, even after dealing with the sudden weapons search. Thankfully, none were found, except the old man with a pistol that didn't even fire. He let the elderly man return to his home after a dire warning. Still, assassins could be among the villagers.

Norah must be what mattered most this instant. August ached to be with her—to discuss and smooth out their turmoil. To make certain she avoided more risks and complied. His heart burned for her in a way he never thought possible. And, with soldiers everywhere, he didn't want to leave her alone too long.

He crept into the bedroom. She lay, wrapped in sheets on the bed, her breathing even. Last night, with sleep eluding him, he'd come to the cottage, twice, to check that she was safe, but never went inside.

He undid his belt and removed his tunic, fingers fumbling. Pulling off his boots, he reached over and placed his hand on her hip. "Norah," he whispered.

She gasped and jerked upright in the bed.

"It's me, don't be afraid." Would she order him out?

"August?" She gripped the sheet to her chest over a cotton nightgown.

"I wanted to be certain you are all right. I shouldn't have woken you." He hadn't wanted her to wake and be frightened that a person was there.

She rubbed her face. "I can't think. Are we going to talk?"

He sat in the chair near the bed, his reproaches further fading at the sight of her wide eyes and tousled hair in the shadows. Yet his trust had been damaged. "Go back to sleep. I'll stay right here."

"No, please, come to bed." She flipped back the sheet. "We'll talk in the morning."

"I'm still not happy about what you were doing. You were irresponsible; the danger is real." He hesitated. Somehow, they had to find their way back to where they'd been.

"I know. You're disappointed and upset, but please come to bed." Her drowsy, sad voice tugged at him. "I love you and promise no more carelessness."

Standing, he slipped off his trousers and unbuttoned his shirt. He climbed into bed still in his underclothes, and she snuggled close, her back to him. She smelled exotic, of jasmine. He pulled the sheet over them both. Finally, he draped his arm over her, the warm softness of her, and tried to sleep. She clasped his hand and held it to her breasts.

August sat at the little table and raked his fingers through his hair. The sun was strong, reflected in the windows, showing they'd slept late.

Norah set two cups of coffee before them and sat. "I don't have sugar, but here's milk." She nudged the little earthenware pitcher toward him. In her faded, flowered robe, blonde hair with reddish hints past her shoulders, she looked so young and vulnerable. The thirteen-year difference stretched between them.

He grasped her hand. "We must mend our quarrel. But I need to be certain that you'll never attempt such activities again. That you are finished, and I can trust you. Our feelings are sincere."

"My love is true, I swear. I should have thought how much it would put you in danger. I was reckless, like I said." She squeezed his hand, her gaze direct and slightly contrite at the same time. "I'm finished. You can search the cottage."

"No, that isn't necessary." He *had* to believe her. "But I'm firm on this. No more."

"I understand. Everything is gone." Her voice cracked.

"I worried more for you than me." He raised her hand and kissed her sweet flesh. "If Schmidt found out, it would have been difficult to protect you. He could go over my head, and the scandal might have ruined us before we could discreetly leave."

She sipped her coffee, her gaze never leaving his. "The authorities in Paris could destroy your career before you're able to retire."

"Precisely." Or he had a chance to disable the U-boat. But, if caught, that alone could annihilate him, in injury or treason. So much to consider. He'd wanted to tell her, but… He shifted in the chair and rubbed his thumb over her hand. "Next year, I hope we'll be safe in Switzerland."

"It was only the saving of Jewish children that compelled me. But I'm done. You can trust in me again." She half-smiled, though it remained sad. "I hated deceiving you."

He strained his utmost to have confidence in her. She was so much a part of him, their lives like puzzle pieces striving to fit together. He leaned across the table and kissed her. "I only want both of us safe, and as 'innocent' as we can manage." An ironic statement, considering his plans.

"I will be. The obedient house frau." With a slight wink, she held up her cup in salute. "Who paints."

"I doubt you'll ever be totally obedient." He smiled, feeling a sense of relief. However, he'd still be vigilant. There were outside forces that could influence or deter them both. "But I appreciate a woman with your spirit. That's what attracted me to you." He released her hand and drank his coffee, the aroma and taste pleasant.

"And I thought it was my clever rendition of bird life." Her smile warmed. Then she grew serious again. "You weren't worried about me the night before last? You didn't wonder how I was here alone?"

"Of course I did. I was here, outside. I walked around the cottage. Twice." He'd fought hard not to enter. "I couldn't sleep." He'd also had a sentry watching the cottage the entire night.

"I didn't hear you, and I had a restless night. Oh, I did think I heard something, an animal creeping about. You must be stealthy like a cat." She stretched, reminding him of a cat herself. Her robe fell to the side, revealing her thin nightgown, her breasts outlined beneath.

His desire flickered, but he doused it. He must contain his emotions. "I might be more bear than cat. More coffee, please?"

"Or a lion." She rose and brought back the pot, pouring them both a second cup of the dark liquid he'd provided. "Can you tell me what happened in Paris yesterday? A communist shot a German soldier?" Her eyes met his. "Or tell me as much as anyone would know."

"It's a turbulent change of events, but not surprising. A young communist shot and killed a German naval officer at a train station. The first time for deadly opposition in Paris. Now Nazi officers are retaliating. Any French arrested for opposing German rule are considered hostages, and many are being executed. Repression will be increased." He stared into her green eyes as he relayed this ugly truth. "That gives me extra worry for you."

"I understand. It's so awful." She drank from her cup, her gaze searching. "I just want us out of this war, some place safe for you and me. A cottage on Lake Lucerne?"

"I'm working on that. As soon as my son graduates next autumn, I can put in my papers, then take him out of Germany." He drank half his cup, stood, fetched his tunic, and put it on. "I have to leave now to inspect the airfield at the tip of this peninsula. I'll return tomorrow. Why don't I bring over my horse, and you have your cousin Jean spend the night here? He can ride Maler, and I'll rest easier knowing you aren't alone."

She rose and stepped up to him, her smile tempting, her eyes moist. "That's a perfect idea, thank you."

He bent, longing to wipe away any hesitation, any lasting doubts, and kissed her, hard, his hands in her hair. Tasting the sweetness of her lips, he pressed her close. She wrapped her arms around him.

He pulled back, stabilizing himself before his resolve melted. "I wish I could stay, but we slept late, and I must bring Maler." He turned from her flushed face, put on his hat, and left the cottage. August's body thrummed like a tuning fork. He yearned to indulge in their passion, but needed to stand aloof, the man in charge, for just a little longer. He hadn't mentioned another horrible incident. The transfer camp, Drancy, just opened outside Paris. He cursed. Drancy was a place to hold Jews until shipped to the soon-to-be death camps.

* * *

Jean nudged Maler into a trot and clung to the saddle as the horse pranced through the tall grass and bushes behind the gardener's cottage. Blue butterflies fluttered into the air like flower petals.

Norah smiled, her tense muscles over the last couple of days finally relaxing. Yet she waited in suspense that Pichon might arrive and beg her to continue with her work. She'd have to turn him down, but the guilt still scratched at her on both sides. She couldn't deceive August again. But she felt frustrated at not being able to assist anyone.

Had he forgiven her? Mostly, she hoped. Could she be the obedient house frau? She'd try but needed more. Her art should suffice. She'd bury her other impulses for now.

"Can I gallop him?" Jean grinned as he rode near her again. He sat well in the saddle, a natural.

"No. I'd prefer you walk him easily. If you fall off, your *maman* will strangle me."

"I'd never fall." He laughed. Maler tossed his head and blew air out his nose. Jean rode him down a path, but still in her line of sight as they'd agreed on.

He rode for another hour then trotted the horse back into the garden, carrying the scent of dry grass and heated animal flesh.

Norah had arranged her paints on a scarred little table from the cottage. "I might as well start my painting of Maler while he's visiting." She placed her previous sketch from the picnic next to a cup of water.

"I like your drawings." Jean dismounted and patted the horse's neck.

"Thank you. Did the soldiers wreck anything in your home while they searched for weapons?" She sat on the rusted stool she'd taken from the shed and opened her paint kit.

"No. *Maman* heard them whispering in German, and they said the Major's name. The soldiers just looked for weapons but didn't cause any destruction." He held Maler's reins and stroked his nose while she mixed her paints. "We had nothing to find."

"*Très bon*. They never came here." August had no doubt ordered his men to be non-destructive. But had he forbidden them from searching her cottage? She swallowed hard. He'd probably want to do that himself, no matter his denial.

"That's because you're the Major's sweetheart." Jean winked.

Her cheeks heated. "Temper your tongue, young man," she said in a deep, fatherly-sounding voice. "It's not always good to say whatever is on your mind."

She mixed the burnished chestnut color for the stallion's coat, and the darker chocolate shade for his mane and tail. She caught how the sunlight reflected over his haunch in a lighter shade.

Adding the tan leather color to the French saddle, she detailed the long stirrups, different from an English saddle.

As she painted, she ruminated that in Switzerland she'd grow as an artist. And love a man who had to leave his country, his daughters, because of tyranny and war. Love him so completely he'd forget the sadness—and she must forget the estrangement from her parents and sister, their anguish over her if they discovered her liaison—and she and August would live a good, contented life.

She painted Maler's white socks and skidded her emotions around her loss of family. A shame she couldn't have both their love and August's. After the war, she might repair the chasm.

As the sun set, a young soldier she'd seen around the Town Hall came to fetch Maler and take him back to the stables. August had said his secretary would do this.

Inside, she served fish soup and bread.

"Did you hide anything up in that attic?" Jean sipped a spoonful of soup.

"Not anymore. I'm finished with that." She ate her soup, which needed salt, something she was out of. The carrots and onions she'd got from Loeiza. "Never talk of it again, please."

"You're safer now, I'm glad. I think *Maman* is doing things she shouldn't." Jean's dark eyes flashed as he consumed more soup and bit into the bread.

"Ignore the adults. You stick your neck out, it gets chopped off. Don't be so anxious for adventure, Jean." Norah smiled to soften her scold. "You should just be a child for now."

When they made up his bed on the sofa, Norah glanced out the dark windows. She still had the feeling someone was watching her.

Jean plumped a pillow he'd brought from home. "I sleep in your old room now. Before, I had to hear my sisters complain they hadn't enough space, sharing a bed."

Norah shut the blackout curtains. "Soon, your little brother will need a bed and they'll have to share again. Do you want to be a butcher like your father when you're older, or something else?"

"Not a butcher. Maybe a carpenter like Monsieur Pichon." He traced a finger over the low table in front of the sofa. "I'd like to create things, not kill."

She checked the lock on the door. "You should ask him to take you on, like an apprentice."

Jean frowned and kicked off his sabots. They thunked onto the floor. "Papa wants me in the butcher shop when I'm twelve."

What a shame to stifle the boy's creativity. She blew out candles. Perhaps Loeiza could change Yann's mind.

"Well, let's get some sleep. Good night, and thank you for staying." She shut her bedroom door, sat, and unlaced her shoes in the weak glow of a candle. She looked at the soles; they needed repairing. Would she soon be wearing wooden sabots?

She washed her hands and face at the washstand August had given her. The water cooled her skin. She tugged off her blouse.

A crunch of footsteps outside. Her skin goose bumped. She jerked her blouse back on, blew out the candle, and peered out the curtain. It was too dark to see anything. Another noise.

She opened the bedroom door. Jean whispered, close to her, "Someone is out there."

They bumped shoulders, then hovered by the window, listening. Both peered around the blackout curtain. A shadow shifted across the garden. There was definite movement. Jean unlocked, opened the door, picked up a large stone, and threw it.

"Come back in here," she ordered, stunned.

The stone struck an object near the hedge. A man, or something, groaned, then footsteps rushed away.

Norah dragged Jean back inside and locked the door. "*Mon Dieu*! Are you insane?"

"I hit him, or it." He panted, his voice excited. "I'm here to protect you."

"You could have been hurt. Don't ever do anything like that again." She hugged the boy to her, his body thin and sinewy. Who was out there? Someone who knew August was out of town. She shivered despite the warm air. "It might have been a large animal."

They wedged a chair under the doorknob for extra security.

Back in bed, Norah wondered if it was the soldier who'd hid behind the bushes when she had left Giselle's. Or had August assigned a soldier to look after her, and they'd just injured him? She stared at the shadowed ceiling, every noise outside twitching her nerves.

Chapter Thirty-six

In the parlor of *Maison dans la Forêt,* as evening closed in, Port captain Ziegler raised his glass, a wide grin on his rosy, round face. "At last. She'll be on her way. The U-2000, the pride of the Reich. The glorious queen of the undersea."

"Congratulations. An honor for all of us." August held up his crystal with the amber liquid, intrigued and apprehensive for different reasons. When the bloated U-boat sailed into the new port, he and Bauer would see what they had to work with. They must destroy the engines, and soon. "I look forward to a tour."

"Finally, we'll see some real action." Schmidt drank deep from his brandy. "The **Führer** will be pleased. Maybe promotions are in order. I'm long overdue. My wife and father will be impressed."

"And you have good news, too, don't you, Herr Major?" Ziegler gulped his drink and poured another. "Your son will soon be able to honor the **Führer**."

"*Ja*, my son is graduating a year early. I'm very proud." August received a letter that afternoon. Everything had changed. He couldn't delay his retirement until late next year. He must rush his plans to keep his boy safe and then take him to Switzerland for college—and create a home with Norah. Christoph just turned sixteen, available to attend military school to serve in Hitler's armed forces. August could never let that happen. He almost bit into the rim of his glass.

Further apprehension was when the RAF had heavily bombed Berlin the week before, on

September 7th, but a telegram he sent to Klara's sister had told him they were fine. And so were his daughters. But for how much longer? He encouraged his daughters' husbands to send them away from the city.

"My son will train to be a pilot in the Luftwaffe. He prefers flying to the army." Schmidt preened. "You should be pleased, Herr Ziegler. So many U-boats are being commissioned. Our forces will be too strong for the enemy." Schmidt poured more brandy into his glass. "And it's officially commanded that all Jews must wear the yellow star of David. That will point out those filthy people."

"The Luftwaffe needs more pilots. The English planes are bombing Northern France *in* the daylight. Brazen." Ziegler shook his large head. Then he slopped more alcohol into his glass. "And most of our troops are in Russia for the siege of Leningrad."

August sipped his beverage, nursing the one glass, savoring the comfortable burn in his stomach. He almost said Hitler was spread too thin, he'd gone too far, but his comrades wouldn't appreciate it. And he'd said so once before. The war had raged for two years, since the invasion of Poland in 1939. Useless destruction to appease a tyrant.

August had foolishly hoped for peace, but that appeared unlikely. "And your sons serve with the navy as young officers?" he asked Ziegler.

"At German Naval headquarters in Kiel." Ziegler raised his glass again, the liquid sloshing.

"You're a proud father." August sipped the fiery alcohol. So many young men who could perish in war. He *must* get his boy out.

"My family depends on me since my papa died when I was young," Ziegler continued with a satisfied smile. "I support my old mother; my brothers help, and my sister is a fine German wife with her own family."

"My father never spared the razor strap. My mother, she's only a meek woman." Schmidt grimaced for a moment, then turned to Ziegler, a glint in his eye. "What do you think of this new instruction that sends enemy aliens to internment camps? Especially the English."

"If they cause problems. We should." Ziegler shrugged, sounding distracted, the result of too many glasses of brandy catching up to him. The man swayed on his feet.

"We want no troublemakers." August bristled and eyed Schmidt. The lie he'd tell this man who reveled in being antagonistic formed on his tongue. This subordinate who had an angry bruise on the side of his neck when August returned from the airbase inspection. "It's a relief I found out **Fräulein** Cooper wasn't born in England. She will get her birth certificate and apply for her birth country's passport." Ironically, he'd need a forger. His plan was to make her Swiss. He clicked his glass to Schmidt's, his smile a warning. "*Prost*."

* * *

Throwing up in the toilet for the fourth time that week, Norah wiped her mouth and groaned. She rinsed her mouth with water, then brewed tea to calm her stomach as she buttoned her tightening trousers. Her breasts were tender. She knew the signs. Sitting with her cup of tea, she worried over what August would say. Her pregnancy would present complications. She wanted his baby, but she'd hoped to be married and ensconced in Switzerland first. She rubbed her belly, her emotions swirling like a whirlpool, praying for a healthy outcome. The Queen Anne's Lace tincture she'd started drinking while living with her cousin had failed.

Two weeks past, August had returned from his inspection, and they'd talked until late, then made love, slow and gentle, as if each caress were his forgiveness—and her commitment to abandon the Résistance. But she noticed in a flicker of a glance he still wondered if she had told the whole truth. And she'd never admitted to him about the night visitor, Jean's rock throw, reluctant to ruin their interlude. Then more time passed, and she had still not mentioned the incident.

After she'd nibbled on dry, toasted bread, she walked to the village market. The pungent smell of fish at the fishmongers made her queasy again. She hurriedly bought turnips, beets, and a small chicken to prepare for supper.

She turned to walk home and cringed when Pichon approached.

He doffed his hat and smiled. "Mademoiselle Cooper, did you still want that side table?"

Norah hadn't spoken to him since before she'd given Giselle the documents. "Ah…yes, I do." He could never come to the cottage to measure for it, that would arouse suspicion. "About this long, this wide, and this tall." She bent and showed him the height she needed. Anyone observing should know she was asking for carpentry work.

Pichon pulled out a notebook and pencil and scribbled measurements. "I think I have it. Would you like pine or oak? Oak is more expensive."

"I'll take a pine table." She might have said that too loudly.

Pichon slipped the notebook back into his pocket, his voice low. "I'm sorry you had to quit. Madame Ropars does her best but isn't as good."

"She'll become better. When the table is finished, send a note through my cousin Jean and then you can tell me the price. We'll meet outside your shop." Norah shifted her basket of food, anxious to get away from him in case their interaction was misinterpreted and gossiped about. Pichon *had* been questioned by the Germans as possibly being part of the resistance.

People hustled or shuffled by on the street, heads down, talking in whispers, circumspect and nervous after the search for weapons. The rumors of hostage killings. Who could be trusted?

"Au revoir. Until the table is ready." She moved away from him.

He stepped with her. "Marshall Petain, our WWI hero, now a traitor, has set up courts in Vichy to execute any Résistance fighters who commit sabotage."

"I can honestly say I know nothing of such machinations here." Norah fought a groan at this atrocity. Vichy was the capital of the unoccupied zone. How much longer would the Germans allow the southern part of France to remain free? And the Frenchman Petain sounded as vicious as the worst Nazi.

"I trust you never share intimacies with the Major that could endanger us." Pichon's voice remained congenial as they stepped along.

"I *never* would. I will warn you to be careful and keep yourself safe. Avoid Captain Schmidt. Please excuse me." She ducked into an alley, and down a slope into the woods. Her feet crunching on pine needles released a resinous scent.

Surprisingly, August waited for her at the cottage. Her pulse danced. Even in his full uniform, now she saw only the man inside it. A decent man!

Her breath hitched. Would he support her in what was coming? He intended to marry her, but did he want to be a father again?

He reached for her basket. "I've come to invite you on a holiday this weekend; a few days spent away from here. To a lake cottage at *Lac Guerlédan*. About 150 kilometers northeast. I think we need the time together."

"That would be lovely." She could tell him then about the life growing inside her. They'd used no protection—their lust raw and irresponsible—she should have expected this. But would he be happy?

They entered the cottage. "Before your people inform you, Monsieur Pichon stopped me in the village and asked for measurements for the side table I ordered."

August set the basket on the table, his smile contemplative. "I don't have anyone following you, Norah. But that doesn't mean that certain people aren't looking to cause problems." He touched her cheek.

"I realize that. We need to have faith in each other, again." She clasped his hand, pressed it against her cheek, and thought of the night visitor. She must believe it was a large animal, reluctant to cause any trouble. And now he'd wonder why she waited so long to tell.

She also tried to dismiss the activity at the secret port, yet it still bothered her. Was August a part of it? The sailors now stationed here were smiling and celebrating, as if something momentous was about to happen, according to Jean. The boy seemed to listen in everywhere despite any reprimands. But she didn't dare ask August about the change in the sailors. "Problems surround us. Do we leave on Friday?"

Chapter Thirty-seven

August glanced out the window of the tiny fishing cottage, fixed up for tourist rental, beyond which sunlight danced across the waters of *Lac Guerlédan.* The lake sat in a bounty of forest, the thick spruce trees hugging the shoreline.

Earlier they'd visited Chapelle Ste-Suzanne where the belfry porch dated from 1760. The ceilings had magnificent paintings dedicated to the saint from the eighteenth century. They'd driven in August's borrowed Citroën to the lock on the River Blavet crossed by an old, corbelled bridge. The water's overflow splashed near the lock keeper's cottage. Then they visited a twelfth century Cistercian abbey, partially destroyed during the French Revolution. Norah wanted to paint it all. He enjoyed the history and her pleasure in the sights.

He turned to her. "We'll eat supper in the village. But first, I have a gift for you."

She smiled and kissed his cheek. "Being here with you is my gift."

He pulled out a large, square, flat box he'd stashed under the small sofa. "Open it. You might think me a selfish man for purchasing this for you."

Norah laughed. "It is something…sexy?" She placed the box on the sofa and opened it. With a quick intake of breath, she pulled out the garment. "A gown; it's beautiful." She held up the berry-colored crepe dress.

He admired it, hoping the dress fit. "Try it on."

She went into the bathroom.

When she came back out, he nearly gasped. "You look gorgeous, so elegant."

"I like the mandarin neckline." She trailed her fingers down the buttons on the bodice. The material was gathered above and below her bust, accentuating it. The waistline fit above her hips. The skirt swung like a waterfall when she moved. "Selfish because you wanted me to wear a dress? You were tired of my trousers, *oui*?"

"I'd rather no one but me admires your legs. And you are stunning." He traced his fingers up her arms to the gown's short sleeves. "The shop owner said it is called a Peggy dress."

"You have good taste. I don't suppose you bought me a slip to wear under this?" She twirled away, the skirt fanning out.

"I didn't think of that." He scrutinized the gown. "But you can't see through the material."

She laughed. "How did you know my size?"

"I guessed." He put his hands on his hips. "I was married, so I'm not totally new at this."

"Did you buy pretty gowns for Klara?" A glint of jealousy in her eyes?

"Norah, I honored her as my wife. But I've loved no one the way I do you." He drew her against him and kissed her lips. Now he wanted to remove the dress, his ardor difficult to control. "My burgundy beauty."

"Thank you. I adore it." She tilted her head. "This will look very *femme fatale* with my scuffed oxford shoes."

"I couldn't guess for high-heels." He laughed. When had he felt so carefree since the war began? He craved this moment of joy before the U-boat, delayed once more, arrived at their port. It was a hatchet that hung over his head. He forced his mind to the present. "Maybe next time we'll visit a shoemaker."

"No, you do enough for me. I was only joking."
She kissed his cheek again, her gaze sincere. "I have
all I need."

After a light supper at a café in the village of
Anse de Sordan, they sat out on their cottage's tiny
porch with a bottle of Pommeau de Bretagne—a
sweet wine that tasted of baked apples and
butterscotch.

The sun drifted low, the weakening rays
sparkling over the lake where a few people in
rowboats glided on the water. A piney scent floated
on the light breeze.

He pointed. "Tomorrow, I'll take you out rowing
in a boat."

"I'd like that." She looked pensive for a
moment.

Their chairs side by side, he clasped her hand.
"I've had a letter from my son. He's graduating early.
Which changes my plans. I must put in my papers
now to retire."

She'd stretched out her legs, bare, slender,
under the gown, but now drew them back. "Will you
be allowed to do that?"

"I decided to request it for medical reasons.
Failing eyesight. It isn't true, but I'll get a doctor's
report stating this." He hated to show such weakness
on paper, especially a lie.

"A forgery?" She stared at him. "But dare you?
Who would forge?"

"I know. Ironic. This man is used by the
Germans, so safe for me. He is in Quimper. He's also
an old friend and very discreet. And there is more.
Enemy aliens are being rounded up and sent to
internment camps. You'll need a new passport, birth
certificate, and so forth. How do you feel about being
Swiss?" He tried to make the abrupt change practical.
"Nina Keller is as close as I can think of for your new
name."

"Then we'll marry under my false name?" She sounded surprised, slightly disappointed.

"For now. When the war is over, we can remarry under your real name." He squeezed her hand. "Does this bother you?"

She contemplated the lake and feathered her fingers over her abdomen. "No, not if it's the only way."

"Don't worry, the war has brought out strange circumstances we must circumvent. At least now we'll marry earlier than first planned." He put his arm around her, sensing there was more she wanted to say.

She sipped her wine. "I guess it's the best solution for me, so I can leave France and enter Switzerland." She slanted her gaze at him. "I shouldn't be surprised the Germans have their own forgers."

"I just want to keep you away from such activities." And away from any members of the Résistance. "This man won't report me for changing your identity. Or falsifying a doctor's testimony."

"I remain above reproach." They fell silent. A dog barked from somewhere. "How will I explain my less than perfect French when we travel?"

"We'll think of a reason. You went to school elsewhere?" He took another sip of the wine.

"*Mais oui*, my father worked in the diplomatic corps." She raised her chin. "I attended schools in England and America at a young age."

"You have a shrewd mind." He laughed lightly, his hand massaging her shoulder. "Keep it simple, not too many details."

"I'm behaving, Herr Commandant." She smiled impishly, then rested her head on his shoulder. "I've never repeated our conversations. I never spied."

He kissed the top of her head. "Any precaution is for our safety. Things may happen, later; well, let's enjoy ourselves." He'd nearly slipped but now was *not* the time. He finished his glass of the too-sweet wine, pushing to the back of his mind any thoughts about fouling fuel-lines, though he yearned to confide in her. He still searched for sugar.

"You have more secrets." She raised her head and watched him, then in his silence she stared off over the lake. "I would like to keep my first name. Just say I had an Irish great-grandmother I'm named after. Which is true."

"Norah it is." He kissed her apple-sweet lips. "My favorite name."

When they returned inside, the sun only a hint behind the trees, he unfastened Norah's gown and kissed her naked shoulder. He inhaled her Jasmine scent. The dress now fallen to the floor, he unhooked her brassiere and caressed her breasts. Her nipples hardened under his fingers. She moaned, flesh quivering, then stroked the back of his neck.

In the bedroom, he undressed them both and lost his worries in the heady feel of her body, her hot flesh, as her tenderness enveloped him.

* * *

Under a sapphire sky, Norah watched the muscles in August's arms bulge as he pulled the paddles through the water with the gentle slosh of dipping oars. His shoulders were muscled in his yellow shirt—she had intimate knowledge of every aspect of his body—and he seemed to row with ease.

They rowed past sandy beaches and inlets. Waterfowl, coots and kingfishers flapped in the reeds, raising the dank smell of damp plants. The thick forest loomed around them. A few other boaters were out. She relaxed into the rhythm, the warm breeze on her face.

Their little boat rocked when he slowed them under the dappled shade of a beech tree.

"This lake, the entire area, is so beautiful," she said. "We'll have to come back so I can sketch it."

"I'd like to bring you back here. *Lac Guerlédan* is one of the largest lakes in this region. But it's artificial, formed where the Blavet River meets the Nantes-Brest canal." He tugged his sleeves up above his elbows again. "It connects those two cities."

"The lake must be very long." She leaned back against the stern, wondering when she should tell him her secret, her mind in a muddle.

"Over three hundred kilometers, with more than a hundred and fifty locks." He laid the paddles in the boat.

"I'm impressed that you know the history in France." She trailed her fingers through the cold water. She must tell him, now.

"The hydroelectric dam was completed in 1930." He watched her with his vivid blue eyes. "When I get proper credits, I plan to work in a Swiss college history department."

"That sounds perfect. As long as you're content." Another concern: If England won the war, would he be prosecuted for serving as an officer under Hitler? She bit her lip and mustn't think of that.

She straightened and leaned forward, her nerves growing ragged at what needed to be said. She slowly rubbed her abdomen.

"I will be content with you. And Christoph studying engineering, away from the Nazis. I want you to be happy, too." He smiled, his expression questioning. "How do you feel after your upset stomach this morning?"

She inhaled slowly, flicked water from her fingers, then met his gaze. She tried not to squirm. "I've had several upset stomachs. I think I'm pregnant."

His eyebrows rose. He blinked. "That's...wonderful news." He reached for her hands, squeezing tight. The boat rocked. "I know we're not married, but will be soon. Are you happy?"

She choked on her words, voice thick. "Yes, but it might cause complications."

"*Nein*, don't think that way." He kissed both her hands, his face alight, a glimmer in his eyes. "This will add to our pleasure."

"Especially since plans have changed, and we're leaving sooner." She relished his joyful reaction, the grip of his hands. Any humiliation melted away. Now it was imperative she leave, before she showed. "I'll be mama Norah Keller."

"I'm the luckiest of men. Soon you'll be Norah Gottlieb." His voice was full of delight, smile wide, easing her nerves. "How are you feeling, other than the morning sickness?"

"I'm fine. Perhaps I need a new identity quicker, so I can visit a doctor and not be considered an enemy alien. And risk being interned." She thought of her lost baby, the pain of it not as sharp. She must protect this child. Their child.

"I'll arrange right away for the papers and find you the best doctor. I'll take care of you." His fingers entwined with hers, firm and strong, his smile sweet, proud. She valued her independence but felt safe in his heartfelt declaration.

A high-pitched wail cut through the air. An Air-Raid siren.

"Oh no." Norah shuddered. The noise reverberated through her.

"Hold on, *liebling*. We must find shelter." August released her, sliced the oars into the water, and rowed toward a pier.

An explosion went off in the distance, echoing along the ground and lake. People shouted from the other boats and began rowing to shore.

She clutched the sides of the boat, hiding her panic as they bumped against a splintered piling near a ladder.

* * *

The villagers scrambled to a stone church, down the stairs, and into a cellar, as the siren screamed. August followed and eased Norah to a wall, holding her close. More people shoved in with smells of body odor, and various foods eaten. The door shut, and someone lit a lantern.

Another explosion. The rafters above them shook. Dust and debris sprinkled down. August leaned over her to shield her from the fallout. "Don't be afraid."

"I'm all right," she whispered into his chest as she pressed against him.

A group of old women clutched their rosaries and prayed. The lantern cast strange light over their faces like some sacrifice was about to take place. Whimpers and moans came from others.

"Who's bombing us, the damned Boche again?" a chubby older man growled.

"*Mais non,* it's the British. I saw Hawker Hurricanes. It's the RAF." A boy who looked in his early teens grinned.

"We're going to die before anyone rescues us," a woman in black cried.

August wanted to take charge, but he was on the wrong side. Instead, he played the cautious man, holding his fiancée against his chest. He didn't want her upset, though it was a useless thing to wish for. But now there was their baby to protect. A baby they'd bring into this world of chaos. Kissing the top of Norah's head, his pride and happiness clouded with the peril of their situation.

What could the RAF be after here? Of course, the nearby dam was strategically important. It was a generation station for the German naval base at

Brest. The RAF would do better to destroy Kriegsmarine Yard Brest—though they'd attacked that port several times.

"I hope the British blow the vile Germans to bits." A man swung his cane in the air. "Chase them out of our country."

Norah tensed in August's arms. He massaged her back. He wanted the destruction to end, but here he was, a German officer among the enemy.

Another explosion, though it sounded farther off. A spurt of dust on his head. A dank, musty stink. Norah shivered. Could he obtain the false papers and send her to Switzerland *quickly* while he took care of matters at the port?

Fritz would escort her on the train if asked. August would think of a subterfuge.

"I'm so tired of this. I already fought in the previous war," a craggy-faced man near the door groused. "The war to end all wars, *merde*. We were fools."

"It's all right, *mon cher*. Calm yourself." A gray-haired woman, skinny and weary- looking, touched his arm. A little girl, probably a grandchild, huddled against her.

"I can't take it anymore." The man pulled a pistol from his pocket. "I'm going out there. I'm no coward, I don't hide. The British need my help."

"No! I thought you got rid of your pistol, Henri." The woman hugged the small girl, who started to cry.

Henri put his foot on the stairs. The woman and child wept, their sobs filling the low-roofed room.

Norah tightened her embrace around August. He must do something.

"Monsieur, it's too dangerous." August adopted his most calming voice, intent on soothing Norah and the disruptor. "Stay with your family."

Henri, face mottled, turned to him with a sneer. "Who are you to tell me what to do?"

"I'm trying to keep us safe." August erased any sternness from his tone. "Your family needs you."

The man, clearly unhinged, pointed the gun at August. Norah gasped. People scooted back into the shadows, away from them.

August slipped Norah behind him and faced Henri. "We must protect our families. Put the pistol down before someone gets hurt." A French civilian shouldn't have a weapon, though he could hardly say so. Would this man shoot him?

"You don't sound from around here. You remind me of a soldier." The gun shook in Henri's hand. "Are you a soldier? A traitor Frenchman?"

August kept his voice low. "We're on holiday from another region. And we must all be soldiers during these rough times." Surely the man hadn't heard a German accent in his perfected French.

Norah poked her head around, her fingers pinching his flesh. "Protect us by settling down, Monsieur." Her voice sounded breathless, afraid.

August reached behind and squeezed her arm, holding her in place.

"Please, Henri," the woman pleaded. The little girl cried louder. "Don't behave so. I know it's been difficult."

August stepped forward, as Norah objected, and the man's gun hand wavered.

"Relax, *s'il vous plaît*." His persona of Major von Gottlieb pressed the pistol barrel toward the dirt floor. It could go off at any moment, shattering him, his future. He recalled that other gunshot in his side, the agonized pain, the pools of blood, and his playing dead to survive. His breath tumbled out. He put his other hand on Henri's shoulder. "The explosions are receding. Please don't upset my wife. She is delicate." He cupped the man's elbow and eased him toward his wife. "See to your family; they need you to be strong."

Henri's shoulders sagged, arm drooping to his side. "I have no bullets anyway." His wife and granddaughter embraced him.

The people present sighed, and said Hail Marys, while some cursed and grumbled.

August felt a tug on the back of his shirt, then a hard pull.

He returned to Norah and sheltered her in his arms with a kiss on her forehead.

"Please don't ever do that again," she whispered harshly, her fingers jabbing him.

He tucked her head under his chin, his muscles unclenching. The real possibility he could have been killed, or Norah injured. But soldiers dealt with that threat every day. "I'll try my best, *meine—mon amour.*"

The All-Clear siren blared.

Chapter Thirty-eight

Relief filled Norah when she saw the gardener's cottage, her home, after the animosity in the church cellar. Especially with the chance of a bomb landing too close. Though she'd reveled in their time together at the lake, August facing off with the man and his pistol nearly unstrung her.

She'd bristled most of the way home, the siren still echoing in her ears, angry at his reckless bravery. But she calmed herself, his hand tight on hers, for the baby's sake and their love. He was a major in the army, after all.

The Citroën had slid into the village on vapors. Petrol was growing impossible to obtain because France had no oil production and imports had been banned or blockaded by the British. Trucks and automobiles, with converters, burned charcoal or wood pellets as a substitute to power the vehicles, emitting the nasty exhaust fumes they drove through.

As soon as he brought in her suitcase, August's secretary ran down the path and saluted. "Major, sorry to disturb you, but you're needed in the village. There's trouble at the tavern. Sailors and soldiers."

"I'll be right there." August turned to her. "I'm sorry I must leave. Promise to rest and I'll see you later." He kissed her, hugging her close, and left with the young man.

Norah unpacked, hanging up the beautiful gown in her wardrobe. When would she wear it again? Soon, she'd have to wear loose-fitting dresses because her trousers would be too tight. How would she hide her condition, waiting for August's retirement permission to come through?

Eating a crepe with Loeiza's apple jam, she thought of the RAF bombing so close here in Brittany. It reminded her again that success for England meant disaster for August before he could take her and his son to Switzerland. Was that neutral country a delusion or a haven?

She lit candles as evening encroached, then sat on the sofa and perused an art book. Feeling drowsy, she leaned back against the sofa.

Someone knocked on the door. She started and sat upright, her fingers tight on the book. August wouldn't knock—he had a key. She rose and asked through the crack, "Who is it?"

"It's Private Fritz. I have something for you from the Major."

She hesitated at the muffled voice.

"It's important," he said.

Unlocking and opening the door a few inches, she peered out. "What—"

A hand pushed wide the door. She staggered back.

Captain Schmidt shoved inside. He closed the door, his eyes glinting. "**Fräulein** Cooper. I finally get to see your love nest."

Norah cringed with apprehension. She backed to the sofa. "Get out of here at once."

"I only wanted to visit with you." He swaggered around the room. "This is a suitable place for the Major's mistress."

She swallowed down the information on their plans to marry. It was none of his business. She stiffened, keeping her voice stern. "You've seen it. Now please leave."

"I'd like to see the bedroom, where the magic happens." His voice a sneer, he made no move in that direction, as if he had to watch her carefully.

Fingers clenched, she held fast to rising anger. "August will be here any minute."

"No, he has to resolve an issue with fighting men at the tavern." He shrugged his bony shoulders. "I'm sure he'll share a few drinks with his comrades."

Mouth dry, she tried a commanding order. "You are *not* welcome here. Leave."

"I think, since you provide such interesting service to him, you could service me as well." His words were taunting, nostrils flared.

Norah fought a shudder. She needed a weapon. She inched toward the kitchen. "You have a mistress in Quimper. Go to her."

"She isn't as pretty as you. She never treats me as a priority. I can pay you well, if that's what you want." Schmidt stepped close, poking his pointed nose at her like a snipe. The stink of alcohol drifted off him.

He must have been the soldier sneaking about at the farm and the 'animal' outside her cottage when Jean was here. She'd try indignance. He wouldn't dare touch her. "You're insulting. Be on your way."

He winked. "You don't mean that. I'll show you what a real man can do."

Pulse racing, she should run out the kitchen door, but hated to show fear. "I have all I need. You can offer me nothing."

Schmidt sidled around toward the rear door, as if he anticipated her action. "Only the best sex you've ever had. You'll want me more than him."

Revulsion roiled her stomach. "I'm warning you to leave now. I'm true to *one* man only."

"Are you?" He cocked his balding head. "Women are connivers. I also know about your little forging scheme."

"I have nothing to do with that." She could honestly reply to her innocence now. A spike of fear slid up her spine. What could she use to 'deter' him?

A cast iron frying pan lay in the sink. "You're drunk. Go sleep it off."

"I'm not too drunk to show you my prowess." Shoulders back, chest out, he resembled a scrawny robin. "So, Herr Major took you off to a lake. How romantic. And I hear you're Swiss now."

Face heated, Norah backed to the sink. "I demand that you get out at once. Or you'll regret it. August will punish you when he finds out."

"You dare to threaten me? I'm in charge right this moment. The Major doesn't think I'm good enough. But you will. I'll claim what's his." He lunged and grabbed her breast.

She cried out and smacked his hand away. She snatched up the heavy iron pan, her breath rapid, her breast smarting.

Schmidt laughed and leaned on the table, fingers splayed. "You'd never strike me." His gaze lowered. "Now I'll grope where you'll really enjoy my touch. Then you show me how you please the Major."

Fury surged through her. She raised the pan and smashed it down on his right hand. The contact— a brutal cracking sound.

He screamed. "You bitch!" His hand turned white, then scarlet. He held it up. "*Du dumme Hure*! Stupid whore!" Pain screwed up his features.

Norah hefted up the pan once more. "Go! Never come near me again."

Schmidt yowled, his face flushed. His hand and fingers were swelling, turning purple. He straightened, snarled and swiped at her with his left arm, like a desperate animal.

She knocked his shoulder with the pan, backing him off. "Get out! If you stay away, I won't tell August." August might kill the captain, causing a scandal.

Face crimson, Schmidt cradled his hand and staggered toward the front door. Sweat dappled his high forehead. "I never get what I want. What I *should* have. You broke bones. *Bitch*."

"That's what you deserved." She followed, the pan in hand, her pulse hammering. She hurried around him and opened the door. "I'll smash your head in next time. Out!"

He glowered at her, mouth agape, eyes squinted, "remember, you're just his whore," then he stumbled off into the darkness.

She slammed and locked the door. Gulping air, she dropped the pan with a clang and pressed on her abdomen. He wouldn't come back, he *couldn't*. She slumped, loose like a rag doll, onto the sofa, head in her hands.

* * *

The tower or fin, bristling with radio antennas and anti-aircraft guns, broke the water's surface. Then the mounted cannon slid into view on a long deck like a great gray serpent. The Atlantic was shoved away in foam-tipped waves and loud splashes. Waves thrust back and smacked the bank where they stood.

August watched in silence, hands clenched behind his back, as the U-boat rose farther out of the water. The creature had arrived. He and Bauer exchanged quick glances.

Seagulls wheeled and cawed overhead, as if angry at this huge interruption to their feeding place.

"*Wunderbar*! She's a beauty, isn't she?" Zeigler practically stood on tiptoes, his cheeks the color of plums, his plump lips in a wide grin. The assembled sailors cheered. The salty wind tugged at everyone's hats.

"She is impressive." August scrutinized the deck. Where would the vessel take in fuel? He schooled his features to appear impassive at his shock at the submarine's size.

"Now we'll destroy the English coastal bases and their fleet." Schmidt stood to one side, his right hand bandaged. When August asked him what happened, his captain said he'd bruised it while out on patrol. He'd visit a doctor when he was next in Quimper with his mistress. His face often contorted in pain.

A hatch opened, and the sailors crawled out on the deck and cheered in their dark-blue, flapping-collar uniforms and caps. The sailors on shore shouted back. Zeigler raised his arm to the officers.

August knew the whole village would hear them and be curious. Rumors would start.

The U-boat's bulk looked swollen, unwieldy. Could it really sail in the open sea with so much extra weight? Hopefully, the abomination would never have the chance.

"I'm so overjoyed I need a drink. When the officers come ashore, we'll celebrate at the tavern." Zeigler looked to August, mouth pursed. "In other ports, they rely too much on deceitful French engineers." He thrust his index finger into the air. "In Lorient, only Germans work on the U-boats."

"As it should be." Though the RAF had bombed Lorient in July, causing serious damage. "You should instruct your men and the newcomers to be more discreet. Everyone will be curious about this massive addition to the Reich." August studied the U-boat again, his neck prickling at what lay ahead.

Zeigler smirked. "Perhaps we should have moved the villagers out of this area, for security reasons."

"We've been careful, and I'll increase our sentries. Cooperation is needed all around." August had no intention of ordering anyone to move, but he must sound in charge, and lull Zeigler's mind. Unfortunately, when August retired, the villagers could be displaced. Yet if the port was rendered useless with a damaged submarine, little may change.

Zeigler stuck out his growing belly. One button on his dark tunic looked about to fly off. "There is much to consider. A ship packed with barrels and cork—to make her unsinkable—will sail ahead of *das boot* for anti-mine protection."

August decided not to point out that seemed to undercut the 'secrecy' of the submarine's progress.

"A celebration this evening. I'll be there." He hoped to learn what he could about the U-boat. And then, in a few days, a comprehensive tour. "I must return to my office. I'll leave you to your business of docking. Congratulations, Port captain."

"I am honored to be in charge of this miracle, Herr Major." Zeigler bowed.

August signaled to Bauer, and they strolled off toward the village. "Another week or so, after a tour, we make our plans. Sand and sugar in the oil and fuel lines."

Bauer nodded, his steps even. "I'll keep searching. She's a frightening giant. A distraction on shore is needed for our purposes."

"A bonfire for the sailors, and schnapps. Some delicious food." August rolled his shoulders to ease the tension. What if they failed? A firing squad would await. "That will bring most of the men on shore."

Bauer slowed. "I'm repulsed by this war. Of course, you've heard about the thousands of Jews being shot in Lithuania. My wife has Jewish friends. She writes me in fear for them."

"The Ponary massacre." August's head throbbed with the horror of it. What decent soldier could carry out such atrocities? Where had the conscience of his nation gone? "Destroying this U-boat will be *our* contribution to defeat the Nazis."

"You must stay with the party, or it's too obvious, Major. I will risk the visit on deck to open the fuel hatch." Bauer, a lithe man, grimaced.

"We'll see what's best." Firstly, he intended to get Norah out of the area. He'd drive her to have her photograph taken for her new passport and identity card. Then, if all went well, he would immediately put her on a train to Switzerland. He had friends there who would look after her.

Regret weighed on him at deserting Saint Guénolé and leaving it in unkinder hands when he departed. Especially if Captain Schmidt was slated to take command. *Mein Gott*, this war must end!

Chapter Thirty-nine

Giselle held still in her rear garden as Norah finished the painting she'd sketched of her weeks ago. Norah had been reluctant to spend time—in case anyone watched her movements—with the mayor's wife since she'd passed her the forging materials.

At a rustle in the bushes, Norah turned her head; since her confrontation with Captain Schmidt, every noise nipped at her nerves. A house martin with its blue head twittered from the foliage.

"My brother has joined my sister in Paris. We don't know where he was hiding. He fled the French army once they capitulated. Together they plan to sneak Jews out of the city and its environs." Giselle sighed. "With new paperwork, they can be sent—"

"Please don't tell me anything. You understand my position." Norah bit the inside of her cheek and added finer lines of paint to highlight the woman's blonde hair, straining to keep her hand balanced. She longed for such successes for the Résistance, but she must walk a narrow path. She also clashed with herself over whether to tell August about Schmidt.

Schmidt might report her to a higher authority for striking him. Could August prevent her from suffering any punishment?

"You seem jumpy. I guess you and the Major have mended your quarrel?" Giselle gave a quick smile, her gaze sympathetic. Her little dog nestled on her lap.

"We have. And I intend to keep it that way." Norah wished it could be different; guilt consumed her at not being able to contribute to the freedom fighters. She dipped her brush into a created lighter shade of purple to show more details of Giselle's blouse.

"Do you know your cousin Loeiza is embroidering messages on napkins and caps?" Giselle leaned close. "She passes them to a man in the Black Market who's part of the opposition."

"I implore you, never discuss such matters." Norah plopped her brush into the cup of water. Her suspicions, and what she'd witnessed, were correct. "How do you know this?"

"I hear things. Many pass on the gossip. I only tell you so you can warn her." Giselle pouted and scratched her dog behind the ears. Blanche stuck out her little pink tongue.

"Who else have you mentioned this to?" Norah prayed not to Giselle's loud-mouthed husband. The former mayor who drank too much and told Yann Norah might be a forger. A man Giselle only alluded to with regret the marriage had happened at all.

"No one. Again, alert her that people know. It might get to the *wrong* people." Giselle stroked Blanche's back. The dog wriggled. "I'm being discreet otherwise."

"Thank you." Now Norah's worry for Loeiza increased. But she'd only insist her cousin stop if Norah knew something specific was about to happen against the resistance groups. She studied the painting. "I think I'm finished."

Giselle put Blanche on the ground and came around to look. "*Fantastique*. It's lovely. You've made me look ten years younger." She lit a cigarette and puffed.

Norah rinsed her brushes. "It's realism, though I've decided I still like the Impressionists. Call me old-fashioned."

"Well, I have something for you, along with payment." Cigarette dangling from her lips, Giselle smiled.

Norah wanted to say, 'please don't give me anything except money,' but the woman hurried into the house on her scuffed high heels, one heel mended with tape.

Norah wiped the damp brushes with a cloth, anxious to leave. Giselle returned with coins and a small paper bag. "It's sugar. A tiny amount. I won't tell you where I got it." She blew out smoke.

Norah almost refused, but the idea of sugar in her coffee won out. She stifled a cough in the strong vapers. "I must go. I wish—"

The ex-mayor stumbled out the rear door, his shirt rumpled, his trousers strained over his plump body. "Colonel Britton, a pseudonym surely, is broadcasting all over the occupied territories, urging resistance." Face bloated, he looked terrible.

Giselle swept up a hand. "Go back inside, Ropars, and rest your clouded mind."

"I did my best for you. You never cared. I had visions for this village. A major fishing port and a canning industry." He grumbled, eyes melancholy, then did as she asked.

"Does he have a wireless?" Norah stuffed down her shock as she packed up. "He could be arrested for that."

"Ignore him. I'll warn him again." Giselle sucked on her cigarette, frowning. "He's become a pathetic man."

"Please, make sure he's cautious. Thank you for the sugar. And I wish you every success in your new endeavors." Norah left the farmhouse. Giselle was lonely, that was obvious, and stuck with a lout of a husband. Norah wished they could be friends, but it was too risky.

She walked down the lane, past the cathedral, the gray-stoned market building, and entered the village. The tavern reverberated with lively talk in German. It sounded like a party, a celebration. She hurried past, then glanced into every corner of the village to make certain Captain Schmidt didn't lurk about.

She knocked on her cousin's door. Marie-Louise opened it. "They're in back, making soap." The little girl, large brown eyes critical in her wide-cheeked face, walked off, leaving the door open, as in *come in if you must.*

"It's good to see you, too, Marie-Louise." Norah entered and set her paint case on the foyer bench. In the kitchen, she divided the sugar and put half in an earthenware jar. She went to the rear door.

Loeiza stirred a huge pot over a fire, and Madame Bolloré was with her. Norah stepped out. Petite Yann diligently dug a hole near the stone wall. A crude wooden soap mold with square slots leaned against the wall.

Children laughed and argued from the next garden. Madame shouted at them to be quiet.

Her cousin turned. "Norah, how wonderful to see you." Sweat clung to her face and tendrils of black hair as she stirred stinky fat and caustic soda. "We're making soap; it's almost impossible to buy it anymore."

Madame Bolloré glanced over, her fat cheeks damp with perspiration, her eyes assessing. "Norah probably has plenty of fancy soaps at her cottage."

Norah gave the woman a quick smile, then turned to her cousin. "Put lavender in there to sweeten the scent. Are Jean and Angelique in school?"

"*Oui*, at the church. Marie-Louise should go this year, but she asked to wait until next year." Loeiza frowned. "It's nice to have her home. She helps me with the garden and housework."

And embroidering messages? Norah couldn't warn her cousin with Madame there. She forced a smile. "Marie-Louise will probably run the school by next year. I brought you some sugar." Norah met the hefty woman's glare. "And, no, the Major did not give it to me."

Loeiza swiped her arm over her forehead. "*Merci*. I can bake something edible again. Yann will be pleased."

"What is all this carousing among the sailors?" Madame Bolloré crammed a stick under the pot and fanned the fire. Then she flipped up her white cap, her forehead shining.

"I have no idea." Norah knew that August seemed agitated and distracted lately. She had her own suspicions as to why. "I'm kept out of any information as well as you."

"They're bragging about something." Madame Bolloré crossed her arms under her pendulous breasts in her faded green gown. "My son sees them outside the tavern, raising their mugs of beer, singing their stupid songs. And there is definitely more activity at the little port."

Norah had felt the same pressure and change in the village yet forced herself to ignore it—though questions constantly huddled in the back of her mind.

"I wish this would thicken faster." Loeiza gripped the paddle with both hands and stirred the smelly mixture, the consistency of gravy. The fumes stung Norah's eyes.

"*Voila!*" Petit Yann flung dirt into the air. "I made a tunnel."

"There are whispers of an undersea boat. My friend was sure of it." Madame Bolloré narrowed her eyes. "Her husband works at the tavern."

A submarine? But what was so secretive about this one that the Germans built the port here, in the deep cleft of water? Norah's throat tightened as anxiety tingled along her arms.

"I'll be off now. Enjoy the sweetening. And we should *all* be careful about what we do and talk about." Norah moved to the rear door. Her warning was for her cousin, to keep her vigilant. But also, to the large woman with a loose mouth. "I trust you don't go near the port, Madame. You don't wish to be chased by a sentry, or shot, and fall into the ocean."

"He'll desert you when he's done with his needs, your Major," Madame Bolloré scoffed. "Men always leave. And we women are abandoned to struggle."

Norah departed, surprised by the sting of that insult. She couldn't still doubt August. Schmidt's nasty comment about her being August's whore added to her discomfort. She shook her head to clear it. Madame was understandably resentful over her husband's desertion. A coward who also abandoned his children.

Despite her effort, Norah was curious about what was happening at the harbor. And now the possibility of a special submarine? Rumors had trickled in for the past year over why the port was so carefully guarded. Her curiosity chafed to understand the reason and what troubled August.

* * *

August steered the motorcycle down the country roads, the vehicle vibrating beneath him, the engine roaring. Norah sat in the sidecar, a scarf snug over her head. They both enjoyed the fresh air on their faces.

They'd left the forger in Quimper where she had her picture taken, given information, and a new identity card and passport were being prepared.

Around a bend, armed soldiers blocked the road. When August slowed the motorcycle, the soldiers thrust Gewehr 24 rifles into their faces.

August stopped the vehicle and thrust up his hand, stifling a prickle of anger. "*Halt mal!* Stop this at once. Lower those weapons." He reached for his identity card. Norah shrank down in the car, her hands gripped together.

A young officer strode over. "Where are you going? Who are you? Get off that motorcycle so we can search."

"I'm Major von Gottlieb, Captain. This is my fiancée, Fräulein Cooper." August flashed his identity card in the officer's face. He had to use her real name since she didn't yet have her new identity. "What is this about?"

The captain stuck out his arm. "Heil Hitler, Herr Major. I apologize for the misunderstanding. There has been resistance activity and an attack on a German naval officer in Bordeaux. Over fifty hostages have been captured and executed. More are planned. We are on guard for French citizens who are undermining the Occupation."

"Your diligence is appreciated." August smoothed down his despair at the executions. "You realize I'm the commandant of this Southern Finistère region. We've had little such activity." And he hoped he'd never be put in such a position.

"We are proud to serve you, sir." The captain grinned. "You have big news in Saint Guénolé, *ja*?"

"Which won't be discussed. I will continue my journey. Carry on, men." August revved the engine. The U-boat had only been in port a few days, but the region already buzzed with rumors. Hopefully, Norah did not understand their exchange in German.

At the cottage, August rubbed Norah's shoulders, then the small of her back. "I hope the ride wasn't too rough for you. A car was impossible to requisition this time."

"I'm fine. Our child will be strong, like his father." She nestled her spine into his hand. "What did those soldiers want?"

"Just checking identities, a little coarse in manner as you saw." He smiled to mask his anxiety.

She looked at him with skepticism but said nothing.

Then she ran fingers through her hair and studied her travel documents. The identification card and passport were still with the forger as it awaited the development of her photograph. "This looks very official. Will your Captain Schmidt believe my sudden change to Swiss ancestry?"

"He'll have no choice." Something in her tone made him uneasy. "Has he bothered you?"

She fell silent, head bowed, and he had his answer. His voice grew somber. "Need I speak to him?"

"*Mais non.*" She turned away. "I took care of it. I don't think he'll approach me again."

August thought of Schmidt's hand, now in a cast, bones broken. Surely Norah had nothing to do with that.

"If he says anything to you, you must tell me." He clasped her hand and led her to the sofa where they sat.

She hesitated. "I said I wouldn't… yet I suppose I should." Her sigh was deep. "But you can't retaliate, please. He came here the evening of the tavern fight and said lewd things to me." Her voice choked. "He refused to leave, so I smashed his hand with a cast-iron skillet."

August's fury burned, blazing through his veins. "He came here? What sort of things did he say to you?"

"It doesn't matter. I didn't mean to hit him so hard, but the heavy pan got away from me." She laid her fingers on his thigh. "Please, do nothing. Captain Schmidt didn't harm me."

"But you kept this from me." August fought the urge to find Schmidt and break his other hand, or far worse. "We agreed to be honest with one another."

"I didn't want you to kill him and jeopardize yourself." Her eyes pleaded with him. "We have plans, a future."

"You never fail to surprise me. Yes, we must preserve our plans." He pulled back his ire and squeezed her hand. He *would* deal with Schmidt. "When we receive the finished documents, you must prepare to go to Switzerland as soon as I can arrange a train ticket."

"I'm not leaving you." She stared him straight in the eyes, mouth firm. "Don't ask me to. I'm staying and traveling with you when the time comes."

His request to retire might take months. By then she'd be large with child, a victim of harassment. "Everything has changed. It could become dangerous here, so you're better off safely away."

"Does it have to do with the celebrating sailors?" Her voice lowered. "Everyone is talking about it."

"What are they saying?" His hackles rose. Zeigler's men were sloppy with their tongues. He must speak with him again.

She took a slow breath. "Something about a submarine at the new port."

He closed his eyes and cursed. Of course, the rumors would fly now that the U-boat had arrived. He should have moved the villagers away from the coast, but his compassion had gotten the better of him. He'd once hoped the U-boat would prove a mistake and never be viable.

Gazing at her again, he spoke softly. "Please, Norah, could you agree with me on this one thing, leaving soon for Switzerland?"

She embraced him; her scent, like sultry exotic nights, filling his senses, her lips soft on his cheek. "I beg you, don't ask me to leave. I want to help. Whatever it is, where I can. And be a comfort to you."

"You are the most stubborn woman. But be aware, I will change your mind later. We must think of the baby." He buried his face in her hair, blown loose and fragrant from the wind, and wouldn't admit he relished having her close, in his arms each night. But how to keep her safe? And dare he confess his plan for disabling the U-boat? She still seemed to keep secrets from him.

Chapter Forty

Norah studied the painting of Angelique and Jean at the church as she sat in her cousin's garden. She had the feeling she was wrapping things up quickly, time was short, and she needed to finish what she'd started. She put away her brushes and recalled that day, nearly four months before, when she'd made the sketch. Then her rush to August to save Jean from the sentry on the beach. How her life had changed since then. "I'm finished."

"Let me see." Jean jumped up and peered over her shoulder. "I am a handsome one."

"You are. I decided to have the church more faded in the background, and you and your sister in sharp focus in the center." Norah liked the effect that made the church impressionistic, and Angelique's blonde waves a contrast to Jean's ebony hair.

Angelique joined her brother. "It's beautiful. You will be famous someday."

Norah smiled at the child. She'd rather hover in the background until settled in Switzerland. Would the war be over? Her family safe in England? Her baby nestled in her arms? And, of course, August by her side, sharing their love. She forced down her worries.

Jean checked the vegetable garden, the carrots they'd planted. Bright green feathery tops pushed out from the soil. Soon they'd harvest them. The chickens clucked and rustled next door in Madame Bolloré's yard. The stench from their pens often drifted over on an inopportune breeze.

"How do you like school?" Norah asked, packing up her paint kit.

"I like mathematics. If I'm allowed to work as a carpenter, it will come in handy," Jean replied, his gaze hopeful. His father could compel him to toil in his butcher shop.

"I like math, too." Angelique smiled. "And drawing, like you. But I draw gowns."

Norah stared in surprise. "I had no idea. You must show me your drawings."

Angelique fanned out her threadbare skirt. "I'd like to fashion clothes in Paris."

If elegant clothes were still being created in the occupied city. She hoped both children could achieve their goals. "Where have you seen any fashion drawings?"

"Someone left a *Vogue* magazine in the church," Angelique whispered as if it was a sin. "I traced the pictures."

"She's not too bad," Jean affirmed in his big brother voice. "She needs colored pencils."

"I'll lend you some of mine." Norah's throat thickened at their sweet innocence, and that the war wouldn't destroy their futures.

"Clothes have less pockets to save material, slimmer skirts, too. Wool and silk is only for the military," Angelique said.

Did the trends mention the cotton pads women wore pinned under their arms to preserve their clothes?

The back gate opened. Norah turned to see Yann standing there, his glare unnerving.

Norah took a quick breath. She emptied the cup of water she'd used into the soil.

"Children, go inside," Yann ordered as he stalked across the garden.

Angelique looked at Norah with sympathy, then did as her father asked. Jean flashed an apologetic smile and followed his sister.

Norah stiffened her back. "Good afternoon, Yann. How are you?"

Yann came to stand beside the chair where she sat. "I know there's something dangerous down at the port. A weapon, an undersea boat, given the rumors." His words clipped out in hostility.

She stood, case in hand. "I wanted to finish the painting of Jean and Angelique. It came out well." She held it up, but his expression didn't soften. "I must return home now."

"Don't avoid this. Those German friends of yours have closely guarded that port, constructed a dome to house something treacherous." He practically growled. "What is there?"

She again met his angry stare. "I truly don't know." But she *wanted* to know. She, too, feared a unique type of submarine.

"You're lying. You sleep with the commandant and you know nothing?" He loomed over her in his usual meaty stink, his lank hair falling against his bony cheeks. "You bring danger to us by being here. After this, you should stay away."

"I have no intention of bringing danger. I'm sorry you think so." She thought of Loeiza, and her embroidered messages. Did Yann know about that? She handed him the painting. "Please give this to Loeiza as a gift. *Bonjour.*"

He grabbed her arm as she tried to pass. "Stop acting stupid. What are those bastards Boche doing at the port? What disaster is awaiting us?"

"I don't have any details. I'm not in league with the enemy. It could put you in danger to know what's there." She pulled her arm free and fought a tremble.

"You've been nothing but problems. A loose woman from the beginning. *Femmes* should be docile and obedient. Don't come back here. I forbid it!" Yann shouted. The chickens next door flapped their wings in distress. "And the Boche better never come near my family, or they'll pay."

"That's your prerogative. Stay safe by remaining away from the port and minding your own business where that's concerned." Norah hurried from the garden, ears ringing. Yann swore he no longer supported the Résistance, but did he suspect his wife?

Sorrow filled Norah that she was now banned; though she'd have to say goodbye to the children and Loeiza anyway when she left the village.

One thing was for certain, she would demand that August tell her the truth about what *thing* had arrived at their harbor. Or would he just reiterate that she travel to Switzerland at once?

September was waning, her pregnancy close to eight weeks. Was she making matters worse by insisting on staying close to him? She yearned for them to travel together before her belly became obvious.

Also tumbling through her brain—she had the perfect idea of how to aid the Résistance and not make it obvious. Yann's denunciation and rejection spurred her on. She needed to assist the anti-war effort. Otherwise, she'd feel a further traitor to England.

* * *

The men clattered down a ladder into the dim, gray tube. Ziegler proudly pointed out the various compartments. Bauer stepped easily through the raised, round separation hatch of each compartment, a process for sealing in case of leaks.

August, at over six feet tall, had to duck as they moved through the engine room, over a narrow bridge between two huge diesel tanks, the control room, officers' quarters, electric and diesel engines, and battery compartments. The crew's tight quarters, where torpedoes were stored between the bunks. Most areas were breath-sucked-in narrow, others a larger space. The torpedo tubes fore and aft. The tower or superstructure with its periscopes, antennae, and anti-aircraft guns mounted on top. So much steel, gears, dials and pipes, most painted pale green with the vital parts bright red. The sub smelled of metal, oil, and men in too-close quarters. Such perilous power!

The U-boat's captain, a compact man of average features, frowned, as if he resented any army personnel in his territory, and said little.

"I am so excited to be a part of this." Ziegler barely stepped over the hatches without stumbling on his chunky legs. "Magnificent. *Herrlich!*"

"I wish the Führer was here." Schmidt swaggered along. "He'd take notice of our good works at the port. Then he would see what my contribution is to the Reich."

August bit his tongue, stuffing down his irritation. The idiot acted like he did everything single-handedly. He was a man who bragged to cover his lack of self-worth. August had plans for him after this tour. Plans that seared in his brain.

Back out on the deck, August took a deep breath, glad to hear the ocean under his feet—and not up the sides of a tube. They inspected the mounted, submersible deck guns, the different escape hatches, and the hatch where the U-boat took in fuel. August shared a glance with Bauer.

Once back on shore, August said to Zeigler, "We will plan our official celebration for this marvel of the Reich in a week or two." The distraction he needed. "And you must warn your men to be more inconspicuous at the tavern. There are too many rumors."

Zeigler grinned, his eyes glistening with pride. "They are young, excited. But I'll tell them."

August stepped to the side with Bauer. "You will help with the planning. Do you think we'll have what we need?"

"I believe so, Herr Major. I'll confer with you later." Bauer lowered his voice. "*Das boot* looks like a floating city, too heavy in the middle to sustain speed and maneuverability."

Bauer studied architecture in his spare time. He'd said he longed to return to Germany and help to rebuild Berlin. They all needed the war to end, the savagery to stop.

August nodded and searched the gathered men as his lieutenant left him. He spied Schmidt and approached.

"Captain, I have something to show you. Plus, other matters to discuss." August clamped his hand on Schmidt's shoulder. "Walk with me."

"I have duties…but of course, Herr Major." Schmidt looked at him with slitted eyes.

They moved past the village, along a desolate strip of land, to the point at the western tip of the Bay of Biscay, where a tall, gray column thrust into the sky.

"What did you need to speak to me about, Herr Major?" Schmidt kept his steps slow.

"You'll see." August pointed. "The *Phare d'Eckmühl* lighthouse was built in 1835, but it's been renovated and enlarged since then."

"I've seen it," Schmidt said, voice cautious. "And inspected the structure." He puffed on a cigarette as he walked.

"Surprise funds came from Adelaide-Louise Davout, the Marquise de Blocqueville. She wanted the lighthouse dedicated to her father." August squeezed his subordinate's shoulder. "He was a marshal under Napoleon, titled the Prince d'Eckmuhl, after his service in the Battle of Eckmuhl."

"This is all very interesting, but—"

"Look at the majesty of it." August swept up his hand, teeth clenching. "At 65 meters, it's one of the tallest lighthouses in the world." A structure of aid and not destruction.

"A true wonder, sir." Schmidt's shoulder muscles bunched. "I really should begin my inspection of our gun placements along the coast, as you requested."

"That can wait. The point contains the ruins of a fortified town, a strategic place from the thirteenth to sixteenth century." August tightened his hold and surveyed the flat land, indented by marshy lagoons. Sentries patrolled the coastline where barbed wire resembled crouched spiders. The ocean slurped and sucked at the land mass; the air held the sweet odor of seaweed.

"Thank you for the tour, sir." Schmidt tried to slide out from under August's grip. He dropped his cigarette and smashed it beneath his boot.

"I doubt you thank me at all. You have no respect for me or the people I care about." August leaned close, his grip firmer, fingers digging into flesh. His anger boiled up anew. "Haven't I warned you on two or three occasions to stay away from Norah?"

Schmidt snorted in his breath and touched the cast on his right hand. "I don't know what you mean."

"I think you know exactly what I mean." August bent over him. "And since my warnings have done no good, I have no choice but to defend her honor."

Schmidt struggled to thrust back his bony shoulders. "Your woman is not German. She's fortunate I haven't reported her for hitting a Nazi officer."

"I might write to your father over your crass behavior." August made it sound very casual over the roar of anger in his brain. "I hear he's quite strait-laced in certain situations. And is very fond of your wife."

Schmidt's face blanched for a moment. "You wouldn't… **Fräulein** Cooper is a slutty girl, and beneath you. She invited my attentions."

"Your words dig a deeper trench. Did you touch her?" August glared into the man's face and, by his reaction, the flash in his eyes, he knew he had. The roar increased.

Schmidt wriggled to be free. "I really must—"

"You are a pitiful man who never learns what is important. Advice has had no effect." All the revulsion toward Schmidt balled up inside him, the heat rushing into his face. August raised his fist and punched his knuckles into the captain's nose.

"Aaaah!" Schmidt cried out, eyes bulging. Blood spurted. He covered his nose.

August rubbed his stinging knuckles. "I might have to write to our superiors in Berlin about your insubordination. Your refusal to follow orders."

Head bowed, Schmidt held his nose, whimpering; blood seeped through his fingers.

"You must understand." August flexed his hand. "A man protects his fiancée's honor. In earlier times, a duel would be appropriate."

"*Eeow, scheisse*. I…understand." Schmidt groaned as more blood dripped down onto his tunic. His cast was soon stained in red. "Like my father— you berate me, punish me. I'm never good enough," he whined.

"No excuses. Work on your own character. You should put ice on that. And carry on with your inspection. But I advise you to request a transfer." August left him, allowing the breeze to cool his ire, abandoning the man to his misery. Disappointment niggled at him that he had stooped to such physical violence.

But he had a party and sabotage to plan.

Chapter Forty-one

At her request, Jean entered and brought Pichon out from the carpentry shop to Norah as the sun settled over the treetops. The smell of fresh-sawed wood followed him. "Mademoiselle Cooper, good eve to you."

Norah handed him the Reichsmarks August gave her. "There is plenty there for the little table. And extra for…to help your family get established. I'm certain you can put it to *good* use."

The funds wouldn't be for any purpose August might have planned.

Pichon's gaze narrowed, then a smile slowly spread. "Uh, I think I can employ the money effectively. *Merci.* Much is needed to be done."

Norah smiled. "I'll give what I can to help. You do have a baby on the way." This was her only means to aid the Résistance and pretend it was for other reasons. If Pichon used it for his family, or different arrangements, it was up to him. She was earning a little money from her painting. Giselle had set her up to paint her friends, who came down from the larger towns.

"I'd also like you to show Jean what you do in your shop. He's interested in carpentry."

Jean's eyes brightened at her request.

"I would be happy to." Pichon grinned at the boy. "An apprentice, of sorts. Jean can help me work on the side table tomorrow. Any interesting news I might like to hear?" He cocked his head toward the harbor.

"None that I know of. I don't bother with such things. I look forward to the table. Please don't mention Jean's assistance to his father." Norah walked away with Jean following. Guilt still nagged her for going behind August's back.

"I'll bring Monsieur Pichon any extra money from you," Jean said as they strolled. "I'm sure the Major won't want you around the carpentry shop too often."

"Are you certain you want to do that?" She hated to drag Jean into this; his father would choke her. But the boy was right about August's feelings. And Jean could further observe the work of a carpenter.

"It's support for a good friend, his family." Jean winked, swinging his arms. "And their baby, like you say."

Norah nodded and handed him four of her colored pencils. "Give these to Angelique. She must meet me somewhere to show me her drawings." She bid him good evening and ambled through the woods to her cottage. She still needed to ask August about the rumored submarine, but he'd come home moody the night before, his knuckles bruised, and wouldn't discuss it.

She had just entered and lit candles, and the oil lamp, when August thrust open the door. The stern look on his face alarmed her.

"What's wrong?" She touched his arm.

He removed his hat, brow furrowed. "Is your cousin doing something she shouldn't?"

Her stomach tightened into a fist. "I…I couldn't say."

"A man was apprehended by the Gestapo in Nantes. They have methods I don't agree with, but they forced him to give up information." August raked his fingers through his dark-blond hair, eyes sharp and worried. "Something about messages passed by embroidery on hats and napkins, aprons, with Breton words and symbols. Loeiza **Menez** was mentioned."

Norah gripped the back of the sofa, her head spinning. "*Mon Dieu*."

"Captain Schmidt is about to raid her home. Do you understand? These implications—"

"Yes!" Her energy flared. "I need to visit her. Right now."

He reached for her, as if to stop her, but she ran out the rear door. Nausea bubbled as her feet struck the ground. Footsteps sounded behind her. "Norah!" he called.

She dashed through bushes, around trees, and into the village. No soldiers were present at the cottage. Panting for breath, she didn't bother to knock and rushed into her cousin's. She bolted the door behind her.

Loeiza sat in the parlor with her daughters and Petit Yann. Fabric spread across their knees.

"What is it?" Her cousin's dark eyes widened as she laid down her sewing.

"Hide your embroidery, you're about to be raided." Norah gasped for breath, her knuckle pressed to her collarbone.

Loeiza clipped thread and hopped up. "Go fetch my little book, *ma fille*."

Angelique darted up the stairs.

Jean joined them, grabbed his little brother, and fled out the rear door.

Marie-Louise shoved the fabric under a loose board half under the sofa, and sat on the cushion, feet on the board, arms crossed.

Pounding began on the front door. Then kicking against the thick wood.

Angelique returned and paused on the stairs, a small book gripped to her chest. Norah hurried to stand in front of her. She snatched the book and shoved it down into her trousers.

"That's my code book. Protect it." Loeiza approached the door. The bolt groaned; the door creaked and splintered. Men shouted.

The door cracked and swung open, pushing Loeiza back as wood fragments flew. Norah shuddered.

Soldiers marched in with their guns raised.

"Search everywhere, tear the place apart," Captain Schmidt ordered, an incensed glint in his eyes. His glare scraped over Norah.

"Please, what are you looking for?" Loeiza asked in a sweet, nervous voice. "You've broken my bolt."

The men scattered, rushing through the rooms. Marie-Louise glowered at them and didn't move. One soldier yanked off the cushions and felt under the one the child sat on. She still didn't budge. Then he opened the sewing basket and dumped out the contents.

"Your comrade has been arrested, **Frau Menez**." Schmidt shoved his face into hers. His nose was swollen, red, crooked, and his eyes had purple bruises under them. He stank of sweat. Had August struck him? "The coward gave you up."

"I don't know what you refer to. You're frightening my children." Loeiza pursed her full lips, her head raised.

The soldiers pushed past Norah and stomped up the stairs.

Norah pressed on the front of her trousers. Angelique huddled beside her.

"I'm going to be sick." Norah fought the bile in her throat. She knew she had to leave, hide the book, before they were personally searched.

Schmidt strutted before her, but he looked unsure. "Are you involved, Cooper?"

Boots tromped overhead; doors slammed. Drawers sounded jerked out.

"I have no idea why you're here." Norah struggled to swallow. Her stomach churned. God, keep her baby safe. "No one in this house has done anything wrong."

Angelique pressed against Norah, sniffing loudly, tossing her hair in melodrama. "I'm frightened."

Loeiza pushed up to them and grasped her daughter's hand. "We are innocent, captain, so leave my home."

"I'm about to be sick." Norah cupped her mouth and wriggled past Schmidt, gulping in exaggeration. She hurried out the rear door. He didn't stop her.

The garden was blanketed in shadow, the sun nearly set. She rushed to the little back gate and slipped out. She ran down the alley, heart thumping in her ears, one hand holding the book in place.

Lungs heaving, she couldn't decide where to go. She reached the beach where the last of the sun's rays lit the sand. The ocean bashed the shore, leaving foamy streaks. Someone shouted nearby and began to chase her. Nerves taut, she dashed along the top of the beach. The Weeping Castle ruins, *Le Château des Pleurs*, were an outline down to the right. The place where Jean had run that day when the sentry grabbed him.

A bullet fired, whizzed past her, and she cried out, nearly tripping. One way blocked, she ducked and scrambled toward *Le Château des Pleurs*. The tide was rising. She splashed between the ruin's columns, the water cold on her feet. Dragging out the book, she searched, then shoved it into a niche far above her head. Dust and rubble sprinkled down on her. More sounds of gunshots. She pressed against a crumbling wall, the stench of mildew. Caressing her belly, her body shook—she must protect the life growing inside her. Chilly water swirled around her ankles.

* * *

"*Halt.* Hold your fire." August reached the sentry on the beach, his breath painful in his chest. "That woman is under my protection, and she panicked after the captain's raid on her cousin's house."

"Of course, Herr Major." The young man lowered his rifle. "I apologize."

August ran down the sand. Had a bullet hit Norah? *Gott bewahre.* She should never have run off. He cursed. Everything he cherished could be wiped away.

Fear curdled in his throat. She seemed to have entered the ruin.

He slowed when he reached it, gripping a column, and softly called her name. "It's me, *liebchen.* You're safe now."

No answer. He splashed into the ruin. Too many shadows loomed. "Norah. Are you hurt?"

A dark form huddled in a corner. "August? I'm not hurt."

He sloshed over and pulled her into his arms. "What were you thinking? Why did you run?" He kissed her forehead as she shuddered. Relief coursed through him, though scolding her for her rash behavior pushed at his lips. "Did you know about your cousin's activity?"

"I only had suspicions." Her chest heaved. "Will they arrest her?"

"Schmidt will question her, but if they find no proof…" August hugged Norah closer, his life's blood in the beat of her heart. "I'll do what I can. Are you feeling all right? You must agree to leave for Switzerland now."

"I'm all right. Please, be kind to my cousin." She buried her face in his tunic. "I don't know. I might…agree to go."

"*Bitte*. Please." He brushed his hand through her hair as the tide lapped his boots. He tipped up her head and kissed her lips. Stubborn woman, he'd make certain she boarded the train. His love for her enveloped him, along with his anxiety for her and their child. She must leave before he and Bauer disabled the U-boat.

Chapter Forty-two

August flung his hat onto the chair in his office. Three days after the raid, he'd received Norah's identity papers and passport with photographs. She was on the verge of consenting to go when the French Résistance bombed the railroad tracks out of Quimper. It would take well over a week to repair.

With the increased petrol shortage, and further restrictions, he couldn't drive her all the way to Rennes to catch another train. He must keep her sheltered here, at the cottage. Her nearly being shot haunted his thoughts.

"Herr Major." Private Fritz appeared in the open doorway, cowlick bobbing in his blond hair. He held out a paper. "I have a message from Lt. Bauer."

August took the paper. "I cannot believe this." He slapped it with his hand. "Bauer had an accident." Visiting an uncle stationed at Lorient, he'd crashed his bicycle on a rough road and broken his ankle. What more could go wrong? August crumpled the paper.

"I'm sorry to hear that. I like the lieutenant." Fritz watched him carefully. He hovered on the perimeter of August's plans, but he served honestly and was always discreet. "I managed to obtain the schnapps for the celebration, sir."

"*Danke*. You're a good man, Fritz. You may go." August turned to the little table near the wall and crammed fifteen puzzle pieces, the last ones, into the *Luncheon at the Boating Party*.

The picture was serene, joyful, far from what he felt. His body tightened like a mangled rope. Now he must be the one to pour debris into the fuel line.

The party was in two days. Sausage and sauerkraut would be served, along with apple strudel, a taste of the homeland. A roaring bonfire, and more schnapps to douse the sailors.

Restless with frustration, he abandoned the office, walked to the stables, saddled Maler, and took a long gallop through the woods. The scent of trees, the rush of air, helped to clear his mind. The feel of horse, the warm animal scent, and firm muscles beneath him served as a distraction.

He turned Maler around, rode to the cottage, and tethered his horse near the front door. Stroking Maler's velvet nose and fine muscled neck, he entered to see Norah with her young cousin, Jean.

"Thank you, Major, for helping my mother." Jean grinned, then left out the rear door.

Schmidt had questioned Frau Menez, but since no evidence was discovered, August insisted she be released. He still had not found the reason Norah escaped to the beach. She'd told him she was merely afraid and confused.

"I gave Jean some money for his family. The children need clothes. I finished another portrait for the mayor's wife's friends." At a snort from outside, Norah glanced toward the open front window. "You brought your horse. Will we go for a ride?" She approached and put her arms around his neck. "What's wrong, *mon amor*? You look disturbed."

He kissed her forehead. They sat on the sofa as he cradled her hand in his. Her nearness soothed him. "I have so much I should explain…"

"Is it to do with what is happening at the port?" Her green eyes were full of concern. "The rumored undersea boat?"

August pressed her hand to his heart. "I've been reluctant, *and* trying to keep you safe. But things have changed." He explained about the monstrosity of a U-boat, its ugly purpose, and the plan he and Lt. Bauer had concocted. Then Bauer's broken ankle.

Norah's eyes grew huge. "The boat sounds horrible and should be stopped. No wonder it's been kept secret. And poor Lt. Bauer. What will you do now?"

He glanced away, then back. "I have no choice but to sabotage the line myself."

"*Mais non*, please! Anything terrible could happen." She pulled her hand free and gripped his upper arms, her gaze frantic. "You can't do this. Put it off. I can't live—"

"Norah, *liebling,* it's what I must do. To deter the advance of the Nazis on your country. To ruin Hitler's schemes." August eased her face to his, his thumbs caressing her cheeks as she trembled. He might sacrifice everything he held dear, including his life. "I'm sorry. This is the only way. I'll be careful. But the killing machine must be stopped."

* * *

From the open front door, Norah watched August ride off, her body tangled with a fear she'd never experienced before. The panic of losing him; just when she was getting over her agonizing incident on the beach.

They had argued for a half hour over his determination to ruin the fuel line. She drooped in defeat. His intentions were honorable, but if he were caught, he'd be executed. And if not for the rail-line bombing, she might have been halfway to Switzerland.

Someone moved near the hedge. She started, then Jean emerged. "I went to pet the horse, but I heard you talking through the window. The major is so brave. I knew he was a good man. What a fat demon the U-boat must be!"

"Bloody hell." Norah dragged him into the cottage and wanted to shake him. "You should not have listened. You can't mention this to anyone. Promise me. You'll risk his life."

"You know I'm a skilled operative." Jean lifted his head, body at attention.

Did he think this a game? Despite all warnings, one night Jean had sneaked to the ruin and retrieved the code book. It should be destroyed. Hopefully, Loeiza would stop her messaging now that her contact was captured.

Norah gave Jean a severe stare; this child who strived to be a man. "I know you are skilled. But don't you dare go near the harbor. I'm begging you. Take the money to Pichon, hurry."

"I'm at your service. I'll do what's needed. This is my war, too." Jean dashed off into the forest like a long-legged deer before she could warn him again. Would he ever curb his impulsiveness?

Norah shut the door and hiccupped a sob from deep inside her. Her eyes blurred with tears. She felt so helpless. How could she stop August? Was there still a chance? She could be a widow before she was a wife. She caressed her abdomen. A woman with a baby and no father. A man she loved beyond reason.

* * *

Colonel Burmester settled in the chair across the desk from August, late the next day. "You had another incident in this village, Herr Major. Military Command is *not* pleased."

August strained to give him an attentive concerned frown. This surprise visit threatened his plans. "We searched the suspect's home, and nothing was found. Captain Schmidt can give you the full report. The man in Nantes lied. He must be protecting someone else."

"Madame Menez is but a woman of little education, I surmise. However, word has it that matters are too *friendly* out here." Burmester leaned forward in the chair, his voice stern, medals clinking on his gray-green tunic. "Changes need to be made. Especially after the explosion at the manor house, with no one yet punished. Harsher conditions must be applied."

"We nearly caught the Maquis perpetrator at the farmhouse raid. But I'm glad you brought up the subject." August made a point of sighing and shaking his head. "My eyesight is failing. I have a doctor's report. I have put in my retirement papers for the good of the Reich. Sent by courier yesterday. I will retire to Berlin, or rather my hometown of Jüterbog, near my family." He rolled a pen on his desk, pushing hard. He would stop to collect his son, then see his family before continuing to Alpnachstad, a village near Lake Lucerne where he already had made inquiries into purchasing a cottage.

Norah should be safely there when he arrived.

"You're a man of impeccable character, but that's not an asset these days. You plan to leave so soon?" The colonel leaned back, gaze piercing. "Interesting. Who would you recommend replacing you, if you had the choice?"

"I would recommend Lt. Bauer. He should be promoted to captain. At the present, he's in Lorient recuperating from a broken ankle, but also inspecting the important shipyard there. He's intelligent and pragmatic." August gave a look of disappointment. "Captain Schmidt, I'm afraid, is too volatile to be in command. He doesn't follow orders."

"Captain Schmidt has requested to be transferred to Paris." Burmester laced his fingers together in his lap. "We have decided to approve it. To keep an eye on him. His SS father has insisted as well." Burmester tapped his palms on his thigh. "Why haven't you moved these villagers farther from the vital port here? Weren't you warned?"

"At first, I didn't wish to cause suspicions in the surrounding area of what was about to happen. The villagers hadn't given me much trouble. If I made a mistake, I regret it and apologize, sir." August smiled sadly for emphasis. "My diminished vision has caused severe headaches as well. I won't stand in the way of success for the Führer."

"I understand." Burmester nodded. "You want the best for our mission."

"Precisely." August hoped Bauer could take command and leave the village and its people intact. And Schmidt sent to Paris? A boon for him. But Burmester might still complicate matters. "Do you plan to stay for the celebration tomorrow night?" The night of September 28th, as planned with Bauer.

"*Nein*. I'm merely passing through on my way to Brest. Taking care of business along the way. I glimpsed the U-boat; she is magnificent." He grinned for the first time, which tightened the jowls on his handsome face. "But first, you must show me how your horse is doing? I purchased one of my own, a fine animal. I cannot wait to bring the stallion home to Munich for my little grandchildren to admire."

"I'd be honored to show you my horse, sir." August stood, relieved the colonel wouldn't be here tomorrow—and hopeful the Gestapo might not question *him*. Though after the sabotage, the Nazi's terrifying police could be swarming the village.

August had gone over the plans and all that could go wrong in his mind until it felt like his brain had split in two. But dangers like this could always lurk. He crushed on his hat. "Let's go to the stables, sir. I think you will be impressed."

Chapter Forty-three

In front of the cottage's empty fireplace, Norah dug the rag into the tan shoe polish, realized she had too much, scraped some back in the can, then inhaled slowly as she braced herself. Tonight, the celebration, and August risking his life.

This was why he wanted her gone from the village. If she traveled when the tracks were repaired, she would be ten weeks along, too soon to show—so she wouldn't have to pretend to be married when her identity card said otherwise. Would her lover be close behind? Apprehension juddered her every nerve.

She polished her scuffed Oxford shoes, hard, then the wooden soles recently glued on due to the scarcity of leather. The military needed it for combat boots. She'd clop around like a horse.

Why couldn't she stop him? Find an underling to destroy the sub. August should be safe with her. She was tempted to attend the party, but that would make him more agitated. He needed his wits about him for this horribly dangerous mission.

The sharp smell of polish made her nauseous. Her morning sickness was still a problem.

A knock on the front door. She jumped and fisted the rag. Peeking out the window, she saw Giselle. Damn, why was she here?

She opened the door. "*Bonjour*, what can I do for you?"

"I'm sorry to bother you. I have another request for a portrait. And news of me. Nothing to do with—

what you don't wish to talk about." The woman had dark circles under her eyes.

Norah sighed and let her in. "Would you like tea?" She had to do something to keep busy.

"No, *merci*." Giselle set down a note with a name scribbled on it on the kitchen table. "My old friend will be in the village tomorrow, on her way to Dournenez on the north coast, where her daughter lives. We're old friends—I said that already—and she wanted to visit me." Giselle stared about, wringing her hands.

"Thank you. I'll be pleased to draw her portrait. You said you had news about you?" The woman's uneasy behavior made Norah more unsettled.

Giselle met her eyes. "I'm leaving at the end of the week. Leaving my husband." She shrugged. "It was inevitable. He's so drunk, he probably won't notice, though I did tell him."

"Are you serious? Where will you go?" Norah swiped a clean rag over her fingers' tan stains.

"To Paris. To visit my sister and brother. We…plan to start a business." Giselle cocked her head. "I created my own travel pass. You won't want the details."

Resistance work. Norah nodded. "Are you certain about the tea or coffee?"

"I'm certain. I plan for a legal separation from Ropars. You know we Catholics frown on divorce." Giselle gave a brittle laugh. She hugged Norah. "I'm happy your cousin is…doing well. I must go. Good luck to you, *ma chérie*. I pray your future with August will be joyful."

"And much luck to you. Find someone worth your love. Be careful, or as careful as you can." Norah returned the hug, her own fears surging over her like an avalanche. Her knees felt like jelly. This evening would seem endless—but she flushed from her mind that it could be the end for August.

The flames lapped high in the darkening sky. Stars flickered out one by one.

"We are proud Germans tonight." Ziegler raised his glass of apple schnapps. "To *das boot*. The triumphs to come for the Third Reich."

The sailors laughed and patted shoulders, raising their glasses. They had gobbled up the hearty German food provided. The pungent aroma of sauerkraut mixed with the smoky scent of the fire.

August ate little, his stomach in a vise. He sipped the sweet, potent schnapps sparingly. Schmidt was not present, planning his assigned move to Paris, no doubt. Or was he watching from a distance?

Yesterday, long after Burmester departed, British Commandos flew an overnight raid on Saint-Aubin-d'Arquenay, in occupied France. About four hundred forty kilometers northeast of **Saint Guénolé. Where would they strike next? He wanted the allies to succeed, but not destroy France in the process. His homeland, his family, suffered enough in this senseless war.**

August turned to Private Fritz. He'd asked him earlier to watch out for Norah if anything happened to him. To get her on the train to the east. He moved to the edge of the firelight with his secretary. "Be sure to tell anyone who asks I had to find relief from too much indulgence. You're better off not knowing any more."

"*Natürlich*, of course, Major." Fritz looked distressed, his glasses fogged by the smoke, but asked no questions. When the war ended, this dependable young man should join his father in making wine and find a nice girl to marry.

Oberleutnant Krause resembled a statue near the fire, no enjoyment on his severe face. The pale, ghost-like Corporal Flach was among the revelers. He smiled at August and lifted his glass. August must slip away from his steely gaze.

Stepping farther across the grass, August removed his tunic and hat in the deeper shadows, tucking them under a bush. The air was cooler as October was almost upon them. He gripped the sack of granules he'd hidden there and crept toward the concrete dome. He'd managed to find sugar and metal shavings to add to the sand. Bauer insisted sugar would be more effective.

Something moved in the bushes. This could be it, a bullet in the back. His neck prickled. Silence followed. An animal, hopefully. He continued his soft steps, listening to the songs and laughter in the background. Ziegler's booming, bragging voice.

Some sailors sang, "Heil Hitler Dir!" or *Hail Hitler to Thee*. A song composed for Hitler's birthday in 1937. Tragic, to worship a vicious dictator. To his government, tonight was treason, but to the world, August was fostering peace. This was not the army he had signed up for.

Down the stairs and feet from the bunker, he watched the sentry march away on his duty. He would walk to the far end of the port, then return. August had fifteen minutes.

He inched to the dome and around to the front and lifted the netting over the gape of a cave. Soon this opening would be covered by lifting shutters, still being built.

A noise, a shadow, then a touch on his arm. He recoiled, grabbed a small wrist, and jerked a body to him.

"It's me, Major, Jean Menez," the boy hissed. "I'll take the sack and crawl up on the deck."

"You'll do nothing of the sort. How did you know?" His anger flamed as he stared at the child, barely visible in the dark. "What the hell are you doing here?"

"I'm small, I can help. Let me do it." Jean reached for the sack.

"Did Norah put you up to this?"

"No, she'd never allow it." The boy tugged at the sack.

"Get out of here, now," he growled in a whisper. The crash of waves further dimmed their voices.

"You need to rejoin the fire. People will notice. No one will notice me."

"I'll have you arrested. You'll be sent to a labor camp if you're caught." August lied to scare him off.

"Shh, someone is coming." Jean stared behind him.

August turned. The child snatched the sack and dashed away into the dome.

Gott verdammt! He listened, music from a guitar, shouts of humor, more laughter and singing. He slipped inside the bunker. Jean had vanished. He couldn't yell for the boy. But if anything happened to him…

He heard movement on the U-boat, light, like a loping cat. How did Jean know where the fuel hatch was?

August wanted to go after him, every muscle cried out to move, but he stood lookout instead. How many more minutes? What excuse? The entire scheme could come hurtling down on him. Now he must protect this child.

The squeak of a hatch opening; then a pressurized hatch was beneath. The sound of a wheel turning. The singing of sailors on the briny wind. Ziegler's loud laughter. August clenched his hands. He listened for the returning sentry.

He was about to step up onto the deck to grab the boy when metal clicked, another squeak. A shadow shuffled across and down the ladder.

"It's done," Jean gushed out.

August snatched his arm and yanked him from the dome and up, along the grass. They reached the bushes. "I won't ask this moment how you knew where to place the material. But you're certain you did?"

"*Mais oui.*" Jean panted beside him. "It was the right hole. And I closed it properly."

Bootsteps came from the bonfire. August dragged the boy deeper into the foliage, his hands scratched in brambles. They hovered, his pulse thumping in his brain. He held Jean so tightly, the boy grunted. A sound of someone urinating close, the unpleasant acidic smell, and the hum of celebrating men in the background.

The person staggered off. August hauled Jean behind the gorse a few more steps along, listening, then released him. "Get out of here. Go home. I'll deal with you later."

Jean saluted, sprinted over the grass, disappearing toward the village.

August groped under foliage for his tunic, then swept it up and buttoned the garment. His belt secured, he put on his hat, battling to contain his anger, his confused elation. *Had* the boy succeeded? He wiped a handkerchief over his face, then brushed leaves from his hands and tunic. The scratches stung.

After walking five steps, a sentry rushed up to him, rifle on his shoulder. "Herr Major, what are you doing out here?"

"I was taking care of business. The schnapps and sausage did not agree with me." August rubbed his stomach and made a grumbling noise. "Is everything under control? No problems?"

"*Jawohl*, sir. I hope you feel better." The young man stood at attention.

"A little better, thank you. You're a good man to be vigilant." August pasted on a smile and strolled toward the bonfire. The little renegade better have been successful.

Chapter Forty-four

Norah walked through the small carpentry shop where furniture, sabots, and toys waited to be finished. The scent of wood pleased her, and she no longer cared who saw her here. August trusted her and soon she would be gone from the village. Still, many tribulations lay ahead.

Pichon's assistant hammered in light taps on a wardrobe in the corner. Jean kneeled by a little table, sanding on the rough wood.

Pichon joined her. "You see, your cousin learns well. When he can get away, I'll teach him the sawing and cutting process later."

"I'm grateful to you. A shame his father won't support his ambition." She handed Pichon several coins. "This is from a hasty sketch I did of Giselle's friend a half hour ago. She didn't want a painting."

"Anything to help is appreciated." He shoved the coins in his pocket. Her last donation to the resistance. Relief and sadness intermixed. They moved away from Jean.

"I will have to leave soon, though won't say where or why. I'm sorry I can't stay around to help with…your family." She smiled, though fought a yawn at her lack of sleep. A yawn that slid over her anxiety. "It has been nice to know you."

"And I you. I pray you'll be safe wherever you're going." Pichon limped to the open front of his shop, where the morning light slanted in. "Ugh. My leg is painful today. Are you aware Giselle Ropars is leaving, too? The village won't be the same, and our efforts more difficult. I wish I could send my wife and soon to be child away. But this is our home. Do you know Pierre and Erwan Kerguelen's sister? She's taking over Madame Giselle's duties."

"I don't really know her." Norah recalled the young woman who jerked on her hair and slapped her after her brother's execution. Now she would be the forger. "I wish her luck."

"I heard there was a wild celebration at the harbor last evening." Pichon shrugged. "Were you there?"

She didn't dare ask, but struggled not to, if there'd been an alarm raised at the port this morning. It needed to be over—August *couldn't* try again.

"I would never celebrate with the Nazis." Norah had puddled in relief when August returned late last night. When she had asked questions, he refused to speak of what happened, other than it was completed. He had held her tight in bed and murmured endearments in his raspy-edged voice, his peppery-scented cologne invading her senses. She'd shivered in happiness, though now the realization of loss seeped in at saying goodbye until he could join her.

Jean hopped to his feet. "Do you like my work? I'm quick at whatever I do. And learn fast because I pay attention." An aura hung around him she could not define.

"It's an excellent job. I want you to give the table to your mother as a gift." Norah pressed Pichon's arm, then signaled for Jean to follow her out. She picked up the paint kit she'd left outside the shop. "Walk with me to your home and ask your mother and siblings to come to the square."

"I'm sorry for you to leave." Jean matched her steps, dark eyes alight. "Wherever you go, I hope we'll see you again."

"I hope for that, too." She touched the boy's cheek. "And you should be less boastful in this environment."

Madame Bolloré hustled out of the boulangerie, a loaf of bread tucked under her arm. The white-snake Corporal Flach sauntered from the alley. "I'll take that loaf, egg-lady."

When he reached for it, she smacked his hand away. "You'll do no such thing. Mind your manners."

He stared at her in surprise, rubbing his hand. Then he grimaced. "I could have you arrested. You villagers won't be protected much longer."

Madame huffed and swept off, past the stone cottages with chalky-blue shutters. "He wouldn't be bad looking if he wasn't so pallid and vile," the woman grumbled.

Flach, the resident bully, enjoyed any torment. Norah gripped Jean's shoulder, and they quickly approached his cottage. The tabby cat perched on the edge of the well watched him scurry inside.

Five minutes later, Loeiza came out wearing her apron, and carrying Petit Yann. Angelique and Marie-Louise followed behind.

Norah handed Angelique the paint kit and kissed her cheek. "This is for you to create pretty gowns. I'll buy another when I'm settled elsewhere."

"*Merci*." Angelique's eyes moistened with tears. "I'm so pleased. And sad. I'll miss you."

Loeiza hugged her older daughter. "She'll be a fine artist. I hate to say goodbye, Norah, but I know it's best for you." Petit Yann wriggled in her arms.

Norah patted Marie-Louise on the head. "And you keep up the good work of protecting your family."

"I will." Marie-Louise gave her a ghost of a smile. "Safe journey."

Loeiza caressed her younger daughter's dark hair. "She will always be brave."

Norah cupped Petit Yann's chin. "You grow up to be a compassionate man." He giggled.

Loeiza set her son on his feet. She embraced Norah in a scented waft of carrot and onion soup.

"I've given up on espionage. Too close for comfort. I must think of my children."

"Where did you obtain so much information to pass on?" Norah whispered.

"The tavern keeper's wife is part of my sewing circle. She listened in on the drunken soldiers and sailors. They didn't know she's from Alsace, near the German border, and understands German." Loeiza sighed. "And I apologize for the way Yann spoke to you. He's been more agitated lately."

Norah squeezed her cousin close, a lump in her throat. "Don't worry about that. I should be in another country by next week. I love you so much; and thank you for housing me for the past year. Your compassion was invaluable."

Loeiza held her at arm's length, her brown eyes tearful. "I'll light a candle that all goes well for you. And your man. Your relationship seems true and loving. I envy it."

Madame Bolloré hovered in her front door, watching. Children, like chicks, clustered about her skirt, or peered over her shoulder. She slowly nodded to Norah.

Norah waved, then gave Loeiza a kiss. "I'll write if I can. Take care of yourself. *Au revoir*, children." She walked away, swallowing back her emotions.

"Wait." Jean followed her over the cobbles. "I don't know if this matters," he whispered. "But Papa just got a pistol. He hid it, but I saw the gun. I don't know what he plans."

Norah cringed, uneasiness creeping through her. What would Yann plan? She must warn August. Yann was a bigger fool than she thought to put his family in this danger.

* * *

August signed to approve payroll then sifted through scribbled budget plans and other documents at his desk. More ridiculous restrictions. Hitler claiming success even while he failed. The Nazis captured Kiev, and fighting continued in Greece. The United States ordered an all-out war on any Axis shipping in American waters. More Jews sent to death camps, euphemistically referred to as labor camps. This last part sickened him, as it was the most horrific. Did the outside world know?

He slapped the dispatches onto his desk. Train service should be repaired by next Wednesday. Norah *would* be on the train, but he had to stay behind for official approval papers to retire. Anxiousness sparking, he waited for news from last night. Had Jean triumphed?

At 11 o'clock, there was a commotion out front. Port captain Ziegler knocked then loomed in the doorway, his face blood-red and sweating. "*Mein Gott*, Major, something terrible has happened."

"Herr Ziegler, sit, please; you look ill." August put on his best shocked face and adjusted the chair in front of his desk. "Fritz, bring coffee!"

Ziegler plopped into the chair, swiping a handkerchief over his brow.

Fritz rushed in with a cup of coffee and handed it to the port captain, then departed. Ziegler's hand shook. The button that strained over his belly was missing.

"Tell me what has happened?" August's heartbeat tripled as he sat on the edge of his desk.

"We discovered…no, the engineers on the U-boat did, after the engines were sputtering. They're damaged. Men spent hours trying to find the problem." Ziegler drank from the cup, sloshing coffee over the brim.

"Dreadful. Did they locate the complication?" August crossed and gripped his arms.

"*Ja*, it seems somehow that sand and sugar were put in the fuel and oil line." Ziegler patted the cup drips with his handkerchief. "How could this happen?"

"Sand and sugar? That sounds dangerous." August tightened his fingers on his arms and silently thanked Jean. "A travesty, *donnerwetter*!"

"The sugar could clog up everything. There were also metal scraps. Cruel sabotage!" Ziegler thrust up a finger. "It must have happened during the party. Your *Oberleutnant* Krause is as baffled, in his laconic way, as I am."

"Can they clean up the lines, repair the engines?" August hoped this would prove impossible. But he put alarm into his question, and concern in his expression.

"We don't know yet. It doesn't look good. An engineer who helped design it is driving up from St-Nazaire." Ziegler slurped down his coffee, then thumped the chair arm. "So much work destroyed. New engines could be installed. But that might not be enough. And will take forever. We must find and punish the saboteur."

"An investigation will begin immediately." August rubbed the back of his neck. Would the sentry who caught him near the bushes mention *his* presence? Schmidt never said a word if he had been spying. It was the chance August had taken. "But I'm short-staffed. My security officer might not be available as he's being transferred to Paris soon. And my top lieutenant is out of commission with a broken ankle. I have other junior officers."

"The Gestapo can send men here to interrogate." Ziegler wiped his coffee-damp handkerchief over his flabby face. "They'll get answers."

"No, we'll handle it. I doubt anyone in the village is involved." August stiffened. He wanted no

Gestapo here. "It's the resistance fighters, the Maquis. Only they would be so diabolical."

"*Gott verdammt*. I'll be ruined, disgraced. This happened under *my* command." Ziegler groaned like a deflating balloon. He set down the cup and dragged fingers through his mass of white hair. "My stellar career is worth nothing. My wife may even disown me."

"Fritz, tell Captain Schmidt to join us, now! *Schnell*!" August had no choice; he must put up the farce of an investigation. Searches in the woods for the Maquis. If he wasn't retiring, Burmester would order *him* to the Front as punishment. August must count on Schmidt being so distracted by his move, any investigation would be negligent.

Chapter Forty-five

In the woods, August spread out the blanket in front of the same rock from their previous viewing. He helped Norah to sit and settled beside her. The sun hovered near the bay's horizon, leaving rays of russet and ochre streaking the sky. And a shimmering line along the water. The cool breeze carried a piney scent.

"Happy birthday, *meine liebe*." He kissed her gently and opened the flask of brandy. "To your twenty-eighth year. I'm forty-one, but the years haven't mattered between us, have they? We are a perfect match." He'd work hard to make certain they fit, a snug embrace, like a jigsaw puzzle.

"I agree. Our love is sweet and strong." She nestled her shoulder against his upper arm. "I still don't want to leave you and board the train the day after tomorrow."

"But you'll be safe, on your way to Alpnachstad." He hoped it would be so, both of them secure, eventually; yet their future remained fragile. He sipped the pungent alcohol, warmth spreading through him, a fire in his stomach, then handed her the flask. This woman with her luminescent hair, the red-tinged blonde, and lively green eyes. Her endearing smile that cared only for him. "You can prepare the home I've purchased for us and our baby. And continue with your art. I plan to take classes to certify me for a historical research position at a college."

What more could he do to undermine this war from the relative safety of Switzerland?

"I'll find scenery to sketch, and birds. And try to be a good German, or rather, Swiss wife." She laughed, voice teasing, and sipped the brandy.

"I know better. You will always be impetuous. But that's part of your charm." He kissed her cheek and caressed her abdomen. "And you can paint Lake Lucerne before the snows come. Our cottage has a view."

"I suppose Switzerland is like Germany in weather." She pressed his hand to her stomach. "Your daughters won't be that far away."

"Gerta will soon make me a grandpapa. Erika is newly married. I hope they can visit." One was similar to Klara in looks, stocky and solid; the other like his mother, their grandmother, blonde and willowy. He longed to hold them close, remembering them in braids and ribbons. But they were grown young women, soon to have their own families. "But I worry about my aging parents."

"Do they have a good marriage?" She ran a finger along his jaw.

"Very good, affectionate." He pictured his father still studying what went wrong in the First War—and lamenting the loss of his eye. His mother delighting in her roses. "My papa may condemn me for leaving the army. It's tragic my brother follows Hitler so closely. I can no longer get near him." He recalled their antics as children, fishing in the stream, climbing walls, the laughter. Sadness briefly engulfed him. Walter, eighteen months his senior, was a martinet now; a fervent Nazi, a man he didn't care to know.

Did he detect heavy movement in the bushes? He shifted close to her, slipping his arm around her. Sentries were not far off.

"At least your son, Christoph, will be safe with us, soon to apply for engineering school." She took another drink after he did. "Will there be any more interrogations about the U-boat?"

"Ah, you talk of less pleasant subjects." He kissed her earlobe, her sweet taste, his voice lower. Did someone listen in? "After Schmidt's intense talk yesterday with Herr Pichon, Herr Ropars, your cousin's husband Herr Menez, and a few others, I hope I convinced everyone the Maquis did the foul deed. Schmidt is packing to leave."

"You took too great a risk. Won't the powers in Paris want to investigate?" She rubbed across his thigh, her tone worried. He smiled at the touch.

Another noise. He glanced around, studying the perimeter. Was all well?

"An admiral is on his way. I must deal with him. And Ziegler, who is in despair. Krause curses himself for not staying close to the dome. The item in question appears permanently out of commission." August continued to speak softly; proud of the destruction, he was not looking forward to any haughty admiral. Again, he'd explain about his eyesight and headaches, and the vicious Maquis. He'd do his utmost to protect Jean.

"I'm grateful it's destroyed. But I wish you could come with me now, away from these problems." She clasped his hand. "And Yann denied having a pistol?"

"Two soldiers searched his home. They didn't find anything." Perhaps Jean was wrong, or his father had second thoughts about owning an illegal weapon. After another sip of brandy, he kissed her lips again, the soft deliciousness. He hated to send her off, this woman he cherished. Someone he'd hold in his heart for eternity. For tonight, he wanted all duty worries to vanish, yet had the feeling something was off here in the forest. A trickle of warning inched along his spine.

* * *

An owl hooted a lament over their heads. Frogs called *croac croac* at a nearby pond.

Norah sighed after the kiss, her body heavy and tingling. The sun was half visible in the bay, a partial yellow yolk. The smoky brandy made her languid. She watched the sun's last rays reflected off August's high brow, defined cheekbones, and cleft chin, the features she loved. His penetrating blue eyes devoured her. His kindness enveloped her.

"And what about you living in Switzerland?" August nuzzled her neck. "You'll miss your family."

"Of course. I once thought my parents' marriage was not so affectionate, too proper and staid. But I learned they love each other privately." She blinked back tears at seeing their faces in her mind, then pulled her cardigan closer in the cooling air. "My sister Agatha and I used to wander the woods, collecting feathers, and pretty stones, then I'd draw them. We laughed a lot. She's four years older." Agatha with her auburn hair and curvy figure. "But once she married, she became the dedicated wife and mother. My father still works as a solicitor, my mum stays busy with her charities."

She'd miss them all and wondered if she would ever see them again. The war might separate her family forever. Would they ever understand her choices? And would Christoph accept her as a stepmother?

She heard a crunch of twigs and stared into the forest. Was a sentry close?

"But I don't regret anything about you and me." She would miss him so completely when she departed—though she labored to be brave.

"Good, no regrets. I want you to be happy." He cupped her face, his smile in shadow.

"I am. We both need to be happy." She caressed down his arm. "In Switzerland we might find a subtle way to aid the rest of Europe."

"Indeed, we should. I thought much the same."

Her love soared, a thrum in her sinew and bones. She kissed him, deeper. "Let's make love."

"Here? You are a saucy woman," he murmured, his hand stroking her breast. Her body twinged, low and sensual.

She laughed quietly. "No, at the cottage." She had the uneasy urge to get back to the cottage.

"The sun has almost set." August squeezed her to him, his lips on her cheek. "We should pack up."

A footstep in the bushes. The frogs stopped. Louder rustling. They pulled apart.

A thin man stalked from the shadows, half blocking the last of the light. "Here you are, whoring with your Boche."

"Yann?" Norah recoiled, bunching the blanket beneath her. "What are you doing here?"

August rose, brushing himself off. "Herr Menez, return to your home at once."

"I'm not 'Herr', I'm *monsieur*," Yann blurted. "You Germans have fouled our heritage."

Norah stood, her breath scouring her throat. Yann had something in his hand. "Calm down, please. Listen to us."

"You interrogate my wife, then pull me in for more questions. While you're screwing my wife's cousin. I'm tired of it all." He held up a pistol.

"Give me that weapon." August kept his voice even. "Or I'll have you arrested. I don't wish to do that."

Norah shuddered, hand at her throat. "Yann, please, hand over the gun. We can talk about this."

"No more arrests! No more talking." Yann sounded strident, a man on the verge of a breakdown. "You've ruined my country."

The owl squawked and flew from the tree.

"Herr, *Monsieur* Menez, I order you to give me the weapon." August thrust out his hand. "You were treated well, as was your wife."

"August is a decent man; you just aren't aware." Norah's words quivered, desperate and pleading.

"None of you are decent. Not even Loeiza." Yann's arm shook. The gun clicked, then a loud blast.

Norah cried out, covering her ears.

"*Scheisse!*" August grabbed his lower stomach. A dark stain spread along his side. She screamed and staggered beside him as he crumpled to the ground.

Another man scrambled from the bushes. He pointed his rifle and shot Yann twice. Yann flopped backwards, supine on the ground, the pistol thrown aside.

In the reek of gunpowder, Norah snatched up the blanket, kneeled, and pressed it against August's wound. Her hands were soon soaked with blood. "No! No! God help us."

"*Liebe*," August gasped, his eyes wide in the waning sunlight.

"Get a surgeon! Hurry, please!" Norah cried to the sentry, bile about to choke her. She nearly collapsed on top of August. She could not lose her love, she *couldn't*.

The sentry dashed off. Yann lay motionless, his shirtfront a black mass in the darkening shadows. August groaned and wheezed to breathe, his eyes glazing. Norah's head pounded, thrashing behind her eyes. Heart bursting like shattered glass, she pushed hard on his wound. Her sobs echoed through the forest.

Epilogue

The train clacked beneath her, vibrating the bench Norah sat on. She shifted on the uncomfortable seat. She wore the berry-colored dress August had bought for her. Loeiza had sewn an extra panel in the front to accommodate the soon to expand baby. Norah touched her belly. At fourteen weeks, she wouldn't show for a while. The doctor she'd visited said she was doing well.

Snow sprinkled against the train windows. Ice crusted at their edges.

She snuggled her coat tighter around her in the chilly car. She touched the dress that showed beneath her coat and recalled the day he'd given it to her, her silly twirl, then blinked back the rising emotions and fisted her hand.

Someone coughed. The other passengers kept themselves bundled and heads down in stale air smelling of tobacco and body odor.

The countryside slid by outside the windows. Fields, trees, hills, rivers. Villages and towns. Snow covered most of the higher elevations. Soon, everything looked swathed in snow. A sharp, white landscape.

The train screeched to a stop in Dijon. More soldiers boarded. Norah pulled her satchel close, her muscles scrunched.

Germans strolled down the aisle, asking for everyone's papers. A thin soldier soon stood next to her seat. "Papers, fräulein."

Her pulse rippling, she showed him her *Ausweis* identity card and travel documents, all officially stamped—and fake.

"You're traveling alone, **Fräulein** Keller?" The soldier leaned over her, tapping the papers he held into his palm. "What is your purpose?"

"I'm afraid I am alone. My companion became ill and had to stay behind. I'm meeting my fiancé in Lausanne." She looked up with what she hoped were guileless eyes. "The war has…kept us apart. We're eager to marry."

"A perfect goal, but you don't sound Swiss." He glanced again at her passport, his statement a bored monotone with a hint of menace.

Her shoulders prickled. "I spent my early years in New York. My late father was in the diplomatic corps. I lost my beautiful accent learning that terrible English language." She forced a timorous smile, praying he couldn't hear the thump of her heart. "I'm relieved to finally be going home."

"You shouldn't travel alone. It isn't safe." He handed her back the papers and moved on.

She exhaled in relief. Closing her eyes, she *longed* to be left alone, the border so close. Still, the horrid evening in the woods kept stabbing into her thoughts. Her last kiss with August, the rustling bushes, Yann staggering from the shadows. The crack of the pistol. She drooped her head as the terror splashed over her again.

After Yann's death, she had stayed with Loeiza, to comfort her and the children. They comforted her. German officers overtook the gardener's cottage.

Loeiza was shocked, but not inconsolable at her loss. Her marriage had long soured. The children were dazed. Angelique cried. Marie-Louise remained stoic. Jean vowed to be the man and take care of his family. Petit Yann asked the most about where his father was.

Yann's aunt, who lived near Quimper, invited the family to move to her farm when ready. The horse, Maler, would be sent with Loeiza for Jean to take care of. He was thrilled.

Norah sighed and shifted again on the bench as August's pale, stricken face, the blotch of blood, her soaked hands, filled her thoughts. He had been rushed to a nearby clinic, then to a hospital in Rennes. She had little word of his condition, her anxiety chewing her up.

Finally, Private Fritz brought her a telegram. August was in Berlin, at another hospital. Condition critical. The RAF had bombed Berlin on October 7th, two weeks before he'd arrived. The city was a ruin; could they keep him alive?

Then on the 20th, the German commander in Nantes was killed by the Resistance. Fifty hostages were shot in reprisal. The Nazis announced this would be the brutal model for future occupation policies. Norah huddled down further as the train rattled on. Would she make it out of France?

Captain Bauer, promoted and now in charge of the Southern **Finistère** region, continued August's fair policies as unobtrusively as possible. Schmidt was ensconced in Paris. Zeigler returned to Germany in shame once the U-boat was scrapped; it was too expensive to build another.

The Germans walked back down the aisle, their glare on everyone. Norah held her breath and stared out the window.

At the beginning of November, a letter had arrived. *Please come!* August had scribbled, *I'm recovering and need you, my great love, with me.* He was in Switzerland—his son in college there—in the house August purchased. She should join him immediately. Weeping with relief, her heart had swelled, her body fervid with love and anticipation. Like a bird, she would find her safe nest—and begin to paint once more. Perhaps one day she would be well-paid enough to send money to Loeiza. Nevertheless, August and their baby must be her immediate priority.

The train lurched off again in a squeal and clacking. About six more hours to Lausanne in Switzerland. August's younger daughter, Erika, who'd been caring for him, would meet her at the station. Of course, Norah knew she'd be interrogated at the border. Her forged papers had worked this far; she prayed they would serve her again.

Her throat thickened in gratitude and joy that she'd soon be in his arms.

The End

Also published by Books We Love

Escape the Revolution
Ladies and Their Lovers (Miss Grey's Shady Lover/ The
Defiant Lady Pencavel)
Rose's Precarious Quest
The Apothecary's Widow
A Savage Exile – Vampires with Napoleon on St.
Helena
Hostage to the Revolution
On a Stormy Primeval Shore
Her Vanquished Land
Ghost Point

Diane Parkinson (Diane Scott Lewis) has written since age ten and lived all over the world. She wrote book reviews for the *Historical Novel Reviews* magazine and worked as an on-line historical editor from 2007 to 2010. She is a member of the *Historical Novel Society*. Most of her novels are set in late eighteenth-century England. She lives in western Pennsylvania with her husband. For further information about the author, visit her BWL author page and her blog:
https://www.bookswelove.com/lewis-diane-scott/
https://dianescottlewisauthor.blogspot.com/